P9-CFD-494

Fever Moon

Fever Moon

CAROLYN HAINES

ST. MARTIN'S MINOTAUR

NEW YORK

This is a work of fiction. All of the characters, organizations, and events portrayed in this novel are either products of the author's imagination or are used fictitiously.

FEVER MOON. Copyright © 2007 by Carolyn Haines. All rights reserved. Printed in the United States of America. No part of this book may be used or reproduced in any manner whatsoever without written permission except in the case of brief quotations embodied in critical articles or reviews. For information, address St. Martin's Press, 175 Fifth Avenue, New York, N.Y. 10010.

www.minotaurbooks.com

Library of Congress Cataloging-in-Publication Data

Haines, Carolyn.
    Fever moon / Carolyn Haines.—1st ed.
        p.   cm.
    ISBN-13: 978-0-312-35161-8
    ISBN-10: 0-312-35161-5
    1. Police—Louisiana—New Iberia—Fiction.   2. Plantation owners—Crimes
against—Fiction.   3. New Iberia (La.)—Fiction.   I. Title.

PS3558.A329F48   2007
813'.54—dc22

2006037820

First Edition: February 2007

10   9   8   7   6   5   4   3   2   1

For Fran and Mike Utley

Acknowledgments

All of my previous books have been set in Mississippi, my home state, but Louisiana has always held a fascination for me, from the wicked temptations of pre-Katrina New Orleans to the primal pull of the swamps, one of the few places left where nature still reigns. I have to credit two people, James Lee Burke and Dianne Agee, with making that world accessible to me. Burke took me there with his fiction, and Dianne took me there in the flesh. It is her home, and it was such an adventure to share it with her, even briefly.

In one instance in the book I've skewed time a bit. Although the practice of leasing convicts for labor was in use throughout the United States, much of it stopped in the early 1900s, as it did in Louisiana.

The idea for *Fever Moon* came from an image, one of the first in the book—Adele guarding the body of Henri Bastion, much as a dog guards a food bowl. From there, it was my job to figure out why she was there, what had happened to her, and who Henri Bastion was that he deserved such a fate.

My editor, Kelley Ragland, and my agent, Marian Young, gave

comments and criticisms that were insightful, helpful, and enriched the story and the characters. Good criticism is a hot commodity in the writing world. I'm blessed.

In that vein, my thanks go to my critique group, the Deep South Writers Salon: Renee Paul, Gary Walker, Susan Tanner, Aleta Boudreaux, Stephanie Chisholm, and Alice Jackson. And to Steve Greene. A special thanks to Dr. Fred Wells, who gave me medical advice. Any mistakes are my own.

Fever Moon

1

THE bare pecan trees of the Julinot orchard clawed the sky as Raymond Thibodeaux drove past. The storm had blown in from the Gulf of Mexico without warning, bringing rain and the first promise of winter's cold. The front passed as quickly as it had come, leaving behind treacherous roads and rising swamps that lapped hungrily at the fringes of land.

Raymond gripped the Ford's steering wheel, feeling the slide of the bald, narrow tires in the slick bog. A full moon broke through the cloud cover and lit the road more sharply than the headlamps of his car as he drove fast toward tragedy. It was always tragedy when he was summoned. Death and loss were his boon companions, met in a land across the ocean, and now he couldn't escape them.

He pressed the accelerator to the floorboards. It was only tragedy that allowed him to burn the gasoline, which was in such short supply with the war on. Folks in New Iberia, Louisiana, didn't send for the law unless there was no other recourse open to them.

As he thought back to the visit that had prompted his drive, he felt a touch of uneasiness. Twenty minutes earlier Emanuel

Agee had arrived at the sheriff's office, breathless, pale, teeth chattering. "Beaver Creek," he managed to spit out. "Hurry."

The boy had disappeared back into the night, leaving only the wet prints of his bare feet on the floor of the sheriff's office. None of the residents of Iberia Parish lingered in the sheriff's office, especially when Raymond was there. It was true that folks avoided him, made uneasy by his melancholy.

Worried by Emanuel's obvious fear, Raymond had stepped out into the lashing rain. There was no sign the boy had really been there. Some folks might say a banshee or a wild creature had stolen the boy's spirit and come to make mischief for the deputy. Even though the rain had swept away all traces of Emanuel, Raymond knew the boy had ducked into an alley, not wishing to be questioned.

Raymond had gotten his revolver, a flashlight, and his hat and headed the five miles to the small creek that was filled with bream and crawfish in the hot summer months.

Beaver Creek was only a bit beyond the Julinot farm, and he began to slow in the sticky mud as he neared the bridge. Much of his work involved pulling vehicles from swollen creeks when the driver was too intoxicated to judge the narrow, rail-less bridges. He dreaded the thought of finding more drowned people. Women and children, the innocent passengers, men at the wheel, the fear of what they'd done frozen into their features. He had no wish to see such things, but it was his job. Joe Como, the sheriff, didn't like to be disturbed in the middle of the night. Joe, who'd Anglicized the name Comeaux for political aspirations, preferred the coffee shop and conversation. The dead he left to his deputy.

As Raymond neared the creek, he could clearly see the bridge, undamaged, in the moonlight. It was October, the Hunter's Moon. With the storm clouds blowing past, the moon shone with a milky white intensity, casting long shadows on the road.

He stopped on the bridge. There was no sign of an accident. Water flowed fast and free beneath the wooden trestles. Puzzled, he walked down the bridge to the bank to check for tracks. He found nothing but the sluices cut into the sandy soil where storm water had coursed.

As he climbed the bank, he heard a sound that caused the hair along his neck to prickle. Laughter slipped through the trees, coming from all directions, surrounding him. His hand upon the slender trunk of a cypress, he stopped completely. His body tensed, and he felt the bite of metal near his spine. He brought his gun out of its holster in one smooth motion, gripped it loosely, and listened.

Laughter seeped around him again, the sound of madness. He could almost sniff it on the wind, and he followed it back to the road, knowing that at last his past had caught up with him.

Walking around a bend, he came upon her.

For one long moment he stood and stared at the woman. At what lay at her feet. At the blood glistening in the moonlight on her hands and face and the rivulets of it tracing the path of the rain along the dirt road. At the long, twisted ropes of intestines that had been pulled from the savaged abdomen of the dead man.

Raymond's heart beat fast. In all the horrors he'd witnessed and caused, he'd never seen anything that chilled him this deeply. He moved slowly toward her, and she turned to face him, her body crouched and wary. No matter that she stood on two legs, she had the grace of an animal, a wild thing caught in the midst of feeding. Her dress was torn, revealing the white of her thighs and a flash of buttock as she swung around, keeping the corpse between them. It was her eyes that held him, though. As dark as swamp pools, they burned.

"Easy," he said. "I'm Deputy Thibodeaux. Don't make me hurt you." He aimed at her heart. She was very thin, too malnourished to be any kind of threat under normal circumstances. He knew most everyone in the parish, but he didn't recognize her. "I don't want to hurt you," he repeated. He realized, too late, that he'd given voice to his personal curse. He'd never wanted to hurt anyone, yet he was so good at it.

The woman laughed, a sound of joy and something else, something indefinable. When he stepped toward her, she dropped to a crouch over the body and growled.

"Get away from the body." He stepped closer, determined to do his duty. In the moonlight her eyes glinted as if struck by some lunar spell. "Get back from him." He was close enough now to see that the dead thing at her feet was Henri Bastion, the wealthiest man in Iberia Parish.

The woman lunged forward, and he sighted on her heart. He'd killed many things but never a woman. She would be the first.

"Back away," he said. "Now!"

She straightened slowly. Her hands fell to her side and she lifted her chin to the moon, exposing a long, slender throat that worked convulsively to release the howl that fought its way out.

The screened door of her cabin banged in the wind, and Florence Delacroix pulled her robe more closely together and inched up by the fire. The leaping flames danced shadows across her face, hiding and revealing a classic profile with full lips and wide green eyes. A moon-shaped scar followed the curve of her cheek. She turned to the boy, who was huddled beside her in a quilt.

"You saw the body?"

Emanuel Agee held the cup of steaming chocolate to his lips and nodded. When the screened door banged again, he cut his eyes toward it.

"It's the wind, boy. Nothing but the wind." She thought that he was a handsome child, black hair and dark eyes filled with intelligence, like his papa. "Tell me what you saw."

"His guts was strowed all over the road. She was standin' over him, laughin'. She look right at me." He blinked. "You think she put a curse on me?"

"No, *cher.*" Florence studied him. "There's no curse on you." She rumpled his hair. "So Henri Bastion met a devil he couldn't

bargain with." Florence stood up and went to her dresser. She rif-
fled through a purse and came back with a coin. Handing it to the
boy, she caressed his head again, feeling the fine hair slip through
her fingers. "You were right to come here and tell me."

"Daddy said to tell the sheriff and then come to you. He say
you look out for me."

"Your daddy is a wise man. You can always find safety with
Florence."

"It was the *loup-garou*," the boy said, his breath so short he almost couldn't say the words. "It took that woman and turned her."

Florence sat back down in front of the fire. "Henri Bastion was
a man with enemies. Someone finally got mad enough to kill him.
That's all."

"She had hair all over her."

Florence examined his face, seeing the fear in his eyes. "Did
she now? Hair all over?"

He nodded. "She killed him, and she meant to eat him."

"Henri would make a tough stew."

"She meant to eat him raw."

"Did you know this woman, *cher*?" Florence asked. She'd run
through the list of women strong enough to kill a man in Iberia
Parish, and she'd come up empty. Henri Bastion was a man in his
prime. A man who, rumors told, beat a prisoner working his farm
to death with his bare hands. Unless Henri was injured or drunk,
no woman would stand a chance against him.

Emanuel shook his head. "She didn't look like no woman I
ever seen." He turned solemn eyes up to her. "Whoever she once
was, she's not her anymore. *Loup-garou*."

She took the cup from the boy's shaking hands. "Do you
want to walk back home tonight or stay here? I'd drive you but
gas coupons are dear."

"I ain't goin' home. Not through the woods at night with a
demon on the hunt. Likta killed myself gettin' here."

There were indeed scratches on the boy's face, neck, and hands where he'd fought his way through briars and vines, unwilling to take his time in case the werewolf was sniffing his tracks. "Then you'd best make a pallet on the floor. Come daybreak you need to be gone. Won't do for folks to know you stayed here with me."

Raymond never gave the woman a chance to run. She seemed enraptured by the moon, her gaze focused on it. He moved in fast, knocking her legs out from under her. She went down hard, the wind forced momentarily from her lungs. The minute Raymond touched her, he knew she was seriously ill. Her skin burned under his hand. She jerked and quivered at his touch like a wild thing, rolling her eyes and gnashing her teeth. She flipped to her stomach and tried to crawl away, scrabbling in the road and revealing her nakedness without a semblance of shame.

"Take it easy," he said, reaching for her flailing wrist. "I'm trying to help you."

She snapped at his hand, growling. Her voice was gravelly, as if her throat were raw. Talonlike fingers clutched at the damp clay.

Raymond twisted her arm, rolling her onto her back. She fought him with a ferocity that was completely silent except for her harsh breathing. He straddled her, trying to hold her down without hurting her. As he sought to capture her wrists, his hand found one firm breast. She writhed beneath him, bucking with a strength that was hard to comprehend. At last, he snapped the handcuffs on her and jumped clear.

As he hauled her to her feet, saliva ran in strings from her mouth, mingling with the blood that had begun to dry on her chin. She tried to jerk free, but he held her by the handcuffs.

Her dress was torn, her feet bare. Mud and scratches covered her legs. Blood was drying on her face and down the front of what was left of her dress. She panted from the exertion of her struggles, staying as far away from him as the cuffs would allow.

Even in her agitation at being confined, she cast a look at the moon that touched the treetops with silver.

"You're under arrest. Come with me." He pulled her toward the car, setting off another fierce struggle. She was weakening, though. Her body carried no extra fat, and the fever clearly burned with an intensity that concerned him.

He forced her into the front seat of the car, cautious of the teeth that snapped close to his face and ears. Normally he transported prisoners in the back, but he didn't like the idea of her teeth sinking into the nape of his neck while he was driving.

At last she tired, and he relaxed the pressure on her. "What's your name?"

She looked beyond him to the moon riding low in the velvet sky and smiled. Her mouth opened, as if she might answer, but she slumped against the seat, her body shaking with chills.

He checked her pulse, which was weak and thready. For the moment the fight was gone from her.

He left her in the car and took a moment to examine the body. Aside from the abdominal injuries, Henri's head had been nearly severed from his body. The wound was such a mess he couldn't begin to determine what might have caused it. There was nothing to do for Henri Bastion but call the coroner.

Raymond got behind the wheel, turned the car around, and headed back to town. In the bright moonlight, he studied the woman's slack face. He thought he might have seen her before, but he still couldn't place her. Her features were distorted, both by the blood and the fever that raged through her. When she was clean, he might be able to recall her name.

Once he'd known all the young women of the parish. He'd danced with most of them, flirting casually, leading those willing to more adventurous activities. The world had been a series of Saturday nights where the pattern of life was simple. The smell of gumbo cooking in a cast-iron pot over a fire, the pulse of a fiddle, a beautiful young woman looking up at him with the promise of a future in her eyes as they danced while the Bayou Teche lapped softly at the bank. He could remember the feel of liquor going down hot, and the taste of kisses under a full moon. But it was a memory that belonged to a dead man.

As he drove down the treacherous road, he let the past slip away. Those nights were gone. He'd had dreams then, normal desires and ambitions. The war had changed all of that. Had changed him in ways he couldn't explain, not to his family or anyone else. The life he'd once expected had been taken from him, replaced with something dark and violent. He had the sense that destiny had led him to this moment on a lonely road with a gruesome murder and a madwoman.

The motion of the car lulled her. Her eyes opened sleepily, and she leaned against the seat, looking neither left nor right but straight ahead.

"Did you know Henri Bastion?" He tried to block the image of Bastion's body, the abdomen gutted and the head dangling by a bit of spinal column and muscle.

"The *loup-garou* is hungry." Saliva dripped down her chin. "I killed him." Her throat worked.

Raymond watched the way she held herself, ready to flee or attack. The legend of the *loup-garou* was strong among the backwoods people. They believed that the legendary creature was a shape-shifting devil who possessed normal people, both willing and unwilling. Often when children disappeared in the swamps, it was never reported to the authorities. The parents assumed that the child had been taken by the *loup-garou*. To call the law would bring only shame on the family. One of their own had gone to the side of the devil. It was better to hush it up and forget it. And pray the possessed body of the child never made it home again.

"Did you know Henri Bastion?" he asked again. There was a long pause, and he glanced at her. She was awake, her gaze on the moon that seemed to follow them. "What was Bastion doing on Section Line Road?"

Her eyes sparked with fever. She sat bolt upright and then slumped against the door. He reached across and felt her forehead. She was burning up. If the fever went much higher, it might cook her brain. She required a doctor.

He turned the car south at the intersection, avoiding town and the jail. Since she was already in the car, it would be best to take her to Madame Louiselle, a *traiteur* who used herbs and prayers to treat the illnesses of those too poor to afford a doctor. There was no time to drive to Lafayette for a physician, and Doc Fletcher, New Iberia's resident doctor, was out of town. If Madame Louiselle couldn't break the fever, the woman beside him would die.

2

THE dense woods closed in a tight canopy as Raymond turned down the narrow lane to Madame Louiselle's. Beside him, the woman slumped against the door, her eyes closed. Raymond put his hand on her forehead, a gesture so intimate that he hesitated. She twitched beneath his touch like something wild and frightened. He accepted that she might die. She'd slipped from consciousness into a place where she was unreachable. Fever. Madness. He couldn't say. He could only drive.

He crossed the bridge that was often flooded after a heavy rain and thanked whatever God watched over him as he pulled up in front of the dark cottage on pilings.

"Madame Louiselle!" he called out as he scooped the woman into his arms and started up the steps with her. She weighed almost nothing. As tall as she was, there was only bone and skin. "Madame Louiselle!" When he made it to the landing, he kicked the side of the house.

The screened door creaked open and a tiny black woman stepped out. She surveyed Raymond and the burden he carried.

"Bring her inside." She stepped back. "Put her there." She pointed to a quilt-covered sofa.

Raymond deposited the limp woman.

"Who is she?" Louiselle asked as she drew a chair beside the sofa.

"I don't know her name." Raymond watched Louiselle's face closely. Madame treated only those she chose to treat. She catered to no one. "She may have murdered a man." He stopped himself from any mention of the shape-shifting demon. "She's burning up with fever."

Madame Louiselle touched the woman's cheek. "Move the lamp closer, *cher.*"

He did as she asked and heard her sharp intake of breath.

"I know this woman, Raymond. Her name is Adele Hebert." She pressed a finger to Adele's neck, checking her pulse. "Two weeks ago she came to me. Her twin boys were sick with the fever." Louiselle slowly straightened in the chair. "There was nothing I could do." She brushed her fingers over Adele's cheek and looked up at Raymond. "Such perfect little boys, just learning to walk. They died in her arms, she trying to force them to drink her milk." She shook her head. "I'm too old for such grief."

"This was two weeks ago?" Raymond hadn't heard of burial services for two children.

Almost as if she could read his mind, she spoke. "Adele wouldn't give up the bodies. She said she would tend them herself. She said they were her babies and no one else had loved or wanted them, so she would bury them herself." Louiselle took a deep breath and stood. "Let me make some tea for her fever. If she doesn't drink, she'll join her babies." Madame placed her fingers on Adele's neck, pressing lightly. "And her sister."

"Her sister?"

"Rosa Hebert."

"The woman with the stigmata was Adele's sister?" Raymond

stepped back. Rosa Hebert had died a senseless, tragic death. A woman with mental problems, she'd been harried and pushed to the point she'd hung herself last winter. Now, here was the sister, found drooling over a dead man as if he were her next meal.

Madame stood up straight. "The Hebert family has seen too much tragedy, *cher.* Adele has lost all she ever loved." She covered the sleeping woman with a quilt.

Raymond said nothing. The death of a child could drive a woman to madness, and Adele had lost two children and a sister. "Is it the fever that sickens her, or is she . . ."

Louiselle stared at Adele's sweating face. Steam rose from her damp clothes in the chill cabin. "This is more than fever." She sighed. "I will not say more now. Take off the handcuffs and wait outside."

Raymond stood his ground. "She's my prisoner."

"And so she will remain, only dead, if you don't leave us alone. Her wet clothes must be stripped."

"She's stronger than she seems. Perhaps very strong." When Madame didn't respond to his words, he unlocked the cuffs and walked outside, but he took the precaution of leaving the door cracked.

He lit a Camel cigarette, blowing the smoke into the cold eddies of air that circled the cabin. The weather touched the metal in his hip and back like an electric wire, reminding him that he had no guarantees in his future. Each step could be his last. Inhaling more deeply, he thought about Henri Bastion's body lying by the roadside for anyone to stumble upon. Raymond hadn't called the sheriff or anyone else. Not yet. There were no phones near Beaver Creek. None here at Madame Louiselle's. His car was not equipped with a radio. Everything electronic had been put into the war effort. Not even aluminum foil could be had here at home. He could do nothing but wait for his prisoner and smoke.

Five cigarette butts were lined on the wooden balustrade of the porch by the time Madame stepped out to talk to him.

"She's dry and more comfortable, *cher*. The fever is less, but I have no medicine to make it leave. It's claimed her as its own, for now. She will live or not. It's in the hands of God and her will."

"I have to take her to jail."

She nodded slowly. "It would be best if she could remain here, so I can care for her."

"No—"

She put up a hand. "I understand she must be taken. Do these things, Raymond. Keep her dry and warm. Give her these herbs every four hours. Pry open her mouth and pour them in. Feed her soup. Force it down if necessary."

He saw in Madame's eyes what she would not say. "What of her mind?"

"Perhaps it is burned away." She shook her head. "There's a point where not even the strongest person can bear more. Adele has suffered." Her fingers lightly touched his arm.

"Do you think she had the strength to bring down a grown, healthy man? He was gutted, Madame. Like a pack of savage animals had beset him."

She looked into the trees that soughed around her home in the wind. "Good and evil walk the earth, Raymond. You know it because you've touched it. No man can measure the power of either. She was covered in blood, some of it her own. She is cut and scraped as if she'd been struck by a wagon, but most of the blood was not hers."

Raymond tossed his sixth butt to the ground. "Thank you. The county will reimburse your expenses."

"No charge. I don't take money for those I cannot heal."

He left Madame on the porch as he stepped through the door. Adele Hebert lay beneath three colorful quilts. Cleansed of blood, her face was angular and pale. Her long hair, now dry, fanned about her head like a dark aura. She looked dead, like a figure in one of the church windows. He crossed himself without thinking, a habit from a past life.

"She is breathing but just barely." Madame touched his arm. "There is great tragedy in this woman, Raymond. Don't let it slip from her to you." Her touch increased to a squeeze. "You carry enough tragedy of your own, *cher.* Whether you deserve it or not."

Raymond felt his breath catch. No one else in town would dare to speak to him like that. He gathered Adele Hebert in his arms, tucking the quilts around her. "I'll return these."

Madame nodded. She stood in the doorway, watching him maneuver the steep steps as he went back to the parish car. As he put Adele in the front seat beside him, he saw no need to replace the handcuffs. She was beyond slumber, almost in a trance. When he looked up, he saw that Madame had begun to light a series of candles. She was cleansing her home of evil. Despite his lack of belief, he felt a chill trace along his spine.

The study was crammed with books, most of them leather-bound. For the past ten years, they'd been Father Michael Finley's closest friends, his comfort in the wilderness. A musty odor of mildew rose from them, and Michael made a mental note to have Colista clean them again when drier weather set in. Humidity left unchecked would ruin them, and some were old and valuable.

He hurried, barefoot and in his underwear, across the colorful rug to answer the ringing telephone. Dawn had not yet broken, and the demanding peals of the phone could mean only one thing—death had come calling. Few people in Iberia Parish could afford the convenience of a telephone. He'd justified the luxury by pointing out that his services were often in immediate demand. There were times that he regretted his superiors' decision to honor his request.

"Hello," he said.

"It's Raymond Thibodeaux. Something bad's happened, and I need you to go out to the Bastion plantation as fast as you can."

Michael hesitated. Raymond had not used his title, but there was no doubt he spoke with the authority of the law. Of all the people he'd expected when he picked up the phone, it wasn't Raymond. A dark cloud hung over the deputy. The scent of death clung to his hair and clothes and in his dark eyes Michael saw torment. Even now, months after Raymond had returned home, stories circulated how he'd been one of the army's most efficient killing machines, a loner shifting through the war zone like a vengeful ghost. Or a man who wanted to die.

"Father, did you hear what I said?" Raymond didn't hide his impatience.

Michael gathered his thoughts. "What's happened?"

"Henri was murdered last night out by Beaver Creek."

Foreboding touched Michael's heart. Something bad had indeed happened. Raymond Thibodeaux rode the vanguard of tragedy yet again. It seemed God cursed him. "Do you know who killed him?" he asked quietly.

There was a slight hesitation before Raymond spoke, as if he weighed his words. "Henri was attacked by some kind of wild beast. You might as well hear the truth because gossip will be all over town by morning. Adele Hebert was found at the body. It's already spreading that she's possessed by the *loup-garou*."

Michael swallowed. The images were vivid in his mind, and they brought to life his dark suspicions that the swamps were filled with unholy creatures. "A werewolf?" He shivered, aware that his bare feet were freezing. "You don't believe that, do you?"

"It doesn't matter what I believe. I'm worried what the town believes. It was a gruesome murder. I want you to go to the Bastion plantation and prepare the family. Don't let Mrs. Bastion buy into the werewolf business."

Michael bristled at Raymond's tone. "Marguerite Bastion is an educated woman. She's not a fool."

"Father, you and I both know it's easier to believe in evil than good. Many people believed Rosa Hebert was a stigmatic. You among them, I think." Raymond's point was quietly made, and it opened the door on the box of Michael's personal demons. It wasn't his belief in Rosa that tormented him, but his lack thereof.

"Rosa was a child of God chosen to bear the marks of Christ's suffering, a living sign of God's love and sacrifice. She was God's emissary. The *loup-garou* is a superstition used to keep wicked children in line by parents who fear to use the rod." The distinction was clear in his mind.

"I somehow don't see bleeding from the hands and feet as an example of God's love."

Raymond was baiting him, and Michael wouldn't allow himself to respond in anger. "Raymond, I know you suffer. You've lost your way." Raymond hadn't set foot in the church since his return from the war. The man mocked and defied God.

"Well said, Father. Still, if wounds opened up in my hands and feet every Friday, I'd hang myself, too."

"That's blasphemy."

Raymond's voice took on a different tone. "You saw the wounds, didn't you? They were real. Not self-inflicted."

He hesitated, wondering what Raymond's angle might be. "Rosa was given a gift and a burden. It was too much for her to carry. She failed our Father and took her own life. There was nothing I could do to change any of it."

Silence hung between them for a long moment. "That's not an answer to the question I asked, but it's an answer to another question. Good-bye, Father, and good luck with Mrs. Bastion."

Michael heard the click of the phone. He replaced the receiver and walked to the window, his bare legs covered in chill bumps. First light would arrive soon; it was pointless to go back to bed. Raymond had left him with images and memories as wicked and sharp as the devil's pitchfork.

His curiosity urged him to the parish jail, but his duty directed him to the Bastion home. He didn't want to drive there in the dark. Not on this night when a strange, moist wind howled down the chimney and the past had reawakened like a sleeping corpse. Adele's anger at her sister's excommunication was fresh in his mind. She'd cursed him and the church. She'd called down the vengeance of God on him because he'd followed his bishop's orders and closed the sanctified ground of the church cemetery to Rosa's body. A suicide could not be buried in hallowed ground.

Adele had taken Rosa, and then the bodies of her twin boys, into the swamps to a secret grave. He'd never gone to counsel her, at first not wanting to agitate her more and then finding it impossible to overcome the inertia that touched him whenever he heard her name. Even if he'd found her, she wouldn't have listened to him. Her grief and fury had obviously driven her mad.

A log in the fireplace snapped as a gust of wind rushed down the chimney. A shower of sparks, vaguely in the shape of a woman, blew across the room. The priest moved quickly, stepping on the tiny burning embers that had fallen on the rug. The fireplace was dangerous, the night even more so.

He'd wait for dawn to face the grief of Marguerite Bastion. This night, he'd pray to overcome his own inadequacies, which were plentiful.

3

CHULA Baker put her car in neutral and set the hand brake before she got out. She left the motor running. It was an old car and sometimes unreliable about starting. The first light of a cold October morning was creeping up the eastern sky, and she saw the clutch of cars and men standing in the road just beyond Beaver Creek. The letter on the front seat of her car was a tragedy for the Lanoux family. What straddled the road and blocked her path was another. Death always came in threes.

She headed toward the men who hadn't yet noticed her approach. Her heavy skirt, belted around a small waist, swung against bare legs. There were no stockings to be had since the war, and post office regulations prohibited a woman from wearing pants. On this cold October morning she wore her skirts long and stout shoes padded with thick socks. Eighteen-hour days had quickly disabused her of a longing for high heels.

"Ms. Chula." Sheriff Joe Como blocked her path. "What are you doin' out here, *cher?*"

She studied his face. Even though the temperature was in the low forties, sweat beaded on his forehead. His eyes looked left and right but never into hers. "Got a letter last night for the Lanoux family. From the army. I didn't want to be out in that storm, but I figured I should bring it on this morning."

"Is it Justin?"

"I can't read people's mail." She thought of the official envelope and the hundreds of others she'd delivered like it. "Never saw good news come in a letter like that, though."

The sheriff spit a brown stream into the still muddy road. "Iberia Parish gone dry up and die. All our young men killed over in Europe. Gotta have an old man like me keepin' the law."

"Joe, you've still got a good thirty years." She craned to see around his body. "What's going on here?"

He moved to block her view. "Been a murder. Something you don't want to see."

"Murder?" Such things didn't happen in New Iberia. At least not out on a public road. If a man wanted to kill, he did it in the swamp where the body could be slipped into a canal for gator bait. "Who is it?"

"Henri Bastion."

She registered the name with even more shock. Henri was the wealthiest man in the parish. His money had bought him the most fertile land, a high-blood French wife, and hellion children. It had also bought fear of him. "How'd he die?"

"We're trying to figure that one out."

She snorted. "How hard could it be? Gunshot, stabbing, what?"

The sheriff finally stared into her eyes. "Looks like some kind of wild animal tried to eat him alive."

"Good Lord, Joe. You said murder, not animal attack." She had no desire to see this mess. She had mail to deliver.

"We got someone who confessed to killing him. Says she's the *loup-garou*."

Joe wasn't the kind of man who joked about swamp creatures. They were part of his background, like hers. A dense web of superstition connected the parish. It had come to the land with the

Acadians and been mingled with the folklore of the Indian tribes and the Negroes. Such a rumor could start a panic.

"I wouldn't be talking any *loup-garou* if I were sheriff." She lifted an eyebrow. "What with the war taking the boys and men, womenfolk don't need another reason to be afraid."

Joe nodded. "Can't help what Adele Hebert claims, though. She says she killed him. Looks like she tracked him through the woods while he was walking, jumped out, and tried to eat his liver."

Chula put a hand on the sheriff's chest. "I'd stop that talk right here. I know Adele. Her brother is Clifton, the trapper. She's no more the *loup-garou* than I am, and if you say that to the wrong person, it'll be all over the parish in half a day and you'll see what real trouble is."

He drew back and she saw she'd offended him. There were times, though, when Joe Como acted like the brains God gave him were insufficient. Chula Baker knew she was viewed as uppity and overly educated. She'd spent time in Lafayette and Shreveport, cities without respect for the values of the rural parishes. She'd gone to a teachers college where she'd discovered a love of learning and acquired the skills necessary to pass the postal department's civil service test—an accomplishment that several men had failed. She'd learned to speak her mind from her mama, who at sixty-two was still feared for her sharp tongue and ability to cut a man in half and leave him bleeding in the dirt.

"I thank you for your concern, Miss Chula." Joe slid back from her.

"I'm not tryin' to run your business, Joe. I'm trying to keep a wild rumor from turning into some kind of vigilante lynch mob." Her softer tone was more acceptable. "People are tired of doin' without. Most every family has buried a son or brother or father. We've carved a living from land that would've killed a lesser people. These swamps've done their worst to us, but we didn't leave. A tall tale about a werewolf on the loose could be the final straw here."

The sheriff took off his hat and wiped his forehead on the long sleeve of his tan shirt. When he looked at her some of the resentment was gone from his brown eyes. "You make a point, *cher.*"

"What does Doc Fletcher say?" While she'd stood in the road trying to talk some sense into Joe, the sun had climbed over the top of the trees. The morning was still chill, but it would be warm and sunny by afternoon. One of the most effective tools in vaporizing foolish ghost stories was a good strong sun.

"Doc was over to a convention in Baton Rouge last night. He'll examine the body when he gets back to the area."

She patted Joe's arm. "Just tell folks you're waiting to get Doc's professional opinion. Tell 'em it's a puzzle, but don't let on like it's anything supernatural."

She felt him begin to tense under her hand. She was stepping across that invisible line again. "I'd best tend to my business and let you handle yours." She smiled innocently and was relieved to see him return it. "Come by for some whiskey. Clifton brought Mama a new bottle last week. She'd welcome your company for a drink." She winked at him. "On the sly, of course."

"You got your mama's bitter tongue, *cher,* but you got your daddy's Irish blarney." His brows drew down. "Good thing, too, or I'd have to predict spinsterhood."

She laughed out loud, a sound that bounced off the wall of trees that defined the edge of the mud road. "There are worse things, Joe. Believe it or not, there are worse things."

Her gaze drifted to the men lifting something from the road, and she recognized Raymond Thibodeaux's muscular back. She felt a pain beneath her breast, a sharp memory of the beauty of his body before he'd gone to war. He'd gone to Europe a lively young man with a quick smile and come home a specter. His dark hair was shot with silver, and some days he walked with a limp, his eyes daring anyone to notice. A bomb had exploded and sent shrapnel into his body. Gossip was that he might become paralyzed.

Moving to the shade, she waited until Henri's body had been

loaded into a truck bed. When Raymond was left standing alone, she walked to him. "Mother and I would love for you to come to dinner, Raymond." It was an invitation extended often, and always ignored. Others in town might accept his isolation, but Chula could not. The memory of his kisses, his hands so expert in touching her, would not be snuffed out by his anger. What they'd shared was gone, but never her affection for him.

"I'm busy, Chula, but thank you."

"Raymond, we've known each other a long time. I know you grieve Antoine, but you can't continue like this. Your brother wouldn't want that."

She saw the fire snap into his dark eyes. So he wasn't quite dead. At least not yet. "You don't have a clue what you're stepping into, Chula. Mind your own affairs."

He bent down to pick up Henri's hat that lay sodden in the road.

"You once loved the fact that I was smart and spoke my mind." Her voice was soft as she remembered a summer afternoon in her shady backyard when he told her he was going into the army, that when he returned he wanted to be a journalist. "The war took your brother, but only you can let it steal your dreams."

His eyes, once a golden brown, bore into her. It was true that the color had changed to near black. "The past is dead, Chula. So is the man you knew. Leave what's left of him in peace."

He took the hat to the patrol car, and Chula felt the gaze of the sheriff watching them. It would be best to walk away, but she couldn't. She'd delivered two letters to Mrs. Thibodeaux, the first last November telling of Antoine's death in a small town, a village of no consequence to either army. Antoine had been the youngest son, the charmer in a family of handsome men.

Six months later, she'd brought the second letter on a beautiful May morning with robins calling from the wild hedges. Mrs. Thibodeaux had opened the door without expression. She'd ripped open the letter, read the words, and looked up into Chula's eyes with an expression of furious anguish before she slammed and locked the door.

Raymond had arrived home two months later, unable to walk without crutches. In a matter of weeks he was using a cane. When the cane was gone, he pinned on the deputy's badge.

"Raymond, there are people who'd care about you if you'd let them. I remember—"

"Don't. Don't remember, Chula. The past is like a dream. It only exists in memory, and sometimes it's best to let it go." He walked away.

Chula went back to her car, feet sliding in the thick cake of yellow mud called gumbo by the locals. She sat for a moment before she started her car, watching Raymond talk with the sheriff.

Henri Bastion was dead, and from the sound of it he'd died violently. Such foolishness. If a man wanted a violent death, he could accomplish it easily by joining the army. There were still plenty of German and Japanese bullets. So why bring it home? That was a question without an answer.

Raymond got out of the patrol car in front of the jail and watched as the sheriff followed Henri's body over to the funeral home. Doc Fletcher would be there directly to look it over. For now, Raymond had a chance to be alone with Adele Hebert. He'd done a bit of digging, and what he'd learned showed Adele to be a hard worker who'd retreated into the swamps alone to raise twin boys. No one would hazard a guess as to the boys' father. She'd shown up in town big with child and refusing to name the father. Doc had given her vitamins and caution to rest, but Adele had seen him only once. As far as anyone knew, she'd delivered the babies on her own.

Adele's parents had died, her father in the Gulf waters and her mother of infection almost eight years ago. It wasn't much information, and none of it explained why Adele would think herself the *loup-garou* or why her sister would develop the wounds of the stigmata. Raymond walked into the sheriff's office hoping Adele would be well enough to give him some answers to his questions.

Pinkney Stole stood up from in front of the potbellied stove when Raymond walked in. The old black man stared at Raymond, waiting for a command.

"She been mumbling," he said. "Talkin' 'bout the moon and such. None of it made a lick o' sense."

Raymond pulled a quarter from his pocket. "Would you get us some coffee, Pinkney? Take your time about it. Tell Mrs. Estella to feed you some pie." He flipped the coin to the old man who deftly caught it with a toothless grin. Pinkney hung out at the jail because he had nowhere else to sleep. Like an old dog, his presence could be comforting or annoying. Now, Raymond wanted to be alone with the prisoner.

Adele lay on a thin mattress of cotton ticking. Her hand was cuffed to the bedsprings, but if she'd moved since he put her on the bunk the night before, he couldn't tell. The gentle rise and fall of her chest told him she was breathing.

"Miss Hebert?" He called her name softly, surprised at the desire he felt to be gentle. There were moments when the past crept up on him and caught him unaware, making him wonder what kind of man he might have been. Such moments always cost him.

When she didn't respond, he went in the cell with a dropper of the medicine Madame Louiselle had prepared. He gripped her jaw and forced her mouth open. The liquid gurgled between her lips, but she didn't swallow.

Afraid she would choke lying flat on her back, he lifted her head until he saw her throat work. Her skin felt cooler to his touch, but she still had a fever. He wet a cloth and put it on her forehead as his mother had done to him when he was a child. The cold cloth made her sigh.

While Joe was captivated by the idea of a woman possessed by an evil spirit, Raymond worried about something far worse.

Infantile paralysis. It came with a high fever, followed by the death of the limbs, and for some, the inability to breathe. Jail was not the place to be sick, but no hospital would take a person with polio, especially not a possible murderer.

He wiped her mouth and stood. He would've been uncomfortable for the sheriff or even Pinkney to see him ministering to the woman. There was no room for kindness or compassion in the world he'd chosen. Those things had been stolen from him by his own actions.

In the daylight, he studied Adele's features. Dark, thick eyebrows grew with a slight curve over eyes set deep. Her skin was sallow, with grayish tints like old bruises beneath her eyes. The nose was sharp and clean. Spanish or French, he'd say. As he recalled, her eyes were gray, and fringed with dark lashes. If she gained about thirty pounds, she would be a comely woman. Someone had found her so and fathered twin boys on her. For all that she was alone now, she hadn't always been.

Her eyelids fluttered, and he thought of young birds in the first flapping of wings. There'd been a blue jay's nest outside his bedroom window, and each spring, he and Antoine had watched the eggs hatch and the fledglings grow. They'd been careful never to frighten the mother bird, fearing she'd abandon her babies. He could almost feel his brother's breath on his forearm as they stood at the window, watching so carefully. Antoine was often with him.

Adele moaned, and Raymond leaned closer. "Adele?"

She looked at him and lifted a hand to shield her eyes from the sun that came in the cell window. She struggled to sit up but was too weak to do so.

"What do you remember?" he asked as he offered a hand for her to pull against. She swung her bare feet to the floor, unaware that she wore someone else's nightgown.

"Nothing." Her eyes darted around the cell, and when she lifted her wrist and the handcuff jingled, she cried out in terror.

"Last night you were on Section Line Road at Beaver Creek."

He saw the frown as she tried to comprehend this information. "Do you remember seeing a man walking on the road?"

She shook her head. "I remember a storm." Urgency touched her face. "I went to check on my boys—"

"Your boys?" he interrupted.

"To make sure the high water wouldn't pull them from their grave." Her gaze faltered, but when she brought it back to his, there was a dare in her eyes. "The moon went behind a cloud, and I lost my way. I fell. I was sick and lost." She looked at the cuts and bruises on her palms. "When the moon came out again, it was red. Red light all around, bright enough to see."

Her words touched Raymond like the fingers of a corpse. "The moon was full last night, but it wasn't surrounded by a red halo. Maybe you were dreaming."

Confusion touched her features, and he saw that she was younger than he'd first thought. Twenty-three at most. "I knelt by my boys, me, and the light around us was red as the storm clouds blew past. I looked at the moon, so big and bloody. The Hunter's Moon, my brother taught me." Something alive slipped into her eyes and her features changed as he looked at her. Her eyes narrowed, her chin lifted, and the lips drew into a thin line. When she spoke again, her voice was deeper, rawer, and her body trembled. "Running."

"Running from what?" He kept his tone conversational. Her words had sent a creep of flesh along his spine despite the fact he didn't believe in the *loup-garou*.

"From—" A gout of blood rushed from her nose. It filled her lap, covering her hands, as if her head had exploded. The blood still pouring, her eyes rolled up in her head and she fell backward onto the bed.

4

————————

HOLDING Adele in his arms, Raymond brushed past Pinkney as the old man tried to come in the door, cups of coffee chattering against saucers in each hand.

"Tell the sheriff I've taken her to Madame Louiselle's. Doc said he couldn't help her, and she's dying."

"Good Lord, look at the blood." Pinkney shuffled from foot to foot, the dishes reflecting his unease. "Good Lord Almighty, there couldn't be no blood left in her. Sweet Jesus, Mr. Raymond. She done gone."

Raymond ran to his personal car and put her in the front seat. "Remember to tell the sheriff." He got behind the wheel and sprayed mud as he drove away. Adele had lost everything else— and he understood what that meant—but she wouldn't lose her life. Not if he could help it.

She was still alive. He could see her eyelids fluttering, and her hands made small motions, reaching out and falling back. He watched so many helpless people die, but Death would not win this time.

"Adele?" He tried to call her back to this world. And he

thought of a young nurse in Europe after the grenade blast. She'd frequented his bedside, demanding that he return to the land of the living. Now he did the same for Adele. "Stay with me, Adele. I know you didn't kill Bastion."

She slumped against the door and he gave up. She was breathing and for the moment she was at peace.

When he pulled into Madame Louiselle's yard, the old woman was gathering herbs along a rickety wooden fence that could barely hold the weeds out. She showed no surprise, not even when he lifted Adele out, blood soaking her gown and him. She walked slowly to them and pried one of Adele's eyes open.

"Take her inside. You'll have to leave her."

He didn't argue. The sheriff would be angry, but what good was a dead prisoner? As he climbed the steep stairs, he was careful of the long shank of Adele's legs and arms. Bones should weigh more. He had the disturbing notion that she was somehow hollowed out.

He put her on the sofa and stepped back. Madame Louiselle's hands grasped his waist, moving him away. She knelt beside Adele and touched her face, lifted her eyelids, opened her mouth, and examined her teeth and gums.

"Can you help her?" Raymond asked.

"The fever is burning her alive." She rose with the grace of a sixteen-year-old.

"What's wrong with her? She's almost lucid one minute and the next, she's talking crazy."

Madame Louiselle walked to the door, turned and waited for him to follow. "She isn't going to get up and run away, Raymond. Come outside and speak with me."

He followed her outside, taking the opportunity to pull out his pack of Camels. He offered Madame one and she took it, tapping it daintily on the wooden rail of the porch. When she put it between her lips, he lit it for her, then his own.

"Do you believe in the sickness of a soul?" she asked.

"You mean mental illness." A series of images slipped into his mind, hot-pan flashes of bayonets, screams in the night, of frantic limbs clawing backward as a soldier clung to the damp earth of a foxhole and cowered from the gunfire that had driven him mad.

She watched his face. "Not a broken mind. This is something else I speak of."

He shook his head. "I don't believe in evil, not like the devil or a demon or the *loup-garou*. I do believe in greed and cruelty and meanness. And weakness. That's the worst of them all."

She studied him. "I'm sixty years old. I've seen many things. When I was barely three, I went with my *grandmère* to treat the sicknesses of those who lived far back on the narrow bayous of the swamp. There were often fevers." She stubbed out her cigarette. "Often death. I learned from my *grandmère* that there are three kinds of illness. What attacks the body can often be cured with skill and herbs. What twists the mind can be addressed by a change in situation, a trip or a move." She finally looked at him. "An illness of the soul is beyond my skill."

Raymond tried to weigh her words. "You're telling me that Adele Hebert is sick in her soul?"

Madame took another cigarette, bent to shield the match, and exhaled. "I examined her, Raymond. I don't know what's wrong with her. This is beyond my experience."

"Do you believe she's possessed by the *loup-garou*?" He didn't bother to hide his scorn.

She looked over her yard. "She's told me nothing. In my years, though, I do know one thing. If *she* believes she is possessed, what you believe doesn't matter. She believes, therefore to her it's true. We are all victims of our beliefs."

"Surely you're not saying that because she *believes* she's the *loup-garou*, she's burning up with fever, shooting geysers of blood from her nose, and tearing a man apart with her bare hands." He flipped the book of matches in his hand.

"I'm not saying anything for certain about Adele. I was making an observation about human nature. There are forces at work you can't see or touch. You know that. In your heart." Madame was unruffled by his anger. "Families still practice the laying on of curses. Some even voodoo. Sometimes the darkness that cloaks the swamp is more than night. Because a woman . . . or man believes."

"Adele Hebert is physically incapable of gutting a man with her hands and teeth. I look at her lying in the cell, and I know, in my heart, that she's innocent. Even if she wanted to do it, she isn't strong enough. Henri Bastion was in his late thirties, a powerful man. From what I could tell, he wasn't struck on the head and stunned. He wasn't shot. He was knocked down in the road and bitten." Henri Bastion's body told a specific story. "That woman lying in there didn't do that."

"And if she were not alone?"

He nodded. "Now you're thinking." Raymond knew the shape of a murderer. He recognized the eyes of a killer each morning as he looked in his broken mirror and scraped the stubble from his cheeks. The small moments of death reflected in his eyes were missing in Adele's.

Madame's gaze was penetrating. She tapped his pocket for another cigarette.

He offered the cigarette and then held a match, meeting her gaze. "I don't understand the *why* of it, though. Why Adele? The question I have to answer is who would do this to her."

"Leave her with me."

"I don't have a choice." He flicked his cigarette over the side of the porch. "No one else will even try to help her, and if Joe doesn't stop flapping his gums, the parish is going to turn into a lynch mob."

Madame drew on the cigarette and exhaled smoke. "Leave me the cigarettes."

He took the pack from his pocket and handed them to her. "I'll be back tomorrow to check on her." Madame didn't have a telephone. If something went wrong, she'd be alone with the young woman. He waited to see if she might raise an objection.

"Have you talked to Bernadette?"

He knew the name of Adele's other sister. There had been four of the Hebert siblings, a small family by most standards. Rosa was dead by her own hand. Clifton lived so deep in the swamps no one could find him unless he chose to be found. Bernadette was married and lived on Bayou Caneche, a small tributary of the Bayou Teche.

"I'm going there now."

"Be careful, Raymond. Superstitions are dangerous, but sometimes it's the lack of belief that puts one in harm's way."

Marguerite Bastion pulled the shawl higher on her shoulders and poured the coffee. Father Michael knew the delicate bone china had cost a pretty penny, like so many other things in the Bastion home. Marguerite Bastion, née Mandeville, a New Orleans beauty, had brought culture and refinement to the wilderness. Even now, in her grief, he could appreciate her aristocratic features, the composure that was part of good breeding. She poured the coffee and offered him a plate of sweets.

Michael wondered again at the match between her and Henri, a man reputed to be ruthless and violent, at least in his business dealings. Marguerite's marriage to Henri had tied the Mandeville political power to Henri's wealth and interest in the Gulf oil fields. It had also bound Marguerite to a life of isolation and hardship.

"Have another bit of tart, Father?"

He shook his head. "Here in Louisiana we're lucky. Most Americans have a hard time finding enough sugar to make sweets." So far his attempts at conversation had failed miserably. Marguerite was far away in her thoughts.

"And they don't have the stink of cane burning in the fields all winter, yes?"

He felt the lash of her anger and knew it wasn't directed toward him. Her husband was being examined like a hunk of dead meat. An autopsy. What was the world coming to? From what he'd heard, any moron could tell that Henri Bastion had been viciously attacked and killed. There was no need to further desecrate the body, leaving his widow to wait to see what would be left to bury.

"Are there arrangements I can help with?" He put his empty cup on the tray. "Death isn't God's punishment, Marguerite. We all must die to return to our Father."

"Forgive me." She drew a ragged breath. "When his body is brought home, we'll hold the wake immediately. The funeral will follow as soon as possible. I want this over, for the children."

"How are the children holding up?" He hadn't heard a peep from any of them.

"They've taken to their beds with grief. They loved their papa. Now they'll have to grow up without a father." She hitched the shawl higher, and a ring of keys jingled at her waist.

Michael had come to offer comfort, but Marguerite sat rigid on the edge of her chair, her posture perfection, her dress impeccable. She was groomed as if she were going into town. Her hair had been braided and pinned so that it crowned her head, and the dark chestnut color was a glory. Even after three children, Marguerite was still a handsome woman, not beaten down by the hardships of the land.

"Mrs. LaRoche is organizing a dinner to be brought over tonight."

"That's very kind but unnecessary. Bernadette Matthews has been cooking for us." She bit her lip. "I don't suppose Bernadette will be coming for a while. Her sister . . ." She faded into silence, her gaze on her lap.

He swallowed. "You've suffered a terrible loss. It's the duty of the community to come to your assistance."

"That's very kind."

"Do you need help with Henri's papers, the legal aspects? Is there anything I can do to help you?" Michael rose to his feet. He rested a hand on her shoulder. "I'm here to help in any way I can."

"Adele must have lost her mind. I heard she was like a wild thing. Have they charged her with Henri's murder?"

"They don't expect Adele to live."

Marguerite walked to the window and looked out over the fertile land. "Perhaps that would be a kindness for her. For all of us. I mean, to spare us all . . . a trial." She straightened her posture and turned to him. "I don't ever want to know the details."

"I've heard Adele is very sick, unlikely to survive the day." Michael walked to stand beside her. "You'll face many decisions in the days ahead, Marguerite. Don't feel that you're alone. The community is here for you."

"Thank you, Father Michael. Now I'm tired, and I must see to the children."

Michael looked out over the land at the rows of cane that rippled in a slight breeze, the tassels catching the rays of the early-morning sun. Marguerite had lost her husband, but she would not go hungry. Henri had left her plenty of money and the wealth of the land. "The ladies will be out directly with the food. If you need me, day or night, just call."

5

THE midday sun was warm across Florence's shoulders. The tightly cinched dress she'd chosen, a rich burgundy crepe de chine, accentuated the sway of her hips as she walked along Main Street. With the war going on most necessities were in short supply, or not to be had at all, but at least shopping gave her a pretense to get out of her house, and she was one of the few people in town with money to spend. She ran her business cash only—no credit to anyone. Her mama hadn't raised a fool. A man wouldn't pay for a pleasure he'd already tasted.

In a storefront window she examined an ornate sofa, daydreaming for a moment of the house she would have when she left Iberia Parish. To flaunt her wealth here would bring trouble down on her head. She sometimes bought a dress or a new pair of shoes—able to pay for leather soles instead of cardboard if such a thing could be found. No large ticket items, though.

She kept her life simple, her furnishings plain. One day, though, she'd dig up the money she'd buried so carefully and simply disappear from the parish to find the life she deserved. One luxury she allowed herself was a monthly trip to Baton Rouge, the state capital. Though she knew too well the rough districts near the river, she'd found a neighborhood in the north part of town where the hedges were high, the shutters always half closed, and where people lived their anonymous big-city lives in quiet comfort. And safety.

One afternoon a month, she allowed herself the fantasy as she strolled the sidewalks shaded by large oaks and exotic palms. She would buy a house there, furnish it with the heavy mahogany antiques she favored, and start life anew. She would present herself as the widow, if not wife, of a lawman. A woman of grace and beauty who had survived hard times. There would be no children, though. Life was too hard and unpredictable to risk that.

A dark car clattered by, and she noticed her reflection in the window. My, but she looked serious. And sad. Since Raymond Thibodeaux had begun to knock on her door regularly, sadness had burrowed deep in her bones. Her love for him had grown with equal measure with her understanding of the darkness that truly claimed his heart. Raymond felt he didn't deserve to live. He'd exiled himself to a half life as punishment for not dying.

She stepped beneath the awning of Marcel's Dress Shop and couldn't be certain if it was the sudden shade or her thoughts that sent a shiver over her. Now Henri Bastion was dead in a brutal murder, and Raymond had involved himself in the defense of a madwoman.

The door of the dress shop opened and the proprietress, Marcel Yerby, waved her inside. "Florence, is something wrong? You look like you're in pain."

Florence fixed a smile on her face. Marcel had a head full of coarse dark hair she rolled on rags each night to accomplish the latest style. She was vain and sometimes arrogant but today seemed in a chatty mood. "My thoughts had drifted to Henri Bastion and the terrible death he met on Section Line Road." Marcel would have all the latest gossip, and Florence knew the value of talk. She had a few tidbits to share herself, gleaned from Emanuel Agee's late-night visit.

Marcel nodded, eyebrows lifting. "I heard Adele Hebert was hovering over the body, snarling, and that a pack of wolves waited at the edge of the road. Raymond had to shoot four of them before he could get to Adele."

Florence felt a pulse of hope. "So, Raymond is finally a hero in the eyes of the town."

"Hardly. He's defending Adele, saying she's innocent."

Florence walked to a rack of dresses and began looking through them. She waited for Marcel to talk. The shopkeeper couldn't keep a secret.

"You'd best beware, *cher*. Raymond Thibodeaux has something going with Adele." Marcel arched an eyebrow. "She's cast a spell on him and aims to take him all the way to the dark side."

"One thing I know, Marcel. Raymond only goes where he wants." Florence pulled a green floral print dress off the rack, pretending to examine it. "Do you think this color will bring out my eyes?"

Marcel looked at the dress. "Men might enjoy your eyes, but that low bodice and short skirt will have them drooling over your figure. Course, the only man you want to notice is Raymond, isn't that right?"

Florence put the dress aside to try on. "I'm not the kind of woman to break my heart on a rock that won't roll." She forced a smile. "So tell me what you've heard about Adele."

"She had twins, but she never named the father."

Florence stopped with her hand on a clothes hanger. "Didn't she work for the Bastions for a while?"

Marcel's plucked eyebrows rose even higher. "Yes, I'd forgotten. Last year sometime. Are the boys his get?"

Florence shrugged. "The boys died during the early October fever." She grimaced. "I hope this cold snap has finally driven the mosquitoes away. If it warms again, we'll have another epidemic."

"Lettie, at the telephone exchange, said that Raymond called Father Finley and told him to get to the Bastion place. Imagine, ordering a priest around."

"Raymond knows how to get things done." Florence kept her focus on the rack of dresses. "Someone has to take charge in this place."

"I'll bet he does take charge." She grinned. "For all that he never smiles and he sometimes limps, he's a sexy man. He stirs the blood." Marcel clicked the dresses along the rack and pulled out a black number with a plunging back and swinging skirt. "This is perfect for you. As to Raymond, he's haunted by death. He brought it to many, and now he regrets his actions. I know you care for him, Florence, but he walks with the Dark Angel. That's what Raymond and Adele have in common."

Florence pulled out a dress and put it in the stack to try on. "Adele has reason to be insane. Her sister bled from the hands and hung herself, and her boys died only a couple of weeks ago. That's too much pain for any woman to endure. That doesn't make Adele a murderer."

Marcel looked around as if she feared someone would overhear them. "Father Finley wrote the Vatican about Rosa, to get her declared authentic. He was very excited by the prospect of a true religious miracle in his congregation. Of course, you'd know this if you attended church."

Florence laughed out loud. "My life is hard enough without spending extra time on my knees."

Marcel tried to block her laughter with a hand. "You are set for hell, Florence."

"Maybe so." She selected another dress. "A stigmatic in the church would have been a tremendous draw. Converts would've flocked like thieves to a bazaar. If Adele is a *loup-garou,* perhaps we can sell tickets."

"You've become jaded, Florence. Not everything is about money." Marcel made a face.

"Trust what I say, Marcel. Everything of any importance is about money." She lifted the skirt of the black dress, feeling the weight of the material, considering the way it would swirl on a dance floor. She'd practiced the steps of the jitterbug. Before the war, Raymond had been quite the dancer. "Raymond knows that money is always the motive. That's why he's become Adele's champion. She has nothing to gain. And I should remind you that neither does Raymond. He only wants justice." It was true. It seemed the only reason Raymond didn't end his own life was because he felt, in some small way, that he guarded the parish against injustices.

"Raymond's sister was in the shop earlier today. She said Raymond has changed so much since he went to war that she doesn't know him. He's a stranger to his family. He used to laugh and carry on, but now he doesn't even smile. He all but left a girl at the altar." She slid a fitted peplum jacket and skirt out of the rack and held it for Florence's inspection.

She shook her head. "Too businesslike. I'm not a secretary, as everyone knows." She took a breath. "Maybe Raymond doesn't need a silly girl to make him giggle." Marcel's words cut her, but she refused to show it.

Marcel returned the suit. "Raymond avoids his family. He avoids everyone he knew before the war."

"Maybe he has better things to do." Florence kept her gaze on the dresses. Raymond didn't avoid her—he sought her out. Sometimes, just before sleep, he would reach out and stroke her face with such tenderness that it fed the secret hope that burned in her heart.

Marcel sighed. "He dated Chula Baker, and he left that other girl at the altar. I heard she's still lovesick and moved to New Orleans to get away from seeing him."

"She was a kitten who tried to love a lion. It was bound to end in disaster." Florence picked up the green-floral and black dresses. "Let me try these on. I've been invited to a dinner in Baton Rouge next month." It was a lie, but it would throw Marcel's mind off the scent of Raymond.

"At the Sinclair home?"

Florence only smiled and disappeared into the fitting room. Marcel's tongue would wag even faster if she didn't have facts.

Teche was the Indian word for "snake," and it was an apt description of the deep bayou that wound like a serpent's coils through the parish and was the lifeblood of New Iberia. Bayou Teche, the snake river, the provider and destroyer. Raymond drove slowly across the bridge that spanned the placid yellow water. The bayou, like so much of life, wore both faces.

As a boy, he'd loved the bayou. He and his father and Antoine had spent many afternoons fishing, paddling softly past the gators, snakes, and snapping turtles that could take off a man's hand. He could still hear his father's voice. "All creatures have a place and a purpose, boys. Never kill except as a last resort. For food, to protect yourselves or those you love. To kill for pleasure shows the worst of any man."

Raymond often heard those words in his nightmares.

He drove northeast, maneuvering the roads still muddy from the storm. Bayou Caneche, a smaller tributary but still navigable by pirogue, fed into the Teche about ten miles due north of New Iberia. No one had been able to give him exact directions to Bernadette Matthews's house, at least not by land. He had a general knowledge of the area. He would find Bernadette, "the normal sister," because she was next on his list to question.

His thoughts drifted to Adele and the dark flutter of her eyelashes against her cheeks, like a moth under a glass. Not one single person in town had claimed to be her friend, or even know her. She was trapped, too. He would have to figure out the properties of the trap before he could spring the release.

The sun was bright; the day beautiful. He passed rippling acres of marsh grass that bent in a soft wind to take the last green bows of summer toward shore. The landscape would soon turn brown and drear, but still beautiful in its own way. The cypress trees had already begun. The furry fronds took on a russet color, reflected in the black pools of swamp water that dotted his travels.

After the war and his long stay in the hospital, he'd come back to New Iberia because it was home. Because there was nowhere else to go. No place had beckoned him, promising the life he'd once dreamed of having—a wife and family, a job, the weekends to drink and dance with his friends. That life was forever out of his reach. Antoine, a boy who'd never anticipated the reality of war, was dead.

The things he'd seen and done had changed Raymond. The consequences of his actions sat beside him in the passenger seat of the car like an always watchful corpse.

Perhaps that was why he felt so compelled to help Adele. In a strange way, they were both prisoners of external forces. He'd gone to war because it was his duty. He'd followed the orders given him, killed when commanded to do so, taking no pleasure in the men who fell before him. Until Antoine. After his brother's death, Raymond had taken satisfaction from the dead. Against his father's dictates, he'd killed with grim pleasure. And he'd learned that killing couldn't stop the nightmare parade of images that haunted his sleep.

Sometimes at night he heard Antoine's whistle, the shrill, clear sound of a hawk that had been their secret signal. *Kay-ie.* The sound would pierce his head. Drops of blood leaked from his ears, and he would awaken to the sound of his own screams.

Adele was haunted, too. She was lost in her nightmares, and perhaps had chosen to let the fever boil her. Madame Louiselle had hinted that someone had cast a spell on Adele. A spell or something more sinister. To him, Adele seemed poisoned, but he had no idea what could cause such behavior.

The question that intrigued him regarding Adele was why? If this delusion was more than a fever dream, who would select an unmarried Cajun woman as patsy to a vicious murder?

If someone had done this to Adele, he would find that person and make them pay the ultimate price the law allowed. He no longer lived for laughter, only for justice.

He came to a narrow dirt trail that led through a canopy of towering trees. There were no road markers, but this was the way to Bayou Caneche. The road wound, clinging to the highest ground as the land on either side became more liquid than dirt. With the smallest rain, the road would flood. Bernadette Matthews lived her life in perpetual threat of isolation. For many Cajuns it was the preferred way of life.

The road narrowed and limbs and branches began to swipe at the car. Overhead, the tree limbs were so dense the sun didn't penetrate, leaving the area filled with tall trees and little undergrowth. The stark beauty of it made him stop the car.

If a man was patient, he could come upon the wild hogs that roamed the swamps. Because of the shortage of meat, the hogs were highly favored as ingredients in the andouille sausage made locally. They were ferocious beasts who attacked rather than ran. Razor-sharp tusks grew from their snouts, and he'd been on manhunts where the missing person was found dead, the hamstring muscles cut by a boar's tusks.

Alligators, too, watched from the sloughs, dead pools, and wallows like the one to his right. Also favored as meat, the beasts ranged up to ten feet in length and were fast enough to bring down a cow or horse that strayed too close. Those who thought the gator's six-inch legs would slow it down often didn't live to learn differently.

While the hogs and gators had a certain value, the water snakes did not. Large moccasins the color of a dead stick would coil in the leaves and dirt, undetectable except for a stench young boys learned to recognize as soon as they were old enough to walk in the woods.

There were many predators and dangers in the woods, but no wolves. And certainly no *loup-garous*.

He drove on, wondering if he'd somehow chosen the wrong

path. At last the trees parted to reveal a cypress cabin set on pilings at least twelve feet in the air. He saw a child's curly head looking over the railing of the porch, and then another. An older girl was swinging in the front yard, a book on her lap. She watched him with solemn eyes. At last a woman with Adele's dark hair and eyebrows stepped onto the porch and waited, her expression neither welcoming nor forbidding. Two children followed at her side.

As he got out of the car, the woman watched him, unmoving. It wasn't until he put his foot on the step that she spoke.

"If you've come to talk about Adele, I got nothin' to say. My sister is a sick woman and needs medical help. She's not responsible."

"I'm Deputy Thibodeaux."

"I don't care if you're Jesus Christ. I got nothing else to say about my sister, me. I got my hands full here with my young-uns. Adele wants to go and put on another circus freak show to ruin the family name, she can go right ahead. Me, I got kids to think about. These here and three more."

Raymond gauged the ages of the children. The girl and one of the boys were old enough to hunt or fish. The Matthews children would not be in school, of that he was certain.

"Mrs. Matthews, I'm a representative of the law. I need to ask you some questions. Could we talk for a few minutes?"

"Don't expect me to ask you in." She turned on her heel, a child dragging at her skirt, and strode inside. Raymond was surprised to see the door and windows screened. It was a touch he hadn't expected.

The sitting room held two rockers in a corner by the fire. Above a stove was a shelf that held a radio and a collection of delicate glass figurines. Pallets for the children, neatly made, were on the floor. A picture of Jesus praying in the Garden of Gethsemane hung with a rosary beside it.

"You children go outside and play." She pointed to the door.

"Is Mrs. Bastion coming today?" the oldest boy asked.

"Maybe later. To get me to work." She waved them toward the door. "Go. Let me finish with the deputy."

The older boy took his brother by the hand and led him outside. Raymond, alone with Bernadette, took a seat in one of the rockers.

Bernadette stood in the center of the room. "Ask your questions. I got supper to cook."

Raymond had hoped for some insight into Adele. Into the strange behavior of both of Bernadette's sisters. "Do you believe Adele is possessed by the *loup-garou*?"

Her lips curled. "I believe my sisters, both of them, wanted folks to notice them. Since the day they were born, they cried and whined, demanding everything. Of the two, Rosa at least believed in God. Adele is sick. She had those babies and then couldn't remember to care for them. She's always been off." She tapped her head.

He rocked slowly in the chair. Bernadette's portrait of Adele contrasted sharply to that of Madame Louiselle. "Who fathered Adele's twins?"

"She gave herself freely. Perhaps one of the men she slept with bit her and made her believe she was the *loup-garou*. Adele was simple. Men influenced her in bad ways." Bernadette leaned forward. "That doesn't mean she'd kill a man, especially not Henri Bastion. She used to work for him."

"Do you know what man she was seeing?" He brought his notepad and pen from his pocket.

Bernadette took a breath. "My sister slept with lots of men. When she worked for Henri Bastion, she was fired because she couldn't stay away from one of the prisoners leased to Henri. A prisoner! She couldn't find a decent man who would marry her, so she took up with a convicted murderer."

The practice of leasing prisoners from the state penitentiary at Angola had once been accepted all over the state. Now it was a special arrangement. The leaser provided food and shelter lowering the cost of incarceration to the state. Henri Bastion had been working a crew since before the war. "Do you know this man's name?"

"Armand Dugas. Adele spoke of him sometimes."

"And he was a murderer?"

"So I've been told. Maybe he killed Henri and fixed it to look like Adele did it."

"Where is your husband, Mrs. Matthews?"

The change in subject took her by surprise. "What business is that of yours?"

"It would be helpful if you answered the question." He didn't want to threaten her, but her evasiveness made him suspect she might be abandoned. The cabin held small luxuries, though, and a single woman could never afford such things.

"Bodine is hunting with Clifton. They took a rich man from Shreveport into the swamp to hunt the wild hogs." She snorted. "This rich man wants adventure. Perhaps he would pay big dollars to hunt the *loup-garou*. We could turn my sister loose and let him track her through the swamps. Imagine her head on the wall of his Shreveport home." Tears sprang from her eyes, and she dashed them angrily away with her fists. "Why must Adele do these things to shame me?"

Raymond put his hands on his knees and leaned forward. "Tell me about Rosa."

"What can I say?" She shrugged, gaining control of her tears. "On her knees from morning to night, praying, crying out for God's mercy. It was horrible to watch."

"Did you see her hands bleed?"

She stepped toward him. "I saw the blood, and I saw the wounds on her hands." Her mouth hardened. "In her room, I found the hammer and spike, too. There was blood on the spike. What would a lawman call that? Evidence, maybe?"

"You're saying Rosa hammered a spike into her own hands?"

"I'm only telling you what I found."

"Why would she want to do something like that?" A greater point was that she would have had to have help. She couldn't hold the spike and hammer it, too.

Bernadette shrugged. "Rosa was Papa's favorite. When he died, she said she saw him standing in the yard, beckoning her. She believed she was destined to die soon, and when she didn't, she believed God had a special purpose for her."

"And Adele?"

"She always walked on the dark side, her. She was wild and willful, always running out at night. She told stories that scared us to death. She told my mother one time that she could fly. Mama believed Adele had special powers. It's true Adele got around the parish. She'd be at one place dancing and then before the night was over at Breauxbridge or St. Martinsville."

Raymond could clearly read the jealousy in Bernadette's face. They were alike, physically. The difference was in their expressions. Even burning with fever, Adele's face had more softness. "Do you believe Adele's possessed?"

"Only by a need to be the princess, all eyes on her."

"What's your relationship with the Bastion family?"

"I work there some, when Mrs. Bastion needs me. I took Adele's place when she was fired. They pay regular."

Raymond made a note. Bernadette's life had been hard, made harder by the public spectacle that her sisters had each created, deliberately or not. "Do you know if Adele had a reason to want Henri Bastion dead?"

"Why don't you ask Veedal Lawrence, the overseer at the Bastion plantation, what happened to Armand Dugas? That might answer your questions about Adele and then you wouldn't have to come here and bother me. Now you better leave before my husband gets back. He wouldn't think kindly of a man sitting in his rocker in his home."

6

JOLENE paced the small office, her face flushed with anger. "We drove all the way out there, and she wasn't home. All of that food! We couldn't leave it on the porch. There were ants everywhere. The high water had them out. We had to feed everything to the prisoners, and let me just say they looked like they hadn't eaten in a week of Sundays."

Michael wanted to sigh, but he kept his expression neutral. "Mrs. Bastion has suffered a terrible loss. She isn't herself, Jolene. You can't hold her to standards of conduct when the situation is so difficult. Her husband was torn apart in the middle of the road, for heaven's sake."

"Where in the world could she be? There wasn't a trace of her. Do you think she's okay? Folks are saying Henri was meeting the devil, walking so far from home on a stormy night." Jolene's pale brown eyes, almost golden, glittered with fear.

Michael blinked. Even he was beginning to be affected by all the wild talk of werewolves. "Probably, he walked to assist his digestion. People with money . . ." He didn't finish his thought, which went to eccentricities.

"There are those who say he traded his soul for wealth." Jolene had stopped pacing and stood in front of him. "What do you think of that, Father Michael? Do you believe the dark master walks the night, his hooves striking sparks on the gravel?"

Ever since Rosa, questions of belief had become difficult. Satan was a reality, and the line dividing angels and demons was clearly defined in his mind and bolstered by the rules of the Bible. When he'd chosen to enter the Dominican Order, he'd done so because he wanted to be a soldier of God, not a teacher or a scribe or a monk who spent his life tending animals and praying. He wanted to wage war against Satan and his demons, against the evil that afflicted mankind.

"If only Satan showed himself with his forked tail and cloven hooves, my work would be so much easier." He forced a smile. "He's a master of disguise, Jolene, but you have nothing to fear. Not from Satan or the *loup-garou*."

"I heard Henri Bastion was a wicked man—"

"Jolene, let us not speak ill of the dead. It does no good." He felt a prick of hypocrisy. Henri Bastion had sat in the first pew of the church each Sunday, his wife and children beside him, but Michael had never seen evidence that the Lord had been able to touch Henri. The prisoners working the fields were evidence of that.

Jolene started to say more but continued her pacing instead. He could see the anger was dissipating, and he spoke softly. "I want to thank you for all the help you've given me this past year. I don't know what I would have done without you. Especially with poor Rosa."

Jolene walked to the chair in front of his desk and placed her hands on the back of it. "Was she a real stigmatic, Father Michael?"

He could so clearly see her desire to believe. In this land where superstitions were the principal religion, people wanted a sign. They needed God to show them that he'd not left them to rot in the mosquito-infested swamps. The months of the past year followed a series of nature's obstacles, from the first spring plague of insects to the snakes and malarial infestations of summer, and on to the latest epidemic of fever that had claimed the lives of at least forty of his parishioners. Many of the young men were dead on the battlefields of France and Germany. The parish suffered daily.

"I saw Rosa's hands bleed. The manifestations of the nails had begun to appear in her feet."

"And her side? Did it bleed, too?"

He shook his head. "Primarily the hands. The wound in her feet was a new development." He closed his eyes to block the memories. The wounds had terrified him, and in his terror, he'd allowed doubt to grow. In his doubt, he'd failed Rosa in the most profound way. Now he would not fail Jolene.

"You really wrote the Vatican about Rosa?"

"I did."

"Were they considering Rosa as a saint?"

"They were." He wasn't lying. The cardinals in Rome had taken Rosa Hebert's case under serious scrutiny. What he didn't tell Jolene was that the Vatican had cast a dim eye upon Rosa. His request that she be authenticated as a stigmatic had met with firm disapproval, and it was too late when he'd understood that the Vatican was not eager for a common American woman to be elevated to the status of miracle.

"Just because she's dead, does that mean they'll stop trying to prove she was real?"

He stood, wanting to pace the room himself, to enjoy the release of action. He forced himself to stand steady, calm, the picture of composed strength. "Because her death was a suicide, the Vatican won't consider her case. Had she died under other circumstances, the investigation would have continued. Suicide is a mortal sin."

Jolene's thin bottom lip slipped into a pout. "That's hardly fair. If my hands opened in gaping wounds and started bleeding every Friday, I might have to consider suicide, too."

"That is a damning statement, Jolene." He shook his head but could not shake loose the sadness. "Suicide is not something to joke about. You are God's creation. You live by His choice, and it's for Him to determine when it's time to call you home."

"Sometimes God overloads the wheelbarrow."

He saw the pulse in her throat and knew she was aware of her blasphemy. In moments like this, he'd learned to review a person's past. It gave him what passed for wisdom among his parishioners. Jolene was in an unhappy, childless marriage. Her waist was thickening and her looks were fading. She teetered on a thin line between doing the good works of the church and becoming a bitter, harsh woman.

"As hard as it is to hear, God has a purpose for all that He puts in our paths. He knows the burden you carry, Jolene, and each day He sees your strength." He hesitated. "My area of study was the history of the Irish church. My anticipation was that I would be sent to Belfast, to work with a country I loved and understood. A country engaged in a terrible war. I had no preparation for this culture in Iberia Parish. I don't understand why God sent me here, but I have to trust that He has a plan."

"Your trust in God's grand design intrigues me. How do you know it's true?"

He touched his chest and thought he heard an echo. "In here. Faith happens in the heart, not the mind, Jolene." He knew the proper words, even if he'd lost his belief in them.

She mimicked his gesture. "There's nothing here but emptiness. I want to feel something, before I'm too old."

Jolene needed to be loved. She needed tenderness. He was moved by her emptiness, but he had no solution for her. "You must pray to God for faith. If you seek it, God will deliver it to you."

"I've spent hours on my knees."

The anger had returned to her voice, and he was suddenly weary. "God demands surrender. You should pray for the grace to surrender to His will."

"So that I can go home to Jacques and cook his supper and fetch his slippers." Her voice rose with each word. "He doesn't love me, Father. All I want is someone to love me."

Michael grasped her shoulders and held her firmly. "God loves you, Jolene."

"It's not enough." A dry sob tore at her throat. "I just want someone to hold me, to make me feel safe."

Michael drew her into his arms. He was violating one of his personal rules with the females of his congregation, but Jolene was on the verge of a total collapse. He felt her bitter tears soaking through the starch of his collar. He held her in his arms, an intimate embrace, feeling only compassion.

He let her cry herself out, then assisted her into a chair. He poured a small measure of brandy into a lovely crystal glass from a set his grandmother had sent from County Cork. "Drink this."

She tried to resist but he pressed it into her hand.

"If Jacques smells liquor on my breath . . ."

"Send him here to talk to me. There is a duty to God we shall discuss." He walked to the window and looked out. Plants grew lush and thick in the Louisiana heat and humidity. Even now, so late in the year, there were blooms on the roses in his garden. While the nuns labored over collards and other winter crops for the Victory Garden that would feed them, Michael had planted an assortment of mums that bordered his paths in bright golds, oranges, and russets—a sunset rush of color and graciousness in the middle of a brutal swamp.

Beyond the garden was a wrought-iron fence, and beyond that a live oak with graceful limbs that swept the ground. He could recall in vivid detail the morning he'd looked out this very window and taken such pleasure in his flowers, his gaze sweeping up to the fence and the tree, and the dawning horror of Rosa Hebert swinging in a gentle wind.

He didn't hear the door close as Jolene left, her footsteps muffled by the vacuum of his private nightmare.

The line of twenty prisoners, mostly Negro men, swung machetes in unison, then advanced and swung again, hacking their way into the purple rows of sugar cane. Behind them, another line of twenty men stripped the stalks and tossed them into the bed of a wagon for delivery to the refinery. In the distance, working another field, Raymond saw the migrant workers, paid labor, hacking and stripping. Haitians and Puerto Ricans had been brought in to work for minimal wages for the harvest, but it was the convicts who interested Raymond. Henri had controlled their lives the same way a human determined the destiny of livestock.

A breeze swept across the field, and Raymond caught the scent of the sugar cooking at one of the refineries. The odor was sickly sweet, nauseating. The men kept working as if they didn't smell a thing. Raymond watched the process, the endless bending and hacking of the first row of men, followed by the quick stripping and tossing of the second. The cane had to be cut close to the ground, for the sweetest part was near the soil. Almost everyone who lived in southern Louisiana had worked the cane fields at one time or another. Such labor had taught Raymond as a young boy that he wasn't interested in farming.

The convicts moved in a steady rhythm across the rippling field of cane. The men would work until darkness stopped them and rise again at first light. The race was on to beat the first frost of the year, which would destroy any unharvested cane. Marguerite Bastion's comfortable future rested on the backs of the convicts and imported poor who toiled in her fields.

Even from a distance Raymond could see the skeletal quality of the men, hear the clank of the leg chains that bound them to the job and to each other. The chains were unnecessary. None of the men looked as if he could make it to the road if he tried to run. They were in pathetic condition. It was ironic that the slaves once used to grow and harvest the cane were better treated because

they were financial investments. If half the prisoners never returned to Angola, it would be that many less mouths for the state
to feed.

He drove on to the house and parked. He was halfway across
the yard when Marguerite stepped onto the front porch. Like
Bernadette Matthews, Marguerite had a child clinging to her
skirts. Unlike Bernadette, Marguerite was beautifully dressed. The
cameo at her throat was expensive; the gold earrings that looped
into a cascade of pearls were real.

"Where is my husband's body?" She lifted her chin and he
saw the Mandeville heritage in her proud stance. What had possessed her family to marry her off to Henri Bastion? Gossip in
town was that she'd been sold for a stake in Henri's empire.
Though he didn't believe the gossip, he knew the reality was that
if her parents refused to allow her to return home, she would
have no option but to stay with Henri. Marguerite hadn't been
taught the skills of survival as an independent woman, and to the
best he could determine, she'd made no friends. In the time he'd
been working as a deputy, he'd seen Marguerite in town only on
Sunday mornings for church, and Henri had stayed at her side,
guarding her contact with others. Perhaps she was a different
kind of prisoner.

He spoke softly. "Doc is doing an examination. I'm sorry,
Mrs. Bastion. I know this is hard for you."

"I want to lay my husband to rest. It's barbaric that you keep
him so you can cut on him more." She held herself perfectly erect.

"There are things we can learn from the body." He didn't
want to go into the specifics of hack marks and teeth angles, stran-
gulation or evisceration. "Doc is working as fast as he can, but to
be honest, he hasn't had much call to do an autopsy."

"Why is an autopsy necessary? Hasn't Adele confessed to
killing Henri?"

He didn't want to go into the reasons Adele might be innocent. "Technically, Adele is too sick to confess to anything. Would

you mind answering a few questions for me?" He put his foot on the front steps and the child at Marguerite's side began to cry.

"Go inside, Sarah."

The child clung to her, crying soundlessly.

Marguerite pushed a strand of hair from her hot face. "Sarah, please go inside. I can't talk with you pulling at my dress."

Raymond leaned down, his intention to talk to the child, to reassure her. The little girl's eyes widened and she tore free of her mother and ran inside. The screen door banged behind her.

Marguerite faced him. "Please, ask your questions and leave. My children are upset and need me."

Raymond pointed to two cowhide-bottomed chairs that lined the gallery. "Would you mind if we sat in those rockers?"

"Certainly. I want to help."

Raymond pulled out the notepad he always carried. "When was the last time you saw your husband?"

"When he walked out the door. He said he would be back in an hour. He put his hat on and walked out." She bit her bottom lip. "I never saw him again."

"He was in the habit of walking every evening, wasn't he?"

The look she gave him was confused. "He also drank coffee every day and ate a biscuit for breakfast. Why are his habits of interest to you, Deputy?"

"Sometimes the patterns of a man's life tell me things. To have an idea of who might want to kill Henri, I need to know his routine. Did he always walk to the same location?"

"I didn't question Henri, about his walks or his destinations. Obviously you've never been married, Deputy Thibodeaux. It isn't a woman's place to ask such things."

"Weren't you even curious?"

She took a breath. "By the time Henri left on his walks, I'd tended the children all day, cooked our meals, cleaned the house, washed and ironed. I was glad for an hour of quiet to compose myself."

"Don't you have some help?"

She nodded. "At different times, both Adele and her sister Bernadette have worked here. Believe me, there's plenty to do for a dozen women."

For the moment, Raymond let the matter of Adele rest. "What type of business did your husband do?" Raymond asked the question casually, but he watched Marguerite closely. If Adele hadn't murdered Henri, someone else had, and motive was at the base of his question.

"He grew cane as you can clearly see. Henri excelled at farming."

"He had no other business interests?"

Marguerite frowned. "He was a planter, Mr. Thibodeaux. Is there something I should know?"

"Veedal Lawrence is your overseer?"

"That's right, since before I married Henri." She looked out toward the fields. "He isn't my choice, but Henri trusted him."

"Is Veedal responsible for the prisoners?"

"Yes. He's in charge. Henri never allowed me to interfere. Henri said the state prisoners were difficult to motivate, and that Veedal had total authority."

"With Henri gone, the burden of the prisoners falls on your shoulders, Mrs. Bastion, but I'll check with the overseer on my way out."

"Thank you, Deputy Thibodeaux. There's so much for me to figure out how to do now, without Henri. Your help is appreciated."

"You said Adele worked for you for a time. What did she do, and why was she let go?"

"Last year she came for the gathering of the summer crops and the cane harvest. She helped me preserve the vegetables to see us through the winter." Her hands smoothed the arms of the rocker. "She worked beside me, a strong, efficient worker, maybe a little peculiar. She kept her own counsel." She gave him a look

of puzzlement. "And now she's killed my husband. I don't understand why."

"Did you fire Adele or did Henri?"

"She simply didn't return to work one morning. I discovered later that she'd come down with morning sickness. She
was pregnant."

"Who was the father?" He pretended to write in his notebook but his attention was focused on Marguerite. Bernadette
had claimed that Adele was fired, but it was possible Henri had
fired her without telling Marguerite. He was getting a picture of
a man who seldom confided his reasoning to his wife.

"Who can say? Adele was often down in the stables where we
keep the prisoners. She was lonely, I know that. For some reason she
couldn't find a man to love." Her smile was sad. "It's difficult here
for a woman, Deputy. So many men have been killed in the war."

"Was there one particular convict she fancied?" He held the
trump. Armand Dugas. It would be interesting to see if Marguerite revealed the man's name.

"Veedal said she flitted from one to another."

"And what did Veedal say she was doing in the stables, exactly?"

"She had some homemade salve and mumbo-jumbo herbs.
She organized baths."

"Your husband allowed this?" Raymond couldn't cover his
surprise.

"Henri said Adele could do no harm. He knew she was a little off, but he certainly never thought her dangerous."

Raymond stood up. "Thank you for your time, Mrs. Bastion."
He walked past her and down the steps. Out of the corner of his
eye he saw the little girl standing behind the screen door. She
held a glass figurine of a horse in her hand, one that matched
those in Bernadette's home.

When he was at his car he turned back to Marguerite, who'd
stood and walked to the door. "There was never any particular
convict linked with Adele?"

"If there was, Henri never told me." She let the screen door bang behind her as she entered the house.

Raymond drove the hundred yards to the stables. The men were in the field, and he hoped the foreman was, too. When he entered, the stench nearly made him gag. He crossed to the small office and walked straight to the desk. He felt no hesitation as he began to go through the papers until he found what he sought.

The prisoner inventory list from the previous year showed one Armand Dugas arriving at the Bastion farm in February of 1941. Dugas was serving a life sentence for murder. No additional information was given. Raymond scanned the other papers. There was no mention of Dugas being returned to Angola. Either he was still in the field, or he was dead.

"What the fuck do you think you're doin'?"

Raymond looked up to find a tall man, freckles burned to a burnished copper across his face, red hair thinning and arms as big as hams.

"I'm checking your prisoner inventory."

"Just because you're wearing that tin on your chest doesn't give you the right to come in here and poke around."

"No, but Mrs. Bastion gave me that right." He smiled. "She also told me to check the condition of the convicts. She's wondering if their food ration is adequate."

"She doesn't give a fuck about the food."

"You must be Veedal Lawrence." Raymond held the papers in his left hand, his right easing ever so slowly to the gun at his side. Veedal didn't look like a man who'd been refused by the army because of physical defects, yet Raymond knew he'd never served a day.

"It ain't no concern of yours if I'm Peter Piper. Now give me that list and get out of my office." Veedal made a grab for the pages.

Raymond stepped back. He took Veedal's measure. He saw the foreman's pale eyes, the way his jaw set and locked, loutish and eager for a fight. "Try that again, and I'll have to shoot you."

"Put that gun and badge on the desk and fight me like a man."

Raymond smiled. "I'd rather blast your dick in the dirt and watch the show while you try to figure how to put it back in place." His fingers closed on the grip of his gun. "Now I want to see Armand Dugas."

Veedal grinned. "I'd like to see him, too. Bastard pulled a runner last fall. Either he made it out of the swamp alive or a gator got him. Couldn't rightly say which."

"You're telling me that Dugas, half starved and in leg shackles, got away?"

"Strange, ain't it? Almost like some kind of magic. I come down that mornin' and his leg irons was lying open on the ground. He was gone and no amount of whippin' could get the others to say what happened."

"He just up and disappeared?" Raymond forced his grip on the gun to relax, fighting his impulse to pull the weapon and slam it hard into Veedal's face, repeatedly.

"Mr. Henri was right upset. Dugas was a good worker, for all of his oddities. The state sent two to replace him, though, so it worked out. Mr. Henri was satisfied."

Raymond had no doubt Armand Dugas's body, or what was left of it, was somewhere in the swamp. Most likely Veedal had beaten him or worked him to death and then dumped the remains for the hogs to eat or the swamp to swallow.

"How many other prisoners have you lost, Veedal?"

The man grinned. "Dugas was the only escapee. We've had eight in the last year die from the fever."

The fever. Another convenient cause of death. "I'm sure you had Doc Fletcher out here to verify the cause of death." He saw the negative answer in Veedal's heated eyes. "You'd best see to it that the men's food ration is increased. Considerably. I'll be back by to check, and if they don't look a little less like walking skeletons, you and I are going to have another talk, and you aren't going to like the gist of what I have to say."

Veedal snapped a salute. "Yes, sir, boss. I'mma gonna do jus' what you say."

Raymond dropped the papers he held to the floor. He walked past Veedal Lawrence. He'd intended to interview the convicts, but the men wouldn't talk to him with Veedal around. He'd come back in a day or two. Check on the foreman's progress.

7

THE sun hung above the treetops when Chula turned down the road to Louiselle Dumont's home. The post office was closed for the day, but there were older residents, or those who lived alone or without transportation, whose mail Chula delivered whenever she could.

She felt the familiar burn of tired muscles between her shoulder blades as she wrestled the car through a patch of wet sand. It would be good to get home to a hot bath, to the supper her mother would have planned for her. There were days she thought she missed the life of wife and mother, but mostly she was glad to remain a daughter. Once she left her mother's home, no one would coddle her. In Iberia Parish, and the rest of the country, the yoke of domesticity rested firmly on the woman's shoulders.

Smoke rose from Madame Louiselle's chimney and Chula felt a pulse of excitement. Madame had begun to teach her the ways of the *traiteur,* the healer, and each encounter with the older woman brought something new into her life. Chula had discovered an innate ability to sense illness. Part of it was her willingness to listen, to truly hear what lay beyond words. She'd come to believe, though, that another part was a gift. Madame had convinced her of that and was helping her learn to accept and hone her talent.

She picked up the letter from California off the car seat and hurried up the steps of the cabin. She was about to knock on the door when it opened. Madame put a finger to her lips and drew Chula inside.

The room was too hot, stifling for such a lovely October afternoon. She was about to protest the heat when she saw the form of a young woman on the sofa, the firelight flickering over her sleeping features. At first she didn't recognize Adele, but when she did, she raised her eyebrows. She'd heard the talk that Adele had been spirited away from the jail—that Raymond was protecting her, for some unknown reason. Chula knew why. For all that Raymond had lost of himself, he was still a man who defended the helpless.

For a time, just out of high school, Chula had believed she loved Raymond. Believed it enough to yield to the hot passion that jumped between them. She felt a smile touch her lips. Those were good memories to cling to when seasons passed and no man sparked her interest. The thing between her and Raymond, though, had been, ultimately, a joining of two minds that could not abide injustice. When the passion had burned away, a bond of friendship as strong as love had remained. At least until the war, when Raymond returned a shell of the man she'd known.

"Chula?"

For a moment Chula had forgotten where she was, or who lay before her in a sweating coma. "Madame, what is this?"

"It's an unusual case, Chula. Like none I've seen."

Chula stepped closer to the sick woman. "Will she live?"

"I haven't been able to break the fever, but it's reduced. I lit a fire to ward off the chills." Madame's voice was in a low register, barely a ripple of noise.

"Fever?" Images of the most recent epidemic came to mind. Delivering the mail, Chula had seen funeral after funeral, coffins nailed shut by doctor's orders against the spread of illness. Some said it came from mosquitoes, others said it was a sickness in the swamp water, and others believed it was bad humors from an evil spirit. Chula and her mother had escaped illness, but many lives had been lost.

"It isn't the yellow jack." Madame's dark eyes held Chula's, telling her not to be afraid. "This is something else. Want to examine her?"

Chula nodded. She did want a closer look. She stepped over to the sleeping woman and took in the paleness of her skin, the purple rings beneath her eyes, the way her hands and feet twitched like a sleeping dog.

She touched Adele's forehead and felt the dry, hot fire that burned within her.

"She had a seizure this morning and bled from the nose. She lost a lot of blood before I could stop it with cold compresses." Madame stood beside Chula.

"Has she regained consciousness?"

Madame shook her head. "I thought she might, but she slips back into her sleep. She doesn't want to leave her dreams and return to this world."

Chula touched one of Adele's jerking hands and held it firmly. She felt the tremors that pulsed through Adele's flesh as an electric current might. Chula inhaled sharply and looked at Madame, who only nodded.

Chula's hands moved up Adele's arms, touching, pressing, sensing. As her hands explored, she tried to clear her mind to register the sensations she felt. Adele's muscles were strung taut, defying the appearance that she slept. There was an inner tension in Adele's body that Chula had never experienced.

"She fights herself," she said, not intending to speak aloud.

"What else?"

Chula let her hands wander to Adele's chest. The drum of her heart reminded Chula of a trapped bird, wings beating in the effort to escape. Panic, fear, the consuming need to be free. "She's afraid. If she continues, the fear will kill her. Her heart will burst."

"Which is why she bled from the nose. The pressure of her beating heart."

Chula stepped back. "The fever has no physical cause, does it?"

Madame took her arm and led her into the kitchen. She closed the door and went to the open window for a breath of cool air. "I'll make some tea."

Chula took a seat at the table while Madame put a kettle on and prepared the teapot. The room was painted aquamarine, a color that Madame said soothed her mind when she was troubled. Chula loved the color and the bright glass jars of preserved tomatoes, beans, potatoes, jams, and fruits that lined the shelves. Often Madame took payment for her services in meat or vegetables. She canned what she couldn't eat, supplies that would last her during the winter or a long flood.

Herbs and different marsh grasses hung in the windows, drying. Madame's gift of healing was her use of the native plants to concoct medicines. Those who couldn't afford, or didn't trust, Doc Fletcher came to her.

"Have you given Adele anything?"

"She holds nothing down."

"Not even water?"

Madame shook her head as she placed tea in a pot. "She acts as if she can't swallow, but I've checked her mouth and throat. There's nothing wrong. She drools constantly."

Hydrophobia. Chula thought about the infection spread by the bite of a rabid animal. "Could it be rabies?"

"I thought it might, but no."

She had a terrible thought, one that would devastate a parish already overwhelmed with disaster. "Polio?"

"No, not that." Madame poured the hot water over the tea. "It's a fever in the brain. It comes and goes. Raymond said she was sensible this morning."

Chula accepted the cup of tea Madame handed her. "Could it be that someone is giving her something to cause the fever?"

Madame's smile was proud. "That thought has crossed my mind."

Chula frowned. "Or is it possible Adele seeks the fever because of something she's done? Maybe the illness is mental."

Madame took a seat opposite Chula. "You are gifted, Chula Baker. You tease out the seed that others can't find. With time you'll ferret out the truth."

"Adele doesn't have much time." She spoke with certainty. There had been the finger of death on Adele's face. "If that fever doesn't break, she'll die before anyone can help her."

"Do you believe she has the right to choose death?" Madame's ringless hand touched Chula's arm.

"Father Finley says that we must live according to God's plan for us. That it's a mortal sin to commit suicide." She spoke slowly, remembering Rosa. "I'm not so sure. There are other questions. These men who go off to war know they'll die. Isn't that suicide, too? To rush a hill into gunfire?" She shook her head. "They're called heroes and given medals. Poor Rosa Hebert was called a sinner and excommunicated."

Madame's chuckle was soft. "The laws of the church, which are man's laws, are often woven to a purpose, *cher*. Not God's purpose, but man's. The question I asked you is one only you can answer. It must come from your heart, not your mind. Law and logic are of no use."

"If I put myself in Rosa's place, I understand. I saw her hands, the awful wound that opened every Friday. I can imagine that all week long she dreaded Friday, when her flesh would rupture in those painful wounds."

"Imagination is an important part of healing. To feel another's illness is to understand it." She patted Chula's arm. "It's also a danger. To feel too much—the illness will trick you."

Chula sipped her tea. Madame was never straightforward with

her lessons. This was one, turned upside down, for her to figure out. "Did you ever see Rosa's hands?"

"I did. She came here, wanting me to make it stop."

That surprised Chula. "Father Finley wanted her to be verified as authentic. I think he saw certain sainthood for her. And lots of glory for the parish."

"You've read the life of the saints. Is this something you'd willingly seek?"

Chula laughed. "Stoning, persecution, burning at the stake, no, I wouldn't choose that, but I'd never have thought of it that way." She sobered before she spoke again. "Could you help Rosa?"

"There was no physical reason for the wounds to open in her hands."

"Was there a mental reason?"

Madame stood. "Isn't that the same question we just asked of Adele?"

Chula rose, too. She drew the letter from her pocket. "I almost forgot."

Madame took the envelope and looked at it. "My sister writes me every month. She says there are no bugs or snakes in California. The sun shines every day. The air is dry and like a kiss." She put the letter on the table. "I would die there." She shook out her apron. "Come back tomorrow if you can. I'm going to steep some tincture tonight. I may need help getting it down Adele."

"Certainly." Chula hugged the older woman. "Will you be okay tonight?"

"The full moon has passed. At least for this month."

It took a moment for Chula to catch the humor hidden at the corner of Madame's mouth.

Chula was still smiling as she drove away from the cabin. Lost in her own thoughts, she rounded a sharp curve with deep sand, unprepared for the car blocking the middle of the road.

She slammed on brakes, cursing. As soon as she brought her vehicle to a stop, inches from the wooden bumper of the other car, she was out and striding down the road past both cars. "Where are you, you stupid son of a bitch?" She was too angry to control her language. "What kind of moron leaves a car in the middle of the road on a curve?"

There was no sign of the person who'd abandoned the car, and she felt the edge of her anger fade. She took a deep breath; the October air held the promise of a chill when the sun went down. Turning, she looked back to see a tall, lean man standing with one foot on the running board of his car. To her disgust, she recognized Praytor Bless. He was grinning like a mule eating briars.

"I would have said something sooner, but I didn't want to interrupt your pleasure in usin' foul language." Praytor took his foot off the running board and stood up tall, his hands at his side. A brown fedora shaded his eyes. Lanky and lean, he wore a starched shirt and creased wool trousers.

Chula disliked the fact that he stood between her and her vehicle. For all that he'd thrown in with Henri Bastion and was said to be building his own fortune, he made Chula uncomfortable. "What are you doing out here, Praytor?" She deliberately chose his first name.

"I could ask you the same." He shoved his hands in the pockets of a nearly new jacket. Chula noted that whatever work Praytor claimed to do for Henri, it didn't require manual labor or sweat.

"I'm doing my job." Her tone belied her smile. "Delivering the mail."

"And I'm doin' mine."

"Which would be?" She was worried about Madame. There were fools who thought Madame practiced some type of voodoo or witchcraft. They couldn't comprehend that she was a healer, not someone who dabbled in curses and plagues.

"Lookin' out for my interests."

She would have to pass him so she started forward, her skirt swinging against her legs. "I've never been clear what your *interests* might involve, Praytor."

"I'm a businessman, Miss Chula. By the terms around here, a successful one." He turned so that he could walk with her to her car. "I got railroad and oil concerns. A little of this and a little of that. I expect my fortunes to grow in the near future."

"Congratulations are in order then. Are you here to see Madame? Are you ill?" she asked, a thin layer of concern in her voice. She could feel her heart beating too fast, but she knew he had no inkling of her dislike for him. Nor would he. The trick to men was to smile as you looked in their eyes, to flatter even when it stretched the biggest imagination. Her mother had taught her survival skills in a world dominated by men. She was no physical match for Praytor and though he'd done nothing untoward, she felt uneasy around him.

"No, ma'am. I just wanted to talk to Madame about some medicine for my sister. She's taken poorly and can't seem to pull out of a slump."

"I'm sorry to hear that. I hope she recovers." She tried to recall if she'd ever seen Praytor's sister and came up with a negative.

"She just needs a tonic to build her blood. Mrs. Dumont will be able to help her, I'm sure."

"Are you having car trouble?" Chula pointed to his vehicle as she passed.

"Not at all. That Ford runs like clockwork. I stopped to see if there were any crayfish in the slough there. I was thinkin' Mama might boil us up some with some potatoes and corn. Maybe pull out my fiddle for a bit of dancin'." He opened her car door. "Would you care to come to dinner?"

She pasted a smile, fighting against revulsion. "How kind of you, but I have plans."

"I didn't realize you were seeing anyone." His tone was sharp.

Praytor Bless had money and influence. He wasn't a man to toy with. "I have plans with Mother." She got in and pulled her skirt in before closing the door. "But your invitation is kind, Praytor. I hope you enjoy the crayfish and the music."

She started the car, focusing her attention on the road, hoping he would take the hint and move his vehicle so she could pass.

For a long moment he stared in the window at her, at last walking to his car and moving it to the side of the road so she could drive by.

She gave him a nod as she passed, her foot heavier on the gas than normal as the first blue notes of dusk seeped through the thick woods.

The sun had set when Raymond watched Praytor Bless exit the road that led to Madame Louiselle's. First Chula Baker had pulled out, going a bit faster than advisable. Then, fifteen minutes later, Praytor. Instead of turning toward home, Praytor headed north, toward town.

Raymond eased down the road and parked at Madame's. He gathered the quilts he'd had Pinkney wash and dry and took them up the stairs. Madame signaled him inside without a word, taking the bedcovers from him.

"How is she?" he asked. His own observations told him that Adele was neither better nor worse.

"She suffers." Madame led him into the kitchen. A large glass bowl contained leaves and brown berries that Raymond had never seen. Madame poured an amber liquid from the bowl into tiny bottles.

"Chula Baker was here." He made it a statement. "And Praytor, too."

"Chula brought my mail, and Praytor came to see what he could learn." Madame wiped her forehead with the back of one hand. She put the bowl down and walked behind him. "He's a nosy man, but Chula is like you, Raymond, out of time and place here. Once she was good company for you."

Raymond leaned his weight on the back of a chair. "I'm not good company for anyone, Madame."

He felt her light touch trace across his lower back, moving along his hip. A tingle flickered up his spine.

"The pain is like a fire, burning low and then growing with new fuel. You live in the shadow of it," Madame said.

He didn't want to talk about his wound. "The pain reminds me of who I used to be and how much I've changed. If I didn't have it, I might forget." He walked to the window to escape her touch. "I'll bring some of Adele's clothes tomorrow."

"She's beyond my help, Raymond. Has Doc Fletcher returned?"

"He has, but he can't do more than you." Doc was a good man, but he would recommend incarceration in the state asylum. Adele would be taken away without even a trial. Joe Como would want him to drop the case. "Did Praytor see Adele?"

Madame moved around the table so that she faced him again. "He didn't come inside. He had no way of knowing she was here."

"Good." Praytor was a mama's boy and a busybody. No one to fear, but someone to stir trouble if he had half the chance. "I don't want folks in town to know she's out here. Could mean trouble for you."

Madame handed him a cup of steaming tea. The brew was black, and Raymond thought of his great-grandmother, an Algonquin Indian who had no use for white men, saying they were a curse on the land and would bring death to all living things.

She'd taught Raymond the cry of the hawk, saying it would bring help in times of trouble. Raymond had taught the call to Antoine, a signal between them when they'd hunted together.

Nanna, as he'd called the old woman, claimed that she could change into a crow at will, and her eyes had been black and sharp. She'd cocked her head when she listened, like a bird, and she could read the future in the dregs of plants she used for medicinal teas. Once she'd drunk a cup of tea so black it was like looking into a hole. The thing she'd seen had frightened her so badly that she'd only say that Raymond faced a great battle and much hardship. She hadn't been lying either. He sipped the tea, refusing to look into the cup.

"Did Adele ever mention the father of her boys?" he asked.

"She never said." Madame stood at the sink and sipped her tea. "She came for morning sickness. She walked all the way here. She said only that she was with child and needed something so she could continue to work."

"Did you ask her who the father was?"

Madame nodded. "I told her that he should help her." She shrugged. "She said he wouldn't. She said he was nothing to her or the baby. That she would love the child enough for two parents. When twins were born, she was delighted. She had them herself, alone. She is a strong woman."

Raymond pondered that as he drank the hot, bitter tea. "She didn't want the father to share in the baby, so she didn't love him?"

"Adele didn't seem to have love in her life, from any source, except Rosa and those baby boys. The man who planted the babies was never a part of her life. A man sometimes betrays the woman who loves him."

Guilt was a physical sensation. Raymond thought of the young girl who'd waited for his return from the war, expecting a ring. He couldn't explain to her that the man she loved was dead. What had come home from the battlefields was only a husk, a man undeserving of love. A half man deserving only contempt.

"Raymond, are you ill?" Madame took his teacup from a hand that shook.

"May I sit with Adele a moment?"

"Talk to her. Try to reach her, *cher*. She needs someone to bring her back. She has lost her children but she is young. From what I can tell, she can bear a child again."

Raymond left the cool kitchen and drew up a chair beside the sofa in the stifling front room. A thin sheen of sweat covered Adele's face, and he wrung out a cloth in a basin of water and wiped her face. She looked only moments away from death. In many ways, it would simplify things if she died. The parish would calm down, and the wild talk of werewolves would dissipate.

And a killer would also walk free, because Raymond knew she was innocent. Not by evidence, but by his gut. He'd come to the badge not because of his knowledge of the law or his desire to apply it, but his job was a symbol of who he'd become, a loner. It suited his view of himself, a man watching life from the outside. He judged others as he judged himself. This woman, though, so harshly served by life, needed his help. Whatever her sins, she was innocent of murder.

"Adele, I want to help you." He spoke softly, wondering if Madame could hear him. "I don't believe you killed Henri. I want to prove it, but I don't know how. I need answers from you. I need for you to wake up and talk to me."

Adele sighed, and a whisper of peace touched her features. In that moment, by the light of the flickering fire, Raymond realized that she might have been beautiful.

"Do you know what happened to Armand Dugas?"

The name troubled her. She turned her head from side to side. Raymond had the sense that she was almost with him, that the veil of unconsciousness was thinning.

"I need to find Dugas if he's alive."

Her hands seemed to push him away.

"Adele, let me help you. Try!"

He sensed Madame behind him, and he turned to look at her. "Can she understand me?"

"I don't know, *cher*. But I do. And I worry for you. Some things are impossible to change." She put a hand on his shoulder. "Come back tomorrow. If she isn't dead, she may be aware."

8

FLORENCE slipped the thin gold wire through the hole in her ear and straightened to judge the effect in her mirror. The gold glinted softly against her jawline. The earrings were the perfect length. She turned slowly and examined the room. The bed linens were freshly ironed and the coverlet new. A peach shawl, draped over the lamp shade, cast a warm, soft light that played to perfection on her olive skin tones.

From the bottom drawer of her vanity she brought out the tiny bottle of real perfume and dabbed her ears, neck, and cleavage before lifting her skirt to apply a drop to her naval and the exposed pubis that showed beneath her garter belt. For tonight she'd purchased silk hose. They'd cost a pretty penny, but the effect was worth it.

She lowered the skirt of the little black dress she'd bought at Marcel's and rocked her hips to see the shimmy of material. For a split second she fantasized about going dancing. There were joints and bars all over Iberia Parish, but dancing was a date, and Florence Delacroix was not a woman men asked on a public date.

She swallowed back the bitter taste of self-pity and walked to the kitchen. Her drink had left a condensation ring on the table, and she picked up the glass and wiped the water mark off the burnished wood. He was late. She finished the bourbon, put the glass in the sink, and walked out on the front porch where a cool breeze brought the singing of insects to her.

The night was clear and through the arching limbs of the live oak in her yard she saw the round moon floating in black velvet. She shuddered as if someone had stepped on her grave.

The high-pitched whine of a mosquito near her ear made her swat wildly, her finger painfully catching the gold hoop in her ear. It shouldn't be so hot in the last days of October. The weather was unnatural. Something bad was bound to happen.

She let the screen door slam behind her as she went back inside to look for her car keys. He was twenty minutes late, and she would not sit and wait for him. One of the lessons her mama had taught her was that waiting for a man was time lost forever. At thirty-four, Florence didn't have time to waste. God had blessed her with firm flesh and sweet curves, but time had already begun to pull and tug. When she studied her face in the bright morning light, she saw the tiny wrinkles that would, in time, be fissures. Her breasts, so ripe and firm, would sag. She'd known older whores who tried to sell themselves and they disgusted her. Time was her most precious commodity and no one wasted it for her.

Her keys were on the vanity and she picked them up, along with her purse. Her high heels clicked on the wood as she strode through her house snapping off lights. The screen creaked and she jutted out her butt to hold it back while she locked the door.

A hand came out of the darkness and grabbed her buttocks, sliding over the curve of muscle to a place more intimate. "I'm sorry I'm late. Were you going out?"

She left the keys in the lock and stepped into his arms. "Time doesn't wait for no man and neither does Florence." His after-shave was sharp and clean like a snapped pine branch. Her cheek brushed his chest and she felt the starch in his shirt. She liked a clean man, one who took pains to show respect for her. She limbered her spine and let her groin sink against him. His response was swift, eager. She laughed, loving the power she held over him. Though folks in town said he was half dead, she knew how to bring life to him. "What kept you, baby?"

"I was out at the Bastion place and then had some things to do before I finished work."

Florence stepped back and in the dim light saw the trouble in his face. She took his hand. "Let's go inside."

"I thought you were going out."

He was teasing her, but she didn't care. She walked backward, pulling him inside by the hand. "I changed my mind." Once he was inside, she latched the screen.

His arms circled her from behind, pulling her against him where she felt again his desire for her. His hands gently captured her breasts, cupping them as he kissed her neck. "I would have called, but by the time I found a telephone I would have been even later."

"You want a drink?" She caught his hands and stilled them. Most of the time she was eager for a man to finish, pay, and leave. Raymond was not a paying customer, though. She wanted to make the evening last, to savor the hours they shared. She was playing with fire, but she couldn't stop herself.

"I'd like that." He released her.

She went to the kitchen and got the ice she'd already chipped and made two fresh drinks. Her body felt both heavy and light. Raymond stirred emotions that she knew were best left alone. Sexual desire was acceptable. That was the boundary Raymond had set for her—clearly set—before he began to see her on a regular basis. He gratified her in a way no other man did, because he could stretch time and sensation in a way she'd never experienced. Because this was more than just sex for her. That was a secret she could not share with him, else he would leave her. In the fantasies of a future life that she wove, he played a starring role.

By the time she made the drinks her hands were shaking. She took a deep breath and forced a smile as she walked back to the front room where he stood looking out the door at the still, soft night.

He took the drink and sipped it. "Thank you, Florence." His gaze remained out the door, at the moonlight filtering through the crooked oak limbs and draping Spanish moss. "It's twenty-six days until the next full moon."

She knew where his mind had gone without being told. "My granny used to tell me stories of the *loup-garou*." She put her arm around his waist, content for the moment to drink and talk. Most men had no use for her memories or her dreams. Raymond enjoyed hearing about her past, and she wanted him to know her when she'd been innocent and untainted.

"Were you afraid of the big bad wolf?" he asked. His hand slipped down her arm, hugging her against him.

"When I was little, before Mama took a house in Baton Rouge." She laughed. "Granny was a gifted storyteller. She would gather all of us children into bed with her, five or six of us all beneath the quilts. The house was heart pine, and the flames from the fireplace would dance on the walls and turn them red. Then Grandma would tell us about Pierre, a man who loved money more than anything else."

"Tell me the story."

She nestled closer to his side, inhaling his scent. "Pierre buried his money in the swamps so no one could find it. He was such a mean man that he left his wife and children hungry. When he went to work in the morning, he put the print of his hand in the flour barrel to be sure his wife used none of it to feed the children. He said they could eat acorns or catch fish, but he wasn't going to feed them."

"Was Pierre a real person?"

Florence shook her head. "I don't know. I never knew him, but he could have been someone from my grandmother's time."

"Tell me the rest."

"Pierre came home every evening and went by himself into the swamp to bury the money he'd made. He was late going out one night, and he traveled by the full moon, wanting to save the lantern oil. When he came to the right place he started digging, but then he heard something in the woods. He was angry because he thought one of the children had followed him to learn his secret hiding place."

" 'Come out and take the beating you deserve,' he said. The only answer was the rustling of the underbrush. He grew angry and lit the lantern and held it up. 'Come out or I'll beat you until you can't move,' he cried.

"Instead of a child, a beautiful woman stepped out of the woods. She wore a gown of white with a silver belt. A silver fur tipped in black was draped over her shoulders. He'd never seen anyone so lovely."

"This rendition of the *loup-garou* is different from what my family told. There was no mention of a beautiful woman as I recall the story." Raymond finished his drink and she handed him hers, swapping glasses.

"This was how Granny told it."

A breeze shifted the tree limbs, scattering the shadows on the ground.

"What happened to Pierre and the beautiful woman?"

"Pierre was so taken with her beauty that he forgot about burying his money. He scrambled out of the hole. 'Are you lost?' he asked. She said no, she knew exactly where she was. She said she'd been waiting to talk to him. He turned to reach for his lantern, and when he swung the light to better see her face, in her place stood a huge gray and black wolf with a silver belt around its neck."

Florence hesitated. She hadn't thought of the story in years, but she was suddenly transfixed by the image in her mind.

"Florence?"

"I remember now that I didn't like the end of the story." She tried to shrug off the feeling that settled over her.

"Will you finish it? I'm taken with this beautiful woman who turns into a beast."

"Come inside." The moon shadows shifting on the ground disquieted her. "I've given myself the heebie-jeebies." She laughed and heard the hollowness in her voice.

Raymond closed and locked the door. When he turned to her he took her glass and his and set them on a small table. With one sure movement he pulled her into his lap as he sat on the sofa. "Tell me the end."

Florence could hear the steady beating of his heart. The sound comforted her. She was a fool to let childhood fears slip around her, she who knew so well how superstitions fed on ignorance.

"Pierre ran through the woods for his life with the wolf bounding after him. He made it home and rushed to barricade the doors, but he wasn't fast enough. The wolf leaped into the house and attacked his wife and children, eating all of them. When it was finished, it changed back into the woman. She was covered in blood. It dripped from her mouth. She looked at Pierre and said, 'Beware that you aren't consumed by your own hungers.' And then she ran out into the night."

"That's a twist I didn't expect." Raymond was amused, and that more than anything eased the dread that had built around Florence. "Your grandmamma was teaching you a moral lesson about greed, wasn't she?"

"I haven't thought of that story in years, but I guess I always hated it because the innocents were killed. If the *loup-garou* had eaten Pierre, it would have been justice."

Raymond's hands stroked her bare arms. He kissed the top of her head. "I've never heard an account of the *loup-garou* that comes close to that. Usually the stories are about howling and salivating wolves and lost children that disappear forever in the dark swamps."

"Half the town believes Adele Hebert is the *loup-garou*."

His hands stopped moving on her flesh. "People are desperate for a diversion. Anything to turn their thoughts from the war and from the plague of fever. Adele has provided them delicious gossip, but I wonder if they truly believe."

"They believe what's convenient."

He lifted her face so that he could look into her eyes. "You're a bright woman, Florence. That's why I enjoy your company. That and certain other talents."

She touched his freshly shaved cheek. A question burned in her mouth, but she knew not to ask. If she hinted that she wanted more than what he gave her, he would be gone. She hadn't known Raymond before he went to war, but this much she knew—his mind was as scarred by what he'd done and seen as his body. He kept both hidden from everyone.

Instead, she closed her eyes and kissed him. She let her body do the talking as she pressed into him, one hand catching a firm hold of his hair and the other working at the buttons of his shirt.

He held her with one arm while his other hand began a slow exploration up her silk-clad leg. He made a noise of appreciation deep in his throat as he found the top of her stocking and then the bare flesh of her thigh.

His fingers brushed lightly up her skin, barely grazing her pubic hairs and the bare flesh of her belly. His touch, so delicate yet so assured, turned her inside out. She arched in his lap, allowing him better access.

"Florence, you're a woman made for pleasure," he whispered into her hair. "Sometimes I think knowing you is the only thing that keeps me human."

His words increased her hunger. If pleasure was what he wanted, she could give that. She was skilled in the ways of pleasing men. She kissed him deeply and then stood up. With a swift motion she reached behind her and unzipped the dress. She let it fall to the floor, revealing the black satin bra and matching garter belt she'd bought in Baton Rouge. He swallowed.

He reached for her and she stepped back, smiling. "I want you to want me more than anything else in life."

His smile hid a near desperate need. "If I want you any more, I'll embarrass myself here on your sofa."

Raymond had more control than he gave himself credit. She knew from past experience. "You can touch me with your hands. Or your tongue. Nothing else."

His answer was a groan.

She stepped close enough for his hands to grasp her right thigh, sliding up the skin, moving to a place where she could barely control her own need for him. But she locked her knees and held herself steady, letting his fingers explore. When she could stand it no longer, she took his hand and pulled him from the sofa. Once he was standing, she unzipped his pants and freed him, satisfied that her merest touch made him inhale sharply.

This was their game, to tease and tantalize each other to near torture. She liked to make it last, because it was these moments that she thought of when she surrendered her body to the lust of other men. It was Raymond she saw in her mind, replaying his touch, his caress, his teasing suggestiveness. And it made her work tolerable.

She'd never known a man who enjoyed the art of foreplay as much as Raymond. He could spend hours drawing his fingers along the quivering skin of her abdomen, circling ever closer to the place that would bring her relief—yet veering away at the last moment, laughing at the way he made her body buck and arch toward him.

And she returned the favor with her hands and lips. Until both reached the end of their endurance and the joining was all that remained to bring about the last and final pleasure. *La petite mort* was the term her mother had used. So fitting, as they lay exhausted afterward, almost too sensitive and alive for the touch of the sheet, yet exhausted to the point of near lethargy.

Whatever sexual bond connected them, Florence had never

known such complete satisfaction. She loved Raymond. Had no doubt of it. She also knew that to express those three words would end their nights together. It wasn't that she was a whore. Her occupation had nothing to do with it. Raymond's aversion to love went much deeper. He would never allow himself to admit his feelings for her, and he would never accept the responsibility that came if she revealed what her heart felt for him.

As she smiled and led him to the bedroom, she felt the familiar stab of pain in her heart. She would satisfy herself with this moment, with this night, which was more than many women ever knew—based on her experiences with their clumsy husbands. Even if this were their last night together, she had truly loved.

She finished unbuttoning his shirt and slid it from his body, and then unbuttoned his slacks. He stepped out of his shoes and pants in one fluid motion, and as she knelt to remove his shorts, she let her fingers trace the purple scar that covered his lower back and right buttocks and made an S down the outside of his thigh. Her probing fingers felt the metal still there, and she leaned to kiss it.

"It doesn't hurt anymore," he said, and she knew he lied. She kissed it lightly and then turned her attention to things that wouldn't remind him of the war or the parts of himself he'd lost in Europe.

His fingers gripped her hair, massaging her scalp, and she felt true joy as she heard his moan of pleasure. This night would be enough for her. She would make it so.

Kay-ie!

Raymond awoke beside Florence, his heart pounding. He'd been dreaming of Antoine. He pulled the sheet over Florence's taut hip, glad that he hadn't awakened her. The night had grown chill, and Florence liked to sleep against him nude. At first he'd resisted staying the night, but the only sleep he achieved was beside Florence. Her warm body and the soft movement of her chest gave him more comfort than he cared to acknowledge. But not even Florence was a barrier against the past, against the man he was.

In his dream Antoine had been standing by the bed. Raymond had reached out to him to beg forgiveness, but Antoine had faded into the night. Then Raymond had heard the hawk's cry. He sat up and in the moonlight from the window he saw that blood had soaked Florence's pillowcase. His eardrum was bleeding. Again. She never complained, never asked, and each time he came to her, the bed linens were ironed white perfection.

He watched the rise and fall of her chest. Her breasts were lush, heavy. Made for a man. Her dark hair spread over the pillow, a froth of curls. The small scar on her face heightened her beauty. He held his hand a millimeter from her cheek, desperate to touch her. Yet he restrained himself. Sometimes, when he looked at her, he imagined he could see her as a child, a perfect, untainted beauty before life had put the pain he sometimes saw in her green eyes.

He'd known brave men, but none more courageous than Florence. She met life with a smile and a tender touch. Those were her weapons, and she used them as a warrior. He didn't have to protect her, because her strength was greater than his.

A wolf's howl came through the night, distant but clear, and he felt the hairs along his arms stand on end. Trappers had almost eradicated the wild creatures from the swamps—the bear and wolves and most of the big cats. A few survived, though. Had it been one of them that attacked Henri Bastion as he walked along the road? He hoped Doc Fletcher would have some idea of the beast that had bitten Henri.

Raymond felt the need for action, but Florence slept so peacefully, and it was so little to give her—a night of companionship after the generous bounty of her love. Her feelings for him were strong, but he couldn't bear to know about them. He came to her two or three times a week, and that told him how much he'd come to rely on her.

The house he'd bought on the edge of town contained the

necessities of life—a bed, a toilet, a lamp. The nights he spent there alone were tests of endurance. Often he didn't try to sleep, avoiding the nightmares that plagued him and the pain that sometimes claimed his body in the darkness. Florence mitigated those things. Sometimes he vowed to stop seeing her, but he always returned. She was the only thing that made his life bearable.

Plaintive and chilling, a cry of loneliness, the wolf spoke again. There was no answer, and Raymond wondered if it was a solitary creature whose pack had been killed.

Adele's face came unbidden, and he had a sudden surge of worry for Madame Louiselle. Guilt and anxiety made him want to leap up, but he held himself steady, listening to the slow breathing of the woman who curled against him.

Adele was weak as a kitten, if she were still alive at all. He had his doubts that she'd survive the fever. His worries about Madame were unfounded, and he forced his tense body to relax. His fingers traced the side of Florence's face, and she snuggled closer to him. Before he went to war, he'd always thought a wife and family were his for the asking. He'd intended to do his duty and come home to resume the rhythms of life he knew in Iberia Parish. His secret dream involved an education—a type of betterment the army had made possible. He'd always been interested in journalism, the writing of facts, a modern-day historian. Journalists dug beneath the surface of things, and he'd always been good at that. Chula, even after their romance had faltered and died, had encouraged him in his dreams.

The war had changed him, though. He'd lost all ambition for an education. He'd come home and, despite the sometimes intense pain of his leg and hip, had settled into the job of deputy. There was little to dig into, but what digging was done in the Iberia Parish Sheriff's Office, he did.

When the sun came up, he had some tracking to do. He'd failed to find Clifton Hebert, but some of the tidbits of gossip he'd heard had piqued his interest. Clifton lived far back in the swamp—no one could, or would, give an exact location. The one thing that all of his sources had been sure about was that Clifton Hebert kept a pack of savage dogs. Hog-catchers. Dogs so vicious and filled with bloodlust that they would jump the wild boars that roamed the swamps and hang on to the nose and ears until the human hunters could catch up and either shoot the boar or wrestle it to the ground and tie it for domesticating. It was said the meat would lose its gamey taste if the boar was castrated and fed corn or grain for several weeks before slaughter. Catching the dangerous boars alive was also part of the insane excitement.

Often the dogs were slashed by the boar's razor-sharp tusks, and the men who hunted boar for sport sometimes didn't come back alive. Raymond had been on several search parties for missing men where a body was found, the hamstring muscles in the back of the legs severed. Once the boar brought a man down, it didn't waste a lot of time finishing the kill. Wild boars were dangerous game for men and dogs alike. Clifton Hebert made his living leading such hunting expeditions.

It had not escaped Raymond's attention that the wounds on Henri Bastion could have been made by savage dogs. Or hogs. Clifton needed to answer to his whereabouts on the night Henri Bastion died.

Other things nagged at him. Rosa Hebert, for one. How was it possible that one family could contain such a wealth of misfortune? His compassion for Adele and Rosa, topped off by his suspicions about what had happened to Armand Dugas, had led his thinking down a long and tortuous road. His calls to the state penitentiary at Angola had gone unheeded. His requests for a state-verified list of prisoners sent to work the Bastion farm had been met with amusement by the deputy warden who took his call.

Strangely enough, it wasn't Henri Bastion's ravaged body that kept pricking his subconscious. It was Henri's daughter, standing by the screen door. She'd clearly been terrified of him.

He closed his hot eyes against his churning thoughts. He had to be up at first light. He'd left his car in town and walked to Florence's, as much for her reputation as his own. Some of her customers wouldn't feel right about her if she was a deputy's main punch. Some of the townsfolk wouldn't feel right about him if they thought he was courting Florence. It was best to be discreet.

Besides, he had work to do and the earlier the better. He closed his eyes and willed himself to sleep.

9

MICHAEL Finley used his finger to pull the starched clerical collar away from his neck. He'd gained weight during the summer, but the cold months would lean him back up. That was his body pattern—to eat and drink and enjoy during the hot days when sleeping through the afternoon was a necessity rather than a vice. During the winter, he chopped wood and found exercise to be more pleasurable—if cold weather ever came this year. November loomed close at hand and except for the storm that had blown through a few days before, there hadn't been even a whisper of cool. Good for the cane and mosquitoes, hard for the people.

He brewed a pot of the strong Louisiana coffee heavily laced with bitter chicory. Since the war, real coffee had become hard to find anywhere, but the population of Iberia Parish had a head start on the rest of the country in learning to accept substitutes. Long used to isolation and self-sufficiency, the settlers of the marshlands of Iberia Parish preferred chicory coffee to the pure thing. It had taken Michael time to develop a taste for the Cajun blend, but now he loved it, topped off with scalded cream. He took a cup out the back door of his kitchen to wander his rose garden.

Try as he might, he couldn't avoid the wrought-iron fence at the back of the garden and the magnificent oak beyond that. Another flood of guilt at the thought of Rosa Hebert threatened to swamp him. She'd known his joy in his garden and that tree. She'd also known how he betrayed her. That's why she'd chosen that tree in which to kill herself.

He stood for a moment in front of a Fire and Ice blossom reordering his thoughts. His first act was to ask God for forgiveness. For Rosa, who'd acted in pain and torment. She'd never meant to harm him in any way. It was his own failing that gave him feelings of inadequacy. He'd let Rosa down when she needed him most, and it was that knowledge that kept the site of her suicide so fresh in his mind.

"Father Finley?"

The voice startled him and he turned swiftly, hot coffee slipping over his hand. "Who's there?" The voice was female, and not one he could place.

"It's Chula Baker. I have a letter for you. From Rome. I thought it might be urgent so I brought it on over."

Chula appeared at the garden gate. If she was aware of the tree behind her and what it represented, she didn't show it. She opened the gate on a metal protest and walked toward the priest, hand extended with a battered letter. "I knocked at the front door, but when no one answered, I figured you might be having coffee here in the garden." She looked around. "It's so lovely. Amazing. Mother's roses are still blooming, too. Your mums are a nice touch, but the heat is hard on them."

He took the letter. "Thank you, Chula."

"Have a good day, Father." The gate creaked like the cry of a banshee, and then she was gone.

Michael held the letter in one hand and his coffee in the other, trying hard to clear his mind. He put his coffee down and tore open the seal. He read the words twice before the pages fluttered from his hands.

Rosa's suicide had undone all he'd worked to accomplish. He had direct orders from the Holy See to abandon his attempts to get Rosa declared an authentic stigmatic. The letter's language was strong and clear—any further efforts on his part would be viewed as disobedience and heresy. He was to focus on tending to the needs of his parish in a "modest and humble fashion." He didn't have to read between the lines to see that he was being viewed as a glory-grabber.

He stepped on the pages as he walked to the gate. Holding the wrought iron like a prisoner might bars, he looked at the oak. It was said that every oak was a sign that Mary had visited. Wherever an oak grew, her foot was said to have stepped. But he could muster no belief that Mary or any other deity had found cause to put a foot down in this accursed land.

His fists gripped the gate as he slid to his knees. The bleak future rose before him, and he surrendered himself to the darkness of disappointment. A miracle had been put in his hands, and he'd destroyed it. His faith in Rosa had faltered. He'd questioned her late one evening, demanding to know if she injured herself. No matter how many years passed, he would never forget the look on her face. Later that night, she'd hung herself. His moment of doubt had made her doubt herself, and she was dead because of him as surely as if he'd knotted the rope around her neck and thrown her from the tree.

Solid hands gripped his arms. Shame at his own weakness touched him as he swiveled on his knees to look into the eyes of Colista LaSalle, his housekeeper.

"Come inside, Father Finley," she said, urging him to his feet with her strong hands. "Come on with you. The garden's no place to be found on your knees by any of the nuns or schoolchildren."

He allowed her to assist him to his feet. "I was praying. For Rosa. And for myself."

"Your breakfast is getting cold." Her insistent grip pulled him toward the back door.

He stepped away from her. "Thank you, Colista." He couldn't meet her gaze. He had no desire to see the questions in her eyes. "I'll be along in a moment."

"You're better now?"

He nodded curtly. "I'll just finish my meditation and be inside in a moment."

She turned and walked inside, never looking back.

Her footsteps faded and he got slowly to his feet. Not all the prayers in the world could undo what had happened to Rosa. The best he could do would be to go inside and eat the hearty breakfast she'd prepared as if nothing out of the ordinary had occurred.

The musky smell of the moccasin drifted to Raymond on the breeze. He froze. If he was close enough to smell it, the snake had seen him. Behind him something large plopped into the water. He could only pray it was a turtle and not an alligator. Around his head a swarm of mosquitoes hummed and buzzed, an irritation he couldn't afford to acknowledge. The snake was a danger that required all of his attention.

His gaze moved from the log in front of him to the pile of leaves and dead limbs, the scuppernong vine that for a moment made his heart pound. The snake, colored to blend in with the environment, was impossible to find. He dared not move until he did, though. Some snakes, like rattlers, gave a warning and only struck if frightened or provoked. Moccasins were more aggressive. The damn thing could be hanging in the trees, waiting to drop on his shoulders.

Lucky for him the water that lapped at the edges of the path was still and quiet. During floods, when the current was swift, he'd seen as many as fifty moccasins, all balled together, spinning in the water. Here, he should be able to spot the telltale V that would ripple across the still surface as the snake swam in lazy zigs and zags. The water gave back a perfect reflection of the swamp unblemished by movement of any creature. He moved his gaze to the land around him. In the muted tones of the earth, the snake was well hidden.

The stench was strong. He'd undoubtedly awakened the creature while it sunned, taking advantage of the warm October morning. He looked behind him, hoping he'd already stepped over the reptile. His gun was drawn and ready, but he preferred to use the machete he'd brought for just this purpose. Before he'd set out to find Clifton Hebert, he'd gathered tools for maneuvering around the swamps.

At last he saw the creature, not four feet in front of him. The snake was so thick and fat that he'd mistaken it for a dead stick. It watched him, completely motionless, waiting for him to step closer so it could strike above the top of his boot.

He took one step forward and brought the machete's blade down, slicing off the snake's head with a clean stroke. When he stood up, he was facing the open jaws of a powerful dog. The animal's lips were curled in a silent snarl. It hadn't made a sound as it approached him. One ear had been torn from its head, and there were scars about its muzzle and over its body. Some had been serious injuries that had been poorly sewn up.

He dropped his gaze. He'd been taught in the service not to challenge a dog with a direct look. He could shoot the animal, but he didn't want to. He had no doubt that at last he'd come upon Clifton Hebert's lair. He didn't want to piss the swamp man off by killing his hound.

"Cesar!" The voice boomed through the trees, echoing so that Raymond couldn't place where it came from. "Come here, you."

The dog trotted back into the swamp, looking as if it walked on water.

"Clifton Hebert!" Raymond called out the man's name. "I'm Deputy Raymond Thibodeaux and I need to talk to you. Your sister is in serious trouble."

"Rosa is dead, and if that Bernadette is needin' help and more money, you tell her to kiss my ass, her."

Raymond filed that away and yelled, "It's Adele."

A curse was followed by the sound of someone slogging through water without a care for any of the dangerous creatures. When Raymond saw Clifton, he was waist deep in the water, a rifle held over his head to keep it dry, coming through the slough at a steady pace. Raymond had grown up in Iberia Parish, and he'd learned that those who didn't tread with caution often died. No one had ever taught Clifton that lesson.

"Where's that fool Adele at?" Clifton spoke while he was still thirty yards away, but it was time enough for Raymond to take in the man's stunning physique. He was possibly six-six or -seven with shoulders as wide as a door frame. His black hair, matted and filthy, grew to his waist. Though it was a warm day, he wore a dark green jacket with long sleeves, the pockets bulging.

"You deaf?" Clifton demanded when he was ten yards away. "Where's my sister at?"

"She's very ill. I took her to a *traiteur.*" Raymond didn't want to tell him Adele was in jail.

Clifton walked out of the water and onto the path, a giant. Raymond was tall, but he looked up into Clifton's face.

"What's wrong with Adele? And why're you comin' to tell me? The law don't normally bring news of sickness." The planes of his face shifted forming a scowl. "Why're you here, Deputy Thibodeaux?"

As if sensing the change in their master's mood, three large dogs, including the one-eared mastiff, slipped out of the woods. None made a sound, but their exposed teeth told of their displeasure.

Raymond kept his attention on the man. "Henri Bastion was killed two nights ago on Section Line Road. Adele was found at the body. She said she killed him."

Clifton didn't move, not even to register a flicker of surprise. "Ain't no business of mine."

"Adele is your sister."

He shook his head. "Nothin' I can do. Adele grievin' her babies. She's not right."

"She claims she's possessed by the *loup-garou*." The swamp around him was so still that he heard a falling leaf touch the water. It was a place of magic as well as danger.

"Folks believe what they will." If Clifton found such a thing ludicrous, he didn't show it.

"She has a high fever. I believe she's hallucinating."

At last Clifton sighed. "Her babies died from the fever. She took it hard. Wouldn't let no one help her. Buried them herself where no one would ever disturb them. Them and Rosa. She took Rosa's body when the church wouldn't have it."

Clifton had moved upwind of him and Raymond had to work not to show a reaction to the stench. "Are you sure it was fever that killed her babies?"

For a moment Clifton merely regarded him, reading the levels of his question. "First week of October, Adele sent word to me to bring some herbs and things. The babies was sick. They was dyin'. I saw them myself, me. There was nothin' to be done. Not even Madame could help."

"Was Adele sick then?"

Clifton scratched at his head. "She wasn't sick. She was wild. She runnin' all around, cryin' and beggin' for her boys to get well. She ask Bernadette for help, but no one could change what happened. After the boys died, she put them in the swamp where she put Rosa's body after she took it." He looked back at the dogs and they sat down instantly. "It hurt Adele fierce that Rosa wasn't in the church cemetery."

"Mr. Hebert, would you mind coming into town and talking with me?"

"I don't have no bidness in town, no."

The dogs stood and moved three steps closer. The hair along their backs was standing on end.

"I'll bring you back here." Raymond felt water oozing through his leather boots, the only thing worth having that the army had given him. The heat was stifling, the odor of the fetid water mingled too strongly with Clifton's unwashed scent.

Clifton shook his head. "No."

"Why not?" Raymond knew arguing would get him nowhere. He'd have to shoot the man to subdue him.

"I stay in the swamps, unless bidness calls me out."

Raymond had never heard of Clifton Hebert being in trouble with the law, but then Raymond had lost two years overseas when anything could have happened, and he hadn't thought to check with the sheriff. Joe, for his part, couldn't put two and two together if his fingers were held up for him.

"Is there a place we can sit down and talk?"

Clifton pointed to the ground. "Sit." He eased to a knee.

Raymond squatted. "Look, I'm trying to help your sister. I don't think she did this."

"Henri Bastion was a righteous bastard. If someone kilt him, they did a good thing."

"Someone surely killed him, and I don't think it was your sister. Is Bodine Matthews working with you?"

Clifton shook his head. "Bodine gone. Bernadette hired herself over to the Bastion plantation, puttin' on airs, her. She wash out Marguerite Bastion's silk panties and think she's good enough to wear 'em. She got so high falutin', Bodine couldn't take no more of her."

"Do you know where Mr. Matthews might be?" Raymond saw him as a possible suspect.

"Me, I can't help you." Clifton started to turn and walk off.

Raymond thought about asking Clifton about his midnight deliveries of liquor. The bottles were untaxed by the state. Instead, he chose a different tact. "Are there any wolves left in the swamps?"

The question stopped Clifton. He turned slowly back. "Most been trapped."

"I thought I heard one last night." Raymond shrugged. "Could've been imagination, but I thought I heard it clearly." He picked up a stick and drew out a rough sketch of the crime scene in a patch of dry sand. "Henri was here, and Adele was here. Henri was savaged by some type of animal. A wolf or"—he pointed at the three dogs—"something like that."

Clifton walked close enough to look down at the drawing in the dirt. "When Adele got pregnant, I tell her I take care of Bastion for her. She never said, but I think he forced Adele. I think those *bébés* were his." He waited until he had Raymond's eye. "I meant it, when I tole her I'd take care of Bastion, yes. He would be gone in the swamps now if she'd say one word, but she never would say."

"You had a grudge against Henri Bastion?" If Henri was the father of the twins, as Clifton suspected, it might give Adele motive to kill him. Especially if she had been raped.

For the first time Clifton smiled, revealing startling white teeth. Beneath the dirt, Raymond saw what would have been a handsome man.

"Name one man that didn't," Clifton said. "Henri cheat his mama outta her last crust of bread. He had a lot to answer for."

"Adele worked for him. There's talk that she was in love with him."

The smile disappeared. "Talk ain't worth nothin'. Adele had no use for Henri. Ask her."

"She's too sick to talk." Raymond rose slowly to his feet, aware that the dogs watched him with eagerness.

"If she gets better, she'll tell you. If she doesn't . . ." He shrugged. "Makes no difference then." He stood and stepped back into the water and the dogs vanished into the underbrush.

"Clifton, don't you care what happens to Adele?"

He kept walking. "I learnt long time ago, it don't do no good to care what happens to anyone. Can't change what's got to be." He was waist deep and moving away. "Don't come back here, lawman, 'less you hirin' me for a huntin' trip."

10

Thank you, Claudia." Chula took the key from her employee. "I'll lock up."

Claudia's fingers closed over hers, holding for a moment until Chula met her gaze. "Don't stay up here 'til the wee hours, Miss Baker. You don't get four hours sleep a night. I know you don't believe in evil spirits, but it's not good to be walking the streets alone at night. There're plenty of bad men out to do harm. Doesn't have to be a werewolf."

Chula gently withdrew her hand and held it palm out. "I swear I'm going home right away. Mother's about to bust a gasket. She has a 'gentleman caller' for me to meet at dinner."

Claudia Breck's pale eyes showed interest. "If he's not right for you, *cher,* send him on to me. There's not a decent man with two good legs who can stand up to finish a dance." With her words the humor slipped from her face. "If this war doesn't end soon, we'll all go to our graves as spinsters. I want children."

Chula put her arm around the plump young woman. "Justin Lanoux is coming home." She'd hesitated about telling Claudia this. "When I took the letter out to his mama, she asked me to stay while she read it."

"She thought he was dead, didn't she?"

"She did, but it was news that he was wounded and has been transferred stateside. When he's released from the California hospital, he'll come home. For good." She saw the hope in Claudia's eyes. She'd been sweet on Justin since she was in fifth grade.

"Is he hurt bad? Did the letter say?"

The letter hadn't specified Justin's wounds, which was what had troubled Chula. "I'm not sure. But he's alive and he'll be home in a few weeks."

"Do you think I should call his mother?"

Tapping her lips with a finger, Chula considered. "I'd wait. You don't want to appear too eager. Mothers are so protective of their sons." She grinned. "Then again, you have a good job. You're quite a catch!"

Claudia laughed. "I can't thank you enough for the job. It's the best feeling in the world to be able to buy a bit of meat when it's available, and bread. My mama is proud of me, even if I'm twenty-two and unmarried."

"You were the most qualified applicant, Claudia. I'm glad you got the job, but I didn't play favorites. You got it because you deserved it."

Color touched Claudia's cheeks. "Some of the people in town have been . . ."

"Cruel?" Chula lifted a shoulder. "They're jealous. Times are hard and your paycheck is steady. Some folks think a steady paycheck is a man's prerogative. A qualified woman should step out of line and make room for a man, even if he can't read."

"They say ugly things about us. About you."

"That's unfortunate." Chula locked the cash drawer. "My mama taught me that sticks and stones are dangerous, but words won't damage any of my bones." She sighed. The day was finally over. She wasn't looking forward to the "gentleman caller" as her mother insisted on referring to John LeDeux, but she was ready to get away from the post office. All day long people had come in wanting to talk about Henri Bastion's death. As the day had faded, the stories have gotten more vivid and exaggerated. Before she'd locked the front door, Chula had heard that Adele was found with Henri's beating heart in her hand and his liver in her mouth. Ridiculous!

"I'll see you tomorrow, Miss Baker. Have fun tonight. Take him to the dance hall and dance blisters on your feet."

"Thank you for the suggestion, Claudia."

Chula turned off the lights and slipped through the door, re-locking it behind her. She'd walked to work, a half mile down a street lined with quiet homes that had once been immaculately maintained. Now, even the residential neighborhoods were show-ing the strain of the war. Paint wasn't to be had, building supplies almost nonexistent. Everything was rationed. The president was urging everyone to sacrifice for the cause, but faith—in the cause and in the president—was wavering. People could sacrifice only so much, and as more and more families lost sons and brothers and husbands . . . it would take years for such wounds to heal.

Anger heated her cheeks as she walked. Men died for the stu-pidest of reasons. This great war was about money. Freedom and peace might be the fringe benefits, but it had grown out of greed. The young men who went to war believed in liberty and justice, but the old men who waged these wars had no such illusions. They had greed and a lack of regard for the cannon fodder they sent to their deaths. This war, like others before it, was about lin-ing the pockets of the rich with gold. History had been her ma-jor in college, and she'd seen quickly enough that all wars were fought for economic reasons.

She walked up the broad front steps of her mother's home and stopped in front of the beveled glass door, trying to shake off her anger. She'd agreed to dinner with John LeDeux because it pleased her mother. LeDeux was a professor at Louisiana State

University in Baton Rouge. He was doing research in Iberia Parish, and her mother had been wildly excited at the idea of introducing him to Chula. Chula was not so enthused.

She opened the door and stepped into the house feeling a swift hunger pang at the mouthwatering odor of roasting pork. Maizy was the finest cook in southeast Louisiana. Though many things were hard to find, the Baker family had plenty to eat. The swamp could be bountiful if one knew where to look, and Maizy had connections.

Her mother met her at the foot of the stairs. "Chula, Dr. LeDeux will be here in fifteen minutes."

"I'll be ready."

"Just this once couldn't you have come home on time?"

It was a familiar complaint of her mother, who admired Chula for having such an important job, but it also fretted her that someone, or something, controlled Chula's time more than she did.

"I'll be ready. What is it that Dr. LeDeux teaches?"

"Biology or botany or something along those lines."

"And how did you meet him?" Chula pulled off one boot and then the other as she walked upstairs.

"I haven't actually met him. Mary Margaret Castalette gave him my name and number and said I might be helpful in arranging some trips into the swamps. I think Mary Margaret was being clever because she knows I have a connection with Clifton Hebert, the star swamp man." Mrs. Baker arched her eyebrows. "She is scandalized that Clifton keeps my liquor cabinet stocked."

Chula's laughter was appreciative. "I'm sure you take great delight in telling her how much you enjoy your toddy."

"Of course."

Picking up her boots, Chula climbed the stairs. "I'll be dressed and ready when Dr. LeDeux gets here."

"Wear something pretty. It might surprise you to discover you've some feminine impulses under that tough veneer."

"Oh, la, and maybe I could muster up a swoon while I'm at

it." Laughter floated down the stairs as Chula closed her bedroom door.

She didn't have time for a bath, but the Baker house, thanks to her paycheck, was equipped with hot running water and indoor plumbing. She used the second-floor bath to quickly wash and change into a dark blue dress with short sleeves and a tucked waist that showed her figure to advantage. It wasn't that she didn't enjoy looking feminine, but her life required her to look efficient. She took her chestnut hair down from the prim bun and shook it free on her shoulders. Touching a bit of liner and mascara to her eyes, she put on lipstick and hurried downstairs just as the doorbell chimed. John LeDeux was a punctual man.

Maizy let him in while Chula chipped ice for drinks and cast surreptitious glances at her mother, who'd struck a pose of elegant patience on the sofa. Thomasina Baker enjoyed putting on the dog, and Chula loved watching her do it. It was like a mini-production of the local theater group that her mother directed. Artful posing, sharp dialogue, fun.

Chula made sure to keep her back to the door as she heard footsteps approaching the living room. She mixed a drink for her mother and herself and turned with them in hand. As her gaze met John LeDeux's, she stumbled slightly, a drink sloshing over the fingers of her hand.

"Good evening, Mrs. Baker." He nodded at Thomasina. "Miss Baker." He gave Chula a smile and a nod. "Thank you for inviting me into your home. It's a rare pleasure to be able to sit at table with a family."

"Have a seat, Dr. LeDeux. Chula, would you do the honors?"

He took a seat in a club chair beside Thomasina.

"Would you care for a cocktail?" Chula asked.

"Anything on the rocks," he said.

Chula filled a glass with ice and poured bourbon over it. She handed it to him, taking in his suit. It fit him well, yet he didn't have the dry, sunless look she associated with academics.

His fair skin was lightly tanned, his hair touched with golden highlights.

"Mother says you're a teacher at LSU, but she failed to say what you teach."

"I'm a social anthropologist. What brings me to New Iberia is the recent events involving a murder."

Chula could see the intelligence in the man's eyes. Surely he wasn't here to investigate a superstitious bunch of gossip. "Your interest is the murder, or the talk about the *loup-garou?*"

"The latter. I'm working on a book that examines the effect of local legend on social dynamic."

"Mob mentality is a dangerous thing to play with, Dr. LeDeux. Surely you don't intend to investigate superstitious gossip?"

"Chula, darling, your blue stockings are showing." Mrs. Baker waved Chula to sit down. "Maizy has made some canapés. I think Dr. LeDeux will find them far more appetizing than your probing."

"Not at all, Mrs. Baker. It's stimulating to find someone willing to discuss the value of local folklore. And please, call me John."

"What's the premise of your book, John?" Chula asked as she took a small pastry from the tray Maizy passed.

"Basically that monsters and bogeymen are a healthy part of the psyche of a community. It's a balance of dark and light."

Chula sat on the arm of the sofa beside her mother and sipped her bourbon. "Healthy?"

"Parents repeat the old legends to frighten their children, to keep them safe. These legends are developed with a specific result in mind. Take the *loup-garou,* for example. The goal is to keep young children from wandering into the swamps and getting lost or hurt by the wildlife. Am I correct?"

"To a point." Chula caught the smile of victory on her mother's face and realized she'd played right into Thomasina's matchmaking plot. Her mother had sought out a man who was Chula's equal. A man who would give her tit for tat in a debate and wasn't put off by her strong opinions.

John leaned forward. "These legends and stories were created to serve a need, but when they exceed the bounds of that need, the delicate balance is destroyed."

"And terrible tragedy can result." Chula took his glass for a refill.

"Yes. In my research, when the balance is tipped, tragedy is the end result. The Salem witch trials is a prime example." His fingers closed over hers as he took the glass. "I'm here in New Iberia to study that process."

Chula swallowed, unable to look away from his penetrating gaze. "I hope there's nothing to study. Adele Hebert is not a *loup-garou,* and the sooner that foolishness is stopped, the better for Iberia Parish."

"The problem with hysteria is that it can't be easily dispelled. Though it may be whipped up out of thin air, it becomes difficult to disperse." John waved the canapé tray away. "The power of the myth or legend is so strong that logical thinking is useless. The young girls who testified at the witch trials fed on each other's emotions. I wouldn't be surprised one bit if more sightings of a *loup-garou* aren't reported. If that begins to happen, the parish is in for some dangerous times."

The sun hovered in the tops of the tree casting orange and fuchsia fingers over the western horizon. Against the violent sky, Adele Hebert's house stood in stark silhouette. Raymond walked up the two wooden steps and across the gallery to the front door. It opened with a twist of the knob.

When he stepped inside, he understood why Adele had felt no compulsion to lock up. The one-room house was sparsely furnished. A table and two chairs, a chifforobe, and a pallet on the floor took up the left side of the room. In the back was a potbellied stove and kitchen shelves. To the right, beside a cold and empty fireplace, was a bassinet. The cradle was fashioned from cypress, handmade with grooves and pegs, a beautiful piece of work, and hung with yellow draperies and ribbons. It was the only thing of beauty in the house, which was immaculate. Though Raymond schooled himself to feel nothing, he couldn't stop the image of Adele, cradling her dying children, that rushed into his mind. Such suffering shouldn't be allowed. Perhaps she had chosen insanity over the pain of reality, but that still didn't make her a killer.

Raymond went to the chifforobe. Two dresses and a night-gown hung from pegs, and underclothes were folded in a neat stack. He took the clothes out and put them in a pile. Adele needed something to wear. A pair of shoes, dusty but in good condition, were added to the things he meant to take her.

He moved on to the kitchen. The shelves were bare. Glass containers used for staples sparkled in a shaft of sunlight, empty, washed. Someone had come in and cleaned the place thoroughly, but who and why? Raymond had turned up no friends of Adele. She was a loner. Her only living sister suffered from embarrassment of her peculiar family. It didn't stand to reason that Bernadette, who lived miles away, had come to clean the house. But someone had. Perhaps to erase the traces of something Adele had been given to eat?

Raymond went to the bassinet, his steps slow and reluctant. He could almost taste the grief in that corner of the room, but he forced himself to move forward. Clifton Hebert's name was carved in the wood, and Raymond was surprised that the swamp man had made this for his sister. Clifton had acted as if Adele were far re-moved from his affections, but the cradle belied that. The cradle was evidence of a bond between brother and sister. He'd spent hours creating a work of art for Adele's babies.

Inside the bassinet were stuffed animals, homemade from calico and flour sacks and stuffed with sweet grasses from the swamps. A floppy dog with button eyes, and a tatter of red cloth for a tongue, was tucked beneath a handmade quilt. Raymond exam-ined the dog and gently put it back in the cradle.

There was nothing in the house to help Adele. Nothing. The disappointment was bitter. He'd hoped to find something that might explain Adele's bizarre behavior. If Adele had stumbled on something tainted—or if someone had given her poison—there was no trace of it in the house. In a way, though, the immaculate condition of the house was evidence. Just nothing he could use in a court of law. He picked up the clothes and left.

Night had fallen by the time he got back to town, and the streets of New Iberia were dark. In some of the homes lights burned, but the town had begun to settle for the night. Raymond pulled up at the sheriff's office and got out.

Pinkney Stole sat on a bench outside the office, and Raymond joined him. Raymond offered the old man a Camel as he shook one from his pack for himself.

"Sheriff Joe was shore pissed that you took the prisoner off." Pinkney puffed smoke into the still night.

"He'll live."

"Question is, will she? She looked dead to me."

Pinkney acted dumb, but he wasn't. Raymond exhaled a blue fog of smoke. "I don't know. In some ways it would simplify things if she didn't."

"That gal didn't kill Henri Bastion, did she?"

Raymond considered the best way to answer. He decided on the truth. "No."

"Then who did?"

"If I had an answer for that, I'd be out making an arrest."

"How come that gal thinks she's possessed?"

"Pinkney, you've got the right questions. The problem is I don't have any answers." He tossed his butt into the street. How had Adele become possessed of such a delusion? Was the family crazy— some defect that led to mental problems?

"Folks is spooked by all that talk of *loup-garous*."

"Folks are stupid." Raymond shook out two more cigarettes. "You had any supper?"

"No, sir. Sheriff Joe didn't bring none by for me."

Half the time Joe forgot that Pinkney had no food or money. Raymond took a dollar from his billfold and handed it to the older man. "When you go to Estella's, keep an ear out to see what folks are saying."

"Big Ethel'll splash it all around."

Raymond nodded. "See what she's saying, what folks are talking. Maybe ask about Henri Bastion and what he was up to. I've heard a few things but no one wants to speak out."

"Folks scared of Henri Bastion. He'd as soon beat a man to death as spit on him."

"I haven't found a single person who mourns his death." That in itself was disturbing. More disturbing was that whoever had killed Henri was still free and roaming the parish. Raymond pulled another dollar from his billfold. "Bring me a catfish po-boy."

"You got it, Mr. Raymond. I'll be back."

Pinkney left and Raymond sat back watching the occasional car that passed. Two couples walked by, hand in hand, on the way to the movie theater. On weeknights movies only cost a nickel, and sometimes Raymond slipped into the back seats and let the Hollywood images remind him of his naïve dreams of romance and love. Now, he often left before the show was over.

A movie would be a nice diversion, but it would be a nickel wasted. Raymond couldn't get his mind off Adele Hebert. He'd talked to most of the principals and had found nothing to prove or disprove that Adele was the murderer. She'd be tried for Henri Bastion's murder at the next session of court. Unless she died.

What he had learned about Adele gave him a picture of the fabric of her life. No one had been able to give her an alibi for the night of Henri's murder. Adele lived alone. Since the death of her children, her behavior had been erratic. She'd been seen at night, by Doc and others, paddling down the Teche or sometimes walking aimlessly about town. Not a single person had lifted a hand to help her. Most knew her as the sister of Rosa Hebert, the suicide who claimed to suffer the stigmata. According to local gossip, Adele had been tainted by her sister's life, as if either sainthood or insanity could rub off.

At the sound of footsteps approaching, Raymond was pulled from his thoughts. Pinkney sat down and handed him a hot sandwich on the fresh, crusty bread that Estella baked each Wednesday.

"Any interesting talk?" Raymond asked as he peeled back the linen napkin and bit into the sandwich spiced with horseradish and hot sauce.

"That place be buzzin'!" Pinkney picked his teeth with a toothpick. "I sat in the kitchen with Ethel, and she said all the Negroes 'fraid to go out at night. They lightin' fires and sittin' up with guns, waitin' for the *loup-garou* to come and try to git the young-uns."

Raymond took another bite of the sandwich. Pinkney did best when he was simply allowed to talk. If Joe Como could ever learn that, he'd find Pinkney an invaluable resource.

"Big Ethel said that yesterday they was two men in the restaurant talkin' 'bout Henri Bastion and how he got what he deserved."

"Did she know the men?"

"No, she didn't. But they was sittin' with Praytor Bless."

Raymond took another bite. Praytor Bless, like Veedal Lawrence, was a healthy man, yet he'd never served as a soldier. Rumor was that he had a leaky heart, but Raymond had seen him hauling huge cypress trees out of the swamp for a pier. Praytor looked to be hale enough, though he'd never cut himself free of his mama's apron strings. Francine Bless controlled the pocketbook.

"Praytor was sayin' that Henri's widow would make a fine catch for some enterprisin' man. When he say it, Praytor get all cocky, like that man gone be him."

Raymond wished for a cold beer to wash his sandwich down.

But he didn't drink in front of Pinkney, whose thirst most often led him to trouble. "Marguerite Bastion was once a beauty, but she has the taste of lemons now." He made a face. "Maybe she'll take up with Praytor. They're two peas in a pod."

"She 'the richest man in Iberia Parish.' That's what Praytor sayin'."

"And that itself will only bring her problems." Raymond hadn't considered the difficulties that lay before Henri's widow. Somehow, though, he didn't think Marguerite would be fleeced out of a thin dime. "You hear anything else?" He took the last bite of the sandwich.

"Big Ethel said some of the local men were talkin' 'bout comin' to see Sheriff Joe. They want the prisoner chained up."

Raymond knew there was discontent that he'd taken Adele out of the jail. "Too damn bad."

"They say she should be chained at all times. Case she turns into the wolf again."

Raymond lit a cigarette. "I'd be glad to let them sit in shifts and watch her. Make sure she isn't growing hair or fangs."

Pinkney's eyes widened, whites showing. "She not gone change like that in the jail, is she?"

"She's a sick woman, Pinkney, not a werewolf. That's a bunch of foolishness. Most people know that."

"Not to hear the talk. Big Ethel said her man's totin' a gun all the time. Gone shoot anything that moves in the woods at night. Not even lettin' his gran'children out tomorrow at all for the trick or treat."

Raymond shook out a cigarette for Pinkney and then stood. It was time to go home. More than time. Tomorrow he needed to go over the autopsy report that Doc Fletcher had sat on for nearly a week.

If the werewolf hysteria was going to build, it would be soon. The next night was Halloween, when youngsters dressed in costume and knocked on doors for treats. Most folks enjoyed a little thrill of creepiness, but this year, he hoped there would be no foolishness. Pinkney didn't have to tell him that the parish was like a powder keg of superstition.

In twenty-one days, the moon would be full again. The November moon, called by the Indians the Snow Moon. But snow was far away from Iberia Parish. His Algonquin great-grandmother, who'd lived in the Appalachian Mountains and watched the change of seasons, had told him the Snow Moon brought man his harvest. He could still remember her eyes, black and shiny. She'd held his hand and warned him to be careful what seeds he sowed because the harvest always came.

"I'll be in a little late tomorrow, Pinkney. Tell the sheriff I'm going to Doc Fletcher's and then to talk to Father Finley."

"Shore thing, Raymond." He stood. "I'm goin' in, too. I don' much cotton to sittin' out here alone."

Raymond walked down the street to his car. Because he was a law officer he received more gas stamps than most. He had fuel for a drive, and tonight he felt the need to ride the parish, get a sense of things.

He found himself headed out Section Line Road toward Beaver Damn Creek. As he drew closer to the scene of the murder, he slowed, remembering his thoughts as he'd driven out the first time, when he'd assumed Emanuel Agee had come to tell him of a drowning.

As he rounded the bend in the road his headlamps picked up another vehicle in the exact location of the murder. He slowed and stopped. When he got out of the car he saw a lone man standing on the side of the road.

Tragedy always drew the vultures, a harmless breed of gawkers who derived some pleasure or solace from looking at accidents and murders. Raymond didn't understand the impulse, but he knew such men weren't dangerous. Still, his hand was on his gun when he got out of his car.

"Good evening, Raymond," Praytor Bless said. He stepped

out into the sandy road where Raymond could clearly see him. Praytor's pants were crisply pressed, his shoes shined. Mrs. Bless made sure her son was well turned out.

"What are you doing out here, Praytor?"

"This is where Henri died, isn't it?"

"Why are you so interested?"

Praytor walked down the side of the road. "If Adele Hebert wasn't under the spell of the *loup-garou,* she must have been some kind of powerful. From what I heard, the body was savaged."

"Why are you so interested in Henri's murder?" Raymond asked again.

"Lots of folk are interested." Praytor's voice was lazy and slow, like his movements. "Most everybody in the parish was involved one way or another with Henri. Business deals, things of that nature." Praytor scraped his foot along the ground.

"What nature?"

"You must get paid by the question, Raymond." Praytor laughed. "Henri farmed, but he also had a hand in running a pint or two of untaxed liquor into New Iberia. You know that. Some of us boys had a little bit of the action. Just a little pocket money. I thought I'd confess in case you stumbled on the information and thought I was a suspect." His smile was wide.

"Does 'some of us boys' include Clifton Hebert?"

Praytor laughed. "Henri handled the transport details, which has left the rest of us in something of a bind."

Raymond should have cared that Praytor Bless had just confessed to running untaxed liquor, but he didn't. "Do you know anyone who might have an interest in seeing Henri dead?"

Praytor leaned against his car and stuck his hands in his pockets. "Most ever'body who knew him. Henri had the Midas touch. We all disliked him, but we couldn't help but do business with him."

"Was there anyone in particular who had it in for him?"

"Not that I could point a finger at. Henri was shrewd. Men like him make enemies. I heard his body was torn to bits. You don't seem to think Adele Hebert did it." Praytor hooked a thumb in his suspenders. "You the only person in town who doesn't."

"I don't think there's such a thing as the *loup-garou*." Raymond stated it flatly. "I'd appreciate it if you told that to everyone you talk to. Adele Hebert isn't possessed by anything except a high fever."

Praytor stood up straight. "Then who did kill Henri?"

"That's what I intend to find out." Raymond turned and started walking back to his car. "I'd get on home, Praytor. As far as I'm concerned there's a killer still running loose in Iberia Parish."

11

RAYMOND sat in the empty examining room as the girl bundled the bloody sheets and began to clean the room. Henri Bastion's body had been released for burial. Doc Fletcher busied himself with the tools of his profession, putting instruments on a tray for the girl to remove.

"I don't have an answer." Doc turned to Raymond after the girl had left the room. "Henri Bastion died from blood loss. That's what I know for sure. I simply couldn't tell which wound was the mortal one. Before he bled to death, he could have been strangled or possibly stabbed."

"Were the bite marks human?" Raymond asked.

Doc pushed a strand of salt and pepper hair from his forehead. His brow was wrinkled, and Raymond could see the exhaustion in his face. Doc's life involved the horrors of accident and disease. He was familiar with death, in many forms, but not in the manner of Henri Bastion.

"The wounds were savagely delivered." Doc cleared his throat. "There were places where the bites were distinctly canine, but at other places . . . perhaps a wild hog." He picked up a pair of scissors and studied them. "I can't say for certain, Raymond. I know you want me to say that a wild animal killed Henri. I can't. There was bruising around his abdomen, and several ribs were broken. I don't think a dog did that."

Raymond looked out the window and saw the Teche flowing quietly by. "Someone struck him with something?"

"That's most likely what happened, but I can't say that absolutely. The damage was extensive."

"Someone struck him hard enough to break his ribs, and then when he fell to the ground, a pack of animals finished him off."

Doc put the scissors down. He walked to the door. "That would be my professional guess. But it's a guess, Raymond. The only thing I can say for certain is that his death was one of the most horrible I've ever seen."

Raymond paced the room. "Doc, did you ever examine Rosa Hebert?"

Doc removed his white coat stained with blood. "I did."

"And?" Raymond pressed.

"She had wounds in her hands identical to those that would be made with a large spike." Doc walked to the door and Raymond had to grab his shoulder to stop him.

"Did she hurt herself?"

"I don't know." Doc's brow furrowed. "She asked me to help her. She said she wanted the wounds to heal. I gave her some salve and bandages."

"Did the wounds come back?"

Doc shook his head. "I don't know. She hung herself two days later." Doc sighed. "I don't know who felt worse, me or Father Finley. Neither of us helped her."

"If Adele was poisoned, is there something that would make her behave this way?"

Doc's gray eyes grew suddenly sharp as he searched Raymond's face. "What are you asking me?"

"I don't think Adele had anything to do with Henri's death.

I think someone murdered him and set Adele up. Gave her something to make her act crazy so that the blame would fall on her."

"Do you have any evidence for this theory?" Doc leaned against the wall, exhaustion in the lines of his face. "Raymond, you're walking a line here. You know that."

"This isn't about me."

Doc lifted an eyebrow. "Oh, really. I've been waiting awhile to hear you say that. A lot of people have been waiting."

Raymond felt the flush touch his neck and begin to creep up his face. Doc was an astute bastard. "Is there some kind of poison that would do this?"

"I don't know, but I'll look into it. Until then, my advice is for you to take Adele to the state insane asylum where they can lock her up. For her own safety."

"I won't do that. She isn't guilty of anything except an illness."

Doc's nod was slow. "I don't know if you can save Adele, Raymond, but I pray to God you can save yourself."

When Doc left the room, Raymond remained. The autopsy had neither helped nor hindered Adele's case. If she had the element of surprise, she might have struck Henri with a bat or a limb, bringing him down for Clifton's dogs to finish off. It could have happened that way, but Raymond didn't believe it. Adele was innocent. And now he'd have to search harder to prove it.

Delayed for over a week, Henri Bastion's funeral—due to a request from Deputy Thibodeaux—was a small and private affair. Michael stood in the church chapel counting the three Bastion children, Marguerite, Jolene LaRoche, who sat in back despite his request that she stay home, Veedal Lawrence, and five other men from the community. Michael had pressed the men into the service of pallbearers. No one wanted to carry the coffin of a man killed by a werewolf. Such contact was too close.

Michael reflected, with disgusted resignation, that had Thibodeaux not insisted on a private service, there would've been at least three hundred souls present. Drawing such a large congregation was, most times, a magician's feat in New Iberia.

From his seat on the back pew, Thibodeaux walked to the front of the church. Michael knew the deputy had been eager to see who might attend a private service. Raymond had hoped to find a lead, a hint of someone come to see his, or her, handiwork committed to the grave.

"Father Michael, thank you for your assistance." Raymond spoke so that his voice didn't carry. "There are things you should know. Confidential things."

Michael was intrigued. Thibodeaux had no confidants. "Go on."

"I spent the morning with Doc Fletcher. He had the autopsy results, but he couldn't make up his mind about the cause of death."

Michael gave the deputy his full attention. "What do you mean? Henri was murdered, wasn't he?"

"Yes and no. Doc said the bites on Henri's body were definitely made by an animal. Dog or hog, he couldn't say for certain. A wild animal could have killed him, or he could have been strangled or suffocated. Maybe even stabbed."

"Doc couldn't tell—"

"He could have, except Henri's neck was chewed away, as were portions of the lungs. There is a possibility that all the damage to the body was done to cover up the real cause of death. Not a supernatural cause, but a very human one."

Michael looked out over the cluster of mourners, who were growing restless as they waited for him to begin the service. "Why are you telling me this?"

"I need your help."

Michael nodded, hiding his surprise. Raymond Thibodeaux asked no man for help. "What can I do?"

"Help me control the fear that's taking over the parish. To-night is Halloween. If something untoward should happen, even a prank, it could spark real trouble."

Michael stared into Raymond's dark eyes. He'd heard a story that once they'd been golden brown. He'd also heard reports that Raymond had single-handedly killed dozens of Germans, stalk-ing them, rushing their foxholes, hiding in bombed-out build-ings in deadly ambush. The man before him generated rumor and legend. Whatever the truth of the war, he suffered. Michael could read it as clearly as he saw his own pain. "I'll do what I can. Which would be . . . ?"

"You believe in miracles, don't you, Father?"

The only answer he could give touched his lips. He had no idea where Raymond was leading him. "Yes. The doctrine of the church is filled with the miracles of Jesus."

"Would it be a miracle if a human being were transformed into a wild animal? Say a wolf, for instance."

The question had already nagged at Michael. "If you're refer-ring to the *loup-garou,* that would not be God's handiwork but the devil's. Evil creatures belong to their master, Satan."

Raymond touched Michael's arm. "That's exactly the kind of talk I don't want to hear from this pulpit today." He rubbed at the weariness on his face. "It's my belief that Henri was killed by someone. Someone strong enough to take down a healthy man, and someone who's still walking the streets of New Iberia. Henri's body may have been bitten by an animal, but it was a human hand that snuffed the life from him."

Michael heard the restlessness of the congregation increase. "If Adele is the *loup-garou,* she would have the strength of a demon and the teeth of an animal, Deputy. That's why the beast is re-ferred to as a shape-shifter. Because it takes on the physical char-acteristics of another creature."

"There's talk of lynching Adele all up and down the street.

A stigmatic is one thing, but a werewolf is something else. Please, Father, don't contribute to a disaster."

Several of the nuns were standing anxiously in the wings. Michael swung his gaze to the congregation. Marguerite Bastion looked brittle enough to snap in two, and her boys were kicking each other. He had to start the mass. "Please take a seat, Deputy. I'm beginning the service." He stepped toward the pulpit, the white robes floating behind him.

As Michael took his place above the closed coffin, he tried to calm his mind, to find that connection that allowed him to comfort others. He surveyed the audience, hoping for divine inspiration in his words. The Bastion children needed more than he could give them. The boys had recovered from their grief and were punching each other in the pew. The girl stared straight ahead as if she no longer remained on this earthly plane.

Marguerite had done her duty as a wife. Henri's casket was cypress, cut and polished by one of the best craftsmen in the state. The wood gleamed a burnished red as light from the windows struck it.

He went through the rituals of the mass of Christian burial, coming at last to his favorite part. He cleared his throat and looked out over the meager congregation. "Henri Bastion's body is here with us, but his soul is in the hands of God. Like all mortals who passed before him and who will pass after, he must stand before God and be judged for the life he led."

Only Jolene seemed to be paying any attention to him at all. Marguerite had captured one son's shoulder in her hand and was pressing hard enough to make tears slide down the boy's cheeks. Michael felt a stab of defeat. Nothing he'd prepared would be heard. Like every Sunday, his words would be ignored. Ten years had taught him the futility of trying to penetrate the dense web of ingrained belief and behavior that comprised the Cajun settlement. Raymond had nothing to fear from him or his words from the pulpit.

He concluded quickly. As he walked to stand beside Marguerite while the body passed, he felt Jolene's comforting hand on his forearm.

The pallbearers hoisted the coffin and began the walk to the church cemetery. He could not go there without thinking of Rosa, denied admittance. In his mind he could see every detail of that morning. Adele had lifted Rosa from the cheap coffin, placed her in the pirogue, and paddled upstream to an unmarked grave in the swamps.

Trying to escape his own memories, he stepped quickly outside to lead the processional to the cemetery.

The last days of October had finally given a break in the heat, and the day was crisp and sunny. His robes blew against his legs as he walked behind the coffin. The best he could do was finish the burial, thankful to God that the heat of summer had broken.

Florence tied a multihued scarf around her head, dark curls fanning out on one side beneath the red cloth, gold hoop earrings dangling. She'd made a peasant blouse with elastic at the shoulders so she could pull it low. To that she'd added a bright purple skirt, cinched around her tiny waist with a gold scarf. Judging her reflection in the mirror, she decided she looked exactly like a gypsy. She'd chosen that costume because she intended to read Raymond's future. She'd set up a table in her front yard, complete with a clear glass ball she'd ordered from Sears Roebuck, which would pass as her gazer's crystal. The children would love it! Her house was always the most popular destination for the trick-or-treaters who walked the town, hoping for something good in their sacks, and she never disappointed them.

Darkness had just begun to fall when she heard a tap at her door. She'd told her regular customers that she wasn't available, but it was too early for trick-or-treaters. She went to the door, surprised to see Raymond standing there in the fading daylight.

"What's wrong?" she asked. His face looked drawn.

"Adele is gone."

Florence drew him inside and closed the door. "Gone where?"

"Madame went into the woods to gather more herbs for her tincture and when she returned, Adele had dressed in the clothes I left for her and disappeared. Madame caught a ride into town to tell me."

"Shit." Florence realized the potential trouble this meant for Raymond. "Do you have any ideas where she went?"

He shook his head. "Home? Into the swamps? I don't know. Why would she leave Madame's? She was so weak she could hardly sit up."

"Crazy people sometimes have tremendous strength." Florence had heard stories from some of the older whores how men, enraged or demented, had committed impossible feats. One man, though small and most often timid, had murdered six whores in a New Orleans brothel after being shot four times by the madam. The story was that he'd kept slashing with his knife even after his heart stopped beating.

Florence touched the crescent scar on her cheek. Crazy people had surprising strength. She knew that from personal experience.

Raymond paced the small room, and she thought of offering a drink but knew he'd refuse. He was wearing his uniform and his gun, and Raymond didn't drink on the job.

"There won't be another full moon for weeks," she said. "No full moon, no *loup-garou*." Her words earned a smile.

Raymond walked to her and touched her cheek, lifting her face. "Thank you, Florence." His voice was rough with emotion, and he bent to kiss her cheek so that she couldn't see his features. Florence caressed his cheek. Raymond was afraid of losing control, of feeling too much. She chose to keep the conversation light.

"You're welcome, kind sir. Would you like your future read? I have my crystal ball ready." Florence gave him a flirtatious look.

He hesitated, and she knew him well enough to know he was thinking of time lost, of fading daylight, of a woman alone in the night, of Halloween and the pranks that came with it, and finally, of her own need for his time and attention.

"A quick reading would be much appreciated, Lady Gypsy."

Few people would characterize Raymond Thibodeaux as gallant, but there were times she saw it. Sometimes his language revealed a man who had explored legend and story between the covers of a book. Sometimes his eyes told her that longings from his past, years dead, still haunted him. For just a moment, she'd seen something so alive in his eyes that she'd almost betrayed herself.

"Come and sit at my table." She took matches to light the candles she'd set up, mostly to give the illusion that she was actually staring into the ball.

They both took seats, and she felt the pressure of his foot beneath the edges of the tablecloth that covered the ground and concealed their legs. She shook off her sandal and put her foot into his crotch, pleased at the expression of surprise on his face. "I see that you are a man who feels deeply," she said, applying light pressure with her heel. "You are a sensual man who finds such delights to be a nuisance when your mind is on work."

Raymond laughed, encouraging her to continue.

"Tonight an opportunity for resolution will present itself. You'll find companionship and release with a dark-haired woman. A very pretty dark-haired woman with curls." She increased the pressure of her heel, arching her foot so that her toes came into play.

"Does the Lady Gypsy see where I can find my escaped prisoner?"

Florence waved her hand in front of the ball as if clearing it. She leaned closer to it, her warm breath misting the glass slightly in the chill night air. A shadow seemed to fill the glass, shifting like fog. She was so startled she gasped.

"Very convincing," Raymond said. His hand had found her foot and was massaging her arch. "What do you see?"

"A search," Florence stammered, unable to shake the disquiet that touched her. "A search through the dark woods."

Raymond eased her foot to the ground and stood quickly. "Are you okay?"

"Of course." She tried for a laugh. "It's a joke. The ball is empty." She forced a glance at it. She'd seen something. Most likely the candlelight refracted in the round glass or a magnified shadow of the movement of her hands. Whatever it was, she'd lost Raymond. He walked over and kissed her on the cheek, darkness hiding the gesture from any who passed her house.

"I'll be back once I've found Adele."

"Happy hunting," she said. Her fingers slipped down his arm, touching his hand lightly. "I'll be waiting."

12

CHULA sat in the window of Main Street Drug Company watching the young children dressed as witches and ghosts scamper down the street as their mothers called out warnings to them. The pharmacy boasted a full soda fountain and sweetheart tables with a view of the town's main street.

She could hear the children's chanting. "Trick or treat, smell my feet, give me something good to eat." Halloween had always been the best holiday of the year to her, and were it not for John LeDeux sitting across the small table from her, she would be at home, dressed as a witch, prepared to scare the children as they knocked on the door for candy.

"It's amazing how many pagan traditions are still part of American celebrations," John said. "Halloween may be the clearest example."

She pulled her attention from a dancing ghost who looked to be six or seven and refocused on the man across from her. His honey-blond hair and tanned skin were better suited to a movie idol than an academic. He was handsome, no doubt, but that wasn't what attracted her. Her intelligence was both her protection and her prison. She'd used her mind to ward off loneliness, but with the exception of Raymond, it had always held others at a distance. Now she turned to the facts she'd studied to find common ground. "Halloween stems from a Celtic ritual, right?"

"Part of Samhain, the beginning of the season of darkness when magic is strongest." He captured the cherry on his banana split and offered it to her.

Chula closed her eyes and bit into the sweet fruit. John didn't realize what an act of faith it took. Suddenly chilled, she pushed her unfinished ice cream away. John stood and removed his jacket to drape around her shoulders. She found the gesture attentive and welcome. "Thank you, John. I think it was your words rather than the temperature that chilled me."

"To the Druids, the winter, or dark season, was part of the natural cycle, as were magic and the casting of spells. On November first, they would dress in the skins and heads of the animals they'd killed and dance around a bonfire. This is the one night when humans could shift into a different form. That tradition may be the genesis of the werewolf stories."

"The pagan touch." Chula slipped her arms into the sleeves of his coat. The scent of a spicy aftershave lingered in the wool.

"Halloween also has a bit of Roman influence." John's smile was self-deprecating. "I can't seem to climb off the lecture platform."

She laughed. Few men had the confidence to make light of themselves. "I enjoy this kind of conversation. A lot."

His gaze touched hers and held. "The Romans worshiped Pomona, the goddess of fruits and gardens, another harvest theme."

"And there's a touch of Christianity from All Saints Day or Hallowmas." She could see she'd surprised him. "I was never a student of religion, much to the sisters' chagrin, but I remember the tidbits that interested me. I loved the idea of it because of dressing up as saints, angels, and devils. I still enjoy costumes."

"Halloween is a mishmash of all the traditions. The children love it, don't they?" He nodded to another group of laughing children. Two were dressed as witches, one as a clown, one a ghost, and another a fairy.

"What's different this year are the parents trailing behind them." She nodded at several adults hustling to keep up with the eager children. "In the past, it was safe for the young-uns to trick or treat alone. Look at that mother's face." The woman who passed by the window looked terrified. "People are really upset by Henri's murder."

She'd turned the conversation to the pivotal place where she wanted to go. "I hope you don't stir up more fear, John."

He picked up her hand from the table and held it lightly. "That isn't my intention. I'm here to observe, mainly. It's rare to have an opportunity to see how people react to folklore, to a myth that seems to have sprung to life from our own prehistory, if you buy into some theories of psychiatry. I want to ask a few questions."

"Questions can sometimes lead people's thoughts in a certain direction."

He studied her. "You have little faith in your fellow man, Chula. As Jung would point out, you see the wolf in all of us."

She couldn't help but smile. "I never thought of it that way, but I think you're right. People panic and they do stupid things. I see it every day. We're fighting a war that makes no sense. Powerful men disagree, and hundreds of thousands of soldiers with no opinion are dying. It's hard to trust an organism that finds itself in such predicaments." She waited for his reaction. If he was offended by her sentiments, it was best to find out now.

John's laughter was unexpectedly loud. "I'm surprised you haven't been hung and burned in effigy around here."

"I'm not exceptionally well liked." She shrugged, hiding the sudden jolt of pain.

"Because you're a woman in a man's job, or because you're a woman with a brain who dares to express herself?"

"Both." She found the admission difficult for some reason.

She'd begun to believe she'd accepted her social isolation, yet now it was pinching her. Why did John LeDeux's presence make it so?

"Have you ever considered moving away from here?"

The question was gently put, but Chula felt as if she'd been physically assaulted. "It wouldn't matter. I'd still be odd man out." She was mortified that her eyes had begun to mist over. "My heart is here, in this land. I could leave it physically, but I would never be a part of the next place."

He squeezed her hand and then released it. "Are you so sure, Chula?"

"My mother's family goes back here ten generations, to the first Acadians who were taken from their homes in Nova Scotia and shoved onto ships. They were forcibly removed halfway around the world to a land that no one else wanted—the marshland and bog that make up so much of this part of Louisiana. We made this our home."

"I feel I should take notes," he said, teasing her gently. "This sense of place is incredible to me. I've followed an academic career around the lower states and I've lived in some interesting towns. There's never been a place I couldn't walk away from."

"To a Cajun, home is everything, John."

"Yet you left to go to college."

"A temporary exile." The self-pity had passed and she could laugh at herself. "I beat it home as soon as I graduated, and now I have this very good job."

He leaned forward and whispered conspiratorially, "You probably make more money than I do."

"Heaven forbid." She mimed horror.

"Will you help me do some interviews?"

"Who do you want to talk with?" She wasn't certain she wanted to be involved.

"The sheriff, his deputy, the *traiteur,* the widow, the young boy who reported the incident—the people most intimately involved."

"What about Adele Hebert?"

"I'd give a lot to talk to her, but I don't know if they'll let me."

"They say she isn't speaking to anyone. She's very ill." Chula had a flashback of the young woman lying in Madame Louiselle's front room, chest fluttering with short, shallow breaths. "She's been in some type of coma. No one expects her to live."

"Will you help me with the others? Your mother said you know everyone in the parish."

She wondered at his motives. Did he see her merely as a means to the end he wanted, or did he see her as a woman? It wasn't a question she could ask outright. "Yes, I'll talk to the people on your list and ask them to speak with you."

"Thank you, Chula."

"There's one warning, John. If you stir up trouble, I wouldn't put it past Raymond Thibodeaux to toss you into jail. He ramrodded the Bastion family into holding a small, private funeral mass for Henri this morning, thereby disappointing five hundred people eager for gossip."

"When can we start? I have classes to teach in Baton Rouge, but if I can set up appointments, I can travel back and forth."

"Raymond is the key to all the others. If he talks with you, the others will."

"I'll pay him a visit first. Now I suppose I should get you home. Your mother will be worried."

Chula shook her head. "Wrong. I'm sure she's clapping her hands with glee that we've found enough to talk about to occupy our late evening."

They left the drugstore, laughing out loud as a child dressed as a pirate capered by. Moonlight peeked through the canopy of trees that lined the sidewalk while Chula talked about the development of New Iberia and how the coming of a railroad would change the town. "The days when the Teche is the heartbeat of the parish are ending."

"Do I detect a note of sadness?"

Chula considered it. "I'm twenty-nine years old and I act like someone seventy, always despairing about how the world is changing. If you asked anyone else, they'd say the railroad will bring New Iberia and the world closer." She hesitated, kicking a pile of leaves from the sidewalk. "I don't want the world closer."

"What about modern conveniences?"

"The price is always too high." She gave him a wry smile. "We're a special place, unique. All of that will change." She caught a glimpse of a figure moving quickly through the bushes in the McLemore backyard.

"What's wrong?" John touched her arm.

"Probably just a child playing a prank." She paused to get a better look. "Mrs. McLemore lives alone. Maybe I should check."

"I'll go with you."

They walked across the front lawn to the back, where the shadows were deepest. Chula scanned the yard, her gaze moving from the storage shed to a clump of azaleas and camellias, past a pecan tree. Nothing seemed out of the ordinary. John stood beside her, and she felt him tense.

"There."

At the very back of the yard where a thick wisteria covered the fence, she saw someone—or something—running. The creature looked neither human nor animal and disappeared into the darkness.

"Stop!" John took off after it with Chula right on his heels.

They dashed to the fence and halted. Whoever it was had made a clean escape.

"Did you see that?" John asked. "What was it? I couldn't tell if it was an animal or a person."

Chula's heart still pounded. "It was probably some older boy, pulling a Halloween prank. Let's go home and call the sheriff." She took his hand and pulled him back to the sidewalk, out of the dense shadows. When they resumed walking, their pace was brisk, almost a jog.

Sitting on the ground with his back pressed against a tombstone, Raymond watched the Spanish moss in the old oaks dance in the moonlight.

"Happy birthday, Antoine," he said. He gave the distinct cry of the hawk. "I can't stay long, but I wanted to visit a moment." He got to his knees and turned to face the stone so he could trace the inscription with a finger. "Antoine Thibodeaux, 1927–1943, Beloved son and brother, he answered the call of duty." Raymond had paid for the stone but hated the inscription. "Beloved son, left unprotected by his brother" would have been far more accurate. His poor judgment had cost Antoine his life. Hell, Antoine had barely become a soldier when he died, had never become a man in the truest sense of the word.

In the months since Antoine had been shot, the earth had mended with a new web of grass, but everything else about Antoine's death was raw. No one in the Thibodeaux family had recovered from the loss, would ever recover. Tony had been the heart of the family, the thing that kept them all together and moving forward when Ambrose Thibodeaux had died in a boating accident. Now they were lost. Each in a different way, but lost nonetheless.

He could no longer speak with his mother. Pain radiated from her, peeling the skin from his bones. Antoine had joined the army, following Raymond, wanting to fight for his country, to make a difference. In both of their idealistic imaginings, the war was going to be something like shooting bottles on a fence post. One German down, two, three, four. Raymond was a skilled sharpshooter, and he'd imagined the war as death from a distance.

He'd learned differently on his first combat assignment. He'd tracked through woods and slipped behind a mortar nest of three German soldiers. He'd shot the first one in the chest and the second in the neck before either man knew what had happened. The third had turned to him, terror on his face, his gaze searching the woods for the bullet that would take his life. Raymond had shot him, because to do it meant saving American lives, the lives of his brother and comrades. But the dreams had started then, the images of bloodied young men holding out their stumps instead of hands, pleading for mercy. Mercy that Raymond couldn't give. He was a reluctant but efficient killer, and the only solace he took from it was that by volunteering for such jobs, he kept Antoine safe.

Tony had followed him into the infantry, because he knew his big brother could protect him. But Raymond had failed. The cold stone against his hands was testimony of his dismal failing. The harvest he'd brought to his family was death and loss and suffering. This was the bitter crop his great-grandmother had warned against. When he felt the urge to live again, all he needed to do was come here and attend his harvest.

The sound of a vehicle bumping over the rough road made him get to his feet. He felt as if he'd fallen asleep, though he knew he hadn't. He'd only been at the grave for ten minutes or so, but the night had taken on a different cast.

When he saw the old truck, his heart sank. He'd avoided the cemetery all day, hoping not to run into his family. His sister parked the truck beside his car and walked toward him.

"What are you doing here?" Her voice was low.

Raymond stepped back from the headstone. Elisha had the look of a witch, dark hair hanging in tangled ringlets. She'd once been pretty, a slender girl with eyes as tender as a doe, and this was what grief had done to her.

He made a semicircle around her, determined to get back to his car and leave. He'd had his moment with Antoine, but he didn't want to talk to his sister. He couldn't face her, or his mother. He'd caused them too much pain already.

"Raymond, please!" Elisha advanced on him. "Won't you talk to me?" Tears glistened on her pale face. "Mama is dying, Raymond. Grief is killing her. Antoine is dead, but you're not."

Raymond wanted to grab her by the shoulders and pull her against him, to hold her against the pain that was tearing her apart, but he had no comfort to give her. "I can't help Mama. I can't help anyone. She sees me and it makes it all fresh again. She sees me, and she thinks how Antoine is dead."

"She sees you and she sees her son." Elisha held out a hand to him. "Raymond, she talks of you constantly, of how you look like Papa, of how you did this or that. Please, come and see her. Before it's too late."

Against the dark night, Elisha moved like a wraith of suffering. She was too thin, her cheeks hollow and lines marking flesh too young and tender for wrinkles. No matter how much he wanted to comfort her, he knew his touch would ultimately bring only pain. "Go home, Elisha. Mama will be worried about you."

"Mama doesn't worry about me." Elisha wiped the tears from her cheeks. "She sits on the porch and rocks. That's what she does, Raymond. She looks down the road, hoping that there's been a mistake and that Antoine will walk home. She slips away more and more each day. She doesn't know or care what I do."

Raymond felt the weight of her loneliness. "I would change things, if I could." He stepped toward her. She was his little sister, a child he'd cuddled like a puppy when she was born. He and Antoine had taken her on their adventures, waiting for her when her legs were too short and stubby for running. My God, she'd become a woman and he wasn't certain how it had occurred.

"Why did you come back here?" Her tone held only confusion, no blame. "You won't see your family. You have no friends. You walk the town like a ghost. Why did you come back?"

He hesitated, but then decided to tell the truth. "Because I have no place else to go."

In the moonlight fresh tears tracked silver down her face. "I don't know who I feel the sorriest for. You or me or Mama."

"Go home, Elisha. It's dangerous out here. You should stay

home at night." Her unrelenting grief had driven away all of her friends and suitors, and that was his fault, too.

Raymond walked to the car and got in. His headlamps caught and held Elisha as he backed out and left the family cemetery. He had to find Adele, before everyone in the parish learned she was on the loose. He had to find her and contain her—for her own safety. He couldn't help his family, and if he failed Adele, he would accept that he was doomed.

Adele was barefoot. That much Raymond could tell from her footprints. She was headed toward town—if she even knew what direction she followed. Using a flashlight, Raymond tracked Adele from Madame Louiselle's and into the thick woods. Trying to find Adele was the only thing that quieted the demons that raged in his memory. Straining his eyes in the darkness, he concentrated on his task.

He stepped cautiously, more afraid of a snake or gator than a predator. The length of Adele's stride told him she had no such concerns. She was running, careless of her footing or what she might disturb. Almost as if she were a part of the swamp.

He considered the story her tracks told. From a coma, Adele had risen, dressed, and stepped into the night. She'd begun to run, and for the last mile that he'd covered, she hadn't slowed at all. A woman who was so weak she couldn't sit up without help was now running. As Raymond's boot slipped into an oozing bog of mud and cold water, he realized he could draw one of two conclusions. Either Adele had played them all, pretending to a weakness that was fake, or she was so ill she didn't know what she was doing. The third option was impossible. She was not a shape-shifter with supernatural strength and powers.

He splashed through the bog and kept going. The waning moon couldn't penetrate the thickness of the woods, and he was forced to rely on the feeble beam of the flashlight. He found the high-arched print of her foot, the impression of the ball deep and the distance between steps nearly three feet. She was still running.

When the trail came to a spring-fed branch, he stopped. The tracks disappeared in the water, and though he cast the beam on the other side, he couldn't see where she'd exited. Or if she'd left the water. He brought the light down into the water, half expecting to see her dark hair and wide-open eyes staring at him from beneath the shallow stream.

He found only dead leaves rotting on the bottom. There was nothing for it but to turn back. He couldn't follow her now, and he certainly couldn't keep the pace she set as he tracked her by flashlight. Her direction was northeast, as if she were being drawn to town.

As long as she stayed in the woods, no one would hurt her. If she showed up on the streets of New Iberia, there was no telling what a panicked resident might do. Raymond hesitated on the edge of the stream.

By refusing to chain Adele to Madame's bed, he'd allowed her to put herself in ultimate danger. She was free and running loose because of him. Because of the decision he'd made. He stood a moment in the moonlight before he began the walk out of the woods.

When he returned to Madame Louiselle's, she took him to her kitchen where a bowl of soup steamed hot in the cool night. She stood behind him, her hands moving over his shoulders, and he listened to the gentle mumbling of a prayer.

When she was finished, she moved to sit across from him. "I'm sorry, Raymond. I wouldn't have left her if I'd thought she might run away."

He pushed his bowl away. "I never believed Adele *could* run away."

"You wanted to handcuff her, and I urged you not to do it."

Madame held his gaze with one dark and curious. "Is it possible I'm to blame for all of this?"

"No, Madame. She was so sick. How could you know?"

"Sometimes it isn't possible to know the outcome of an action. Sometimes you have to act on faith." She leaned forward. "How's your back?"

To his surprise, the pinching pain was gone. "Better. Thank you, Madame. I have one question. When you saw Adele last, was she quiet?"

Madame nodded. "She asked for water, and she understood. She was coming around, beating the fever back. I went to gather some roots to brew her a calming tea. I had it in my head that she would be ready for a warm bath when I returned. I was only gone an hour or so. When I came back, she was gone, and I went to town for you."

Adele had moved from near invalid compliance to running wild in less than an hour. It was a repetition of a pattern that confirmed Raymond's dark suspicions.

"Madame, did anyone come to see Adele?"

The old woman's face showed sudden understanding. "It's possible, *cher*, but I didn't see anyone. I was half a mile away."

Raymond stood up. "Thank you, Madame. And don't worry. We'll find her." On his way out, he put his hand on her shoulder and gave it a squeeze.

When he was in the yard, he pulled the flashlight from his pocket and examined the ground. It took ten minutes, but he found what he was looking for. Tire tracks led up to the house. Someone had come to visit Adele while Madame was gone. To visit and to dose her again with the concoction that made her run like a wild thing through the woods.

He knelt down to study the story of the tracks. The tires were in fair shape. Better than fair. Since the war, rubber was near impossible to find and most residents made do with tires so bald they had no tread. Raymond slowly rose to his feet, aware that his back made no complaint.

Praytor Bless's car had good tires. Somehow, Praytor, or his mama, had managed to obtain them. It would be worthwhile to pay a visit to Praytor in the near future.

13

_____

THE sound of childish laughter disappeared on a gust of wind as Florence picked up her crystal ball and started toward the front door. Trick or treat was over. She'd handed out fortunes of adventure and wealth—along with apples, oranges, and the much sought-after peppermints she'd found in Baton Rouge. She was out of energy and treats, and something in the night had set her nerves on edge. She wanted to be inside with her door locked, waiting for Raymond to return. Tonight, she needed the comfort of his arms, the sense that for the dark hours of the moon, someone was there to protect her.

Her hand touched the handle of the screen door when she heard something behind her. Turning, she clutched the crystal ball, prepared to use it as a weapon if necessary. Her gaze scanned the front yard where shadows shifted as the wind blew the oak limbs beneath the moon.

She thought to call out but found her voice paralyzed. The screen creaked as she pulled it open and turned to step inside.

A strong hand on her ankle tore a scream from her throat, and she plunged headfirst in the front door, kicking at the grip that snared her leg. She was on her stomach, her only defense her feet. Her heel connected solidly with something, and that made her thrash harder.

"Hold on there, wildcat," a male voice said, and there was a whine in the words. "Florence, calm down. You likta kicked me in the head."

She flipped onto her back and sat up to find Praytor Bless kneeling on the top step and rubbing his shoulder.

"You 'bout dislocated my shoulder there, Florence." He stood up. "I came to get my fortune told."

Anger washed over her in tides of red, but she forced herself to control her breathing and bite back the curse she wanted to hurl at Praytor. She took in the fact that Praytor had on a freshly ironed shirt, but she could smell whiskey on his breath.

"You scared the life out of me." She got up and retrieved the crystal ball that had rolled across the floor. "You're too late, Praytor. I've stopped gazing."

"I was waitin' for the young-uns to leave. Thought it would be more fun if it was just the two of us."

She looked past him into the night. "Another time. I'm tired."

"Seems to me you're tired a lot of nights."

He was already halfway in her home. Outside she'd been threatened by her own imaginings. Praytor wasn't a man she feared, but she was also careful to maintain a certain front with him. He collected information, his sharp eyes seeing things that others missed. Tonight, he was drunk.

"Go home. Come back tomorrow. We'll both enjoy it more."

"Goin' home wasn't in my plan." His gaze narrowed. "You don't look busy right now. Maybe you got plans for later on?"

She sighed, calculating. It would be easier to take the ten minutes necessary to service him, but something in her rebelled. "My plans are none of your concern, *cher.* Go home and come back tomorrow." She forced a smile. "I'm tired, Praytor. I want to give you full service, and I can't tonight." She touched her head. "My head is pounding."

He stood there, staring at her, and she felt a tingle of warning glide over her skin like the lightest silk. Praytor had always reminded her of an insect, something that waited in a dark crevice to trap and devour other, weaker species.

"You refusin' me?"

She swallowed. "Only for tonight. Come back tomorrow." And when his car pulled up, she'd lock her door and refuse to answer it. She moved forward to the door, determined to show him she wasn't afraid. "I'm tired, *cher*. My head aches. Tomorrow we'll have some fun."

She looked past him and felt something inside her chest grip. Someone—or something—was hiding behind the oak tree beside the road.

"What?" Praytor read the expression on her face and turned to look. "Who's out there?"

"Someone." Florence found her voice was breathy with fear. "There's someone behind that tree."

"Someone spyin'." Praytor's voice was edged with anger. "I'll drag 'em out and teach 'em not to be spyin' on me." He stumbled down the steps and lurched across the yard toward the big oak.

Something big took off running, moving fast. Florence heard the small cry of fear that escaped from her as she watched the shadowy figure disappear into the trees across the road. She couldn't be certain what she'd seen—a person or some type of large animal. The night was too dark for details.

"Hey! Hey, you, come back here!" Praytor charged into the road, stumbling.

She heard the sound of a car, and saw, too late, the headlights of a vehicle coming fast down the road. Praytor was illuminated in the vehicle's lamps, his face showing horror.

The driver stepped hard on the brake, swerving at the last

instant, so that the car careened through the woods across the street, the headlights bouncing up and down as the car bumped over ruts and shrubs.

Florence recognized the car. She ran past Praytor without a glance and into the woods where the car had come to a stop.

"Raymond," she said, pulling the driver's door open. "Raymond." He sat behind the wheel, still gripping it. "Raymond." She thought her chest would explode with her fear. "Can you hear me? Can you move?" She thought of the metal in his back and the things he'd never told her but that everyone else in town repeated—one day the shrapnel would shift and his spinal cord would be severed.

"I'm okay," he said at last. "Who was that idiot standing in the road?"

She couldn't stop the trembling. When she touched his shoulder she felt the solid muscle, the warmth, and she felt tears form in her eyes and fall down her cheeks. "Praytor. He's drunk."

"He's going to be dead when I get out of here."

Raymond shifted and slowly moved his feet from the floorboard to the ground. He stood, moving carefully as if he, too, wasn't certain that something hadn't changed.

She wanted to throw her arms around him and hold him, to attach herself in a way that she could make certain he wasn't hurt. She stepped back, though, and let him lead the way to the road where Praytor sat in the ditch, the smell of vomit strong around him.

"Praytor, I'm going to kick the shit out of you to the point there won't be anything left but empty boots." Raymond staggered slightly.

Florence held back, forced to watch the scene between the two men play out, helpless to stop whatever was going to happen. She didn't care about Praytor. Raymond, though, was another matter, and Praytor Bless was known to carry a knife and fight dirty.

Praytor's response was another stream of vomit.

"Shit." Raymond shook his head. "You aren't worth the effort." He turned, looking from Florence to the headlamps of the car still shining into the woods.

He stepped toward Florence, and she felt a smile touch the corners of her lips. She moved to meet him when the sound of another car echoed on the empty night air. She saw headlights, and then the car slowed and stopped. Chula Baker jumped from the passenger side of the car.

"Raymond, I've been hunting for you everywhere." She ran toward the deputy as a tall, handsome man in slacks and a jacket got out from behind the wheel of the polished Studebaker. He stood by the car, watching but not interfering.

Chula took a deep breath. "We saw something in Mrs. McLemore's yard. Something strange. I finally tracked down Sheriff Joe, and he told me to find you."

Raymond stood taller. "What did you see?"

Chula's laugh was nervous, and Florence assessed her. Chula Baker was disliked by the town because she didn't act womanish. Talk was that she'd acquired book learning and lost her femininity. Uglier talk implied that Chula and her employee, Claudia Breck, were *une gouine*. Florence watched the way Chula stood, feet planted solidly, her gaze holding Raymond's as she spoke. Florence admired her.

"There was something in the backyard. We were walking by and I thought at first it was a prankster. But . . ." Her voice faded.

The man stepped forward, his hand going to Chula's arm for support. "Whatever it was moved curiously. We couldn't tell if it was human or animal." His voice was low, calm.

The image reminded Florence of what she'd seen. "I saw it, too. It was here, just before you wrecked." She walked closer to Raymond, Chula, and the man. "Praytor was going to chase it in the woods, but he was too drunk to run."

Raymond's face in the headlights of the car was severe. "Did you get a clear look at who it was?"

"No," Chula admitted. "It was dark. Honestly, it could have been an animal."

"And you?" Raymond looked at Florence.

"It was behind a tree, and it moved through the shadows."

Raymond glanced toward Praytor, who'd passed out in the ditch. "Thank you, Chula. I'll check Mrs. McLemore's right away."

"Glad to help, Raymond. This is John LeDeux, a professor at LSU. He's working on a book, and he'd like to talk with you when you have time."

"About what?"

Florence saw the way Raymond bristled. She stepped a little closer, envious of the way John LeDeux touched Chula, the accepted show of support and friendship a man might properly show a woman.

LeDeux offered a smile. "I'll explain it all to you when you have a free hour. Right now, let me help you get your car out of the woods." He removed his jacket and handed it to Chula. Without a backward glance he walked across the road and into the woods where the car waited, the headlights casting strange shadows in the trees.

Michael took the last popcorn ball and dropped it into the paper sack the little hobo held out. "Please don't trick me tonight," he said, smiling at the boy who was no older than six. "I hope to see you at mass Sunday morning."

"Yes, Father," the boy said. "Thank you." He ran to his waiting mother.

Michael watched as the woman put her hand on the boy's shoulder, keeping him tightly under her control as they walked away. He'd seen that same gesture all night long—mothers protecting their young.

He locked the front door and turned off the light. His treats had been demolished by the dozens of youngsters. The parish house was always popular with trick-or-treaters because Colista made the sticky popcorn balls, candied apples, brownies, tiny pecan pies, and other delectables that were highly sought after. Colista said it was his duty to tempt the young children into the ways of the Lord, and a little popcorn and syrup were a small price to pay.

"Doesn't matter how you catch their souls, Father, as long as you draw them to the church," she'd told him as she'd arranged the trays of treats beside the front door.

He had to agree. Bribery wasn't always a bad thing.

He went to the sideboard and poured a small glass of port wine. The night was cool, and he wanted something to warm his blood. Or numb his mind. Images of Henri Bastion's drab funeral were lodged in his brain.

Deputy Thibodeaux had ordered the coffin hammered shut with headless nails—an act to thwart the curious from gazing at the body. The undertaker had refused to answer any questions. Even Doc Fletcher had been tight-lipped and brusque. Raymond had buttoned up the town officials in an effort to calm the talk and stop fear from growing.

Michael took a seat before the small fire he'd built and sipped the port. The sweet, fiery taste soothed him. At least the cool weather would thin the insect population. The rampaging fevers would end. The latest news on the war seemed more hopeful than ever. American troops were crawling across Europe, routing the Germans. There was hushed talk that victory would soon be at hand.

He got out his missal to read the Scriptures for the following day. Preparing the homily had always been one of his favorite parts of the job. Rome dictated the Scriptures, but it was up to him to bring the interpretation to the residents of New Iberia, to explain it with parables and stories that made it relevant to the hard life of many of his congregation.

When he'd first joined the priesthood, he'd had no doubts

about his calling. He'd known in his blood that the Lord had work for him, and he'd walked away from the rich history and relative comfort of his Boston family with the idea that he would eventually be posted to Ireland, where his family roots were embedded in the limestone. The focus of his studies—and interests—had lain with helping to settle the plague of violence that had rent Northern Ireland and pitted brother against brother. Instead, he'd been sent to the dark marshlands where language, culture, and tradition all worked against him.

In the ten years he'd served as priest at St. Peter's, he'd found more questions than answers. Until Rosa. Rosa Hebert had been a gift from God, a messenger sent directly to Michael, a sign that God had not forsaken him and the people of lower Louisiana. Rosa, with her terrible suffering and the miracle of her wounds, would have been—should have been—the indisputable fact of God's love and existence, for him and his congregation.

Rome had not seen it that way.

The Vatican had balked, finding reason after reason not to investigate the miracle, holding back approval or even acknowledgment of something so powerful. And while the cardinals debated the propriety of Rosa Hebert's selection to bear the marks of Jesus, Rosa had begun to deteriorate. With each of her doubts, his own grew.

He'd seen it and been unable to give her the comfort and strength to stop the process. He'd been so caught up in the possibilities that her fame would bring that he'd been unable to help her. He'd failed her, and he'd failed himself. And in the process, he'd failed God.

He got his pen and paper from the desk and returned to the fire, pushing his feet out to warm. The parish house was drafty and cold, but cold was better than summer. Even his mind worked better in the cool months.

He jotted a few notes, pausing at the sound of tapping on the study window. He looked up, but the pane was empty. He returned to his work, but his concentration was fragmented. Lately, thoughts of Rosa had tormented him more than usual. All of this business with Adele and her transformation into the *loup-garou* was a mockery of Rosa's true suffering. Satan could manifest himself, he knew it for a fact as surely as he knew that God could mark the hands of a woman with the wounds of a spike. What he couldn't determine was whether Adele was Satan's revenge, or if she were simply a woman deluded with grief and fever, as Raymond insisted.

The sound of breaking pottery made him stand up. He went to the study window and looked out over the garden. The moon wasn't full, but it was bright, and he could see the paths that led among the dying roses. The last cool snap was finishing them off. In the moonlight, the mums were different gradations of silvery gray.

Nothing seemed amiss, yet he'd distinctly heard the sound of something breaking. The wind hadn't been strong enough to blow over a pot. He put the pen and paper away and walked to the back door.

"Colista?" She'd gone home earlier in the evening to attend to trick or treat at her house, but it was possible she'd come back. "Colista?"

No one answered and he felt the emptiness of the house in a chilling way. Moving to the back door, he opened it and stood on the threshold, reluctant to step outside. If someone was in the garden, he didn't see them.

Then he remembered that it was Halloween. In all likelihood, one of the young boys from the church had decided to play a prank of some kind. He smiled, stepping out onto the garden walkway paved with bricks molded and fired by slaves.

A gust of wind blew his cassock against his legs and he heard the creaking of the garden gate as it moved on rusty hinges. The sound was like cold fingers tracing his spine. His first impulse was to turn and run back inside. Exactly what the prankster hoped to accomplish.

Forcing his stride long and his shoulders back, he walked to the gate to close it. He'd just touched the cold wrought iron when he looked beyond at the oak tree.

A cry escaped him as he stared at the sheet-draped figure of a woman swaying gently in the breeze on the end of a stout rope.

"Rosa!" He cried her name as he ran forward. "Rosa! No!"

14

THE first pale light of dawn filtered through the bars of the cell, now empty, where Adele should have been. Raymond stood at the open door, weighing the cost of his actions. Last night, when he'd seen Elisha, he hadn't realized how much she reminded him of Adele. Now, looking at where Adele should have been, he knew he was right to avoid Elisha and his mother. No matter his intentions—and he had intended to protect Antoine, Elisha, his mama, and Adele—whoever he touched ended up suffering. As soon as Adele was found, he would leave. He was a man more solitary even than a *loup-garou*. Adele had captured his tender feelings because he saw himself in her. In her, he'd seen his possible redemption.

Now she was alone in the woods, hungry, sick, and possibly drugged. He'd not found any proof to show she was innocent of a gruesome murder. If the townsfolk panicked, they would kill her. As soon as the sun was up good, he intended to find Praytor Bless, or at least Praytor's car. He wanted to check the tires for a match with what he'd found at Madame's.

The door burst open and Pinkney blew in with a flapping

coat and the smell of autumn. "Big Ethel's on a tear! She jus' heard her gran'baby's been missin' since eight o'clock last night."

Raymond turned slowly. He'd been up all night, and his body was sore from the automobile accident. No physical pain compared to the dread he felt at Pinkney's news. "Missing? You mean ran away or—"

"Gone missin'. Peat Moss, thas her name, went to go to the outhouse and she never come back in."

A splinter of hope touched Raymond. "How old is Peat Moss?"

"She four."

His hope withered. This was a young child missing, not a wayward teen. "She's been missing since eight? Why didn't they report it?"

"They ain't got no phone and they been huntin'. Didn't have time to drive into town and track you or Sheriff Joe down."

That was the hard truth of it. Even if the family had come into town, there was no guarantee Joe could have been found, and Raymond had been out all night following Adele's trail—he was certain that it was Adele roaming the night. His problem lay in the fact that he'd told only Florence that Adele had escaped from Madame's. He hadn't warned anyone. Now a child was missing.

"How did Big Ethel find out the baby is missing?"

Pickney had recovered his breath, and he tipped the old fedora he loved back on his head and swelled his lungs with air. "Big Ethel was in the kitchen at the café cookin' some ham and biscuits when her son, Leroy, bust through the back door, all upset and lookin' for volunteers to search the woods."

"Is Leroy still there?"

"Was when I left. I got the biscuits and came straight here to tell you."

"Thanks, Pinkney." Raymond picked up his jacket and the snap-brimmed hat he wore in cold weather. His gun was already strapped to his waist. He started toward the door.

"What about your biscuit, Mr. Raymond?"

"Enjoy it, Pinkney. When you see Joe, tell him I need to talk to him. Tell him to sit right here until he talks to me. Tell him it's important."

"Should I tell him about Peat Moss?"

Raymond nodded. "Tell him." He stepped out into a wind that blasted him in the face with grit. His impulse was to run, but he forced himself to walk as he made the three blocks to the café. Instead of going in the front, he went to the back door. He could hear Big Ethel when he was still twenty feet away.

The back door was screened, and he stood for a moment, letting her cries wash over him. Grief had come to another household because of him. He stepped inside and saw her seated on a stool, her apron thrown over her head as she rocked and howled. Two other cooks supported her, patting her back and whispering softly. There was no sign of Leroy.

The first wisps of smoke rose from the oven, and Raymond walked over to it and turned it off, pulling the pan of scorched biscuits out. One of the cooks nodded her thanks, but she made no effort to leave Big Ethel's side.

"Is Leroy still around?" Raymond asked.

"He went to find Clifton Hebert." The woman spoke with resignation. "Say he gone get Clifton to find Peat Moss."

Raymond stepped closer. "Ethel, can you talk to me?"

She heard him because her rocking slowed. The two cooks stepped back, waiting a moment to be sure she could support herself, and then returned to their work in the kitchen, tut-tutting and whispering low prayers. Ethel wiped her eyes and pulled the apron down, her fingers working the rosary beads she clutched.

She was a heavyset woman with caramel skin and hair touched with gray. "My gran'baby been gone nearly twelve hours. She's only four."

"I know." He tried to organize his questions. "She went to the outhouse about eight o'clock. Tell me what you know."

"She was dressed like a ghost. She'd been trick-or-treating, though her daddy was set against it. Got a sack full of things. Leroy said she went outside, liked to show she was grown up and could go by herself. When she didn't come back in, he went to check. She was gone." Tears moved silently down her face. "She was jus' gone. Peat Moss is a good chile, jus' a little slow to catch on to things. She never cries, never fusses. She's just good." She turned her head and sobbed.

"Is it possible Peat Moss simply wandered into the woods?"

Ethel's sobs subsided. "She likes the woods. Never was afraid of the dark like other children." She inhaled raggedly. "You think she wandered off?"

Raymond wouldn't lie to her, not even for comfort. "Is there anyone who might have stopped by to get her? A relative took her to spend the night?"

Big Ethel shook her head. "Not without tellin' her maw. Nobody woulda took her. She only four. She don't spen' the night away from home."

Raymond had no children, but he'd been around his younger siblings and his cousins enough to know that a four-year-old wouldn't deliberately walk into the woods on a dark night. Not alone. Not on Halloween. Not without either force or temptation.

"Was anything else missing?"

Big Ethel bit her bottom lip and shook her head. "Leroy didn't say. Only thing he said was that he was gettin' volunteers with guns and when they found whoever took Peat Moss, he was gonna kill 'em. He say Clifton Hebert can track a ghost and that they gone have Peat Moss home by nightfall."

Raymond kept his expression carefully neutral. The one thing he didn't need was a vigilante group roaming through the swamps. "We'll do everything we can to find her." He heard the emptiness of his own words and looked down at his boots, so worn and caked with mud.

At the sound of knocking, he looked up to find Pinkney at the kitchen door, his face a mirror of doubt and anxiety.

"Mr. Raymond, got a message for you. It's important."

"What is it?"

Pinkney looked at Big Ethel and shook his head. "Best you come out here a minute."

Raymond patted Ethel's shoulder as he walked past her to the door. "What is it?"

"Father Finley done called. Says there's a body hanging in his oak tree where he found Rosa Hebert."

The sun was moving higher in the branches of the oaks when Raymond pulled into the priest's house, his old Chevy clanging and grinding. His collision in the woods had damaged the car, but it was too early for a mechanic to be open. The car ran, and he had no choice but to drive it.

Instead of going to the front, he walked around the house, past the garden to the oak where he'd cut Rosa Hebert down. At the sight of a white-shrouded body swinging gently from a huge, arched limb, he felt dread touch him. The body was too small to be an adult, but it could easily be a four-year-old child.

He looked around for Father Finley but the priest was nowhere in sight. He caught a glimpse of the black-clad priest in a window of the house. Like last time. When Finley had called to report another body hanging from the tree, the body of Rosa Hebert, he'd remained in the house while Raymond and the coroner had done their jobs.

Raymond walked forward slowly. There was nothing for it but to lift the sheet and see what was beneath it. He heard the creaking of the rope as the wind teased the tree limb. His fingers felt numb as he lifted the sheet.

"Sweet Jesus," he said, dropping it. He turned away and took a deep breath. The remains of Kyle Fenton's scarecrow was beneath the sheet. He walked to the trunk of the tree and sat down on a gnarled root because his legs were weak. It was a scarecrow, a pair of pants and shirt stuffed with straw and wired to a pair of crossed boards.

When he looked up, Finley was approaching him. The priest was pasty with worry. "Who is it?" he asked, stopping twenty feet away.

"Not who, what. It's Kyle Fenton's scarecrow."

He watched the emotions play across Michael's face. First there was relief, then anger that boiled into rage. "What little bastard would play such a trick?" he asked. He walked to the rope that was tied off around the tree trunk and began jerking on it. "What terrible little bastard would do such a thing?"

Raymond rose and went to the priest. He grasped Michael's hands, already raw from the bark of the oak, and held them. "It's okay. It's okay." He heard the priest's dry heaving as he struggled to check back his emotions.

"Who would do this?" Father Michael looked to Raymond as if he might have a real answer.

"I don't know. Someone who wasn't thinking. A kid." He untied the rope and lowered the scarecrow to the ground. "I'll send Pinkney over to clean this up."

"I thought it was Rosa." Michael's legs nearly buckled as he sat down on the root Raymond had vacated. He put his face in his hands. "I failed her, Raymond. I lost my belief in her, and she hung herself."

Raymond held the rope in his hands, helpless to do anything else. He felt sharp compassion for the priest, a man who was deviled by a Hebert sister just as he was.

15

A stand of sugar cane stood tall in the morning sunlight as Raymond pulled into Leroy Baxter's front yard. The cane was disconcerting. The men of the family should've been out chopping and harvesting. The first heavy frost was overdue.

The tarpaper and tin cabin was abnormally quiet. Raymond got out slowly, waiting for the sheriff to lead the way. Joe Como had felt it was his duty to talk to the missing girl's mother. There had been no trace of Peat Moss Baxter in fifteen hours, and Joe was politician enough to want the family to see he was personally on the case.

"I want to take a look around the outhouse," Raymond said. He wanted no part of the pain and grief that Joe would have to confront.

Joe gave him a helpless look, tucked his shirttail in, and walked to the front steps. He was knocking at the door as Raymond disappeared around the back of the cabin. Raymond heard the wail of Aimee Baxter and kept walking.

The outhouse was some twenty yards from the cabin, and he knew there would be nothing to find. Whatever tracks had once been there were gone. Leroy and a dozen men had brought Clifton's dogs over to try to follow the trail of the missing child. Raymond had mentioned to no one the irony of Clifton most likely tracking his own sister with the very dogs that had savaged Henri. This latest development, though, made no sense.

Even in her fevered madness, he knew that Adele would not harm a helpless little girl. Yet Peat Moss Baxter was gone, and there seemed no other explanation for it. Talk all over town was that the *loup-garou* had taken another victim. It was only a matter of time before Joe demanded that Adele be brought back to the jail. So far, the sheriff had been too distraught over the disappearance of the child to think through the logical steps he should take. He'd assumed, like everyone else, that Adele was still weak and incapacitated at Madame Louiselle's. But Joe would demand to question her, eventually. At that point, Raymond knew the town would be out of control. No one would listen to him when he tried to explain there was something else afoot in Iberia Parish.

The outhouse gave up no secrets, and he went back to the patrol car. In a moment, Joe came out, his armpits and back covered in sweat. The muffled sounds of Aimee's sobbing settled around them as they drove away.

"Go to Madame Louiselle's and get Adele. Bring her back to the jail." Joe stared out the front window of the car as he spoke. "I tried to tell Aimee that Adele couldn't have harmed her child, that she's too sick to have done anything, but there's a lot of crazy talk that she was on the loose last night. All those reports of something scuttling around town aren't helping. Whatever bastard hung that scarecrow . . ."

Raymond drove without answering. Sunlight filtered through the trees, creating a flashing effect of black and white. He was aware that Joe sat beside him, sweating in the cool morning, but Raymond was no longer in the car.

The winding downhill road of a small village stretched before him. Sunlight touched the walls of shops and houses, their colors muted by age. He carried his rifle as he walked, boots echoing on the empty stones of the street. He was part of a cleanup detail. The infantry had met fierce resistance, and after weeks of heavy casualties, they'd taken the town of Trieste. Most of the soldiers had moved through the village, leaving Raymond and a few others to bring up the rear. After the noise of the fighting, Raymond welcomed the quiet.

As he moved along, he stopped to examine the bodies of German soldiers. Medics had evacuated the American wounded, and Raymond could still see the horror of the mangled men. He'd become an apt judge of death. He could read it on their faces, his friends and comrades he couldn't help. It was better not to look, to focus on the enemy instead, to count each lifeless body as a step toward victory.

In the heart of the town he walked from the shadows cast by the old buildings into the sunlight, stopping at the town square. Five Germans had fallen there, and he walked toward them, struck by their pallid youth. They looked no more than fifteen, and he knew the rumors that Hitler was drawing his army from boys who should have been in school were true. The war was turning, and Germany would lose, but not before a madman had devastated the population.

One of the boys groaned, and Raymond knelt down, pulling a dead body out of the way. The boy's face showed suffering and no fear.

"You got a live one."

Raymond looked up to find Antoine walking toward him. His younger brother looked exhausted, and Raymond realized yet again that Antoine was still a child himself, only eighteen.

"He's hurt pretty bad." Death had left a marker in the boy's eyes. He knew he was dying. His torso and legs were buried beneath the weight of his dead comrades, but Raymond could see that his abdomen was destroyed.

Antoine shifted from foot to foot. "What're you going to do? The medics are gone."

Raymond stared into the boy's eyes. His blue gaze was unrelenting, a dare. "Leave him to finish it in peace." He made the sign of the cross and stood.

"We can't just leave him." Antoine's voice broke. "He's a kid, Raymond."

"What else is there to do? I can't shoot him like a sick dog." Raymond spoke with anger. "By the time we find some medics, he'll be dead." Fighting for freedom for the world was one thing, but watching a child die was something else.

"Maybe we could carry him."

Raymond shook his head. "He's too far gone. Half his guts are missing." If the boy were a farm animal, Raymond would put him out of his misery. "We'll find Jimbo and get him to radio for a medic." Raymond knew the boy would be dead in a matter of minutes. He walked past his brother. "Let's go."

He'd made it twenty yards when he realized Antoine was not following. He turned back. Antoine was running to catch up with him, his boots ringing on the stones. The sharp report of a weapon cracked the morning light. Antoine stumbled, his face showing puzzlement before he fell to the street.

Raymond looked at the young German. His icy smile never faltered as he held the pistol in his hand.

"Hey! Raymond!"

He turned to find Joe red-faced and angry.

"I been talking to you for five minutes. What's wrong with you?"

"Sorry." The wheel of the car was slick beneath his hands, and he felt the bone chill that memory always brought him.

"I'm thinking we should transfer Adele to Lafayette. The sheriff there will take her."

He couldn't argue with Joe's logic, except Adele wasn't in custody.

"You got a problem with that?" Joe was belligerent.

"No."

"Get her then. I'll call up to Sheriff Burke and set it up. Bring her by the office first. I got some questions for her."

"Sure." Raymond felt numb. Joe was going through the motions so he could tell his constituents that he'd questioned Adele. She hadn't been conscious long enough to answer anybody's questions, but Joe could say he tried. If someone didn't kill her first.

Raymond pulled up at the courthouse and waited for Joe to get out of the car. "I'll be back," he said as he put the car in first and pulled away from the curb. Only Madame and Florence knew Adele was missing. Raymond would find her—before anything else could be laid at the door of an innocent woman. He would find her, protect her, and then do what he did best. Bring desolation down upon the head of the person responsible for Adele's troubles.

Michael took the cup of hot coffee with a shaking hand. His body was covered with quilts that Jolene and Colista had warmed by the fire, yet he couldn't stop the fits of sudden shaking that made his bones rattle. He was cold, but most of all, he was guilty. That soft underbelly of marbled culpability had been exposed to Raymond, and Michael was still unnerved by the deputy's tenderness.

"When Sheriff Joe finds the boys who pulled that prank, they'll get the thrashing of their lives." Colista wrapped another blanket around Michael's feet. "It was a cruel and fearsome thing to do to a man of God."

"These days children have no discipline." Jolene, who'd paced the study for half an hour, finally took a seat in one of the chairs near the fire. "Do you have any idea who would do such a thing?"

Michael shook his head, then cleared his throat. "No." It was more of a croak than a word. "I should've walked out to the tree and examined what was there before I called anyone. I failed Rosa, yet again."

"Don't be foolish, Father Michael. Anyone seeing a hanging figure in a tree would have called the law. Anyone—" Jolene's words were interrupted by the sound of the doorbell.

Colista hurried to the front of the house as Michael sank deeper into the quilts. He had no desire to talk to anyone. He wished Jolene and Colista would leave him alone in his shame, let him writhe in the bitterness of his own craven fear.

"Father Finley is not well."

He could hear Colista's sharp voice that let him know whoever was at the door was being insistent. In a moment he heard the front door slam and the sound of scuffling footsteps headed toward the study.

The door opened and Marguerite Bastion stood in the doorway, her boys squirming in front of her. In each hand she pinched the ear of a son. "Tell him!" She jerked the boys' ears painfully.

"I'm sorry, Father, we put the scarecrow in the tree." The smaller of the boys choked out the words.

"I heard them laughing about their prank." Marguerite twisted their ears again. "They are vile children."

Both boys howled and Jolene stepped forward, her hand reaching out to stop Marguerite.

"This is none of your affair," Marguerite said to her. "I'm trying to save their souls. They've learned that lying is a form of sport, that cruelty is good, and that everyone around should fear and obey them."

The younger boy sank to his knees, tears streaming down his face. "Mama, please. Let go my ear." He could barely speak.

Michael stood up, a waterfall of quilts dropping around him. "Mrs. Bastion, let the boys go." She was clearly furious at her children, and Michael felt his own anger burning. But they were children, unaware of the ramifications of their prank. To any other person, it might have been a Halloween spook. These children couldn't know the wound they'd opened.

"They've been sent by Satan to destroy me." Marguerite

stepped back from them. "They lie and make up horrible tales. I want them sent to the reformatory today. They won't get a penny of Henri's money. Not one penny."

"Mrs. Bastion, the boys are just being children—" Jolene stopped at the look on Marguerite's face. She bent to help the boys to their feet. "Go into the kitchen with Colista and wait there."

The boys needed no second invitation. Running footsteps hurried down the hall. When the boys were gone, Father Michael turned to Jolene. "You are my greatest support in this town, Mrs. LaRoche. You've made the worst of times here bearable, and you've been a true friend in my times of greatest need, but I need a word with Mrs. Bastion alone."

Jolene gave a nod of support before she left. Michael turned to Henri's widow. "Whatever those boys did, I can't condone physical brutality."

Marguerite took a deep breath. "You have no idea. The boys are out of control. They lie and spend their time creating mischief. Henri let them do whatever they pleased, and now I'm paying the price. I fear what they might have done. What they might do in the future." Tears glinted in her eyes. "For the sake of their souls, I think they need to go to the reformatory where they can learn penance for their behavior."

Michael put his arm around her and felt the thinness of her bones. She'd lost weight, heightening even more her look of aristocracy. The Mandeville name went back to fifteenth-century France, woven with the Bourbon heritage for centuries. Perhaps now Marguerite could use her name and influence to help bring culture and civilization to the parish.

"The boys need a firm hand, Marguerite. That's all. I'll help you. The community will help." So much had happened since Henri's death that he'd failed to give Marguerite the kindness she needed. She was overburdened with responsibilities.

"I bore those boys, Father. They are my blood. But they are bad children."

"The boys have suffered the gruesome death of their father. It's made them rebellious and wild. The prank they pulled . . ." He waved his hand at the window. "It was cruel and upsetting, but I'm sure they didn't understand their actions." He felt her tense but continued. "There's no need to rush to action. Perhaps you could bring them to me each day for guidance. I'll be glad to talk to them. Maybe a trip to New Orleans, to your family, some exposure to a more civilized life."

"You don't understand, Father Michael. I can't control them." She ignored the tears that slipped down her cheeks. "They're capable of anything. Henri allowed this. He said his sons would rule the parish. He taught them that they would pay no consequence."

"They're still young. Such things can be corrected."

Marguerite walked to the doorway. When she spoke, her back remained to Michael. "You keep them, then. You correct their behavior." She faced Michael slowly. "Henri taught them cruelty. Perhaps the church can undo what is done. I cannot."

She walked down the hallway, slamming the front door as she left the house.

Michael stood, stunned, until Colista tapped at the door, her face furrowed in worry. "Father, those boys haven't had a meal in almost a week. Should I feed them?"

"Certainly." He turned away so she couldn't see his face. "Call Joe Como. Tell him the mystery of the scarecrow has been solved. Ask him if he can come talk to me."

16

MARGUERITE Bastion aimed the Packard straight out of town toward Baton Rouge. Raymond watched her go, wondering what sent her off like Satan himself was biting at her heels. He was just glad she was gone. He had business at the Bastion plantation, and he could better conduct it if she wasn't there. He was playing a hunch and there was no time to waste. Desperation tugged at his shirtsleeve, reminding him that Adele's life hung in the balance and a little girl was missing in the swamps.

He went to the plantation because Adele had worked there. Had possibly become impregnated there. It was a place she might go. Besides, he had run out of other places to search.

Raymond parked on a farm road that led back to the fields and was used by the trucks to carry the cane stalks to the refinery. Sunshine warmed his shoulders and a sticky sweetness caught in the back of his throat as he stepped over the stubble that bled sap into the ground. He skirted the edges of the fields, staying among the cover of the brakes.

He heard the prisoners long before he saw them. Their leg irons clanked, muted in the dirt as machetes thwacked against the cane. The rhythm of the stroke was a background pattern in his head. Circling the field, he found a position in a thicket where he could watch. Veedal sat his horse in the shade, a tin cup of water in his hand. The men never looked up. They worked with the rhythm of something mechanical.

It was high noon before Veedal called a break. "Sit in the shade," he ordered. "There's water and food. If there's any fighting, the loser gets ten lashes. The winner gets five." He spurred the horse and the animal shot forward, leaping into a row of cane.

The men shuffled to the shade, too weary to argue. Raymond walked out of the brake toward them.

He'd seen men too beaten to show fear. The last time he'd seen it, he'd lost his brother. These men were fated to die at hard labor in a swamp where their bodies would find a shallow grave, if not be eaten by wild animals. Raymond had no reason to expect help or pity from any of them.

"I'm looking for Armand Dugas." He looked around the group. "Anyone can help me, maybe I can help him."

One of the prisoners was ladling food into tin plates that were being passed down the line. A dirty chunk of bread passed hand to hand. The men eyed it, ignoring him. For all of the hard work, the men had sufficient food. Marguerite must have intervened after his visit.

"I'm a deputy here in Iberia Parish. I'm not making promises, but I could put in a word for the man who helps me." They looked at him, smelling his desperation. He pushed harder. "If Armand is dead, I need to know how and why."

"Armand is lucky," a tall man with dirty yellow hair said. "He got out. Don't matter if it's dead or alive. He's free now."

Raymond nodded. "Armand isn't my problem. Adele Hebert is."

That caught the attention of several of them, quick glances that fell back to the rich black alluvial soil. As he worked his way down the row, dark brown eyes held his a moment longer than the others. Raymond stepped closer to the middle-aged Negro. "What's your name?"

"Daniel Blackfeather."

Raymond could see the Indian heritage mingled in his features. The man's eyes held a stillness that was absent in the others. "Adele's in trouble. She's accused of killing Henri Bastion."

Daniel's smile was slow. "She shoulda done it here. I woulda helped her and she wouldn't be in trouble now."

A few chuckles and grunts of assent passed down the line. Raymond had no time to wade gently into the conversation. "Adele's in the woods and she's in bad shape. There's a search party out, and if they find her, they'll kill her. If you can tell me something that might help her, I'll see what I can do to get you off this plantation. I'm not making a promise, except that I'll do my best."

Daniel took a bite of bread and chewed it slowly. Several of his teeth were missing. "Adele brought us food when she could. She took a fancy to Armand. She believed he was an innocent man." He looked around the group, reading the faces of the men he was chained to. "Armand was goin' to escape. Adele was helpin' him."

Down the line the chains rattled. Another prisoner stood up. "Shut up and eat, Daniel. Veedal don't want us talking."

Raymond looked in the direction of the plantation house. Veedal would indeed return, and he wouldn't be happy at Raymond's presence. "Tell me about Dugas." Raymond directed his request at Daniel.

Daniel held out his tin cup for water. Raymond filled it from the barrel, and he wasn't certain if he'd given an advantage or gotten one. His fingers touched Daniel's as he passed the cup to him. "Tell us about Adele," Daniel countered.

"You know Henri is dead." A nod went down the line. "Folks are saying Adele murdered him. Adele Hebert is not a *loup-garou*. She's been set up, and Armand Dugas figures into what's really going on. If Adele was ever kind to you, now's the time to pony up." He eyed the line of men. Most failed to meet his gaze, and he knew no help was forthcoming. When he returned to Daniel, he saw something else in the stillness of his eyes.

"Armand had friends." Daniel's gaze never faltered.

"You steppin' too close to your grave." A tall black man in the middle of the line stood and walked toward Raymond, dragging his chain and forcing the men on either side of him to stand. Even twenty pounds underweight, he was a large man, his skin shining in the October sun. "You get caught out here talkin' at us, we're the ones gone pay."

Raymond looked at him. "You're already dead, mister. You just don't know it." He turned back to Daniel. "Tell me. Anything might help Adele. Please." If begging would help, Raymond would beg.

Daniel's gaze shifted beyond Raymond to the path Veedal would take when he returned. "Armand was from Baton Rouge. He ran a string of women, prime snatch for the big men sittin' at the capitol." His pause was brief but eloquent. "Armand did somethin' else for those men. When someone stirred up too much trouble, Armand made him go away."

Raymond could guess the rest of it. "Dugas was convicted of murder and sentenced to Angola. Who'd he kill?"

Daniel looked down the line of chained men. "Armand tole me he didn't kill no one. He was tried for killin' a whore name of Aleta Boudreaux. Thing is, no body was ever produced. Accordin' to Armand, this woman never existed. They made her up and sent him to the chain gang for killin' a ghost."

Dugas had been tried, convicted, and quickly sent to the swamps to work where his chances of survival were slim to none. It was an effective means of getting rid of someone who might know too much.

Raymond pressed the prisoner. "The night Dugas escaped. Tell me about it." He kept watching for Veedal's return.

"Adele brought food when she could. Veedal didn't like it, but it gave him a chance to mess wid her. That night when she come down, he wasn't overly suspicious. The fat bastard put his hands on her, tried to kiss her. Adele was a smart one, though, she brought him some whiskey she'd stole from Bastion's private bottle." Daniel rubbed his ankle where the leg iron had rubbed the skin. "She played him. He drank the whiskey and ten minutes later he was on his hands and knees runnin' in circles like a dog."

Laughter moved down the line of men.

"The liquor had a potion in it?" His words were rushed.

"Must have, but it sure upset Adele to see Veedal the way he was. See, Adele and the Missus grew herbs, for healing and such, up behind the house. Sometimes one of us would go and help work the ground." He shrugged. "I figure she used something from there."

The chains rattled. "Veedal was slobberin' and gruntin' like a boar hog in the river mud." The thin blond man grinned at the memory. "He was actin' crazy. Armand finally hit him in the head wid a shovel. That put an end to his crawlin' and growlin'."

Daniel reclaimed the story. "Then Adele got the key from the wall and unlocked Armand's chains."

Raymond stayed focused on what the men could tell him. Veedal would be back any minute. He had to make his questions count. "For Dugas only?"

The men shifted down the line, the play of metal on metal the sound of hopelessness.

"No one else would go. We wouldn't survive the swamp."

"So Dugas took off on foot and Adele did what?"

He shrugged. "She'd been feelin' poorly. She said she was gonna go home to the swamp. Said her brother would bring her fish and meat and she'd stay home."

"Do you think Dugas got away?" Raymond asked.

Daniel shrugged. "They hunted him for days. They tried to make us tell where he went, but we had nothin' to tell. Armand was a friendly man, but he never talked to us about his plans. We didn't know nothin' we could tell if we'd wanted."

Raymond had one more question. "Were Adele and Dugas lovers?"

Daniel laughed and the chuckle passed down the line of men. He held up his chains. "I been here two years. The chains never come off. Never. Dugas was chained just like me."

"Were Adele and Henri lovers?"

Daniel shook his head. "Adele was a kind woman. If she slept with Henri Bastion, it wasn't 'cause she wanted it."

Raymond was already moving when he spoke again. "I'll be back to see what I can do." He stepped into the cover of the brake as Veedal rounded the point of land that hid the plantation house, his horse covered in a nervous sweat.

The overseer put the men back to work and Raymond slipped among the dense trees toward the house. It was at least a half mile, and he felt the pressure of time slipping away from him.

Each step brought a pinch of pain in his back, but he kept going. At last the white house, like a dream, could be seen among the trees. He skirted the yard and went to the back, searching for signs of a garden. About fifty yards from the house he heard the soft buzz of bees. The busy drone drew him toward a thick wall of azaleas. He moved forward cautiously, until he saw the hive boxes hidden among the foliage.

Beyond the beehives he found the herb garden choked with weeds. Some of the plants—peppers, thyme, basil, dill—he recognized as everyday herbs necessary for cooking spicy Cajun foods. Others he didn't know.

Always listening for the sound of Marguerite's car or Veedal's horse, he wasted precious time searching for a container. At last he found a dishpan and began the tedious process of gathering samples. He collected even the plants he knew.

He was about to leave when he noticed a band of wild grass bordering the south side of the garden. The beaded heads, heavy with black grains, dipped and crested in the breeze. Coastal Bermuda contained a small black head, but this was different. He stepped forward for a closer look. The peculiar growth seemed out of place so he grasped a handful of the grass, pulling it by the roots, and added it to his collection.

Madame Louiselle would be able to help him identify the plants. It was possible that Adele's strange behavior could be accounted for by something growing right in the Bastion yard. He felt an unfamiliar tension between his shoulder blades and was surprised to recognize hope. If something in this garden proved responsible . . . it was almost too much to believe. But if it was true, then he'd have the how. All that would be left would be the who.

Raymond sped into town, the dishpan beside him on the car seat. He was headed toward Florence's house when he spied Chula coming out of the post office. She carried a satchel of mail.

He slowed as he pulled beside her and stopped. "Chula, are you going out toward Madame Louiselle's?"

"I could be." She leaned on the window. "What's that?" She pointed at the dishpan.

"If you're going out toward Madame's, you could save me a lot of time by taking these to her."

"Hand them over." Chula reached into the car. "I need to check on her anyway."

Raymond hesitated. "Thank you, Chula."

"I'm glad to do it." She lifted the pan to her hip. "Whether you like it or not, Raymond, I hold you in high regard."

She turned and left him in the idling car as she walked down the street, the mail satchel swinging at her side and the dishpan on her hip.

Raymond revved the engine and accelerated. Chula Baker had inherited her mama's high-handed ways, but he couldn't stop the smile that touched the corners of his mouth. He could only thank his lucky stars she was an ally and not an adversary.

By taking the herbs, Chula had freed him to search for Armand

Dugas. Raymond knew the price of hope, but he couldn't help but believe the convict was not only alive but in possession of knowledge that would help him prove Adele's innocence.

Florence let the crisp air flow over her face from the open window of the car. She caught her hair in one hand, restraining the dark curls from tickling her face. She was almost afraid to glance at Raymond as he drove. He'd been distant, more tense than usual. The weight he carried had grown heavier, and she knew it was Adele. Whatever Adele's ultimate fate, Raymond had assumed the responsibility. His fate was now bound with Adele, for better or worse. Adele had softened him in some ways, yet made him more distant, too.

His invitation to ride to Baton Rouge had been so unexpected that she'd failed to ask why they were making the trip. It was county business, because they rode in the patrol car on gasoline paid for with county coupons. But when business was done, there would surely be an element of pleasure. Why else would he have invited her to ride with him?

She'd chosen a red top with sleeves that tied on her arm and a tight black skirt, the kind of dress any woman might wear for a day of shopping in the state capital. Shopping. Or lunching. Or going to a movie or even a live performance at one of the supper clubs.

On either side of them the marshes stretched like a sea of grass. The sky was cloudless and blue, and she caught the scent of dead fish and mud. Beyond the vista she knew so well, she saw another reality. Hovering on the horizon was a different image, a cottage in a shady, respectable neighborhood with shuttered windows and a quiet lawn. She was traveling to Baton Rouge—and the future she dreamed about—with the man she loved. Surely this was the first step in that direction.

When she did chance a look at Raymond, she saw a hardness

in the set of his mouth that made her anxious. Whatever he chewed was bitter. Once his business was done, he'd come around to feeling better. She'd make sure of it.

"Has there been a sign of that missing child?" she asked.

Raymond glanced at her as if he didn't know who she was. He blinked. "Joe's got a search party out. Clifton Hebert's leading another one."

"Do you think Peat Moss is still alive?"

His grip on the wheel tightened. "I don't know."

Exasperated, she asked, "Raymond, why are we going to Baton Rouge?"

"Business."

He was never a talkative man, but his silence was like a wall between them. "Why did you ask me to ride with you on county business?"

He sighed. His hand moved toward her and then returned to the steering wheel. "Did you ever hear of a man named Armand Dugas? He worked around Baton Rouge."

Florence felt the point of his question like a knife. The fantasy of a life in Baton Rouge with Raymond died a violent death. "Is this Armand Dugas in the life?"

"Yes."

"You brought me along with you so I could help you track down a pimp?"

"Yes." He didn't look at her.

She focused her gaze out the window. The open stretches of marshland were behind them. Cypress trees crowded close to the road, their limbs bound by vines and moss. They hadn't passed another car for miles.

"Did you ever hear of him?" Raymond asked.

"No." She blinked back tears, and when she wiped her cheek her finger found the thin ridge of the crescent-shaped scar. Raymond had never implied this was a date. She knew they were in the county car. This had only ever been business. For all that she prided herself on her practicality and lack of sentimentality, she felt the searing heat of disappointment and betrayal.

His hand touched hers, his fingers tracing her own until they caught around hers. "Florence, I didn't mean to hurt you. I should have explained."

"But you were afraid I'd say no."

He didn't answer, and she knew she was right. Her jaw ached from grinding her teeth. "Why is this Armand Dugas so important?"

"I can't be certain, but he may have the answer to Adele Hebert."

"Do you ever think of anything except Adele Hebert?" She turned on him. "What about that child? You're hauling me off to Baton Rouge while that little girl is still missing. What about her? Why is it only Adele you feel the need to protect?" Anger and hurt fueled her words.

He was surprised by her outburst and that made her even angrier. "Don't you think people talk? They say you took Adele Hebert from her cell and hid her in the swamp so she can't be made to pay for what she did. They say she's cast her spell on you."

"Who says that?"

"The men who pay me for the pleasure I give them." She flung the words at him, hoping for pain. He viewed her as a whore with useful contacts; she would show him what contacts she had.

"They're wrong."

"Where is Adele Hebert? That's the question everyone asks, Raymond. You told me Halloween Night that she had escaped. Folks in town think you have her. Have you hidden her?"

Raymond put both hands on the wheel. "No. I wish I had, though. Adele could be dead in the swamps. Will you help me?"

She turned away from him. "Do I have a choice?"

"With me, always."

17

CHULA shoved the letters into the postal slots, her quick fingers sorting with experienced speed. Madame's cottage had been empty when she'd gotten there, so she'd left the herbs with a note on the top step. Worried about Madame and Adele, she'd returned to chaos at the post office.

Claudia worked beside her, fumbling each piece of mail she touched. It was easy to see that Claudia was in a terrible state, and Chula could easily guess the reason why.

"Did you talk to Mrs. Lanoux?" Chula asked.

Claudia dropped a stack of letters that scattered across the wooden floor. When she stooped to retrieve them, a sob escaped her. "I went to visit, but . . ." She pressed her face into her knees and wept, hunkered into herself like a child.

Kneeling beside her, Chula recovered the mail and put an arm around her coworker. "How bad is Justin?" The day she'd delivered the letter to the Lanoux family and she'd learned that Justin was wounded and headed home from the war, she'd feared his wounds were life-changing, but hoped that time would mend him.

Claudia lifted her tear-stained face, anguish evident in her features. "Mrs. Lanoux said I couldn't see him. She said he wouldn't see anyone. She said he refused to come out of his room, that he sat in the dark and wouldn't talk or eat. Oh, my God, Chula. Remember how Justin used to pull pranks and get into mischief. What have they done to him?" She hugged her knees and wept silently.

Chula gently rubbed Claudia's back. There were questions to be asked, but she sensed that Claudia had no answers. "Give him time, *cher.* He wasn't in the hospital a long time. Maybe his wounds aren't as serious as we suspect. It's hard for a man to be hurt, even a little."

The bell on the door jingled and the smell of Wild Root hair tonic wafted into the post office. Chula looked up to find Praytor standing at the counter looking down at them with a calculating eye. He made no attempt to hide his thoughts. Chula rose and stepped forward to shield Claudia from his gaze.

"Can I help you?" she asked. She held her place, refusing to step closer to the counter. Behind her Claudia scrambled to her feet and fled the room.

"Didn't mean to interrupt." Praytor grinned.

"Do you want to buy stamps?"

"Actually, I'm here on criminal business." He leaned against the counter.

"What can I help you with, Praytor?" She forced herself to sound pleasant. There was something about Praytor that gave her the creeps. He was a mama's boy who she'd viewed as Henri Bastion's toady. Now that Henri wasn't around to boss him, he seemed lost. Not a good thing, in her opinion.

"Sure looked like an interestin' game you were playin' when I walked in." He grinned at her.

The mail slipped from Chula's fingers, and she clasped her hands behind her back before she slapped him across the face. "We don't have time for games at the post office. Now, did you need some stamps?"

He tapped the service bell on the counter but muffled the sound by wrapping his long fingers around it. Chula thought of a spider. "I saw you going out to that old conjure woman's place. You got business with her?"

Chula's first impulse was to tell him to kiss her behind, but she schooled herself to show nothing. "I took some mail to her and a few other people out that way. The same as I'd do for your mother if you weren't all the time in town."

"You see anyone out there? Maybe someone hidin'?"

Chula bit her lip as if she were thinking. "No. Fact is I didn't see anyone. Madame wasn't at home. Why do you ask?"

"Where's that professor man?" Praytor countered.

Chula frowned, caught off guard. "John's interviewing some people, why?"

"Sheriff Joe needs his help. Asked me to step in and fetch him."

Chula wasn't certain she believed what Praytor was telling her—that the sheriff was suddenly interested in Dr. John LeDeux. "Where's Raymond?"

"Last seen headed out of town with that whore beside him in the front seat of the patrol car. Seems like they took a day off for a trip. The sheriff is a mite upset."

"Did Raymond have a lead on the missing child?"

Praytor shook his head. "I don't think that little pickaninny took off for Baton Rouge, and that's the direction Deputy Thibodeaux was headed. I doubt Raymond is sniffin' that trail. Must be something else he's caught the scent of."

Chula ignored his insinuations and picked up the mail she'd dropped. "Raymond wouldn't leave his duties, Praytor. The sheriff knows that if you don't." It didn't make a lot of sense that Raymond had taken off to Baton Rouge with Florence, but she was sure he had a good reason. "Tell Joe I'll call around and try to find John."

"Now would be better than later." Praytor pulled a knife from his pocket and began to scrap at a rough spot on his hand. "Got a splinter that won't come out. Maybe I'll take a ride out to Madame Louiselle's, see what she can do for it. I got it in my head somehow that she can help me with several things."

Chula put the letters on the counter. Her hands were sweating. "If you need John right now, check with Aimee Baxter. He said something about talking to her about how Peat Moss disappeared." The Baxters lived on the other side of the parish and there wasn't a telephone within five miles of them. She had to divert Praytor from Madame Louiselle's.

In the back room she heard Claudia blowing her nose, and her assistant stepped back up to the counter, her face reddened from crying. "I can watch the counter if you need to find Mr. LeDeux," Claudia said.

"Shall I get him for you, Praytor, or can you manage it yourself?"

"Thanks, Miss Chula. I'll go find him for the sheriff. Joe seemed like it was urgent." Praytor tipped his hat at both of them as he opened the front door.

"Please ask John to call me or come by when he's finished with the sheriff." She forced a smile on lips that felt paralyzed.

The bell jingled as Praytor left.

"Chula, are you okay?" Claudia asked. "You're like a sheet."

"I have a bad feeling." She put her palms on the counter for balance. The search for Peat Moss, Praytor's visit, Madame's absence, the fact that Raymond had left the parish at such a critical time—she wasn't certain what, exactly, had churned up such anxiety. She simply had the sense that tragedy had crossed the parish line and was headed straight for town.

Colista collected the dishes from the table, her face pinched and her hands shaking. Michael sat across from the Bastion boys, wondering what duty required of him. In the brief time they'd been in his home, he was at a loss. The boys were savages. It had crossed his mind that if the church had refused to consider his stigmatic, the Holy See would never consent to exorcisms for two boys.

He put his napkin on the table. "I've sent someone to your home to talk with your mother." He wondered if Jolene was brave or just crazy since she'd taken on the chore of trying to reason with Marguerite. She was the boys' mother and she had a duty to them—if Jolene could make her see it.

"Won't do no good." The older boy, Caleb, banged his spoon against the empty soup bowl. "Daddy said we didn't have to mind her and her high-bred ways. I'm still hungry."

Reaching across the table, Michael grasped his wrist. "Stop it."

"You're not my daddy, and I don't have to mind you. You're just an old maid in a dress." Caleb laughed out loud and his brother, Nathaniel, joined him.

"Your mother wants you put in the reformatory. If I don't intercede in your behalf, that *will* happen." If he'd hoped to threaten them into good conduct, he saw that it was a vain attempt. "The reform school is an awful place. Terrible things happen to the children there."

"I want some cake." Nathaniel looked around the dining room with sudden interest. "Got any cake here?"

Michael knew better than to call to Colista. She'd reached the end of her tether. Caleb had hit her in the face with a piece of bread, and Nathaniel had poured his soup on the floor. Michael felt helpless to deal with the boys. He'd never met such a force of complete lawlessness and deliberate maliciousness.

"There is no cake, but if you reform your conduct, perhaps Colista will bake you one tomorrow."

"I want it now." Nathaniel edged his glass of milk along the table.

"Knock that milk off the table, and I'll punish you." Michael knew he'd drawn a line, and there was no retreating.

"You gone spank him?" Caleb asked, amused.

"I'd prefer not to, but I will." Michael eased back his chair. If action was required, he intended to deliver it swiftly. They were children, after all. Whatever Henri had had in mind when he'd allowed them to gain such an upper hand on adults, he couldn't say. What would happen to them if Marguerite abandoned them would only teach them more cruelty.

Nathaniel looked at his brother for guidance. Caleb kicked the leg of the table repeatedly.

"I want to talk to you boys," Michael said. "It's important."

"What we gone get if we talk?"

He thought about it and saw a way to give Colista some needed relief. "Ice cream from the drugstore. We'll walk there and have a treat. But first you have to answer some questions. Important questions."

The boys stilled. "We can pick out our own flavor?" Caleb asked.

"Certainly." Michael felt an indefinable shock. It was as if they'd never had ice cream at the soda fountain. Their father had controlled the parish, yet the idea of an ice cream had accomplished more than threats of bodily harm.

"What you want to know?" Caleb clearly wanted control of the conversation.

"Your mother said . . ." He had to phrase it delicately. Marguerite hadn't actually said anything, but she'd implied. "The night your father was killed, do you know where he was going?"

Nathaniel picked up his spoon and began to tap it against the table. Michael ignored him, honing in on Caleb. "Tell me everything you can remember about that night."

"He went down to the shed." Caleb kicked the table faster. "The *loup-garou* got him."

"What shed? What was he doing?"

"The tractor shed. He went there sometimes."

"Why?" Michael forced his hands to release their grip on the arms of his chair.

"That's where he met her. The bad woman. That's where they did it." The expression on Caleb's face was neutral, which made his revelation even more shocking to Michael.

"Your father was meeting a woman?"

"That's what I said." Caleb looked at him.

Michael felt his nerve falter, but he had to be sure. "They were having, uh, relations, in the tractor shed?"

Caleb nodded as something broke in the kitchen. Michael heard Colista mumbling a rosary. Sweat trickled down his spine. "Did he meet this woman the night he was killed?"

Caleb picked up the salt shaker and shook the salt all over the tablecloth. He looked at his brother and they both laughed.

Michael was stabbed by a pang of pity. Henri had stolen the boys' childhood. By allowing them to run amok, to see the business of adults, he'd taken their innocence and their childhood.

He cleared his throat. "When Henri was . . . finished in the, uh, shed, where did he go?"

"He walked. Like he did ever' night. Put his hat right on and took off down the road. Sometimes we followed." Caleb was losing interest in the conversation. He glanced at his brother. "Can I have a double scoop of ice cream?"

"Yes, just a few more questions." Michael wanted to hit something. The things these boys had witnessed had damaged them. Henri had not been a guardian of his children, and now Michael better understood Marguerite's frustration. Still, she'd implied that her own sons might have killed their father. To say he was concerned by the circumstances would be an understatement.

"Hurry up, Father Michael. I want to go to the drugstore," Nathaniel said. "I'm still hungry."

"We'll hurry." He cleared his throat again. When he'd spoken to Joe on the phone, the sheriff had asked him to get as much information as possible. "Did your father walk in the same place all the time?"

"Yeah, down the road to Beaver Creek. That's what he did.

He'd finish at the shed and then take off walking like he had ants in his pants."

"He always went to Beaver Creek?"

"We followed him sometimes. When he went down to the shed, Mama would lock us out of the house." He drew images in the salt he'd poured on the table. "She said we were the sons of Satan and that we weren't welcome in her home. Daddy would come back and make her let us in."

"The night your father was killed, did you follow him?"

"Yeah." Caleb laughed.

Michael heard the back door slam, and he knew Colista had been listening and that she'd fled the premises. If the boys were going to confess to the bloody murder of their father, she didn't want to hear it.

"What did you see?" Michael asked softly.

"We heard Daddy screamin'." Caleb leaned over and punched his brother so hard on the arm that the younger boy fell from his chair. Nathaniel sat on the floor and began to cry.

Michael grabbed Caleb's arm and pinned it to the table, forcing his attention back to him. "What did you see?"

Caleb leveled a kick at his brother's head, but Michael managed to divert it. He tightened his grip on the boy's arm. "Tell me what you saw."

"I seen the wolf woman come out of the woods, all pantin' and slobberin'. She jumped on him and rode his back. When he stumbled and fell in the road, she tore out his throat. She was on her hands and knees, growlin' and slobberin' blood." Caleb kicked the table so hard the dishes rattled. "I never knew Daddy could scream like that."

18

RAYMOND clutched his notebook in his hand as he walked out
of the courthouse in Baton Rouge. The court record on Armand
Dugas told the same story that Daniel Blackfeather had relayed.
The state had prosecuted a murder one charge without a body—
or any evidence that the elusive Aleta Boudreaux had ever existed. The follow-up on prisoners was abysmal. There had been
the order of the judge to send Dugas to Angola on a ten-year
hitch that had begun in 1940. There was no record of an appeal
filed on Dugas's behalf or any other record of the trial. There
was only the paperwork on Dugas's transfer to the state prison;
nothing on his lease to the Bastion family.

Dugas's legal trail ended at the eighteen-thousand-acre prison
farm bordered by the Mississippi River, and Raymond had no
doubt that was the location where Dugas was expected to end his
life—and as quickly as possible. The men who had orchestrated
his trip there had anticipated that Dugas would become one of
the hundreds of unmarked graves in the prison cemetery. The
pimp had been smarter than anticipated; Raymond believed Armand Dugas was alive.

As Raymond walked to the car, he felt regret settle over him. He'd wounded Florence. It had never crossed his mind that she'd think his invitation to ride to Baton Rouge was anything other than work-related. His life was about work, except for the few hours he spent with Florence. He'd been so focused on finding Adele—before someone else did—that he hadn't thought of what Florence might think or feel. He'd asked her to "take a ride to Baton Rouge" simply because he hadn't known how to ask her if she'd mind using her connections to help track down a pimp.

When he'd left her on River Street, where the nicer cathouses were located, she'd refused to even look back at him. He checked his watch. He'd agreed to meet her at four, and he had to get a move on.

Driving through the business district of the capital, Raymond noted the stately buildings where lawyers plied their trade. The war had destroyed his innocence and taught him that men of power never bothered to concern themselves with the havoc wreaked upon the poor and weak. Because of the oil beneath the Gulf waters offshore, Iberia Parish was becoming a primary interest of the politicians. Henri Bastion had controlled Iberia Parish in ways most folks didn't understand. The average parishioner saw the Bastion plantation and understood that Henri was wealthy. The sugar cane plantation was only the visible evidence of Henri's power and wealth, though. His interests extended to the railroad that was being built across the Atchafalaya Basin and into New Iberia as well as drilling rigs out in the Gulf of Mexico. Henri pulled the strings on everything, from the untaxed liquor that flowed into the parish to Adele Hebert. Henri had touched her life and driven her insane.

Though he didn't believe in the *loup-garou*, Raymond believed that greed and envy drove men to madness, and he was beginning to picture Henri as a man of voracious appetites. Raymond had to find out which of Henri's interests had brought about his brutal death and how Adele had become caught in the middle. But first he had to find Florence and make amends. He took a folded legal document from his inside jacket pocket and put it on the seat of the truck.

When he turned along River Street, he slowed. Florence was here somewhere, making a lazy afternoon visit with women who earned a living at night. Realizing the full impact of what he'd asked of her made him pull out a cigarette and light up.

The houses, two- and three-storied, and now shuttered and quiet, spoke of a time of luxury before the war. Once elegant private homes in Grecian or Federalist style, the houses were well-known addresses for upper-class whores far removed from the hot pillow joints along the riverfront. It was this River Street section where a man with money came to rent the attentions of a young girl or the exotic beauty of an octoroon.

When he spotted Florence sitting on white wicker furniture on a front porch secluded by elephant ears and banana plants, he parked and walked up the sidewalk to the front steps.

Florence stood, nodding subtly to him. "Callie, this is my friend Raymond. He's the one looking for Armand."

"Callie," he said to the young woman who looked no more than sixteen. She was beautiful with a milky complexion, green eyes, and chestnut hair. "I need to find Dugas. Someone who helped him may be in serious trouble."

The girl looked up at Florence.

"Raymond is telling the truth," Florence said. "He doesn't want to put Armand back in prison. He only wants to help Adele Hebert; she's the one who helped Armand escape."

"He'd kill me if I told where he was." Callie kept her gaze on Florence, trusting only what she read there.

"But he is alive?" Raymond said.

Callie flicked a look of distrust at him. "I know a man who calls himself Armand Dugas. Could be he's someone else, just using that name."

"Could be," Raymond agreed. "Could you deliver a message?"

"Maybe. If I see him. Armand is only seen when he chooses to be. Sometimes he just shows up, then disappears like a whisper."

"Tell him Adele Hebert needs his help." Raymond wrote down the sheriff's office phone number and handed it to Callie. "Tell him to talk only to me." He started to say more but stopped. It was possible Armand had slipped back to the bayous to settle his score with Henri Bastion personally. Adele might not be his highest priority. "Tell him to call me because if he doesn't, I'll find him. And then, if it's too late to help Adele, I'll make sure he goes back to Angola."

Callie's nervous gaze shifted to Raymond and back to Florence.

"He means it, *cher*. Adele is his personal mission. If he fails her, he's going to be a very mean man to deal with." She kissed the top of Callie's head. "Take care, baby."

Raymond tried to put his hand on Florence's elbow as they walked down the sidewalk, but she shook him off. "I'm not your paid escort, and you don't have a right to touch me." She got in the passenger seat.

Sliding behind the wheel, Raymond studied her profile. It was going to be a long ride home.

The golden light of late afternoon had faded, leaving the sky misted with pink. Chula sat at the wrought-iron patio table across from John. With John's return from his unsuccessful attempt to find Clifton Hebert, her anxiety had abated, but unrest nibbled at her. She touched his hand on the table, an unconscious gesture that startled her once it was done. When had she become a woman who initiated such an intimate move? Since she'd met John, Chula felt as if she stepped from an amber prison, like an insect trapped for eternity. At night she was troubled with dreams, kisses and moments of passion, the cries of a baby—things she'd sealed away inside herself since she and Raymond had called it quits.

"Chula, are you okay? You're unusually reserved." John sipped the iced tea Maizy had prepared.

"Praytor was looking for you earlier. Did the sheriff talk to you?"

John was surprised. "To me? Why?"

"Someone told him you were writing a book about the *loup-garou*. He's looking at you as an expert. He's feeling a bit desperate from what I hear."

John brought her hand to his lips and kissed it. "If it means I can spend more time here in New Iberia with you, I'll be an expert. Chula, my feelings for you are strong."

She let her hand linger in his for a moment before she withdrew it. What he offered her was so large she couldn't look at it head-on. Not yet. "That little girl, Peat Moss Baxter, is still missing. It's been almost twenty-four hours." She looked at the oaks that made the backyard so beautiful. "I hate for night to fall. People are so afraid. They aren't thinking rationally."

He stood up, offering his hand to her.

She put her palm in his and felt the electric friction that was both pleasurable and dangerous. "Let's go find Joe and get this behind us. Gossip around town is that Raymond has gone AWOL. Joe is really on edge. I went to Madame's today, but she was gone and so was Adele. I'm getting worried, John."

"Even with Raymond gone, can't the sheriff handle it?"

Chula couldn't help but smile. "Joe's a superstitious fool. He means well, but Raymond does most of the work."

They turned at the sound of footsteps. Maizy all but rolled her eyes. "Miss Chula, Mrs. LaRoche is here to see you. She's in the parlor. I gave her some brandy to help calm down. She's in a state. I tried to call the doctor, but she won't hear of it. She says she's got to talk to you right now."

Chula didn't waste any time wondering why Jolene LaRoche had shown up on her doorstep. She knew the woman from church, but they'd never been friends. Chula strode through the house, trusting that John would follow. She found Jolene slumped on the sofa, her hair disheveled, her dress stained with sweat and dirt. "Jolene, what happened?" She knelt in front of her, picking up a limp hand and chafing it.

Jolene's green eyes focused slowly. "I . . . I went out to talk to Marguerite Bastion." Her wild gaze found John standing in the doorway but she didn't seem to register his presence. "Father Finley has the older boys." She stumbled. "Marguerite's boys. I went to talk to her. I . . ."

Chula picked up the brandy Maizy had poured and held it to Jolene's lips. She helped her take a sip. "You have to tell me what's happened. I can't help unless I know."

Jolene closed her eyes and took a breath. "I didn't know where else to come. Raymond isn't in town and the sheriff is off on a search. Pinkney told me to come to you. He said you had a car and could find Raymond."

Chula patted Jolene's arm. "I'll do what I can, if you'll tell me what happened. Are Marguerite and the children okay?"

Jolene shook her head. "The older boys hung the scarecrow in Father Finley's tree. Marguerite brought them and left them. She wants them sent to the reformatory. I went to talk to her, but when I got to the house, no one was there except the little girl, Sarah." She covered her mouth as if to keep something from surging out. "I heard her singing in the back of the house. Oh, God." She rocked back and forth.

Chula held her still and offered her more brandy. Jolene sipped, her gaze once again shifting around the room until it stopped on John. "Who are you?" Jolene asked.

"He's my friend." Chula gently turned Jolene's face back to her. "Is Sarah okay?"

Jolene nodded. "She was singing. I've never heard her make a sound in her life. She comes to church and never says a word. I'd wondered if she was mute. But she was singing a lullaby. I knocked, but there was no answer. The door was unlatched, so I went inside. I was worried about Sarah. It seemed she was all alone. Marguerite's Packard was gone. No one was there except that three-year-old child."

Chula sensed slow movement behind her and realized that John had taken a seat in one of the chairs. He sat very still, drawing no attention to himself.

"Did you see Sarah?" Chula asked.

"I walked back through the house, following the singing." Tears moved down her cheeks disturbing the dirt smudges. "It was so beautiful. I was captivated. Like something in a painting. And then I saw her." Wide green eyes riveted into Chula's. "Sarah was sitting in a rocking chair with a woman. I was so shocked. The baby was sitting on the woman's lap, singing and touching her hair. I came up behind them, and I wondered who was holding Sarah and where was Marguerite.

"When Sarah saw me, she stopped singing. It was as if her voice disappeared. She stared at me, and then the woman in the rocking chair turned. She moved so slowly. She turned and looked at me." Jolene had grasped Chula's hand and held it so tightly that Chula thought she might be crippled.

"Who was it?" Chula asked.

"It was Adele. Adele Hebert sat with that child on her lap."

Chula couldn't believe it. "Are you sure?"

"I'm positive. When she saw me, she put the baby down very gently and stood up. Her clothes were torn. She was almost . . . naked. She started toward me and I lost my nerve. I screamed and ran. In the parlor I tripped on the rug and fell. Adele jumped over me and ran out the front door. I got up and chased her. I don't know what came over me, but I chased her into the swamp. I was afraid she'd cursed me and I wanted her to take it back." Jolene wept in earnest now. "I don't want to turn into a wolf when the moon is full. I don't—"

Chula swallowed her impatience. She eased up on the sofa and put an arm around Jolene. "You aren't cursed. I swear it. You're fine."

"How can you be sure?" Jolene asked.

"The *loup-garou* has no power in the daylight." She looked at John as she spoke. She was playing into the myth, giving it more steam by adding even a simple bit of foolish comfort, but she had to calm Jolene and keep her quiet until Raymond could be found.

"She's right," John said. He came to stand beside her. "You're completely safe, Mrs. LaRoche. The werewolf has no power in the daylight."

"Are you sure?" Jolene asked.

Chula nodded. "So sure that I'm going to run you a bath and find some clean clothes. I want you to get cleaned up and by that time, I'll be back."

"You're leaving me here alone?" Jolene's grip on her arm was fierce. "Please. Not alone."

Chula looked at John. "My friend will be down here in the parlor, and Mother will be home any minute. John will call Father Finley. When you've had a bath, Maizy will give you something hot to eat."

"Where are you going?" Jolene asked.

"To find Sarah Bastion," Chula said. "I can't believe her mother left her alone in the house. I'm afraid if Marguerite doesn't come back, the child might wander into the woods and be lost."

"She's already lost," Jolene said. "Just like that other little baby girl." She twisted her hands in her lap. "They aren't children anymore. They belong to the *loup-garou*."

19

Cars lined the road beside the sheriff's office. As Raymond drove by, he felt a stab of concern. Joe Como wasn't known to work late, yet his car was parked beside the vehicle of Praytor Bless and some others he didn't recognize. Only an emergency would draw folks into town, burning their gas ration. When Raymond saw Pinkney standing out in the cool night, he stopped and rolled his window down.

"What's going on?" he asked.

"You in a worlda hurt. Sheriff's been rantin' and ravin' all evening 'bout how you disappeared. He called Lafayette and they said no one has seen you. Praytor Bless"—his lip curled—"said you went off to Baton Rouge with your ho—with Miss Florence." He nodded at Florence.

"Did they find Peat Moss?"

"No, sir. No sign of that baby. The swamp done swallowed her up." Pinkney was almost dancing with anxiety.

"Has something else happened?"

"Mrs. LaRoche been by, hysterical 'bout somethin' at the Bastion plantation. Those bad Bastion boys done confessed to prankin' Father Michael with that scarecrow. He brought them in to talk to the sheriff. That's what's happenin' now. Sheriff Joe and Praytor got those boys in there tryin' to make 'em tell things."

"What things?"

"They sayin' they saw Adele Hebert runnin' loose in town last night. They sayin' she was howlin' at the moon and slobberin' and that she got after them and tried to catch them."

"Bullshit." Raymond spoke before he thought. He opened the driver's door. "Pinkney, would you drive Miss Delacroix home?" The thing he wanted to tell Florence would have to wait. He picked up the papers from the seat as he got out.

"Me?" Pinkney looked confused. "Sheriff don't let me drive the county car."

"It's okay. Just take her home and make sure she gets inside safely and locks her doors. Then come right back here."

"Okay," Pinkney said, nodding. "I can do that. I can drive Miss Florence." He walked around and slid behind the wheel. "I'll be right back."

Raymond stepped away from the car as Pinkney put it in gear. The vehicle jerked forward, and he thought he heard a faint curse from Florence. It was the first word she'd spoken since they left Baton Rouge. He'd had no opportunity to tell her his regrets or to try to make amends. She was having none of him.

Shit was coming down like an August rain, thick and relentless. Everywhere he turned, things had shifted out of his control. There wasn't a moment of any day that he didn't feel the shrapnel in his hip and back. Most days he could put it out of his mind, ignore the sensation of metal on bone that could one day be his invitation to paralysis. The long drive to Baton Rouge had aggravated his discomfort.

Before he went inside the sheriff's office, he walked down to Praytor's car. The light from the window of the sheriff's office was bright enough for him to check the tread on the tire. Expecting to find a match to the prints he'd discovered at Madame's, he felt disappointment as he ran his hand over the rubber. There was a little tread left, but not much. Not like the prints he'd found. Someone else had been at Madame's.

He walked into the sheriff's office as Praytor drew back his hand and slapped the older Bastion boy.

"Listen, you little brat, you're going to tell us what we want to know," Praytor said.

Before anyone else could react, the boy launched himself at Praytor. He wrapped himself, monkeylike, around Praytor's right leg and sank his teeth into the thigh.

"Oh, goddamn!" Praytor tried to shake the boy off. "Goddamn!" He spun, slamming his leg and the boy into a desk. The boy hung on, gnawing ferociously.

The younger boy climbed onto his chair and began to scream. "Bite him, Caleb. Tear out a hunk!"

Joe stood frozen in panic near the cells. Raymond took four strides and grabbed Caleb Bastion by the back of the pants and dragged him free of Praytor's bloody leg.

"You fuckin' little monster!" Praytor drew back his good leg and aimed it at the boy's head. As he delivered the kick, Raymond pulled Caleb out of range. He deftly caught the heel of Praytor's silver-tipped boot and flipped him backward. Praytor hit the floor so hard it knocked the breath out of him and for a moment he lay stunned.

Still holding on to Caleb, Raymond grasped the younger boy by the scruff of the neck. He propelled both of them into a cell and slammed the door locked. He turned to Joe. "What were you thinking? They're children."

"Where have you been?" Joe looked over the desk to see if Praytor was alive. "You likta killed him. His leg is bleedin' bad." He glared at the boys who were hanging on to the bars with both fists. They grinned back at him.

"Cockroaches have survived since man crept out of the muck. It'll take more than a bite and a fall to kill Praytor."

"Very funny. Where the hell have you been?" Joe tucked in his shirttail.

"We'll talk later."

"Where's Adele Hebert? These boys say she was running loose through town last night."

"Yeah, I heard that from Pinkney. Running and howling and slobbering. Aren't these the boys who hung a scarecrow in a tree to torment a priest? Pretty reliable witnesses, I'd say."

Joe looked at the boys and sighed. "Yeah. They did that. They told the priest that their daddy was meeting Adele in the tractor shed and that they saw her turn into a wolf and kill him."

"And you're willing to believe every word."

Praytor shoved at the desk as he slowly sat up. He glared at Raymond. "You're not so damn smart. The boys saw Adele runnin' loose in town. You know it's true, too. You're protecting that crazy bitch. She's killed a man and taken a young-un and still you won't put a bullet in her brain and get it done."

Raymond felt the pressure in his chest, the tightening of his scalp. After Antoine was killed, Raymond had become a killing machine. He'd taken any risky assignment, launched himself at the Germans as if he were invincible. He shot and stabbed and bludgeoned, but it was all too late. Nothing he'd done had been able to erase the sight of Antoine lying dead. In all of the violence, he'd accomplished only one thing—to add to the horror of his memory. When he'd finally been stopped by shrapnel and sent home, he'd vowed never to lose control, not of his temper or his heart. Now, though, the idea of smashing his fist into Praytor's face was almost irresistible. "Praytor, why is it so important to you that Adele die? Surely a courageous man like yourself isn't afraid of a werewolf." He howled softly.

"Stop it." Joe stepped between them. "Where is Adele, Raymond?"

"She's safe." He had no intention of saying anything in front of Praytor. Had he wanted to confide in Joe, he wouldn't do so with an audience.

"You didn't take her to Lafayette."

"I know. She's somewhere the likes of Praytor Bless and his mob can't get her."

"If I want her, that old conjure woman won't stop me." Praytor slowly gained his feet. "Neither will you, Thibodeaux. Folks around New Iberia deserve protection. Everybody knows you're under the spell cast by Adele Hebert. Next full moon, you gone grow long teeth and hair. We'll be shootin' you along with her."

For a moment Raymond could see nothing but a starburst of crimson. He fought to maintain control and willed himself not to beat Praytor to a pulp. "Most folks in town tolerate you, Praytor, because of your mama. They know you're a coward and a fool, but out of respect for Mrs. Bless, they don't say it to your face. Get out of here before I kick your ass up one side of Main Street and down the other."

Praytor stood for a moment, then turned and limped out, a scattering of blood droplets flying from the wound on his leg as he stomped out the door.

Joe took a seat behind his desk, straightening a stack of papers. "Where've you been, Raymond?"

"Following a lead in Baton Rouge."

"With Florence Delacroix?"

"Yes, sir." He held Joe's gaze. "Whatever else you think, Sheriff, don't buy into this idea that Adele Hebert is the *loup-garou* and that she's running loose all over town."

Caleb Bastion shook the bars of the cell. "You either stupid as pig shit or lyin'. I'm telling you, Adele Hebert's runnin' loose in town. Halloween night she was in Mrs. McLemore's backyard. I seen her and so did that post office woman. Likta scared her and her sweetheart into runnin' home." He laughed. "She can cover some ground, I'll tell you that."

"Raymond, I want you to go and get Adele now. I want her in a cell and locked down." Joe placed his hands on top of his desk, fingers spread. "Don't argue, just go do it. If she is runnin' all over town, there's a chance she has the Baxter child."

Raymond knew he had no choice but to obey. If he didn't pretend to go and get Adele, Joe would send someone else. By pretending, he could at least gain some time to try to find Adele.

"Yes, sir," he finally said. He walked to the door. As he pulled it open, Chula Baker tumbled into the office, her hair askew and her body trembling.

"Raymond," she said, grasping his forearms and hanging on. "Raymond, you've got to go to the Bastion farm. That foreman is killing two of the men." She gasped. "I tried to talk to him, but he said if I didn't leave he'd gut them on the spot. You have to stop him."

Raymond pushed past her, realizing too late that she had a little girl with her. He almost tripped on the child as he ran toward the street where a pair of headlights came straight at him.

He could hear Joe talking to Chula, trying to calm her. He knew what was happening. Veedal had somehow figured out that Daniel Blackfeather had spoken with him. Now Veedal intended to make Daniel pay the price. Daniel and someone else, someone who hadn't talked but who would make a prime example to the men of what happened when any of them broke the code of silence.

Flames from a bonfire leaped into the November sky. Raymond drove straight for it, cutting across the fields, the patrol car bucking and twisting. Instead of slowing, he pressed harder on the gas. The scene before him came directly from hell.

Veedal had erected two wooden crosses. Two human forms hung from them, the limp weight of the bodies dragging at the ropes that held them. Both men were either unconscious or dead. Huddled in front of the crosses were the rest of the convicts, and walking in front of them, tapping the handle of a whip, was Veedal Lawrence.

"Lawrence! Back away from the men!" Raymond yelled at him through the open car window. "Back away now!"

Raymond pinned Veedal in the headlights, hoping that the foreman would step away from the prisoners. Veedal saw the approaching vehicle as it bumped over the field, and he turned back to the men on the crosses. He raised his right hand, the barrel of the pistol pointing at Daniel Blackfeather's chest.

Raymond pushed the gas to the floor, gripping the steering wheel with all of his strength as the front tires dug into the row, plowed upward, and launched forward. The center of the wooden bumper struck Veedal in the thighs. The foreman disappeared beneath the car, the surprise on his face almost comic.

Before Raymond could bring the car under control, he was thirty yards past the bonfire. He got out and ran back, ignoring what felt like a surge of electrical voltage that started in his back and made him clamp his mouth to keep back a cry of pain.

By the time he got to the cross where Daniel Blackfeather hung, he was limping severely. "Help me," he called to the convicts.

In one clanking mass, they rushed forward to hold up Daniel's body as he cut him down. They moved to the second man, the tall blond-haired fellow, and cut his bonds, too.

"Get water," he told them.

"There ain't none here."

"Put Daniel and the other one in the car." Raymond was sweating. He could feel it pouring from his head and down his back. His legs were on fire. "Where are the keys to your leg irons?"

"Veedal's got 'em." The men turned in unison to look at the foreman. Blood leaked from his mouth and he made strange floundering movements with his arms.

Raymond walked over and searched the foreman's pockets until he got the keys. He unlocked the first man. "I'm taking these injured men to Doc Fletcher's. I want you to unchain everyone else. I want you all to go up to the stables and get some water and food. Don't try to escape. If you run, they'll track you down and kill you. You'll be part of a sport. Now load Veedal up in my car."

"Leave him to us." A small black man stepped forward. Scars ran across his face and arms.

Raymond shook his head as he picked up the pistol Veedal had dropped. "He's going to the doctor along with the other two."

"You can't take him. You can hardly walk." The man stepped closer to Veedal so that he could look down on him. "We should have him."

Raymond pointed to three other prisoners. "I'll drive the car back over here, and we're going to load all three of them. If Veedal dies on the way, I won't grieve it. But I'm not leaving him to die in the dirt."

"You don't know what he done to Blackfeather and Smith." The small man's eyes burned.

Raymond looked down at Veedal. The foreman's eyes were clouded with pain, but he was conscious. And he was scared. His fingers clasped Raymond's boot, squeezing, begging.

Veedal Lawrence deserved to die, for all the things he'd done in the past. He'd had no mercy on the men he was charged to oversee. If Raymond let him live, would he regret it? Raymond shook free of Veedal's grasp. His hand tightened on Veedal's gun, and he brought the barrel to point at Veedal's forehead. Pain, like an electric current, sang along his spine as he stood in the dancing shadows of the fire.

The convicts were completely still. The only sound was the crackle of the bonfire and the rasp of Veedal's breath.

"Kill him." A convict stepped forward, leg irons clanking. "Do it."

Raymond's finger tightened on the trigger, almost involuntarily. Killing was the price he paid. He brought death. That was his job.

"Do it!" The prisoner stepped closer. "Do it!"

Raymond forced the gun down to his side. "No. Let him stand trial for what he's done."

He walked back to the car and drove slowly to where the men waited. His back hurt, and he was afraid he would lose control of his legs. He had to get medical treatment for the men. He had to get to Adele.

20

MICHAEL stood at the window of Doc Fletcher's guest room trying to calm his thoughts. Behind him, the sound of labored breathing came from the bed where Veedal Lawrence struggled to live. Instead of generating sympathy, the sound was like a rasp against Michael's skin, agitating and annoying. He'd administered the last rites, but he was finding it impossible to offer comfort to the man in the bed. His preference would be to walk out, but instead he surveyed the room, seeking strength in the orderliness of his surroundings. Men like Doc, a few men, had imposed order and civility on the swamp around them. It was possible to tame the wilderness, but now Michael better understood his distaste for Iberia Parish, for the primitive impulses that ruled land and creature. That nurtured men like Veedal Lawrence.

The horror of it was unsettling, and Michael tried to remember what the old physician had told him about the history of the house during spring socials as they sat in the shade. Built in the early 1800s by a North Carolina planter who'd settled in Acadia and tripled his wealth in rice and cane—until he backed the wrong side of the Civil War—the house had gracious rooms, each with a fireplace and crown molding that showed the intricate craftsmanship of a superior carpenter. It was a lovely house where time seemed frozen in the past, a place where the very ill came to either be cured or to die.

Outside the window the lawn sloped past elegant live oaks, a croquet field, bird baths, and a large pavilion to the quick waters of the Teche. Michael knew this because he'd spent many a Sunday afternoon on the pleasant grounds. Now, fog shrouded the familiar scene and muffled the sound of a tug headed downstream. Looking outside was like trying to see through multiple layers of cheesecloth. Only the harshness of Veedal's breathing was sharply in focus on this bleak November morning.

It was the fact that Veedal lived that brought Michael to his dilemma. Boday Smith had recovered, but Daniel Blackfeather was still in surgery to repair internal injuries. Had Raymond not stopped Veedal, Daniel would be dead.

Michael turned so that he could see the Bastion foreman's sweating forehead. Veedal Lawrence had risen from the muck of the swamp in the form of a man, but he wasn't even an animal. He was an aberration.

And Henri Bastion had condoned such brutality, or at least had done nothing to stop it. Michael had never considered himself naïve, but now he saw that he'd sought a form of blindness brought on by his ambitions. He hadn't seen what was happening on the Bastion plantation because he refused to look. The children, Marguerite, the prisoners, possibly even Adele—all had suffered at the hands of Henri Bastion while Michael had thrown open the doors of the church to the town's wealthiest man. Now Marguerite was missing, Sarah Bastion was in the care of Chula Baker, and the boys remained in jail until Marguerite could be found.

In the fog that swirled in heavy sheets, Michael thought he saw a woman standing in the middle of Doc Fletcher's lawn. Something about her touched him like an icy hand. He rubbed the window, trying to clear the condensation for a better view. As a breeze caught the fog and shifted it, he saw her again. She stood, arms dangling, staring in at him as if she could see into his soul. Her dark hair, wet from the fog, clung to breasts almost bare. Dark eyes looked at him from under arched brows. "Rosa." He took a step back and whispered her name.

When he looked again, the lawn was empty. His mind had merely played a trick on him. The scarecrow, the horror of Veedal Lawrence, the fact that Marguerite had disappeared, leaving behind her children without anyone to care for them—it seemed impossible. Yet it was real. The woman on the lawn, a harmless apparition, was not.

He heard a tap on the door and turned to find Sheriff Joe Como standing in the doorway. He signaled Michael out into the hall after a contemptuous glance at Veedal.

"Marguerite is gone. Like she vanished. I tried to track her down to all the places she might go, but it seems like she's vanished," Joe said. "Did she say anything when she left the boys with you?"

Michael thought for a moment. "She said she was done with them, and they should be sent to the reformatory."

"Praytor Bless feels the same way." Joe's smile was slow in developing, but when he recounted the story to Michael, he chuckled. "You shoulda seen that boy ride Praytor's leg. I'll bet he bit a plug out of Praytor's thigh, right through his pants."

Michael didn't doubt it. The boys were out of control. "And what will happen to them?"

"They're safe enough in the jail, for the moment. We'll cross that bridge when we get to it. I'm hoping their mama will come home and assume her responsibilities. Save the county a lot of trouble and expense. Course if Praytor presses charges, that's another thing, but somehow I don't see him admitting in open court that he was bested by a twelve-year-old boy."

"And Raymond?"

Joe shook his head. "Waitin' for Doc to evaluate him." Joe

slapped Michael's shoulder. "If you think of anything Mrs. Bastion said, might give us a clue where to start lookin' for her, let me know." He walked down the hallway and took a left to Doc Fletcher's kitchen.

Michael walked back to the window. The fog would lift, eventually, exposing the town once again. But not the New Iberia he'd once seen. A core of darkness had been exposed. Raymond had seen this, and Michael finally understood why the deputy made him feel uncomfortable. Raymond had looked into the darkness— a thing that Michael had been unable to confront.

Stories about Raymond circulated through the town. How he'd killed a dozen Germans in an ambush in a small French town. How he led a charge against a mortar and planted the dynamite to destroy a bridge. Raymond the hero, the man who faced the enemy without fear.

Yet he'd thrown the medals he was given for bravery into the Teche. A parishioner had seen him do it. And there was the whispered story that he'd begged to be killed when it seemed he might be paralyzed. A week ago, Michael had seen that as weakness.

"Father?"

Michael turned reluctantly to the bed. He had no compassion for Veedal. No matter how he flagellated himself, he couldn't work up any. His distaste for the man was so intense he could barely look upon him.

"Yes." He gazed at the pillow.

"Send Thibodeaux in here." Veedal spoke in a gasping voice. His lungs had been damaged when the car struck him.

"He's busy." Michael wouldn't give Veedal the satisfaction of knowing that Raymond, too, was critically injured. He'd been strung up with weights and pulleys in a hospital bed in the hope that traction would pull the muscles of his body enough to relieve the pressure of the shrapnel.

"I got something to tell him."

The man's gasping was purely annoying. Michael prayed for

compassion and swallowed his curt retort. "Tell me and I'll make sure he hears it."

Veedal's laugh was low, a creepy sound of amusement. "Tell him I'll see him in hell."

Michael drew back. As he stared into Veedal's eyes, he saw the life leave. A blue film clouded the pale irises and the air left his lungs with one last gasp.

The night was summer velvet, a lush softness of black stitched with the thrum of crickets and the distant cry of an owl. A small creature squealed, prey for the predator. Raymond watched the moon rise, a cold luminous disk surrounded by a strange red glow like the aura of a saint. The pale face of the moon was carved in blood, the light tainted with violence.

A stillness settled over the trees, and Raymond listened. Her footfalls came like promises. When she stepped from a grove of water oaks, he heard the gasp that escaped him. She moved with the fluidness of the wild, her limbs gliding without effort.

Her tattered gown touched the flesh of her thighs and floated away, revealing the milky curve of taut muscle. Her waist was girdled by a silver belt that caught the bloody light of the moon and gave it back in a warm glow.

She circled him, moving downwind for a better sniff. She lifted her head like a dog, tasting the air, using her primitive senses. Unable to move, Raymond simply stared at her. He didn't fear her. Had never feared her. It was impossible to fear a creature with such grace and command of her body.

When she was satisfied with his scent, she walked closer, her dark hair lifting in the slight breeze that moved the treetops.

"Adele," he said.

"It's time to run." She reached for his hand and took it, her warm tongue licking his palm so that he shivered. "With me, you can run again. I can make you whole."

He couldn't resist her. The moonlight glinted red in her eyes. "Are you happy?" he asked.

"I'm free," she whispered, leaning into his ear. He felt the coarseness of her whiskers now. Her nails grew thick and long. "I'm free, Raymond. Taste what it feels like to be free. Of the past, of pain, of everything. We can run through the woods, hunting together. No pain. Running."

He felt her teeth at his neck and he made no effort to resist. He'd never wanted anything more than to surrender to her, to give himself utterly to her.

"Raymond?"

He tried to ignore the voice calling to him. Someone touched his shoulder, shaking him, forcing him up from the forest where the moon was misted in a nimbus of blood.

"Raymond, we need you to stay with us."

He opened his eyes and took in his surroundings. Whatever Doc Fletcher had given him had not stopped the pain but had removed the worst of it to a distance. He knew where he was, and he had a burning sense of urgency, yet he couldn't move a muscle to get up. Events were wrapped in impenetrable layers. He could clearly see the pale tea roses on the wallpaper and the rich plum velvet of the draperies and knew where he was. The how of it escaped him, though.

Chula Baker stood at his bedside, a tall, well-groomed, fair-haired man in tow. He vaguely recognized him. "Chula?" He thought perhaps she was an apparition, someone from his long-ago past, before the war. He heard a soft tapping on the window and he looked outside. Adele was just there, waiting for him. "What are you doing here?" he asked Chula.

"Doc said you were doped up, and he wasn't kidding. For a moment there, I thought you were gone." She held his hand, stroking it. "Sarah, the little Bastion girl, is at the house with Mother. We'll take care of her . . ." She looked back at the man. "Raymond, I'm worried about Madame Louiselle. When I took those herbs to her, no one was home. And Jolene LaRoche swears that Adele Hebert was at the Bastion house, rocking Sarah. I know it's impossible. Adele is in a deep coma. But Jolene swears it. She's terribly upset and repeating the story all over town. Now people are beginning to say that Adele has done something with Marguerite."

Raymond forced himself to focus on Chula's face, where worry etched lines between her eyebrows and on each side of her mouth. The man's face mirrored that concern. Raymond fought the lethargy and the strong desire to slide beneath the moon mist and his compelling dream. "Jolene saw Adele? When?" He closed his eyes and saw Adele in the moonlight, a wolfish gleam in her eyes as she stalked him with promises of freedom.

"Jolene said she was at the Bastion house earlier today." Chula spoke clearly and firmly, demanding his attention. "As soon as I heard, I drove out there and got Sarah. She's not injured." She frowned. "She's so strange, though. She doesn't talk."

"Did you see Adele?" He tried to swallow and his throat was dry. Chula stepped to the bedside and offered him the glass of water on the night table.

"I haven't seen her. I thought she was at Madame Louiselle's."

Raymond fought the drug that tempted him back to sleep, to his dreams. He tried to push himself up in the bed and felt the bite of the shrapnel in his back. "Am I paralyzed?" he asked.

"You aren't paralyzed. They're worried that the metal has shifted, that it moved closer to your spine. Doc says you have to stay in bed."

Raymond saw the compassion in her eyes. When he'd been hit by the grenade, he'd come as close to being a cripple as a man could without ending up in a wheelchair. The possibility hung over him, the pain in his body a constant warning of the doom that awaited him. Instead of the anger that normally came with that thought, he felt the need to get up. "Help me get out of this mess." He waved at the weights and pulleys.

Chula shook her head. "No, Raymond. If you aren't careful, you'll—"

"I have to find Adele."

"I can go back to Madame Louiselle's." She motioned for the man to come forward. "John will go with me."

Raymond assessed the man. There were few people he'd trust, but Chula had good sense and a level head. "I need to know that Madame is okay, and I need an answer about those herbs. Someone gave Adele something, and I may have found it. Adele is innocent, Chula. No matter what people say, she's done nothing wrong."

"Folks in town don't believe that. Joe told me that Praytor Bless is organizing some kind of trap. For tonight. He's out for blood."

"I can't lay here and let that happen."

"Wait until I get back from Madame Louiselle's. Then if you want to get up, I'll help you."

Raymond nodded. He had no choice. He was strung up like a bird on a spit. If Chula wouldn't help him, no one else would. "Hurry," he said. "Adele left Madame's, but I'm hoping she'll go back there. Hurry!"

21

FLORENCE cut the precious lard into the flour, added butter-milk, and worked the ball of dough in the wooden bowl. Her actions were more aggressive than necessary. As her fingers teased out the texture of the biscuit dough, her mind was on Raymond and the insult he'd dealt her the day before without so much as a thought. All night long she'd expected to see him at her door, but she hadn't seen hide nor hair of him. If there was any justice in the world, Adele would have eaten him.

She understood that Raymond had not intended to cause her pain. He wasn't a man who would deliberately set out to use and humiliate a woman. Not even a whore. She slammed the dough onto the wooden table and began to roll it out.

What hurt so badly was that Raymond hadn't even thought of the cost to her. Had he talked it over with her, acknowledged even that he needed to put her in a position that could only bring her pain—that would have made a difference. They could have gone to Baton Rouge together, as partners seeking information. But Raymond's actions had clearly shown her that he saw her as a whore first, a woman second, and a partner not at all.

Tears fell into the biscuit dough and she smashed them with the rolling pin. She hadn't made biscuits in ten years, preferring to pick up her breakfast at the café each morning. Raymond's cruelty had driven her back to the kitchen, back to the routine of her childhood when the texture of simple daily chores had put order in a life filled with the chaos of her mother's profession as a whore.

She sniffed and wiped at her eyes with the shoulder of her dress. She'd punched the dough so much the biscuits would be tough and inedible, but it wasn't about eating anyway. It was about cooking and the solace that came from working the dough.

Something rustled outside her kitchen window, and she looked up into the blind white eye of swirling fog. She was taken aback. It was nearly nine o'clock and the fog hung over her house like God was deliberately trying to cut her off from the rest of the world.

It was a vaguely creepy thought, and she clapped her hands together to shake off as much flour as possible. In her bottom kitchen drawer she found the biscuit cutter and began the job of punching out the circles and arranging the biscuits on a baking sheet. The morning was cool, and the hot oven felt nice, reminding her of fall mornings when her mother had baked. Sometimes a special john would join them for biscuits and syrup, but Corrina, her mother, mostly made it a point to share breakfast time only with Florence.

She pushed the pan in the oven and stood, the sense that someone was watching her so strong that she walked to the window and studied the shifting whorls of fog. Though she knew the heavy mist was a condition caused by the heat of the earth and the coolness of the night air, she still rubbed her arms and shivered. Scientific facts didn't go far toward warding off the heebie-jeebies.

While the biscuits baked she went to her bedroom, dressed, and brushed out her hair. Raymond had hurt her, but life went on. She had to get a grip on herself. She'd known all along that Raymond was damaged goods. Before he'd gone to war he'd dated a beautiful young woman, a dark-eyed Cajun beauty from the next parish over. Florence had noticed them all over town—in the drugstore eating Coca-Cola floats, at the movies, walking along the Teche, riding in Justin Lanoux's big Plymouth convertible while they laughed and drank frosted pastel liquor from paper cups.

Florence had watched them living a life forever outside her sphere. She'd fallen in love with Raymond because of his smile and the way his hand hovered so protectively over the young woman's slender back. His gaze had been attentive, tender. She'd laughed up at him, her finger tracing his lips. Florence had watched them and gone back to her house to wait for the paying customers.

When Raymond had returned from the war only six months before, she'd seen him in town, walking with a cane. She'd thought it odd that he never went back to his mother's house but instead bought his own place on the edge of town, a handsome old house left empty when the Gautreaux boys were killed. In a matter of weeks Raymond had gotten rid of the cane and pinned on the deputy sheriff star.

The war had stolen things from him. The first was his smile and the second was the young woman. Gossip around town was that she couldn't take his darkness, his moods, and she'd moved to New Orleans to mend her broken heart once he told her he would never wed. Florence didn't care when she'd gone; she was only glad she left.

Raymond had been home for a month when he first tapped on her door, asking if she was busy. She'd unlatched the screen and let him in, her heart hammering in a way that made her feel alive and angry. Angry because she knew this day would come when she'd pay the price for loving him.

She bent over the oven, pulling the pan of hot biscuits out. When the knock came at her door, her thoughts were so focused on Raymond that she expected to see him standing in the fog when she opened it. Instead, Pinkney Stole stood on her porch, hat in both hands and eyes unable to meet hers.

"There's a phone call for you, Miss Florence, up to the sheriff's office."

"For me?" She was shocked. Her mother had passed away two years before. No one else had cared enough to keep in touch with her. "Who is it?"

"Girl won't say. She axed for Mr. Raymond first, but when I tole her he was laid up and hurt bad, she—"

Florence grabbed the door frame for support. "Raymond is hurt?"

"Yas'm, he's hurt bad. Might never walk again is what Sheriff Joe says. He—"

"Where is Raymond?"

"He's up at Doc Fletcher's house all hooked up to weights and things. They mean to stretch him out, try to ease that metal off his spine."

Florence smelled the biscuits, a scent that had always meant morning and a new day. It clotted at the back of her throat like a gag, and only her grip on the door frame held her upright. "What happened to Raymond?"

A worried frown touched Pinkney's face. "You'd best come on to the sheriff's office with me, Miss Florence. That gal is gonna call back and it was long distance. She said it was urgent for Mr. Raymond."

Florence had completely forgotten the phone call. She rushed to the kitchen and turned off the oven. On her way to the door she picked up her purse and keys. "Let's go," she said, taking Pinkney's elbow to hurry him along.

"You gone leave them hot biscuits to ruin?"

She hurried back to the kitchen and pulled a paper sack from beneath the sink. She dumped the biscuits in the sack and grabbed a jar of scuppernong jelly. "I don't have any butter," she said as she slammed the door locked behind her.

She climbed into the driver's seat and put the car in gear as

Pinkney hustled into the front seat, the momentum of the car slamming his door. "Lord, Miss Florence, you likta took off my legs."

"Tell me about Raymond!"

"He went out to the Bastion place yeste'day to stop that Veedal Lawrence from killin' a couple of prisoners. Raymond ran over Veedal. He dead now. Raymond's at Doc's house."

Florence knew that whatever Raymond had been doing at the Bastion farm, it had involved Adele Hebert. She didn't know—or care—what he was doing as long as he was okay. "Doc says Raymond won't ever walk again?"

"Says most likely. Says that metal's been in there shiftin' and movin' a little each day."

As Florence reached the fog-blurred edge of town she saw nothing of the ghostly buildings. Instead, she remembered Raymond's long, lean body in her bed, dark hair sprinkled over his legs. Her hand traced the scar that started at his lower back and ran down to the shallow indentation near his buttocks and grooved his flesh to his hip bone and then down his thigh. The wound, even after a year, had been red and puckered with dips in the firm muscle where flesh had been torn away.

"Pinkney, I'll let you out at the office. I'm going to Doc Fletcher's." Be damned what people thought. Raymond was injured.

"No, ma'am. You need to talk to that gal. She sounded mighty upset, and she said she had to talk to Mr. Raymond or you. Sheriff tole me to bring you right back to the office. Said he'd skin me alive if I didn't."

"I don't have time to talk—" but before she could finish her sentence, she realized who was calling. "Okay." She pulled in at the curb in front of the sheriff's department. There were cars parked all around, men talking in clusters, their faces tense with worry. "What's going on?" she asked Pinkney.

"Posse or some such. Gone find that *loup-garou*. Good thing

Mr. Raymond is tied down in bed or he'd kick some ass around this place."

Florence passed Praytor Bless holding forth vehemently about something. His face was swollen, his lip puffed and crusted with blood and he walked with a limp. He stopped talking as she walked by, and she ignored him. When she walked into the sheriff's office, the telephone was ringing.

"New Iberia Sheriff's Department," Joe said when he answered. He cleared his throat. "I'll accept the charges." There was a pause. "She's right here." He handed the receiver to Florence.

"Hello." She held the receiver tight, as if pressure on the black handset could clear up the buzz on the line. She heard Callie's voice.

"It's me, Florence. I found the thing you and that lawman was lookin' for. I gave him the message and he said he needed to talk with that deputy. He said tonight at ten at Mitch's place up Bayou Teche."

"That won't work. Raymond's hurt."

"It has to work."

The line went dead and Florence held the telephone to her ear, knowing that Joe and Pinkney and the two Bastion boys in their jail cell were listening to her. "Yes, I'll give him the message," she said into the empty telephone line and then hung up.

"What's that all about, Miss Florence?" Joe stepped closer to her as he asked. "Something I need to know?"

She shook her head. "No, sir. I'm sorry you were troubled by such a call. It won't happen again."

"I had to accept charges for that call." Joe's mouth was a line of annoyance. "Sheriff's office ain't no place for personal long-distance calls. That woman said it was police business."

"She lied. When the bill comes due, you tell me and I'll pay you back." Florence nodded at him. "Now you have a good day, Sheriff. I've got to get back to my chores."

She walked past them without ever looking. She got in her car and headed east, toward Bayou Teche and Raymond.

The afternoon sun slanted in through the plantation blinds, illuminating the room in a warm glow. Raymond woke from the grip of the dream like a man surfacing from deep water.

Everything in the dream had been bathed in tints of red violence. He'd felt as if he were drowning in carrion shadows. Surprised that it wasn't night, he blinked against the golden glow of sunlight that was a blessing. When he tried to swallow, his throat was dry and sore, and he couldn't shift his legs. He felt as if something heavy had been laid across the lower half of his body, restricting all movement. For a moment he was thrown back in time to the first moments of consciousness after he'd been injured in the war.

The blast of the grenade against his back had been percussive, a combination of sound and movement that had initially puzzled him. His body had been smacked hard and he'd fallen to the ground. He'd known something was very wrong, but he couldn't figure out what. His legs hadn't responded to his commands. His thoughts had been addled. He'd opened his eyes and stared into the ground, remembering Antoine. His baby brother. The person he loved most in the world.

He felt moisture build beneath his eyelids and trace its way through the crow's-feet and into his hair. He should have been the one to die. That was the truth he lived with, the reason he lived alone and isolated. Raymond had found that he was very good at war. The adrenaline, the danger, the rush—all for a cause he believed was right. He did his duty. After Antoine's death, he became superb at his duty. The problems began when he tried to sleep at night. What he saw was Antoine, a wounded ghost stalking the night, his eyes filled with dread at what Raymond had become.

In the doctor's bedroom, Raymond felt the sun on his face. He would keep his eyes closed and delay reality for just a bit longer.

"Raymond?"

The woman's soft whisper was like a touch. He knew the voice, but it wasn't possible. He'd lost her by his carelessness. Somehow he must have slipped back into a dream. "Florence?"

Her cool fingers wiped the tear from his temple. "I'm here."

He forced his eyes open and looked at her, a woman of such beauty. She was bathed in sunlight, almost as if the glow were internal. "Am I dead?"

"I don't think so." She smiled. "You're trussed up like a hog at butcher time, but the doctor says you aren't close to dying."

He tried to shift his body and felt the pull of the weights. Doc Fletcher was trying to stretch out his spine. He remembered the discussion before the pain shot. Raymond had consented to the treatment, but traction wouldn't help. He knew that. The metal moved toward its own destiny. It was too close to the spine for removal, and though Doc was trying his best, Raymond accepted that no one could halt or delay destiny. If the metal moved in one direction, he would be paralyzed. If not, he would walk with a minor degree of pain. This was the card fate had dealt him.

"Untie me," he said. "I have to get up."

"You're talking to the wrong woman." She sat up straighter. "I won't have a hand in watching you cripple yourself. Besides, I couldn't undo those knots if my life depended on it."

"Did they find Peat Moss?"

She sighed, and he knew she was debating all that she should or should not reveal. "No."

"Daniel Blackfeather?"

Florence held his gaze. "The two prisoners are going to be fine. Veedal Lawrence is dead."

Raymond tried to feel something, anything. Regret for what Blackfeather and Smith suffered was all that surfaced. "I killed a lot of men in the war. Men I didn't know. I killed them because if I didn't, they'd kill me. Because they were the enemy. I left one boy alive with the thought of getting a medic for him, and Antoine died because of it."

He swallowed dryly and Florence gave him a sip of water.

"Veedal Lawrence is the first man I've taken any satisfaction in killing. I wish I'd done it last week, when I figured out what kind of man he was. That's my curse, Florence. I'm intended to kill— I'm good at it—but too late. I get it done, but only after the innocent have suffered."

Florence took a cool cloth and wiped his forehead. "You'd best put your thoughts and energy into healing instead of killing."

"Have they caught Adele yet?"

"No. Praytor Bless is organizing a big hunt. Folks have seen Adele roaming around the town." She took a deep breath. "If what they say is true, Raymond, Adele must be flying from place to place. She's covering a lot of ground."

"Hell, if she can change into a wolf, why not a bird? Or a damn bat? Maybe she's flying all over the parish." He tried to sit up but the weights tugged at his legs. "Goddamn it, cut me loose from this."

Florence put a restraining hand on his chest. "Chula Baker stopped by. Madame Louiselle was with her and she sent a poultice for you. She told me how to apply it."

"I don't want a damn poultice; I want up!" The slightest pressure of her hand pinned him to the bed, and his weakness was infuriating. At least Chula had found Madame. She should have awakened him, though. "Can you find Madame? I've got to talk to her!"

"Why are you so willing to risk everything to save Adele?"

The question pushed him back into the pillows. He owed Florence this answer. "It isn't what you think, Florence. It's just . . ." He turned away from her gaze. "She's lost everything she ever loved—she's probably insane—but she didn't kill anyone. If I can't figure a way to stop this, she's going to be executed for a crime she didn't do. All because she can't defend herself."

"She's helpless? Is that it?"

"Yes. That's it." He felt relief. Florence did understand.

She got up and walked to the window, adjusting the wooden slats so that he could see the first tinge of amber touching the cypress trees that grew along the Teche. When she turned back to him, he found he couldn't fathom the expression on her face.

"Is it only the weak who're worth protecting and saving, Raymond?" She waited half a moment for his answer and then walked to the door. "I'll get us both some coffee. There's someone waiting to talk to you."

She was gone before he could frame a reply.

22

RAYMOND drew on his tiny resource of strength to force his eyelids open. He found himself staring into the black gaze of Madame Louiselle. She looked at the potion lying on the table beside his bed and back at him. Though she didn't speak a word, he heard her. "You're a hardheaded fool, Raymond Thibodeaux. Suffering should never be voluntary."

"Madame, what about the plants I brought you?" He hated that he was flat on his back.

"Harmless. They're all common for cooking, to calm nerves, some of the cures I taught Adele." Her expression didn't change. "Except for one."

She reached into the pocket of her apron and brought out a small piece of purple cloth. "This I don't know."

Raymond felt like an invalid as he tried to push himself into a sitting position with the weights tugging him back down in bed. Sweat touched his hairline, and he felt the heat climbing into his face. Humiliation made him turn his face from Madame.

"Lie still." She put her cool, dry hand on his forehead.

Raymond wanted to curse and rage, but he forced himself to

fall back on the pillows. He was helpless. The thing he'd dreaded most had occurred.

Madame took the small cloth and unwrapped it. She picked up the bundle of grass. "This I don't know," she said. She rewrapped it and put it in his hand. "Is there someone who can tell you what it is?"

"Maybe Doc—"

She shook her head. "I took it to him. I heard you were hurt, so I chose to be your legs."

Her words stung him, but he steeled himself not to show it. "Doc didn't know?"

"He hasn't studied the native plants. Doc Fletcher believes that true healing comes from a pill at the drugstore." She smiled and reached into her apron pocket and brought forth a pack of Camels. She offered Raymond one and then lit both cigarettes with a match she struck on her thumbnail. "Doc doesn't concede that the pills he finds so valuable come from the same plants that grow wild in the swamps."

"I'd hoped you might have an answer for me." His rage had passed and he was left with disappointment.

"Is there someone else who might help you?" she asked.

Raymond shook his head. "No. But thank you, Madame." He took the cloth from her and held it gently. "Have you seen anything of Adele?"

"No." She went to the window and looked out at the Teche. "She wants to die, Raymond. You must accept that. Whether it is starvation or a bullet, Adele has chosen this."

"I don't believe that. Someone is using her. Someone is setting her up to take the fall for a murder she didn't commit." It was hard to argue passionately from a sick bed. He handed the cigarette to Madame. She went to the window and threw both butts outside.

"How did you get here, Madame?" Raymond was slowly coming to himself.

"Chula brought me, but she left with her new man to go and search for Peat Moss."

"I can call the sheriff to give you a ride home."

"I'm not ready to go yet." Madame picked up the poultice. "Why are you so afraid to heal yourself, Raymond? Why do you choose not to be whole?"

He knew the answer. He'd spent the last six months ferreting out the truth. "I don't deserve to heal."

"Ah, a challenge for any healer." She put the poultice across his legs. "When your woman finally cuts your free, put this on. There's a powerful gris-gris in it. Perhaps even strong enough to fight your darkness."

She leaned down and her lips brushed his forehead. "The guise of darkness can fall away, Raymond. If you wish it."

Her soft-soled shoes made no noise as she slipped out of the room.

Sarah Bastion sat on Chula's lap as they waited on Vermillion Road for the others who would make up one of the search parties for Peat Moss Baxter. The fog had lifted at last, returning the world to a more normal view.

Chula's fingers sifted through Sarah's fine, dark hair. She'd had to cut several snarls out of it, and washing the child had been a battle. Beneath the dirt Chula had found bruises and cuts that showed long months of neglect. If Chula had her way, none of the Bastion children would be returned to their mother.

Sarah seemed content to lean against Chula and stare into the woods; her behavior was troubling Chula. She was too quiet, too docile. Except when Chula attempted to leave her. Then Sarah had clung ferociously to her, hanging on to her leg or skirt or whatever she could attach to. The end result had been to bring her along. A search party was no place for a child, but leaving her behind was worse.

The cry of a hawk drew their attention to the woods. The child cocked her head but didn't utter a sound. Chula wondered if Jolene LaRoche had spun a total fantasy of what she'd seen—and heard—at the Bastion plantation. As far as Chula could tell, Sarah was mute.

"John will be back soon." She spoke to reassure Sarah, because she'd seen the child's gaze follow John. Sarah seemed to like him, and Chula acted on instinct, giving the child reassuring information. John had stepped into the woods, undoubtedly to relieve himself. He was too much of a gentleman to disclose such details. Chula smiled at the thought. A few months in the swamps would cure him of his modesty.

"Sarah, do you know where your mother went?" Chula spoke to the child at regular intervals, hoping that normal interaction might encourage the little girl to speak. Sarah continued to search the trees for a sign of the hawk.

"Shall we go for a walk?" Chula eased Sarah to the ground, got out of the car, and held out her hand for Sarah to take. The child was compliant. She took Chula's proffered hand and clung to it. Together they walked along the road. The day was warm, perfect, and Chula felt her body revive with the gentle exercise. They walked for half a mile, rounding a bend in the road that hid them from the car.

"Your brothers are safe," Chula said. Though she watched closely, she could see no reaction on Sarah's face. She seemed to have no regard for any member of her family. "If we find your mother, you can go home."

Sarah stopped, her face stricken. She stood braced as if her legs had locked. Urine spattered the dirt road, running down her legs and flooding her shoes. Chula looked up from the child to find Clifton Hebert standing in the edge of the woods, a pack of lean dogs at his side.

"Sarah, it's okay," Chula said softly, rubbing the young girl's back. "It's okay." She felt Clifton's gaze on her, and though she'd never been afraid of him, she didn't trust the dogs. Their mottled coats showed battle wounds, and the bright gleam in their eyes let her know they considered her prey.

"Have you come to help us look for Adele?" Chula called to him.

"Adele, no." Clifton stepped forward. The dogs sat without a single command. "I need a word with Bernadette, me." He looked around, taking in the fact that Chula and Sarah were alone. "Where are the others?"

"We're early." Chula forced herself to remember that Clifton Hebert came to her home on a regular basis to bring liquor. He frequently sat at the kitchen table and shared a cup of coffee with her mother, pouring the hot liquid into his saucer to cool it, in the old way. To be afraid of him was ridiculous. Even worse, her fear would transfer to the child, who was already afraid. "Sarah, this is Clifton." She forced a smile into her voice. "He's the best trapper in Iberia Parish. Maybe in all of Louisiana."

"She is not your *bébé,* no?" Clifton frowned, trying to fit the child into what he knew of Chula and her mother.

"This is Henri's little girl." Chula pulled Sarah against her leg. "She's staying with me for a bit."

Clifton assessed the little girl. "The little colored child is dead."

Despite her best effort, Chula felt fear trace along her spine. "How can you be certain?"

"My dogs followed her trail. She went into the woods. The scent was strong and the dogs were on it, yes. I was certain I'd find her, me. But the trail stopped." He held out both hands. "Vanished. Like the little girl was lifted up and taken by a bird."

Unpleasant images darted through Chula's brain, and she struggled against them. "Could someone have picked her up, Clifton?"

He shook his head. "The dogs circled, noses to the ground, smellin' the trees and the dirt." His dark eyes were intense. "There was nothing for them, yes. She was taken."

"By the *loup-garou*?" Chula had to ask.

"By something not like us, *cher*. Call it whatever you want. It's in these swamps."

She tightened her hold on Sarah's shoulder. She looked back down the road, relief palpable as she saw John striding toward them. She waved at him. When she turned back to Clifton, he and the dogs were gone, not even a leaf stirring in their wake.

Florence slipped the kitchen knife into the pocket of an apron she'd borrowed. She picked up the tray of coffee with sugar and real cream and a plate of peanut butter cookies that Myra Fletcher had prepared.

"Try to get Raymond to eat something," Myra directed.

If the doctor's wife was surprised that the town whore had arrived to play nursemaid to Raymond Thibodeaux, she showed remarkable fortitude in hiding it, Florence thought as she lifted the tray. "Raymond's hardheaded."

Myra laughed. "I remember him as a teenager. He and Antoine cut our grass during the summers." Myra straightened the cups on the tray Florence held. "No men could work harder and Raymond taught Antoine, like a father would have. Despite the age difference, they were so close. When Antoine was killed, something died in Raymond." She met Florence's gaze. "When laughter dies in a man I'm not sure it can be mended."

Florence had no reply.

"Doc has seen some horrible things, Florence. He's seen some of the worst that man can do to man. Somehow, he's managed to hang on to his humanity. He can sit down at the dinner table and tell a funny story. He isn't . . . consumed by the evil of man."

Florence cleared her throat. "Raymond suffers, Mrs. Fletcher. I know he does. But there are times I see beneath the pain." It was amazing that she stood in the Fletcher kitchen having this conversation with the doctor's wife. She stood a bit taller. "I don't know if Raymond will ever let himself love again, but he can. He's capable."

Myra put her hand on Florence's arm. "If he's crippled, Florence, he'll want to die. He'll do whatever he has to to get out of a body that's failed him."

"I know."

"Do you?" Myra stared into her eyes. "Maybe you do. I see you love him. Just don't put yourself in front of a hurricane and expect to walk away without being hurt."

Florence smiled. "I thank you. Most folks wouldn't take the time to care if I got hurt or not."

"Most folks don't take the time to think about anything at all." Myra patted her arm and left the kitchen.

Florence started back to the bedroom. She passed two young black girls cleaning the room where Veedal Lawrence had died. The smell of bleach was strong, as if they hoped to sterilize the very idea of Veedal out of the floor.

Doc had put Raymond on the east side of the house, removed from much of the activity. The hope had been that he could rest. Florence made her way down the polished hallway lined with colorful prints of birds. A man named Audubon had come to Louisiana back before the War Between the States to draw the exotic birds, and Doc had bought or traded for some of his work. One day, when she had time, she wanted to examine the paintings, to study the intricate detail and shadings of color that made the creatures seem ready to fly from the frame.

She passed an exterior door that opened onto a small front porch, screened and private for those patients who had recuperated enough to sit and watch the traffic pass on the Teche. She'd stepped beyond the door when she heard Father Michael's voice.

"Are you sure you haven't seen Adele?" he asked. "If you're hiding her, it could go harshly for you."

Florence stopped. In the long list of her sins, eavesdropping would be a minor offense. Raymond would want to know anything she might hear about Adele.

"My sister has been taken by Satan, Father. The spirit of sin has blackened her soul. You must pray for Adele's soul. When they find her tonight, they'll kill her. Pray for her soul."

Florence put the tray on a small table so that the cups didn't rattle. She wasn't certain who the female speaking was, but it stood to reason that it was Bernadette Matthews, Adele's remaining sister. Who else would be begging a priest to intercede in Adele's immortal judgment?

Florence slipped down the hallway and out the front door, making her way quickly around the house so that she stood hidden in the dense camellias outside the small screen porch. She had a clear view of the priest and the untidy woman who talked with him.

Bernadette's resemblance to Adele was startling. There was the same dark hair and arching eyebrows. A closer examination showed the eyes beneath the brows were lackluster brown, the skin blotched. Where Adele was thin and angular, Bernadette was stouter, but they shared the same genes. Bernadette's stance was aggressive, her expression angry.

"The *loup-garou* may be only a legend, Father, but Satan walks the back roads of Iberia Parish. Surely you haven't lost your belief in the devil?"

The priest looked past Bernadette and into the live oaks near the pavilion. "I believe in Satan, Bernadette. I believe strongly in the devil. Sometimes it's easier to believe in evil than in good. That, perhaps, is my greatest sin."

Florence saw the struggle in the priest's face. Her opinion of Father Michael had shifted. She'd always believed him an ambitious man, but she'd not counted on the humility and concern that touched his face. He was a priest, but that didn't elevate him from wrestling with the same doubts that afflicted all humans.

Florence had simply never expected Michael Finley to be so honest about his struggles.

"My sister, *Adele*, has given herself to darkness." Bernadette stepped in front of the priest, demanding his attention. "She's taken a child, Father. Maybe to try to replace her own dead boys, I don't know. But Adele can't care for a young-un. She couldn't care for her boys, no. I tried to help her. I tried to show her what babies need." Bernadette sat down hard in one of the cowhide rockers. "Before her babies died, Adele was strange. She and Rosa both."

Father Michael wiped his cheek and Florence couldn't tell if it was perspiration or a tear. "Rosa was a good woman, Bernadette. She didn't ask for the stigmata."

"Did she have it truly? Or did she pull a trick, yes?" Bernadette shook her head. "Both Adele and Rosa grew such desperation to be special, to have all eyes on them and tongues waggin' their names. Even as little ones. Rosa was always praying. She would go out to hang the clothes and come back inside to tell us some conversation she'd had with the Holy Mother Mary. The clothes would still be in the basket." Bernadette got up and began to pace. "Adele was as bad, in her way. She made up stories all the time. Stories that frightened us. While Rosa spoke with angels and saints, Adele danced with demons, yes. The things she told us were gruesome, and she did it because it was her nature. She'd chosen darkness even then."

Bernadette paced to the end of the porch where Florence was hidden. The camellia bushes were thick, but she held her breath as a small brown wren burst from the foliage, startling Bernadette so that she drew back. Florence felt exposed and wrong, yet she couldn't leave. Not now.

"What is it you want me to do?" Michael asked.

"I don't know," Bernadette finally answered. "I want you to see the truth of Adele. Some will try to save her." She smoothed her hands down the front of her dress. "She can't be saved, her."

"They'll kill her, Bernadette. You know that, don't you? They won't have any mercy."

"Perhaps, in the end, that will be the greatest mercy of all, yes." Bernadette leaned against the support. "Pray that God has mercy on her soul, Father. That's what you can do."

23

———————

Raymond was careful to remain still, as if he were asleep. The drugs Doc had given him were finally wearing off, and he needed to figure a way to get out of the bed. The empty cookie plate sat on the windowsill beside the coffee cups. In an afternoon breeze off the Teche, gauzy sheer curtains billowed inward, draping Florence in a diaphanous gown as she perched on the edge of a chair beside his bed reading a magazine. She brushed the material away, recrossed her legs, and continued to read. She was, without a doubt, the most physically perfect thing Raymond had ever seen.

He'd eaten the cookies only to please her. While she'd been gone to refill the coffee cups, he'd managed to determine that he wasn't paralyzed. He was still a man, and as soon as he was alone, he intended to get free of the traction and get on with his work. Adele and Peat Moss were somewhere in the swamps.

A tap at the door sent Florence to her feet. She answered it, stepping back to reveal Elisha. His sister stared at him, her expression unreadable. He tried to sit up, but the pull of the weights fought him. He struggled to one elbow. "Go home, Elisha." His voice was sharper than he intended. It was bad enough that Florence saw him like this, but he couldn't bear that Elisha should see it.

"I heard you were injured." Elisha hesitated in the doorway. She glanced at Florence, her gaze shying to the floor. "I'm sorry. I didn't know you had company." She backed out of the doorway.

"Wait." Florence crossed the room and grabbed Elisha's hand. "Wait. Please. Come in and see your brother."

"Florence!" Raymond's voice cracked.

"It's only his fear that makes him so bearish." Florence didn't release her grip. Slowly she drew the younger woman into the room. "He's afraid he'll be an invalid. That is such a gruesome fear, it pushes out his manners and"—she glared at him—"his common decency."

Raymond closed his eyes and swallowed the curses he wanted to hurl at Florence. If this was payback for the trip to Baton Rouge, she'd succeeded. "I'm okay, Elisha. I'll be out of here soon."

"They say you killed Veedal Lawrence. That you deliberately ran over him."

His sister's eyes held no condemnation, only curiosity. The scene replayed in his head, the expression on Veedal's face, the solid thump of his body against the bumper, the way the car bucked over the body. "It's true." He felt no remorse or guilt, and he wanted Elisha to see that. To truly know him, so she'd leave him be. "I'd do it again, too."

"All of my friends were frightened of him." She walked to the side of the bed and picked up his hand. "It was a good thing you did, Raymond."

He found his throat suddenly constricted, so he squeezed her fingers instead of answering. As a child, Elisha had worn her dark hair in braids and had helped Antoine work on harnesses and leather goods. Her nimble fingers had often been stained by the

Neatsfoot oil used to soften the leather. She'd been Antoine's helper, his devoted little sister.

"I'm sorry." The words came out as a whisper. "I'm so sorry."

Elisha's tears wet his hand as she clung to it. "Raymond, come and see Mama. Please. Come to dinner Sunday."

He shook his head. "I can't. What I did . . . How can I face her when I know how much she misses Antoine?"

"We all miss him." Elisha sat on the edge of the bed, his hand held between both of her. "You miss him. But you're here, Raymond. Alive. And we miss you." She lifted his hand and kissed it. "I miss my oldest brother as much as I miss Antoine."

"The Raymond you loved is as dead as Antoine." Raymond couldn't look at her.

"I don't believe that." Elisha rose gracefully to her feet. "Still, I'd like that chance to look for myself. Dinner Sunday. I'll cook your favorites." She walked to the door and looked at Florence. "Thank you." She closed the door behind her as she left.

Outside the window a jaybird squawked a protest. Florence leveled her gaze at him, waiting. One eyebrow lifted slowly. When he didn't say anything, she leaned angrily on the foot of the bed frame.

"If you lose the use of your legs, will that be penance enough? How about if you're paralyzed from the chest down? Will that be enough? Maybe you can't use your arms, either. Would that be punishment enough?" She grabbed something from the bed. "Here's the poultice Madame Louiselle sent to you. Why won't you put it on?"

Raymond had no fight left. Elisha's visit, Florence's hot words. Even Madame had pointed the finger of self-destruction at him. Was it so much easier to carry the weight of guilt than to free himself? "Cut me out of this"—he waved his hand at the traction—"mess. I'll put the poultice on."

Florence didn't bat an eye. She pulled a kitchen knife from her apron. "On one condition."

The corners of his mouth lifted in a smile. "You're one tough lady, Florence Delacroix."

"I am."

"What's the condition?"

"That I drive you wherever you go. There are things I need to tell you. Things I overheard."

There were a million reasons Florence shouldn't go with him. She would listen to none of them, so it would be a waste of breath to go down the list. "It's a deal."

The sun dipped behind the trees leaving the sky almost colorless. Michael walked with Jolene along the side of the road, searching for prints as Sheriff Joe had told him. The sheriff had split the volunteer searchers into three groups. One had gone with him, another had gone with Clifton Hebert, and Michael's group was under the direction of Praytor Bless. They were working the southwest corner of the parish close to Adele's home and not too far from the place Henri Bastion had been killed.

Out of deference for Jolene, who looked like she might keel over at any moment, Praytor had assigned them the job of walking along the roadway, searching the damp sand for tracks or impressions. It was a job unlikely to yield anything, but it had to be done. The other volunteers, of hardier stock, were deeper in the swamp, sweeping systematically to the east. Praytor himself was somewhere in the woods, a tracking hound he'd borrowed from Angola prison dragging him through the sloughs and bogs.

Michael could occasionally hear the dog's mournful bay. He couldn't tell if the animal was on the trail or if it had lost the scent and was complaining. Michael could only hope that if Adele was in the section of swamp they searched, that it wouldn't be Praytor who found her. He had no doubt Praytor Bless intended to kill her on sight.

"Do you think Marguerite has left for good?" Jolene asked.

Michael glanced at her. She was still shaken by her experience at the Bastion plantation, and she stayed within arm's reach. Several times a small animal scurrying through the dead leaves had made her jump almost into his arms.

"Maybe." He turned the conversation. "I hear Joe wants to run for the United States Senate."

"That's why he changed his name. Easier to spell." She kept pace with him though she'd begun to breathe harder.

"He's probably right about that." Michael stopped to inspect what appeared to be the heel print of a small child. "Look!"

Jolene knelt beside him, her finger hovering over the indentation in the damp sand. "Peat Moss?"

Michael had prayed for a miracle. He'd asked God repeatedly for the return of the child, a truly helpless being who'd done no wrong. The print looked exactly like a child's, but he wasn't a tracker and he didn't want to arouse the search party and then be ridiculed. "I'll find someone to examine it. Stay here."

"Alone?" Jolene looked at the lengthening shadows on the road. The sun had dipped lower, burning red now through the bare trunks of the trees. The sky was fired with pink and orange, moving toward mauve and purple on the eastern border. Night would be falling soon.

"I have to go into the swamp. Wouldn't you rather wait here? Mark the spot?"

Jolene looked at the swamp and then at Michael. "I'm afraid."

He clamped down on his impatience. "I won't go far. I'll just go in deep enough to find someone. Then I'll come right back. If you yell, I can hear you."

"What if she comes out of the woods? What if she's watching us and just waiting for a chance?" Jolene's voice rose with each new question. "What if—"

He grasped both her arms firmly. "You're frightening yourself, Jolene. You have to get a grip." Her eyes widened in alarm and her spine stiffened, the impulse to fight back showing in her face.

"That's better." He softened his grip. "You're okay. I'll be right back." Before she could protest, he jumped over the ditch and hurried into the woods. As he stepped into the trees, he realized how close it was to night. The canopy of tree limbs overhead blocked out the little sun that still illuminated the sky.

"Praytor!" He decided to abandon all pretense of masculine poise. "Praytor! I've found a track. A child's track!"

There was no answer, and for one awful moment, Michael had the sense that the men who'd stepped into the woods to hunt had disappeared forever, swallowed by the dense swamp.

"Praytor!" If there was an edge of panic in his voice, he didn't care. "Anyone!"

His voice rang against the tree trunks, echoing back at him. A movement to his left caused him to freeze. He'd caught it out of the corner of his eye, and he turned slowly to face it. In the dimness of the swamp, he could see nothing alive.

"Father, protect this your servant from the ways of evil." He made the sign of the cross. He was far beyond worrying about appearing ridiculous now. If the men of the search party were having sport with him, they could enjoy themselves. "Praytor! Somebody answer me!"

Just at the edge of darkness, something moved, shifting silently from tree to shrub. He saw it. This was no trick of imagination or flight of fancy. Someone was in the swamp nearby. Someone who wouldn't answer his cry for assistance.

The trees around him were dark silhouettes now. Ahead was a black slough with cypress knees cresting from the water like the spine of some ancient sea monster. He backed up until he felt the bark of a tree at his buttocks.

In the total silence, something slid from a log into the dark water with a gentle splash. Turtle. Snake. Gator. He couldn't be certain.

Turning to face the opposite direction, he saw only the trunks of trees and the underbrush that seemed uniform. He'd walked less than fifty yards from the road, but somehow he'd gotten turned around. With the sun setting and darkness falling over him, he couldn't be certain which direction would take him back to the road and Jolene.

"Jolene!" He called her name, hoping he could find his way back to the road when she responded.

There was no answer. It was as if he'd stepped into a place bewitched. That was utter foolishness! He didn't believe in magic. A search party of grown men didn't disappear in the forest.

He didn't believe in a woman who turned into a wolf.

Movement through the underbrush caught his eye. This time he distinctly saw the shape of a human. Someone on two legs. But the person had moved with such speed. And without making a sound.

Michael touched the crucifix that hung around his neck. For the ten years he'd been in New Iberia he'd avoided the swamps. He'd known, deep in his soul, that something lurked in the soft black soil rich with damp leaves and seeping springs. Something waited here just for him. He'd avoided it for years, and now he feared he would confront it.

"Father, give me strength to face the test before me." He prayed with his eyes open, his gaze scanning the trees in front of him, turning slowly, hoping and yet dreading to face the attack when it came. "You are the creator of all things. This is yet one of your creatures. I will not fear it with the strength you give me."

The creature stepped out from behind a tree. In the stillness of the woods, not even a leaf seemed to stir. Michael couldn't tell what it was, exactly. It walked on two feet, but with a peculiar stoop, as if it might drop to all fours. Whatever it was didn't move. It watched him, as if it waited to see what he would do.

"Adele?" He called to her, because it could be no one else. "Adele, let me help you. With God's help, you can overcome this." He had doubted Rosa Hebert and her bleeding hands. God forgive him, he had doubted her, wondering if somehow she were marking herself. He did not doubt the dark vision before him, though. It was Adele, and she stood in a way that was not completely human.

She didn't move, yet she seemed to drift closer. He felt the tree at his back as he withdrew. He had to show more courage. He couldn't fear her or he wouldn't be able to help her. But he did feel fear. It was a blade in his gut, turning his legs to jelly and his bowels to mush. Still, he held his ground.

"Come back with me, Adele. Everyone is hunting you. They'll try to kill you. If you come with me, I can keep you safe." His own words seemed to calm him. God had sent him to this place. He wasn't alone. If God had not intended him to help Adele, then why was he the one who found her? He took a step forward. "You have to come back with me. You need medical care."

She moved so quickly that he almost couldn't believe it. She was there, and then she was gone. He'd been staring right at her. Somehow, in the dim and failing light, she simply vanished.

"Adele?" He looked around but night had fallen thick and heavy. He had no idea how long he'd been in the woods. It was almost as if he were awakening from a dream. "Adele."

At first he thought he was hearing things, but the sound of the child grew louder. It was a cry of discomfort and peevishness. Not fear or danger. He forced himself to move forward through the underbrush to the place where he'd seen Adele standing. As he moved, the sound of the crying child grew louder.

When he parted the hackberry limbs, he saw the vague shape of a child squatting. The little girl looked up at him and gave a cry of fear. She started to scrabble away, but he caught the hem of her dirty dress and clung to her.

"Peat Moss?" he said.

At the sound of her name she stopped scuttling. "Mama!" She began to cry softly. "Mama!"

He cradled her in his arms. "We'll get your mama." He held her tightly against his chest as he rose. In the distance several lights were headed his way. The search party.

"Over here!" he cried out. "Here!"

"It's the priest," Praytor Bless called out and the searching men turned in his direction.

"I've got the child," Michael called, still unsure that he truly held the missing girl. "I've got her!"

The hound and Praytor broke through the underbrush. "Well I'll be damned," Praytor said, holding the light on Peat Moss's tear-dampened face. "Is she okay?"

"I think so," Michael said. "I can't be sure until we get her someplace where we can look her over."

"How'd you find her?" Praytor was scanning the area, the dog straining at the leash.

"Adele. She was here."

"Here? How long ago?"

"Minutes."

Praytor pushed past him, letting the dog take the scent. "Get the baby out of here. The rest of you, go with Father Finley. I'm goin' after that she-devil, and I'm gonna get her."

Florence pulled the patrol car into the shallow ditch only a few yards from the cluster of people milling around in the road. Raymond put his hand on the door release, but Florence restrained him. "Give them a moment. The child's just been returned."

Staring out the window, Raymond saw Peat Moss's dark head poking from beneath Big Ethel's arms as she cradled her grandchild, laughing and hugging the young girl.

"It's a miracle! God sent down a miracle to us!" Big Ethel smothered the girl with kisses.

Behind Big Ethel were Leroy and Aimee, both touching Peat Moss's hair and arms and legs as if they didn't believe she was real. The priest and Jolene stood in the background. Michael Finley looked dazed, and he kept glancing back into the woods as if he expected someone else to appear.

"She wasn't even a mile from her home," Florence said.

It was true. Though half the parish had hunted for Peat Moss, she'd been close. "She was hiding under a bush." Raymond repeated what Pinkney had told him when the old man had run into Doc Fletcher's home to tell him the child was safe.

"Do you think she managed alone in the woods?"

He watched the excited crowd. "She doesn't look like she was hurt." He opened the door. "But that's what I need to ask her."

He felt the bite of his injuries as he went toward the Baxter family. When he held out his arms for the child, Big Ethel released her to him. Peat Moss smiled as she touched the badge on his shirt.

"Peat Moss, were you alone in the woods?" he asked.

She only laughed and pointed at her mother. Aimee took her. "She's tired," Aimee said. "Can you ask her questions tomorrow?"

"Doc said she was fine." He looked to the mother for confirmation. In all that had happened, it was difficult for him to believe the child had been returned unharmed.

"She's okay." Aimee closed her eyes as she hugged her child. "By the grace of God, she's okay. Father Finley gave us a miracle. There's a celebration tonight in the Julinot orchard. Come share our joy." She turned to Leroy, and he folded both of them into his arms.

Raymond let them go. He was left standing with Jolene and the priest as the crowd began to thin.

"You're a hero, Father Finley," he said. "You found the child when the whole community was searching for her."

"I . . . Adele helped me."

"You saw Adele?" Raymond's question was sharp. He looked around, as if she might be nearby.

"She was there. She led me to the girl."

"Did she say anything?" Raymond asked.

Michael shook his head. "I tried to talk to her, to convince her to come back with me. I warned her that people were trying to kill her. Praytor is out there now, determined to bring her in. Dead or alive."

"Did she understand?"

Michael shook his head. "No. I don't think she did."

"Was there anything that might help me find her?"

Michael reached into his pocket and brought out a piece of bread. "The child had this in her pocket. Someone gave it to her. I think Adele did it. Adele was trying to help her."

Michael took the bread, noticing the strange texture. It was stale and old with hard purple and black granules throughout. He put it carefully in his pocket. "Thanks. I'm glad you found her safe."

24

THE bar was long and dark, a place where local men came without their wives for an hour of groping a strange woman on the dance floor and drinking and gaming away their paychecks. Arguments were settled with fists or knives, and several stains on the floor looked suspiciously like old blood.

Walking through the door, Raymond met a wall of resentment. Strangers often meant trouble, or at least competition. He held Florence's elbow, daring all who looked to make a move. His body was still weak, but he carried a gun tucked in his waistband, hidden by his jacket. The gun nudged his spine, reminding him with each step of the other deadly metal that shifted beneath skin and muscle. The poultice was wrapped into place, and the pain had lessened to the point that he could walk without limping.

Midway through the bar, he stopped. Because he had no jurisdiction in St. Mary's Parish, Raymond had left his badge behind. The air in the bar had changed from resentment to interest. In Florence. To the patrons, he looked like the luckiest man in the world. The men's gazes lingered on her, as lewd as a touch. Raymond eased her closer to him. She didn't need protection, exactly, but he wanted it clear that she was not available. His glance swept the narrow room. If Dugas was there, Raymond couldn't begin to guess which man he might be. There'd been no picture of him attached to the court paperwork.

He saw a table at the back of the room and moved toward it. Florence held close against him. She kept her gaze down, but it did nothing to prevent the men's looks from raking over her body, probing her breasts and thighs. Raymond had never taken Florence into a bar before, had never felt the surge of anger that came when another man looked at what he considered his own. Though he'd lied to himself about it, in the past weeks he'd grown proprietary of Florence. He'd come to see her as his, deceiving himself about his true feelings, salving them with the knowledge that she made a living by pleasuring men. The thrum of blood through his muscles told him more about his feelings for Florence than his brain had ever let on.

"Is he here?" Florence whispered as she took the seat beside his. They were both sitting with their backs to the wall where they could watch the entire bar. The problem with the seats was the lack of an exit. To get out if trouble arose, they'd have to go all the way to the front door.

Raymond examined each patron. They appeared to be mostly fishermen and swamp men, those who lived on the fringes of society. They'd not been drafted because their births had never been registered. When they died, there would be no embalming or paperwork. They would disappear into the swamps where they'd lived.

Three men sat at the bar, another two at a table with three women, all of whom looked the worse for wear. Florence was like an exotic flower in a ditch full of weeds. He shifted his chair a bit closer to hers.

"Did I ever tell you how I came to get this scar?" She touched her cheek where the thin line of a crescent moon was barely discernible in her olive skin.

"No." This wasn't going to be an entertaining story. He could see it in her clear green eyes.

"When I was thirteen, Mama was working on River Street in Baton Rouge. It was one of the better houses, and we lived about two blocks south of there. We had our own place, and I was going to a private Catholic school nearby. The house was small, but there was a garden." She smiled and Raymond knew she was far away from him in time and place.

"It was a fall morning. Mama was asleep, and I went out to pick some flowers for her. There were butterflies all in the garden. Those big orange monarchs. One of them landed on my hand and just stayed. I felt like I was a princess in a story, and the butterfly was just about to turn into my fairy godmother."

Her laugh was raw, and Raymond felt his heart tear. He didn't have to look at her to dread what she was going to say. For so long he'd walled himself up with his own past that he'd never looked at what Florence pulled behind her. Now he was going to hear it whether he liked it or not.

"When I looked up, there was a man in the garden. He'd followed Mama home. Before I could do anything, he grabbed me by the hair. He put a knife to my throat, and he told me what I was going to do. When I tried to get away, he cut my face. He said he'd carve my eyeballs out."

"Florence, I didn't know."

She held up a hand. "Right there in the dirt of my mama's flower garden with those butterflies all around, I got my first taste of pleasuring a man."

He saw the tears in her eyes, and he knew she'd never allow them to fall. He put his hand over hers. "I'm sorry. I'd never have asked you to go back there. Florence, I was wrong." Her hand was trembling, and he held it to his chest.

"Mama moved us to Shreveport the next day. She left the house she worked at on River Road because the man had followed her from there, had come back to her home and taken the only thing of value she had." She stared at him. "When you asked me to go to River Road, you were asking a lot more than you knew."

"I was wrong." He pressed her hand tightly to his heart. "I was wronger than I've ever been in my life. You deserve so much better than that."

"What is it I deserve, Raymond?"

"Someone better than me. Someone who's not half dead."

Her smile was sad. "That makes it so much easier, doesn't it? You just tell me how much more than you I deserve and that way you don't have to try to meet my needs." She withdrew her hand. "You and that man in the garden have something in common, you know." Her words, weighted with sadness, were spoken almost too softly for him to hear. "Neither one of you gives a damn what I need. It's all about your needs." She stood up. "I've got to powder my nose."

He grasped her wrist, but lightly. "I may have acted like that in the past, Florence, but it's not true." He reached into the inside pocket of his jacket and withdrew a folded paper that he handed to her.

"What's this?" She didn't look at the paper but into his eyes.

"I had this drawn up in Baton Rouge while I was in the courthouse the other day. I knew how much I'd wronged you. This can't make up, but it shows my intent."

She slowly unfolded the paper and read it. When she lowered it, she had tears in her eyes. "Why would you do this?"

"If something happens to me, I want you to have my house. Sell it or do what you want. There's money in the bank. Enough for you to have a different life. If I can't give you a new life, at least I can give you the means to get one for yourself."

She turned abruptly and headed to the washroom. When she left the table, every man in the room watched her hips sway beneath the navy-blue skirt she wore. Raymond almost stood, ready to challenge any of them. Ready to pound his fists into all of them.

He felt the tap on his shoulder and swung around, eager for the challenge. The man who stood before him was ageless, his face a weathered brown that hid more than it revealed.

"You must be the lawman lookin' for me." The man smiled, revealing strong white teeth. "I like the looks of your deputy."

"If you're Armand Dugas, I'm looking for you." Raymond ignored the reference to Florence. He needed information, not a fistfight. Florence was right about one thing. This wasn't about him, and if he intended to help Adele, he needed to act on that.

The man shrugged. "Names change on necessity. I was told Adele Hebert is in trouble."

"She's accused of murder." Raymond saw Florence come out of the restroom and hesitate. He signaled her over. "This is Florence Delacroix."

The man assessed her. "I knew your mother," he said. "If you ever think about moving to New Orleans—"

"She's not moving anywhere." Raymond felt again the pulse of angry blood. He let his gaze bore into Dugas. "You were charged with murder." He let that fact lie between them.

"A woman who never existed." Dugas moved to hold a chair for Florence. "A charge that could never be proved, and therefore never unproved."

"Why would they hang a false murder on you?" Raymond wasn't certain how Dugas figured into Henri Bastion's death, but somehow he did. Whatever thing had been done to Adele had taken root at the Bastion plantation. Dugas was the only lead Raymond had.

The smile left Dugas's eyes. "I knew too much. It was safer for me to be dead. No woman died by my hand, though I wouldn't put it past them to kill a woman just to have a body." His teeth were white in his tan face. "As it turned out, evidence wasn't necessary at all. I was convicted, and I ended up with Henri Bastion, a man who had no hesitation about working a prisoner to death, which was my expected fate."

"Henri was just a happenstance?"

Dugas considered the question. "I don't know."

"And Adele?"

He turned away, hiding whatever emotion surfaced. "She's a good woman."

Raymond knew Dugas wasn't telling the entire truth. "Was Adele in love with you?" he asked.

Dugas shook his head. "Had you seen me, you wouldn't ask. I doubt I weighed a hundred pounds. My body was covered in sores and lice. Another month, I would've been dead."

"Then why did she risk so much setting you free?"

"I was the only man who'd try to escape. The others thought they'd die in the swamps. We were starved near to death." His hand drifted to his bicep, which Raymond realized was smaller than his other arm. "They feared the gators more than Veedal Lawrence."

"Veedal is dead," Raymond said.

Dugas showed a spark of surprise. "How?"

"I ran over him."

When Dugas laughed, he tilted back his head and let the sound dance around the bar until it was absorbed in the beer-sodden wood.

Raymond waited for the other patrons to return to their drinks and conversations. "If you aren't the father of Adele's children, was it Henri?"

Dugas looked shocked. "Adele had children?"

Raymond believed the man was truly surprised. "Twin boys. They died a few weeks back from the fever."

"Damn Henri Bastion!" Dugas's face twisted. "He had a woman, but it wasn't Adele. She wouldn't spit on Henri Bastion." The lines beside his mouth deepened. "He was such a bastard. He may have taken her by force, but she never said anything. She wouldn't kill him, but she knew I would have. That's why she agreed to help me escape, so I wouldn't kill him." He struck the table with his fist so hard that all noise in the bar stopped. Dugas glared around the room and people went back to their conversations.

"I'm sorry, Dugas."

"It wasn't in Adele to harm anyone. She had tenderness for all living things." His gaze shifted to Florence. "Adele was good-looking. She could have worked regular, had a good life. She refused. She said she wanted to be a teacher. Taught her sister's daughter to read, she did."

Raymond felt as if Adele had shifted out of focus. "Are you confusing her with her sister, Rosa? She was spiritual."

Dugas shook his head. "Adele was a gentle person. She hated to see anything suffer. Man or beast. She wanted to be a healer, like the old woman in the swamps she talked about all the time. She worked for the Bastions to save up money."

The picture of Adele drawn by Dugas was in sharp contrast to Marguerite Bastion and Bernadette Matthews's depiction. "I've been told that Adele was free with her body."

Raymond felt Florence's gaze like a hot touch, but she didn't say anything.

"Adele is a beautiful woman, Deputy Thibodeaux. There's no doubt she could have any man she wanted. Her interests, though, were not physical." Dugas spoke with certainty. "If I hadn't been running for my life, I would have taken her as a wife." His hands slowly clinched. "With Adele, I might have had a respectable life."

Florence sat forward. "When Adele's boys died, she got sick, too. She thinks she's the *loup-garou.*"

Dugas studied Florence. When he spoke, his tone was quiet. "Adele is not a murderer. She may be a saint, but she isn't a killer."

He stood up. "Adele was a good girl, a pure woman. By action and thought. Those who say otherwise have something to hide and a reason for slandering a kind woman. If you have more questions, ask them fast. There's a boat I have to meet."

Raymond stood. "What can you tell me to help prove Adele's innocence?"

"Only that she isn't capable of killing." He took two steps away from the table, headed for the back door.

"Where can I find you if I need to talk to you again?" Raymond asked.

"Speak to Callie. She'll get a message to me. Since I escaped from the Bastion plantation, I make it a point never to stay in one place too long. I never killed that woman, but that doesn't mean the state won't send me back to Angola."

25

Beneath the leafless branches of the pecan trees, a sense of joy had replaced the weary dejection of the searchers. Word had spread quickly that Peat Moss Baxter had been found unharmed. A large bonfire, built by Chester Julinot out of downed wood from his orchard, danced in the cool breeze. Julinot's wife, Annie, stirred an enormous pot of gumbo. The nightmare that had haunted the community was ended.

Chula accepted the bottle that Clifton Hebert handed her. She put it to her lips and took a small swallow of the whiskey before passing it on to John. The liquor was a hot contrast to the sweet relief of the little girl's rescue. And by Michael Finley, of all people. The priest hated the swamps. He hated the darkness of night in the woods. It was ironic that with all the seasoned hunters searching for the child, it was the priest who found her. No matter. All that mattered was that she was safe and there would be no more talk of the *loup-garou*. Relief was like a kiss, making the cool night a promise of better days ahead.

"Celebrate the miracle," Clifton said to John. "Drink to the health of the *bébé*, yes."

"To the safe return of Peat Moss." John took a long drink and handed the bottle back to Clifton. "Thank you, Mr. Hebert."

"At least folks will stop fretting about the *loup-garou*," Chula said, her hand automatically going to rub Sarah Bastion's back. The child had fallen asleep on a blanket on the ground, her tiny hand still clutching the hem of Chula's skirt. "I hope Adele is okay."

The waning moon hung over the small gathering, and a breeze blew the smell of the gumbo toward them. Chula's mouth watered. She was starving. Sarah had fallen asleep without so much as a complaint about hunger, and Chula was uncertain whether to wake the child to feed her or to let her sleep. The decisions of motherhood didn't come naturally to her.

"Praytor still hunts the demon spirit," Clifton said, swigging from the bottle again. "He's out there alone with a dog from the prison. 'The *best* trackin' dog in the state,' he says." He laughed. "Maybe the gators will get him and the dog, too." He drank again. "My dogs are the best, but they won't work for Praytor, no. He pay me money to borrow the dogs, but they won't hunt for him. He brought them home and said they wouldn't track."

A breeze fluttered the sleeves of Chula's jacket and she drew her legs up beneath her skirt and covered Sarah with an edge of the blanket.

"There's still no sign of Adele," she said. "She was so sick. I don't understand how she's able to survive out there. I'm afraid Praytor will kill her if he sees her."

Clifton looked up at the moon. "I thought Adele might find me. Always before, she find me when she need me." He drank long from the bottle. "Bernadette, she find me." He made a face. "I'd best go round up my dogs." He handed the bottle to John. "Keep it." In several strides he disappeared into the darkness.

"I'll get us some gumbo," John said. He knelt beside Chula. "Are you okay?"

"There's been so much violence in Iberia Parish in the last week. I don't believe in the *loup-garou,* but there's something going on. Since the night of the full moon. Like a moon curse." She stared up at the planet that half winked back at her. "John, do you think Praytor will find Adele?"

John considered her question. "She can't stay out there forever. She's sick."

"He'll kill her."

"Why are you so certain of that?"

She thought about Praytor. "It's what he is. It's how he can prove he's a real man."

John went to get the food, and Chula watched him, thinking about Praytor. He'd taken no bride, preferring to stay with his mother and sister. She'd thought at first that he was shy, but it had begun to occur to her that Praytor's reluctance to go to the altar had to do with the available women. Since she'd gotten the post office job, he'd asked her out.

She pushed Praytor out of her head and watched John as he chatted a moment with Annie Julinot before he took two bowls and a hunk of fresh bread. His arrival in town had changed her life. In a matter of a few days, she'd experienced a sense of belonging. Not *to* a man, but *with* him. He was her equal, and Chula found security in the fact that she couldn't best him. Sarah, too, had initiated a huge shift in her world. The little girl had awakened a dormant maternal instinct that was stronger than the tidal pull of the moon. Chula touched the child, marveling at the softness of her skin, the perfection of her tiny body. Sarah was the most miraculous creation Chula had ever seen. And possibly the most dangerous.

Marguerite would come to her senses and reclaim her daughter, and Chula would suffer. Even though Sarah was obviously scarred by her life with Marguerite, no court in the land would take a daughter from a mother. Chula would lose the child, unless she took her and ran.

She looked around the orchard. About twenty people were there, most of them releasing the strain of the long search for

Peat Moss. Bottles were passing and Robert Beaumont had pulled out his fiddle. Soon couples would be dancing beneath the leaf-less pecans. It was the rhythm of life in this place she loved. Trouble had passed, and now it was time to laugh and dance. The tax man or the devil might come knocking at the door in the morning, but for this moment, there was something to celebrate and music to dance to.

"Thank you, John." She took the gumbo and shifted to make room on the blanket. "Will you have to leave soon?"

He put his soup aside and took her hand. "Leave with me, Chula. Come back to Baton Rouge. Bring Sarah and pray her mother doesn't care enough to search for her."

His words touched her deeply. "Is that a proposal of marriage?" She forced a smile though the moon was a blur of silver through her unshed tears.

"I want to marry you, but not yet. It would be insulting to act like you had to be legally bound to a man to chart the course of your life. Come with me. If you don't like living with me, you and Sarah can leave, no strings attached."

"My job is here. In New Iberia. My home is here."

"You're an educated woman. You can get a job anywhere. You know that as well as I do. Your roots are here, and it will be painful to tear them out. But they'll regrow."

Chula tried to imagine a life away from Iberia Parish. She'd gone to school for four years. She'd been away, but while she'd lived the life of a college student, she'd also kept the ties to her old life, the one she would return to. She'd never truly left New Iberia. Not in spirit. To steal a child and run away with a man would end all ties. She thought suddenly of the letter from Madame Louiselle's sister in California. How had the sister ended up so far from home? It was a question she'd never asked Madame.

John's fingers laced through hers. "Think about it, Chula. If you want to keep the child, and I think you should, you're going to have to take her and run. I'll marry you tonight, if that's what you want. I want you to love me, to choose to marry me because it's the thing you want to do most in life. But I'll take you any way I can get you."

The passion in his voice calmed her. She touched his cheek. "I have to think about it."

"Good." He leaned down and kissed her cheek. "You have a very capable brain, and I'm sure you'll come to the proper conclusion."

Chula was about to lean into his arms when she heard a car approaching. The headlamps cut across the field, slowly highlighting the different groups of people. The headlights found her and stopped. The driver turned the car off and in the darkness Chula heard the sound of two doors slamming. In a moment Raymond and Florence stepped into the glow cast by the bonfire. Chula felt a pang as she realized Raymond's posture was perfect, but his face was lined with pain and worry.

"Evening, Deputy Thibodeaux." John held out the bottle. "Care for a swallow?"

Raymond took the bottle and passed it to Florence. "I'd better hold off." Florence held it at her side.

"It's been a hard few days for the town." John signaled them to a place on the blanket. "I have to return to Baton Rouge soon, but I'd like to have that talk with you tomorrow if you have time."

Chula checked the sleeping child and moved her gumbo before she stood up. "It's for a book about legend and folklore. About the use of myth in a community."

"A book?" Raymond sounded unsure. "I'm not the person you should talk to. I don't believe in *loup-garous* or ghosts or witches. If that's what you want to talk about, I'm the wrong man."

"Not at all," John said. "Just hear me out. Could we meet at eight?"

Raymond nodded slowly. "Okay. At the sheriff's office. Or even better, at the café."

"Thank you. Now I'll get you both some gumbo. I want the ladies to eat before they swoon from starvation." John started toward the gumbo pot, his tall frame suddenly highlighted by another vehicle pulling into the field.

The car roared into the gathering. Before it could stop, Joe Como flung open the passenger door and ran toward Raymond.

"Come on, Raymond! Praytor Bless was just found down Section Line Road. He's been torn almost in half by some kind of wild animal."

Raymond felt as if his body were being restrained by some invisible force. He started toward Joe's car, but he moved in slow motion. Florence started to follow and stepped into the bowl of gumbo, splashing the hot liquid over the blanket. Chula threw her skirt over the sleeping child to prevent the hot soup from scalding her. Raymond saw the horror on Chula's face, and the pain on Florence's. The sound of the crowd, gathered round to hear the sheriff's news, was like the roar of a boat motor tangled in weeds.

"I'll take Miss Delacroix home," John said, and his words snapped Raymond out of the confusion.

"Thibodeaux! Get in the damn car and follow us!" Joe was already back in the passenger seat of the vehicle he'd arrived in.

Raymond turned away from the sheriff and to Florence. "I'm sorry to leave you like this. Will you be okay?" It was the respect a man gave a date, and he wanted everyone to hear it.

Florence nodded, the surprise and pleasure clear on her face. "You go on. Mr. LeDeux will see me home just fine."

Her formal response made him smile. With Florence, it could have gone either way. She just as easily might have slapped his face. He turned to Chula. "Use what influence you have to keep this under control."

Joe reached across the seat and laid on the horn. "Raymond, get your ass in gear!"

Raymond hurried to the patrol car and fell in behind the sheriff as they bumped out of the orchard and onto Section Line Road. In the rearview mirror he could see several pairs of head-lights come to life. The mob, never far from the surface of any group, had sprung to life.

Joe's driver, a man Raymond recognized from Joe's morning coffee calls at the café, drove carelessly, taking corners with reck-less abandon. They drove fast until they came to the bridge over Beaver Creek. Rains to the north had flooded the waterways in Iberia Parish, and the creek rushed dangerously close to the wooden platform. Once across, they picked up their pace again until the lead car swerved onto the side of the road.

Raymond parked behind and was out of his vehicle before Joe could swing open his door. The lead car's headlamps revealed a lump of what looked like dirty clothes on the side of the road surrounded by an ominous pool of black.

Dread crept up Raymond's spine. Peat Moss was safe. The panic over Adele had calmed, but this would torch it high. He walked forward, swinging his flashlight beam onto the thing in the road. At first he couldn't make out what it was. Then the light caught a glint of metal, and Raymond recognized the fancy silver toe guard on Praytor's boot. He knelt for a better look, swallowing the bile that threatened to rise up his throat.

"Is it Praytor?" Joe asked the question as he stood behind the headlights of the first car.

"I think so." Raymond grasped a piece of cloth and pulled. The thing rolled wetly and an arm flopped onto the road. The beam of light found what was left of Praytor's face. The teeth were there, along with the cheekbones. Most of the flesh had been savaged.

The body had been doubled over on itself. Raymond un-folded it, pulling arms and legs in the direction they should have grown. The entire abdomen was gone, revealing the glistening sinew of the spine. He stood up slowly.

"Are you sure it's Praytor?" Joe asked.

Tired of staring into the glare of headlights, Raymond walked over to speak to the sheriff. "It's Praytor. Or what's left of him."

"Shit." Joe shook his head. "How'd he die?"

"It's going to be hard to tell. Most of his internal organs are gone."

"Shit!" Joe wiped the perspiration from his forehead with his sleeve. "Shit!"

A long, mournful howl wafted out of the woods. Raymond stumbled as the sheriff jumped into him. At the sound of rustling in the bushes, both men drew their guns. The sound of the sheriff's driver locking the car doors was clear in the crisp night.

"Stay behind the headlights," Raymond said as Joe started to move forward. "We have the advantage here."

They stood side by side as they tried to penetrate the blackness of the swamp. The beam of Raymond's light bounced feebly off the trees. The rustling grew louder, followed by a piteous howl that seemed to last an eternity.

"It's over there in those bushes." Joe pointed toward a dense clump of black. "Shoot it."

Raymond put his hand on the sheriff's gun, pushing the barrel down. "What if it's a hunter or a kid? Or it could be Adele. She got loose, and I haven't been able to catch her."

"You're responsible for what happens here." Joe raised the barrel. "Tonight, I'll shoot first and worry about it later. If Adele is here, I mean to kill her." He cocked the gun.

Raymond pushed the barrel down again. "Stop it, Joe. I'll go check." He started toward the bush. Halfway there, he turned back. "If you shoot me in the back, I'll come back to haunt you."

The slight lift of Joe's barrel dropped and he lowered the hammer. "You're either a brave man or a fool. If that she bitch tries to jump you, I'm firin' and I'm gonna keep on firin' 'til she's dead."

Raymond continued toward the hackberry bush. He caught the reflected glint of two red eyes, and for a moment a balloon of irrational fear almost choked him. He forced his feet to move on, his gun out and ready. He would shoot her if he had to. A clean shot. So there would be no suffering. But he didn't want to kill her.

"Adele?" He spoke softly, so that Joe wouldn't hear. "Come out and let me help you."

The bushes quivered, as if she trembled inside them.

"Come on out." He spoke with kindness. "If you don't, men are going to keep hunting you until they kill you."

The bush shuddered more violently.

"Adele." He spoke as he would to a wild dog.

The eyes moved toward him, and a large red hound stepped free of the bushes. It cowered to the road and crawled on its belly, whining and groveling. A lead dragged behind it in the dirt.

"Here, boy," Raymond said, kneeling to stroke the terrified animal's head. "It's okay."

The dog pressed against his legs, whining. When he picked up the lead and stood, the dog lifted its head and howled, the sound echoing back from the thick trees of the swamp.

26

C<small>LIFTON</small> Hebert found the body." Joe sipped the coffee Pinkney had brought him from the café, his hand trembling so that the hot black liquid slopped over the side of the cup, burning his fingers.

"And where did Clifton go? He just left a dead body on the side of the road?" Raymond rubbed his jaw and felt the stubble of growth. "What was Clifton doing out on Section Line Road? He doesn't live anywhere near there."

"He was trying to round up his dogs." Joe leaned his head on his hand, elbow propped on his desk. "I'm too old for this job, Raymond. All I ever wanted to do was keep things safe 'til the war was over. Then I wanted to run for the state house, maybe see about keeping New Iberia's interests in the front seat of the government beef wagon." His hand was trembling so that he put the coffee down. "I never bargained for any of this."

"None of us did, Joe. Well, maybe Praytor did. What was he doing running through those woods alone?"

"Jolene LaRoche told me that when Father Michael found

Peat Moss, Praytor seemed determined to bring Adele in. Alone. Like he wouldn't be bested by a priest."

"Sounds just like Praytor." Raymond had trained himself to keep his feelings numb, and now he was glad for it. Praytor was a fool. Still, it was a gruesome way to go, and if no one else missed Praytor, his mother would. He sighed. "Before everyone goes off the deep end thinking it's the *loup-garou,* I want to point out that both Henri and Praytor had a lot of enemies. A lot of the same enemies. Praytor was hooked into Henri's business."

"That's supposed to mean what?" Joe sat up, forcing his back to straighten with a grimace.

"Two men with similar interests and enemies die in the same manner." Raymond said it slowly so the impact could sink in. "If a werewolf were out there, how would she target two men so much alike?"

"And the girl. Don't forget the girl."

"Peat Moss was uninjured. In fact, it would seem someone took care of the child. She'd been given food. Hardly the handiwork of a *loup-garou.*" He was reminded that the bread and cloth-wrapped grass were still in his jacket pocket. If Madame and Doc couldn't help him, he'd have to go to someone who could. Maybe the university in Baton Rouge.

Joe stood up and withdrew a dollar from his billfold. He handed the black man the money. "Pinkney, go get some soap. Those boys need a bath."

"Sure thing, Sheriff." Pinkney was out the door.

Joe walked over to where Raymond sat beside a potbellied stove. The two Bastion boys, fists gripped around the bars of their cell, listened to every word. "Raymond, I don't believe in *loup-garous.* I don't believe in spells and curses. But I do believe when a man takes on a job, he owes his boss some loyalty. You shoulda told me Adele was runnin' loose."

Raymond felt no compulsion to defend himself. "You're right. I should have."

"I ought to fire you." Joe held his gaze steady.

Raymond's estimation of the sheriff rose a notch. "You should. I would."

"Why didn't you tell me?"

Raymond tried to align the reasons, to give only the most important. "She was so sick and weak, I figured I'd find her before anyone realized she'd left Madame Louiselle's, and I was afraid you'd let it slip and start a panic."

Joe nodded. "My tongue wags sometimes."

"You talk to people. It's your nature."

"And you don't talk to anyone, Thibodeaux. You drift through life like a ghost. If you feel, nobody can tell it. Hell, Adele Hebert's the first thing you've shown any interest in since you got back from the war."

"Are you going to fire me?" Raymond suddenly realized how much he'd come to rely on his job. The force of his emotion surprised him. Florence was right. Adele had become his personal crusade. It didn't matter if she'd killed Henri and Praytor. She was a wild creature, acting on instinct. Acting without the restraint of civilization. Raymond knew what that felt like. After Antoine's death, he'd been wild in his pain. He'd done things, savage things, which were lauded in a time of war.

Joe didn't answer. He walked to the front window and looked out on the street. He stood staring out into the town.

From his own desk, Raymond could see that shops were open. Another day of business had begun. The latest war news was good. American troops were kicking ass all over Europe and Africa. The prediction was another five months and the boys would be coming home. That hope was reflected in a boom in spending. Those who had anything left were eager to buy new goods. Life was moving forward again. Maybe even for him. For such a long time now, he'd been outside time and place, a dead man still alive. Adele had become his mirror, showing him a reflection of half-life, and Florence had ignited his will to live.

"Joe, I'd like to stay."

Joe faced him, a silhouette against the window. "I'm not gonna fire you. You're a better lawman than I am. You're braver than most men here and folks respect that. Folks need more than respect, though, Raymond. You think I'm prone to gossipin'. I sit around with people and before long, we're swappin' a joke or two, and when I leave, maybe they aren't quite as afraid as they were before I got there. You fall short there, Raymond. You can chew on that while I go see if Doc is ready to do the autopsy on Praytor."

The front door closed on Joe, and Raymond sat with his hands flat on his desk. Joe spoke the truth, and Raymond had learned something about himself and the sheriff. He stood slowly, pain biting like a wild dog. It was another irony that though he had no compassion for Praytor's fate, he thought he might know what it felt like for teeth to rip into his body.

He stood and retrieved his hat. Clifton Hebert had "stumbled" upon Praytor's body, made a call to the sheriff's office, and then disappeared into the swamps with his dogs.

The murder scene was troubling to Raymond. The similarities in the attacks, the convenient way the bodies had been so savaged that cause of death was disguised, the fact that Praytor and Henri were business associates. Also troubling was that the hound Praytor had borrowed from Angola had been untouched in the attack. If Praytor had been coming out of the woods, the dog either pulling him or at his side, why had a so-called savage animal gone after Praytor instead of the hound? Predators were smart. They killed the weakest and easiest victim. The hound should have been killed first.

He got a rifle from the cabinet beside the cells.

"You goin' to kill that *loup-garou*?" Nathaniel Bastion asked.

Until the boy spoke, Raymond had forgotten the two were in the jail. "There's no such thing as the *loup-garou*." Raymond found a box of cartridges and picked them up, too.

"Who you gonna kill?" the boy asked.

"Hopefully, no one. I've had enough killing." He walked to the cell. "Where do you boys think your mama went?"

The older one, Caleb, shrugged. "Away from us. She'da left sooner, but Daddy would of caught her and brought her back. She says we're the spawn of Satan." He grinned. "I reckon that's somethin' to live up to."

Raymond studied both boys. "You boys are liars and hellions, but you're not beyond saving. You told Father Michael your daddy was meeting Adele Hebert down in the shed. You told him you saw her jump your father. None of that was true."

They looked at each other, delighted. Caleb turned a bland face to Raymond. "We never said that."

"You said you followed your daddy down to the shed and that he met Adele there for sex. Father Finley didn't make that up."

Caleb shook his head. "We never said that."

Raymond felt his patience unraveling. "Boys—"

The front door opened and John LeDeux walked in, hat in hand. He nodded at Raymond. "Hello, boys."

Raymond took a breath. "I'm sorry, LeDeux. I forgot about our appointment."

"Not to worry. I had a nice breakfast down at the café and figured your schedule had changed with Praytor's murder."

"Can we postpone this talk?" Raymond tried to hide his impatience. On the long list of things he needed to do, talking with a professor wasn't high up there.

"Maybe I could ride with you wherever you're going and talk on the way. Truth is, I have to leave for Baton Rouge after lunch, and I really need to speak with you first."

"I'm going into the swamps."

"All the better," John said. "Chula tells me that a bit of exposure to nature will make me less of an academic. She says it as if my profession is some kind of condition I should want to cure."

Raymond found it hard not to like the man. "It's up to you.

Maybe when you go back to the university you could take some-thing for me."

"Sure thing. Whatever I can do to help."

Raymond gave Caleb and Nathaniel a glare. "I'll be back, and when I get here, you boys have some explaining to do. I'd think you killed Praytor except you were both locked up."

"Maybe we turned into bats and flew out the bars." Caleb laughed and his brother joined in. "I had a taste for that old bas-tard!" He smacked his lips.

The boys were still laughing when Raymond stepped onto the street.

Florence sat on her front porch and watched the patrol car speed away. Raymond had a passenger, a man who, from a distance, looked like the professor courting Chula Baker. Good for Chula, finding a man who met her toe to toe. Folks were jealous of her because she had her own money, her own job, and her own mind. Chula lived in a manner that plainly said she didn't need or care what they thought.

The university man seemed a good match. She rocked the chair slowly with the balls of her feet. What kind of man was Raymond Thibodeaux? She had only a partial answer. Just when she thought she had Raymond pegged, he did something unex-pected. She'd learned things lately. Raymond cared for her. Cared enough to provide for her like a wife. She knew something about herself, too. She wanted Raymond's respect as well as his love. At the bonfire, he'd shown her what it felt like to legitimately share his affections. That taste had started a big hunger.

The old rocker creaked, reminding her of the long-ago fall days when she and her mother sat on their small front porch and the smell of the river came damp and clean on a strong breeze. They'd rocked side by side, talking about Florence's future, about the things that dangled just out of reach for her. Catholic school would lead to college, an education that would allow Florence the luxury of steady work. She'd wanted to be a teacher. Strange that she shared that dream with Adele.

When she'd been raped in the garden, everything had changed. Even though her mother had urged her to return to school, Florence wouldn't. She couldn't. She was no longer the pretty young girl favored by the nuns. A moment in time had stolen the future from her. Perhaps that was what drew her so forcefully to Raymond. Tragedy had changed both of their worlds irrevocably. She couldn't say if either of them would be able to overcome the past. She could only hope.

She pushed herself out of the rocker. It was a sign of old age that she was sitting out on her porch trying to make sense of life, when life wouldn't hold still long enough to examine it. She was only thirty-four but time was slipping away. She'd come to a place that required a decision.

To that end she went into the house and changed into a blue-dotted dress, the most conservative thing in her wardrobe. She didn't bother drawing lines down the backs of her legs to pretend she wore hose. She merely strapped on her black shoes and started walking—before she changed her mind. She had some money in a savings account, but most was buried. All together, it was enough to buy a house. Maybe in Lafayette or somewhere close. She'd find a job, something other than selling her body, and she'd wait for Raymond to court her proper. She'd meet him as his equal. Whatever it took, she could make this happen and leave behind the little girl crying in a garden.

The day was cool and brisk, and she took pleasure in walking through town. She passed the post office and hesitated. It might be nice to speak with Chula. On an impulse, Florence went into the post office.

"Florence," Chula said. She was behind a partition and she was alone. Her hair was pinned up in an untidy bun, her dress deliberately plain, but her smile was warm. "How may I help you?"

"I'd like my mail." Florence cleared her throat. "And to tell you thank you for last night. You treated me with kindness."

"And the same could be said for you." Chula came toward the counter, and Florence saw that Sarah Bastion clung to her skirt. Chula's hand went to the little girl's head. "She won't let me leave her sight, so I just brought her to work."

Florence studied the little girl. She didn't have to be a gypsy fortune-teller to see the child had endured suffering. Whatever went on at the Bastion plantation must have been awful. All of the children were scarred—the boys devils and the girl a mute. "She's a pretty little thing."

Chula picked up the child and swung her onto a hip. "She is that. I just wish she'd talk. She hasn't spoken a word since I've had her."

"Jolene's telling it around town that she was singing."

Chula hesitated, obviously censoring whatever she started to say. It amused Florence. Folks said Chula spoke her mind—another exaggeration about the postmistress. "Jolene was upset. She came tearing up to the house, hysterical. It's hard to know what she saw and what her mind created."

"That's a kind way of putting it."

Chula laughed. "I guess I'm not much good at diplomacy, but I should at least get credit for trying." She sat Sarah on the counter. "Jolene came into the house crazy as a run-over dog. I wouldn't put any stock in what she *thinks* she saw."

"None of it makes sense." Florence leaned against the counter. "You've known Raymond a long time."

Chula nodded. "We dated in high school. Turned out we were better friends than romantic partners. Truth is, Florence, I'll always have a tender place for Raymond. It's hurt me to see him suffer so."

Florence took a big breath. "I want him to love me. Do you think he will?"

Chula settled the child on the counter as she sorted another handful of mail. "I saw a difference in Raymond last night, before the sheriff came to get him. I saw—" She smiled. "I saw just a hint of the man I used to know. I think you're good for him, whether he likes it or not."

"That gives me hope." Florence stood up tall. "Thank you, Chula. I saw Raymond headed out of town. Do you know where he went?"

"John and Raymond have gone to hunt for Clifton Hebert." Chula shook her head. "Those dogs of his worry me. They could tear a man apart."

"And Adele?"

Chula stroked Sarah's hair. "If you'd seen her, Florence. She was so weak she couldn't hold up her head. Like you say, none of it makes sense. How could a dying woman kidnap and then care for a small child? Where would she find the strength? And to kill Praytor Bless." She shook her head.

"Folks say Praytor had a heart condition, but that's not true. His mama got him out of the army somehow." Florence felt a chill touch her bare arms and she rubbed them.

"Only thing wrong with Praytor's heart was greed."

Florence was surprised to hear Chula voice her own thoughts. "He was a conniving man. He had his finger in a lot of folks' business."

"No matter what he had, he always wanted more," Chula said. "Listen, John has to go back to Baton Rouge today, but he'll be back on the weekend. Why don't you plan on having dinner with us Saturday night? I'll invite Raymond, too."

Florence looked to see if Chula was joshing her. An invitation to the Baker home for dinner was not a social event; it was a political statement. Chula's generosity would cost her in the town. "It might not be a good idea for me to come," Florence said. "Lots of people don't think I should socialize with—"

"*Lots of people* let Henri and Praytor walk around town, doing business, intimidating people all over the place. You know what, I say *lots of people* can kiss my ass."

Chula's wide smile drew a matching one from Florence. "That's bold talk, but you'll pay for the rest of your life."

"I'm not so sure I'm staying here."

Florence felt a chill touch her. Only that morning she'd decided to leave New Iberia. "Where will you go?"

"I'm not sure." Chula kissed Sarah's head. "Somewhere safe for this little one."

Florence understood then that Chula had no intention of giving the child back to Marguerite. She nodded her agreement with that decision. "You're educated. You can go anywhere."

Chula nodded. "It'll break my mother's heart, but I think she already knows. I can't imagine belonging anywhere else. But talking with John has shown me that I don't really belong here, anyway. I grew up here. I live here. But I don't belong."

Chula didn't have to explain it. Florence understood. Sometimes tragedy damaged a person's roots so deeply that they could never take hold again.

"Come to dinner," Chula urged.

"Okay." Florence was still reluctant. "Be sure Raymond knows you've invited me."

"I'll tell him the plan." Chula lifted Sarah off the counter and to the floor. "Now I'd better get to work. I've got mail to sort." She was about to swing around with the child when the bell over the door rang.

Florence stepped back from the counter and turned to leave. She inhaled sharply. The ghost of Adele Hebert walked into the post office. It took only a few seconds for Florence to recognize Bernadette Matthews, Adele's sister, but she was so startled she took two involuntary steps back from the approaching woman.

The three women looked at each other in uncomfortable silence that was broken by the sound of Sarah Bastion wetting the floor.

27

SUNLIGHT flashed through the trees, blinding Raymond and then dissipating as he hit another stretch of road with dense foliage. The world of shadow and the world of light. He'd been caught between, in limbo, but events had forced him through to the other side.

John rode in the passenger seat, quiet and thoughtful. Raymond appreciated the other man's patience, his control.

"What did you want to talk about?" Raymond finally asked. They were almost to the site where Praytor's body had been found. John hadn't complained about the breakneck speed, but Raymond slowed the car. He had no idea what he hoped to find there. He'd searched the area twice already. There had to be something that linked Praytor and Henri to their killer.

John cleared his throat. "I heard some talk in the café this morning. Folks blame you for this. They think you've been cursed by the *loup-garou*. They think Adele Hebert put a spell on you, and you set her free."

Raymond considered ignoring this, but he found himself answering. There was something about John, his willingness to listen, his easy confidence. "Adele is a contradiction. In all this time, I still don't know who she is. Her sister calls her a whore, yet a convicted murderer tells me she's a saint."

"Which is it?" John asked.

Raymond remembered Armand Dugas's words—that a person who impugned Adele had something to gain from it. "I'd come closer to believing the convict. He had nothing to—" He stopped. Bernadette had certainly gone a long way to paint Adele in the worst light. Because of childhood jealousies? Raymond slowed the car. What did Bernadette have to gain? That was the answer he should be seeking.

"What's wrong?" John shifted so that he leaned against the passenger door.

"Probably nothing." Raymond searched the woods that had once again closed around the car. "It's just strange that Adele's sister seems to *want* Adele charged with murder. Both Bernadette and Praytor seemed determined that Adele would pay for Henri's death. I was wondering why."

"That's peculiar."

Raymond turned off the heater in the car. The hot air was annoying. "Bernadette gains nothing that I can tell. Neither Adele nor Bernadette benefits from Henri's death. Only Marguerite benefits, financially. I would've said Praytor Bless might benefit, but he's dead. I'd begun to believe Praytor was behind this."

Sunlight dappled the front seat, and John shifted again to block the light from his eyes. "Both Henri and Praytor are killed by the *loup-garou,* and the town wants to blame it on a half-starved woman who's delirious with fever. It's so much easier for all of us if something evil is out there because then we don't have to look at how capable we are of violent acts, of murder. And worse."

Raymond's fingers clutched the steering wheel. He drove through a canopy of trees and then into sunlight that almost blinded him. The scent of pine, so clean and pungent, filled the car, and from far away he heard the cry of a hawk. "What are you saying, John? Say it plain."

John sat forward, surprised at Raymond's tone. "The belief that each of us contains the primitive, the wild. The duality. The wolf within. It's part of my reason for wanting to write the book."

Raymond could feel the sweat beading on his upper lip even though the air coming in the open window was crisp. "Tell me about your book."

"It's a blend of psychiatry and anthropology. The human animal creates myth and legend to explain the duality of our nature. We're both domesticated and primitive. It's the eternal struggle. In religious terms, it would be good versus evil. The werewolf legends are just examples where the primitive side has won. We recognize ourselves in the wolf, and it terrifies us."

The dream image of Adele, cast in the carrion glow of the moon, came back to Raymond. She was alluring, exciting. And primitive. Raymond reached into his jacket pocket for his cigarettes. His fingers found the crust of bread the priest had given him and the purple cloth of grass that he'd stuffed in his pocket when he left Doc's house.

He grabbed the pack and matches. He lit a cigarette and tipped the pack toward John, forcing his brain to slow and think. He thought of Antoine, and how his brother's death had changed him. He'd killed and killed and killed, a primitive creature savaging all who got close. He'd still be killing if he hadn't been wounded. The government had given him medals for his actions, but Raymond knew he'd not acted out of bravery or nobility. He'd killed out of pain. The wolf had taken over, and Raymond knew he could never afford to let that happen again.

John lit a cigarette, his brow furrowed. He spoke slowly. "Raymond, are you okay?"

"Yeah, why?"

"You're bleeding."

Raymond touched his right ear. When he looked at his fingers, they were covered in blood. "I know Adele didn't kill either of those men. I can't prove it, and I can't explain how a woman so sick she couldn't hold up her own head is running wild through the town. Adele is not a *loup-garou,* and if I can't prove that, she's going to be shot on sight like a mad dog."

John pulled a handkerchief from his pocket and offered it. "I wish there was something I could do to help."

Raymond wiped the blood from his jaw and steered the car around a sharp curve. "What I have to figure out is who would want to pin this on Adele. I'm positive someone is giving her something, but I just can't prove it."

"What would they give her?" John leaned forward, the cigarette dangling from his fingers.

"I thought I had it figured out." Raymond pulled the bread and the bundled grass from his pocket and put them on the seat. "This is what I need to have examined at the university. Maybe someone there can tell me what that is."

John studied the bread before he unwrapped the purple cloth. Raymond drove for what seemed like a mile before John spoke.

"Whatever this grass is, there's some of it in this bread."

Raymond kept driving for a moment. "I thought it was the same, too, but I don't know what it is." He began to slow.

"It would take someone with a microscope and more knowledge of botany than I possess to be able to say for positive."

"Can you find that person for me? If I can figure out what she was given, I might be able to find out who gave it to her."

John carefully rewrapped the two items. "Raymond, I can't tell you the who, but I may know how. The werewolf legend comes from French history." John threw his butt out the window. "Between 1520 and 1630 there were over thirty thousand werewolf trials in France alone. Seemingly normal people were afflicted with behavior attributed to lycanthropy. They had tremendous strength."

"I appreciate the history lesson, but—"

John held up his hand. "Just listen. Many of the residents of these isolated villages were near starvation. A type of mold, ergot, infected the rye. This mold is a hallucinogen. The person under the influence develops delusions and what's been described as su-perhuman strength. They ate bread tainted with—"

Raymond slowed the car to a stop. He turned to John, a terri-ble suspicion beginning to grow. "Where does that mold grow?"

"I haven't researched it, but probably almost anywhere there's a damp climate."

Raymond cut the wheel sharply, sending the car bumping into the ditch on the opposite side of the road. He spun the steering wheel again and punched the gas. The patrol car straightened and hit a stretch of washboard that jarred both men almost off the seat.

John righted himself. "I gather our plans have changed."

"I know part of what happened now." Raymond pressed the gas pedal to the floor. The car bounced over the rutted road. "And you're going to help me figure out the rest."

Sarah Bastion's shrill screams echoed off the beaded lumber walls of the post office. Chula tried to cradle the child in her arms, but Sarah fought her with surprising strength. Flight seemed to be her only thought, and she was determined to escape.

"Can I help you?" Florence asked, her hand on the drop-down countertop.

"No." Chula wrapped her arms around the little girl and picked her up. "Excuse me." She carried Sarah into the back of the post office where the bags of mail remained to be sorted. She had no idea what to do for the child, how to help her, or what had caused such a fit. One moment Sarah had been clinging to her skirt, seem-ingly content, and the next she'd been hysterical.

"Sarah," she said softly, "it's okay." Chula gave up trying to pry Sarah's fingers loose and simply held her tightly. "You're safe with me. What's wrong?"

The screams stopped and gradually the crying lessened. Chula rocked her back and forth gently, humming softly against her hair that smelled of Ivory soap.

Bernadette's voice came clearly into the back room. "That child needs a spankin'. Whip some manners into her. Always pokin' into folks' bidness, spyin' and whinin'.'"

Chula gritted her teeth. The Bastion children had seen enough brutality to last a lifetime. If Chula had her way, Sarah would never have a hand raised to her again.

"The little girl's life has been tough lately." Florence lazily drawled the words. "If a whipping would do any good, I might just try to pound some compassion into you."

Bernadette's voice was bitter. "I came here to get my mail, not be smart-lipped by a whore."

Chula peeked around the doorjamb. The last thing New Iberia needed now was a fistfight between two women, and Florence looked ready to snatch Bernadette bald-headed. She turned her attention back to the child.

"Sarah, I have to go out there." Chula felt as if she were battering the child. Sarah was in such a state that she was almost rigid. "I'll be right back."

Chula walked to the door.

"Please!"

The one-word cry was electric. It bounced over the hardwood floors and struck Chula like a spear. She turned back to look at Sarah. The little girl stood with her hands clenched at her side, her eyes burning.

"Don't leave me!" Sarah ran to Chula and threw her arms around her legs and held on. "Don't leave me! Please don't leave me!"

Chula balanced against the doorjamb. She couldn't move her legs. The child held her in a viselike grip. At the counter Florence and Bernadette were watching. Florence bit her lip in sympathy, and Bernadette looked as if she'd been dipped in flour.

"She can talk." Florence's smile stretched wide.

Bernadette ran out of the post office. The bell jangled as the door slammed with enough force to rattle the glass panes.

"What devil got under her skirt?" Florence asked, humor in her voice.

"I don't know and I don't care. Florence, can I press you into working the counter?" Chula lifted the child with her. "The mail is sorted alphabetically. Just go through until you find the name."

Chula strode to the back door of the post office and stepped out into the cool November air. She and Claudia had set two overturned Coca-Cola crates under a cypress tree. She carried Sarah there and eased her down.

"Now that I know you can talk, you're going to have to tell me some things." She kept her voice easy but firm. "Do you know where your mother went, Sarah?"

The little girl shook her head. "Don't come back."

Chula wasn't certain if Sarah was saying her mother wouldn't come back or that she didn't want her to. What had terrified Chula was Bernadette Matthews. Sarah was afraid of almost everything, but Chula had seen her wet herself twice. Once when Clifton Hebert and his dogs came out of the woods and again when Bernadette had shown up at the post office.

She grasped Sarah's hands and pulled them free of her skirt so that she could kneel and face the little girl. "Sarah, I'll do everything in my power so that you can stay with me. I'll fight to keep you, and I won't let anyone else hurt you."

Sarah's grip loosened.

"Why are you so afraid of Mrs. Matthews?"

Sarah frowned. Her gaze focused beyond Chula to the back door of the post office. "Adele." She said the name softly and began to pull away.

"Oh, Sarah!" Chula pulled her close and held her, rubbing her back and kissing the top of her head. "I'm so sorry for all the bad things. I'm so sorry." She took the child's hand. "You're going to be safe, Sarah. I won't ever let another person hurt you." She tightened her grip for a moment on the child's hand. "No one will harm you again."

Sarah pulled her hand free of Chula's. "Adele!" She ran toward the alley beside the post office.

Chula started to follow and stopped. Adele stood in the alley. Her torn clothing revealed limbs that were painfully thin. Long red scratches covered her legs and arms, and her face was gaunt. Her dark eyes, almost hidden by the tangle of her thick black curls, were focused on Sarah Bastion.

"No! Sarah!" Chula made a dive for the child, scooped her up, and ran toward home.

28

THE patrol car flew along the roads. Raymond held the wheel, fighting the sandy road and the sense that time was slipping away from him. Things had begun to shift into focus. There was only one person in town with a direct connection to France. While the Acadians all came from French blood, it was diluted, mixed. But the Mandeville blood was pure, and he knew this because Marguerite Mandeville Bastion made it a point for everyone to know. Marguerite was the person in the parish most likely to know of the ergot fungus and the gruesome history of the hallucinogen. Marguerite would benefit most from Henri's death. But it wasn't Marguerite who fed the fungus to Adele. That had to be Bernadette, who was living above her means with her man gone. The two women had conspired together—Marguerite to be rid of Henri and get his money, and Bernadette to punish Adele.

In his mind Raymond walked through Adele's house, taking in again the smell of strong cleaner. She'd been sick with fever. Her babies had died, and she'd buried them herself in the swamp beside her dead sister. Adele had been obsessed with grief and death, yet her home was immaculate.

John leaned against the car door, seemingly relaxed. He didn't ask, waiting instead for Raymond to reveal whatever he chose.

"I searched Adele's home," Raymond said. "I went through everything. There wasn't food of any kind in the house."

John picked up the cigarettes from the seat. He had to lean over and protect the match to get a light. Leaning back against the seat, he gave Raymond his full attention. "What are you thinking?"

"Adele has no friends, and Bernadette hates her. The person who cleaned her house was removing evidence."

Raymond navigated a sharp turn, almost losing the car in a deep pocket of sand. When he was straight again, he asked, "What happened to the people who ate the fungus? Did it wear off while they were in prison?" He could keep Adele safe—away from Bernadette and everyone else—until she came to her senses.

John drew on the cigarette and tapped the ash out the window. "At that time, there weren't trials, like now. The people accused were executed. Hanged and burned at the stake."

Raymond pushed the accelerator to the floor. "We have to find Marguerite. Now."

Michael checked to be sure his collar was crisp and straight. Throughout the night and early morning, he'd come to one conclusion. Being a hero was every bit as good as he'd dreamed. He'd found Peat Moss—stumbled upon her, actually—and he'd told everyone the truth of how it happened. Yet he was viewed as the man who'd saved a child from the jaws of the *loup-garou*. The aura of fame that he'd craved for so long had been settled upon his head by happenstance. God did work in mysterious ways.

He heard footsteps in the hall, and he gave one last look in the chifforobe mirror. A series of his parishioners had been by all morning to congratulate him. Not just the middle-aged women, but the men and some of the younger people. Their view of him had changed, now catching the reflected glory that God had blessed him with when He'd sent him to save Peat Moss.

He opened the bedroom door, smiling, prepared to receive another congratulation. His grip on the door tightened, and he felt the air leave his lungs. He tried to shut the door, but he wasn't quick enough.

Adele Hebert pushed past him, bringing the smell of dead things into the room. Her body was savaged by the thorns and brambles of the swamps, and her face was obscured by a tangle of wild black curls. She was both exotic and terrifying, and Michael fell back from her.

She closed the door, shutting off his only means of escape by leaning against it.

"Holy Father, bless me and watch over me." The prayer came to his lips automatically. Her gaze bored into him, and he fell silent. She circled him, moving with a grace and confidence that belied her sorry physical state. He could see bruises that must have gone to the bone, cuts and lacerations crusted with mud and infection. It was a miracle that Adele was able to stand and walk, much less move with the fluidity of a panther. She was more beast than human.

"Adele." He spoke softly. This was the second time she'd shown herself to him. While everyone in town had hunted her for a week, she'd allowed only him to see her. She'd brought Peat Moss to him. Adele had played a role in God's plan for him, and perhaps his work wasn't finished. Over the past ten years he'd prayed for a miracle. When Rosa Hebert had developed the stigmata, he'd felt that God had personally answered his pleas. Now here was a second chance.

He felt the pinch of his left shoe on a blister. The pain was ordinary and familiar. A little reminder from God that this woman standing before him was just another wayward soul, an ordinary human in terrible trouble. "Adele, everyone is hunting you. They think you killed Praytor. And Henri. But you didn't harm the child. You didn't hurt Peat Moss."

Her head cocked, as if she were trying to comprehend the real meaning of his words. The fact that she hadn't attacked gave him confidence. Maybe, like Rosa, she'd come so he could save and protect her.

"Adele." He took a step toward her. "Let me help you."

She faced him squarely, the fire reflected in eyes that glittered yellow, then red. "My sister," she whispered, her voice hoarse and unearthly.

Michael faltered. She sounded inhuman, as if some being spoke from deep within her. "Rosa?" He stumbled over the name.

"Help me!" Adele took a step toward him.

The only sound in the old house was the crackle of the fire and a board moaning in the hallway. Like something creeping down the hall.

Michael could stand it no longer. "Colista!" He broke for the door. When he gained the hallway, he slammed the door shut behind him and twisted the key in the lock. "Colista! Call the sheriff!" He backed away from the door just as Adele's body slammed into the other side. The door shook, but held. Michael backed away, turned, and ran toward the safety of the kitchen and the telephone.

29

FLORENCE tapped her fingernails on the countertop. An hour had passed and there was no sign of Chula—or anyone else. Something was happening south of town—she'd seen Joe Como flying down the street in his car and then Pinkney running, his old coat flapping behind him like a tattered ghost. He'd looked like he'd seen something resurrect and walk from the cemetery. By the time she'd gotten out from behind the counter and run to the street in her heels, he was too far gone to flag down.

She was stuck at the post office, waiting.

Impatient and bored, she walked outside, listening. She could almost hear a faint buzz in the air, a charge, like before a lightning strike. The heel of her shoe caught in a sidewalk crack, making her stumble. "Damn it," she mumbled, bending down to check her shoe. When she looked up, a monarch butterfly fluttered so close she could have reached out and touched it. She backed away from the butterfly, the thud of her heart like a hammer. It was November. Butterflies were long gone from the area.

Something bad had happened.

That was the only explanation for Pinkney's race down the

street and Chula's unexplained absence. Florence had checked all over the postal building and out back, but Chula and the child had simply disappeared.

There was a telephone in the post office and she picked it up, her hand shaking. There was no answer at the sheriff's office. Her voice shook as she asked to be connected to Chula Baker's home. Counting the rings, she tried to swallow the dread that lodged in her throat like a thick scream.

"Hello." Thomasina Baker's voice was precise but harried.

"This is Florence Delacroix calling from the post office. Is Chula there?" Florence forced a calm note in her tone.

"Damn it to hell, I was supposed to call you. We have an emergency here, Florence. Sarah Bastion is . . . ill. Chula had to bring her home, and we're waiting on a call from the doctor. Can you manage the post office a bit longer? Chula asked me to call and tell you that Claudia should be there any minute, but I've been running around like a scalded dog."

"Is Sarah okay?" Florence felt some of her apprehension ease. "She was talking earlier."

"We're not sure. She saw Adele and now she won't stop crying."

"Adele? Here? At the post office?" Florence looked behind her at the back door. It was half ajar, like she'd left it when she went outside to look. If Adele was roaming the streets, insane, and she decided to come in . . .

"Joe Como just left here to go to Father Finley's. Adele was there, last account."

"At the priest's home?"

"That's what Pinkney said."

"And Raymond?" If Joe had Adele cornered, Raymond needed to be there.

"He's off with Professor LeDeux. Neither said where they were going."

The sound of the back door opening at the post office made Florence almost drop the telephone. Claudia walked in, the empty mail sack slung over her back. She gave Florence a surprised look.

"Thank you, Mrs. Baker. I have to go now." Florence hung up the telephone. "Chula's at home. Sarah is sick." She didn't bother to explain anything else as she rushed out the front door. Ten yards from the post office she stopped and removed her shoes. Her bare feet dug into the dirt as she ran toward home and her car.

Louisiana's nod at the coming winter was scattered in drifts along the narrow road. The wild sycamores, a few yellow leaves still clinging, glistened an eerie pale white in the morning sun. Raymond hit a pile of leaves at eighty, blowing them over the window and blinding him for a brief moment. His foot never eased off the accelerator.

Raymond took a sharp curve and entered town at breakneck speed. He didn't slow. The streets were dead. No traffic, no one out and stirring. He crossed the Teche and headed north. He had the sense that he was too late, that time was slipping beneath the wheels of the car faster than he could drive. His fingers cramped from his grip on the steering wheel, but the pain balanced the hot wires that stabbed his back and hip. Doc Fletcher had told him to remain in bed, that movement might make the shrapnel shift closer to his spine. That wasn't an option.

Raymond pulled up in front of Bernadette Matthews's home. Both men got out of the car, and Raymond hesitated. "Maybe you should wait here."

"Are you expecting trouble?" John asked.

"Maybe." Raymond didn't know what he truly expected. The house looked empty. There wasn't a sign of any of the children.

"I'd rather go with you then." John's tone was reason itself. "It might be helpful if I knew what to anticipate."

"Adele's sister Bernadette lives here." Raymond was aware

how rash his actions were. He couldn't prove anything—he was acting on instinct.

He took the steps two at a time. John followed close behind him. Raymond pounded on the door.

"It's Deputy Thibodeaux. Open this door or I'll break it down!" When he heard nothing, he kicked the door as hard as he could. The cypress, a wood as tough and strong as the swamp, held solid. Raymond kicked it again and felt the jolt of pain sharp as a blade in his spine and radiating down his leg. It infuriated him.

"Open the door or I'll burn the house down!"

"Hey! You!" A boy appeared out of the woods, a rifle in his hand. "Quit kickin' my house, you!" He called over his shoulder. "Hey, Stella, come out the woods and help me. Some men tryin' to tear our door down."

A young girl appeared at the edge of the woods about twenty yards from the boy. She held a book in one hand and used the other to shade her eyes. Raymond recognized them from his previous visit to the house.

"Mama's gone," the girl called out as she came toward them. "Come back later. She'll be home then."

Raymond was ready to charge into the house when he felt John's hand on his shoulder. "Don't frighten the children," he cautioned. "If you want answers, those kids may have them."

"I'm Deputy Thibodeaux," Raymond said. "Can we go inside and talk?"

The girl and boy exchanged glances. "Mama told us to stay outside today."

"Just for a chat," John said easily as the girl came closer.

Raymond saw the book in her hand and remembered his conversation with Dugas. "We're trying to help your aunt Adele," he said. "Maybe you know something that will help us help her."

"Well, sure." The girl came forward. "Mama said Aunt Adele was in big trouble."

"She is that," Raymond said as he stepped aside for the girl to open the door. They entered together. A foul odor like decomposing seafood came from somewhere in the house, and Raymond wondered if Bernadette had left shrimp heads in the trash.

"Stella, what's your brother's name?" John talked to the children in the front room while Raymond walked back to the kitchen. The contrast between Bernadette's home and Adele's was startling. The counter and sink were loaded with dirty dishes, some growing mold. The trash can overflowed with things that Raymond didn't want to examine.

When he opened the cabinets, he found mostly empty shelves. A bag of cornmeal was alive with weevils. Several jars of what looked like tomatoes held a strange yellow cast. Raymond couldn't help but wonder what the children were eating. He had the urge to swipe everything from the shelves and watch it hit the floor in a satisfying crash of broken glass.

He heard the murmur of John's voice and realized the professor had developed a rapport with the children. Shifting the preserved tomatoes, he found a glass container far in the back. He pulled it from the shelf and examined it in the sun. The meal contained black and purple particles. Like the bread. Here was the link that firmly tied Bernadette to the bread, but still no evidence that would mark her as the person who deliberately contrived to frame her sister for murder.

With the jar in his hand, he walked toward the front room and was nearly gagged by the smell coming from the back of the house. "You okay?" he asked John.

"We're fine here. Are you ready to go?" John's eagerness to depart was evident in his voice.

"I'm going to check that smell."

"Mama said not to go back there!" The boy's voice was panicked, but Raymond ignored him. He heard John's reply, his soothing voice.

Clutching the jar, Raymond stopped outside the bedroom

door, which was locked with a padlock. Concern at what he might find on the other side made him hesitate. Bernadette Matthews, in her jealous misery, was capable of anything. It was possible that, at last, he'd find Adele.

He walked into the front room where John sat with the girl, going over a book. Stella was absorbed in relaying the story, but the boy watched him, wary.

"I'm going to get the tire tool to open the door."

"Mama say to stay out that room!" The boy rose to his feet.

"It's okay," Raymond said. "I have to do this, son. John, maybe it would be better if you took the children outside." He handed the professor the jar of meal as he ushered them outside.

Leaves crunched beneath Raymond's feet as he went to the car. John took the children twenty yards from the house to a tree where a swing hung. Raymond could see that the professor spoke with animation, moving his arm in a large circle. As Raymond returned to the house, he could hear the girl's clear voice talking rapidly about some character from the book. Raymond closed the door behind him as he went back inside.

The wood splintered as he pried the hasp loose. He pushed the door open slowly. The odor was like a wall. He heard it then. The buzzing of insects, a sound that haunted his dreams from the carnage of war. Fighting the memory and the smell, Raymond stepped into the room. His gaze fell on the bed. The body of Marguerite Bastion in the first stages of decomposition riveted his gaze.

Michael mumbled the "Hail Mary" over and over, trying to focus his mind on the words and shut out thoughts of Adele. She was in his room now, the door locked tight from the outside and wooden shutters nailed over the window. Even sitting at the kitchen table he could hear her fingernails clawing at the thick oak panels. If he let his imagination wander, he could feel the flesh of her fingertips tearing, the searing pain of cuticles rubbed raw. He gripped the edge of the table until the cup of hot tea that Colista had prepared rattled dangerously.

"Father Michael." Colista's voice was soft. "The sheriff just pulled up. He's got Pinkney with him."

"And Raymond?"

Colista craned to look out the kitchen window. "No, sir. Only Pinkney."

Michael had pinned his hopes of controlling Adele on Raymond. For some reason the deputy had formed a bond with Adele. He'd protected her. Without him to intervene, Michael felt certain that Joe would simply shoot Adele. Joe would feel no need to try to take a foaming, bloodied, mad woman in alive.

"I'll bring the sheriff." Colista hurried to the door.

To quiet the trembling of his hands, Michael sipped the tea, which was heavily laced with brandy. Laced, hell, Colista had poured the teacup more than half full of the fiery liquor. He took a deep breath and drained it. He had to get himself together. Warmth surged into his stomach and he stood, his legs steady. When Colista led Joe and a wild-eyed Pinkney into the kitchen, Michael met them with a firm handshake.

"She's locked in my bedroom," Michael said.

"Then she's contained?" The relief in Joe's face was almost comical.

The sound of a body slamming into wood echoed down the hall, followed by a howl of rage. Colista, who'd hovered in the hallway, dashed across the kitchen to the sink.

"For the moment," Michael said. "She's working at the door pretty good and if she manages to loosen the hinges, she could take it down."

"Lordy, lordy!" Pinkney edged toward the door. "That little gal hardly looked strong enough to turn a knob."

Joe glanced at the teacup on the table, and Michael asked Colista to pour the sheriff a cup of tea. "Make it exactly the way you made mine," he told her. "And make Pinkney a cup, too." He gave Colista a smile. "Dutch courage. It may be the only thing we have." Whether it was the brandy or the fruit of his prayers, Michael had found a bit of steadiness.

Colista made the tea and put the cups on the table. The sounds of rage and fury echoed down the hall as the three men drank without saying a word.

"Where's Raymond?" Michael finally asked.

"Fired. Or he will be as soon as he gets back. He's up and disappeared again." Joe kept his gaze on his cup.

"We might need him here." Michael kept his tone level.

"If it weren't for Raymond and his high-handed shenanigans, we wouldn't be here *to* need him. Adele would be locked in a cell."

Anger made Joe's voice rough, and Michael understood his frustration with the deputy. Raymond acted as if he had all the answers. He never bothered to explain any of his actions, which were often rash. Adele would be safely locked away in a mental institution or the state prison were it not for Raymond. Joe was right about that.

"I see your point, but Raymond has a bond with Adele. He might be able to reason with her. I'm afraid if we go in there and try to take her, you'll have to kill her."

Joe sighed. He met Michael's gaze. "Have you ever thought she might be better off dead?" He leaned forward. "There's a crowd growing outside. They were down at the sheriff's office when you called. Some of 'em are friends of Praytor, though I didn't know that he had friends. Others are simple folk who're scared senseless. Once they hear Adele is here, in this house, they'll come in and get her."

Michael knew the three of them couldn't stop a mob. "You're afraid they'll hang her?"

"Worse. I'm afraid they'll burn her." Joe didn't flinch as he spoke. He held Michael's gaze. "That's supposed to be the way to kill a *loup-garou* and stop it from passing the curse on to others.

It's the evil eye they're afraid of, Father. The plan is to catch her, put a flour sack on her head so she can't look at them, and then burn her."

"That's barbaric!" Michael pushed back from the table and stood. "We can't allow that to happen."

Joe got up and walked to the window. "Lettie at the telephone exchange has been busy since you called to tell me Adele was here." He pointed down the street. "Look what's comin' and then you tell me that a bullet wouldn't be a kinder death."

30

THE Matthews children were quiet in the backseat as Raymond drove to town. "Where's your mother?" he asked. The camaraderie John had developed with them had disappeared as soon as Raymond insisted they get in the car.

"Bernadette may be in danger." He wasn't trying to intimidate the children. If Bernadette wasn't involved in the murder of Henri, Praytor, and now Marguerite, then she might easily be the next victim. "If you know where your mother is, you need to tell me." Raymond watched the children in the rearview mirror.

"Gone," Stella answered.

She was probably eleven or twelve. Raymond met her foxy eyes in the mirror. She was frightened but determined not to show it. He admired that.

"Gone where?" he asked more gently.

She shook her head, and Raymond couldn't tell if she didn't know or refused to tell. He glanced at the boy who sat beside her. He was maybe eight years old, his dark eyes alert. "Son, where's your father?"

"Gone," the girl said.

"I was speaking to your brother." He had to find Bernadette before more blood was shed. If Bernadette had Adele, Bernadette would kill her. Florence had told him what Bernadette told Father Michael—that death would be a blessing for Adele. More so for Bernadette, if she was guilty.

He focused on the boy, who seemed more willing to talk. "Son, I need to find your pa. Right now." It was possible that the missing Mr. Matthews might know where to find his wife.

John turned in the passenger seat so that he could face the children. "If both your parents have abandoned you, you'll become wards of the state and go to the orphanage in Baton Rouge."

The girl's lip quivered. "You can't do that."

"No, I can't," John said. "But he can." He pointed to Raymond. "And you'd better believe he will. Now where's your father? I know you don't believe it, but we're trying to help you."

"He left us, him, 'bout tree month ago." The boy's accent was thicker than the girl's. "Mama'll be back though. We aren't 'bandoned."

"Where is she?" John asked. "No more foolishness."

"She go this mornin'. Took Adrian, Charles, Letha, and Joann. Lef' me and Stella."

Raymond drove fast, but he watched John and the children in the rearview mirror. The last time he'd been at Bernadette Matthews's home she hadn't had a car. Which meant she was driving Marguerite's.

"Did she say where she was going?" John pulled a packet of Juicy Fruit gum from his pocket and offered the children a stick. The boy took one without hesitation, tearing off the wrapper and cramming it into his mouth. The girl was slower, but she took a piece also.

"She didn't say. She don't tell us her business." The girl answered before she popped the gum in her mouth, as if her grudging reply paid for the treat.

"Why did your father leave? Did he find work over in Houma?" John kept it casual.

The boy's tone was matter-of-fact. "He just lef', him. Say he's never lookin' back at us. Say he's filled up with craziness."

"Shut up!" the girl hissed at her brother. "You keep flappin' your lips, they'll take us away for sure!"

"That's not true." Raymond spoke softly. He didn't understand how it was possible that the children would want to stay in the Matthews's home, but their desperate desire to stay was plain. "I'll do everything I can to find your father. I promise you that."

"He won't take us." The girl was bitter. "He says we're not his."

"I'm sure your father was angry when he said it." The answer to several questions was close, and Raymond edged toward it. "I guess your father was upset because your mother spent so much time at the Bastion plantation." The Bastion boys had said Henri was meeting someone in a tractor shed, a woman. Caleb and Nathaniel had deliberately lied, to lead Raymond and others to think the woman he was meeting was Adele, but now he knew it had to be Bernadette.

He couldn't fathom Bernadette's reasons for interest in Henri. He remembered the crystal knickknacks, the niceties of a home with an absent man. Financial would be his guess. And somewhere along the way, Bernadette and Marguerite had gone from competitors to conspirators. A man like Henri often drew his enemies together against him. "How often did your ma work at the Bastions?"

"Mama went sometimes in the evening to help Mrs. Bastion," Stella said. "Daddy said she should stay home, but Mama said she needed the money 'cause Daddy wasn't always working." Stella looked down at her lap. "Mrs. Bastion gave me the books. She gave Vincent a gun. She said we were good children. She's so pretty and . . . different. She said she'd teach me how to be a lady."

"Where're the rest of the kids?" Raymond asked.

"At Francine's." Stella spoke as if she were exhausted. "Mama took them there because of the smell in the house."

"But she left you two? All by yourself in a house with—" He broke off the sentence.

"Mama told us to play outside. She said to get our toys and books and stay out the house. She said she'd come back and clean up the dead fish." The girl's concern was growing. "She should've been back. She's been gone hours."

They'd reached the outskirts of the town, and Raymond slowed, checking his impulse to rush. The information he was obtaining was worth taking a bit of time. "Your mother and Mrs. Bastion must have been good friends?"

Stella nodded. "Mama said Mrs. Bastion was a generous woman. She gave Mama a beautiful necklace. Gold." Her hands went to her neck, as if her fingers could magically weave the necklace. "Mama said it was a reward for all her hard work, and Mrs. Bastion was going to give us a lot of money. After the wedding."

Raymond forced his fingers to relax on the wheel. If he was too eager, the girl would back away. He remembered something Pinkney had told him, some gossip from the café where Praytor was talking about who would marry Marguerite. She was the richest woman in town was how Praytor had described her. No doubt Praytor thought he was lined up to share that wealth.

"I'll bet your mother and Mrs. Bastion and Praytor Bless were all good friends." Raymond spoke casually.

Stella leaned forward, pushing her face toward the front seat. "They were. Mrs. Bastion said she was going to marry him. I was going to be in the wedding. In a pink dress. Brand-new."

He nodded. "You'd be a pretty bridesmaid. Mrs. Bastion must've been a regular visitor. She sounds like she was fond of your family." The children had no clue to the horror in the back bedroom, and he hoped they'd never have to know the truth.

"She came by sometimes." The boy had crept forward on his

seat so that he was close behind John. "She got sick the last time she came and passed out."

"When was that?" Raymond asked.

"Tree, four, maybe five days ago." The boy shrugged. "Hard to remember."

"Did she go to the doctor?" Raymond asked.

"Mama told us to go down to the bayou and catch some fish for supper." The boy's face brightened. "I caught six."

Raymond's foot twitched to press the gas pedal, but he held himself back. "Six fish. Cat or trout?"

"Catfish. Mama fried 'em up."

"When you got back was Mrs. Bastion still there?"

"She gone. Her car gone, too."

They entered town. He turned right and headed to Florence Delacroix's. He had no other place to take the children, and he had no doubt that Florence would be kind to them. He pulled into her driveway and was almost to the house when he saw Florence's car headed toward him at a reckless speed. He pulled between two oaks and got out. Florence's car slewed to a stop. Her door flew open and she ran toward Raymond, her face telling him that something bad was afoot.

"Adele is at Father Michael's house!" She spoke as she ran. "They have her cornered. They're going to kill her!" Florence stumbled on a tree root and Raymond caught her before she fell.

Her bare arms were firm and warm in his hands. Her body heaved, struggling for breath. Taking a deep breath, she looked up at him. "They'll kill her if you don't get there."

Raymond stepped away from her. "Will you look after Bernadette's children for a while?"

Florence's eyes held a question as she captured Raymond's gaze. She started to say something else, but when she glanced at the children she stopped.

Raymond pulled her aside and spoke softly. "Marguerite Bastion is dead. At Bernadette's house. Call Doc Fletcher and tell him I think she was poisoned, but we need an autopsy. I've got to go."

The children stood in front of John, his hand resting lightly on the shoulder of each. Raymond walked back to them. "You'll have to stay here."

"You can't leave us here," Stella said. "She's a whore."

Before Raymond could respond, Florence turned to the girl. "Yes, I'm a whore, but I'm a whore with hot chocolate and ham sandwiches."

The boy stepped free of John's light grasp and walked toward Florence. "I'm goin' wit you, *cher*. Stella can sit on the stoop and starve if it suits her. Me, I'm goin' wit you."

Michael stood on the front porch as a mob of forty or more men pushed through the gate and onto his front lawn. They trampled the bed of mums he'd spent hours tending. The bright yellow and orange heads lay crushed and bruised, destroyed beneath the cardboard soles of their shoes.

The crowd was mixed—Negro, Cajun, Indian, French, and German, rich and poor. Michael recognized most of the men, but not all. Some had come from deep in the swamps, hearing the news in a form of telepathic gossip that Michael had never been able to understand. They carried guns and rope. And sticks—dry kindling. Joe was right, Michael realized. They intended to burn Adele.

"You folks should go home." He waved a hand to shoo them away from his door. "The sheriff has things under control. Go on home before someone gets hurt."

"We come for the *loup-garou*." Leroy Baxter stepped out of the crowd. He held a length of rope in both hands. "We got to get her in the daylight, before she turns. Now you best get out the way, Father Finley."

"Peat Moss was returned to you without harm, Mr. Baxter."
Michael moved to the first step. He kept the advantage of height,
but he wanted the crowd to know he didn't fear them. He had
failed Rosa miserably—had become a victim of his own fears—
but he wouldn't allow Adele to be burned. "You should be at
home celebrating God's miracle instead of here, trying to do
harm to a woman who is sick."

"She the devil," Leroy insisted. "We do God's work. We send
the devil back to hell."

"She isn't the devil." He wasn't certain what Adele was, but
even if she was the devil's child, she would not burn. From deep
inside he summoned strength. "She's ill!" He roared the words,
empowered when the crowd backed up a step. "Leave this to the
sheriff and the doctor! Get out of my yard!"

The crowd backed up again, and he saw doubt touch the faces
of some of the men as they shifted from one foot to another.
Heat like the kiss of a July morning touched Michael's face. All
of his life he'd craved the power to sway a crowd, and now he
had it. He felt as if God had touched him, giving him words and
the voice to speak them.

"God is the judge of Adele Hebert, not you! Whatever you believe Adele to be, it's not your place to decide her fate. Now leave
this to God and go home to your families." Several men in the
front turned to leave. Michael nodded at the rest. "Go home."

Michael saw movement in the back of the crowd. The person
was short, but he was making his way to the front, pushing and
shoving. Foreboding touched Michael when Bernadette Matthews
stepped out of the crowd to stand beside Leroy. She was the only
woman in the gathering, and her face was twisted with anger.

"Adele is evil." She spoke to Michael before she turned to
address the group. "She's my sister, but she's evil! She's accepted
Satan as her master! She's bewitched the priest! Perhaps she's bitten him and tonight he'll roam the parish trying to steal our chil-

dren. Adele has killed two men already. Maybe more. Marguerite Bastion is still missing!"

A ripple of movement came from the crowd, and in one surge, the men moved toward the steps. Michael spread his feet for a steadier base and held his ground. "Stop!" He turned to the doorway where Colista stood, her face ashen.

"Hand me my gun, and get the sheriff out here." He spoke softly, but Colista scurried to obey. In a moment she returned with the shotgun he'd fired only twice in his life. He took the handful of shells she offered, glad that Colista knew more about weapons than he did.

As he turned to the crowd, Joe Como stepped out onto the porch with him, his pistol drawn.

"I will not let you harm a mentally ill woman." Michael fought back his terror and lifted the barrel of the shotgun so that it pointed into the crowd.

"I'll shoot the first six people who try to come up these steps." Joe raised the pistol. "The woman inside is sick. We're taking her to the hospital in Lafayette, and no one here is going to stop us."

Michael stood shoulder to shoulder with the sheriff. The crowd shuffled and milled, but no one stepped forward. Bernadette looked behind her, assessing the crowd, before she faced Michael.

"You're under her spell, you, and the sheriff, too."

The crowd inched forward again. To his left, Michael saw Raymond Thibodeaux running toward the mob. Raymond's gun was drawn, and the look on his face told Michael the deputy was serious about using his weapon. Michael had never thought he'd be so glad to see Raymond.

"Go home. All of you. Go now before it's too late to turn back." Joe pointed to the road. "No harm's been done. Leave before I start making arrests."

Bernadette barked, and it took Michael a moment to realize the sound was laughter.

"Arrest us, Sheriff Como," she said. "Put us behind bars." Her strange canine laugh came again. "The only folks you can keep in your jail are children."

"Go home!" Michael pointed a finger toward the street. "Get out of my yard, Bernadette Matthews, before I press charges."

From behind him came an anguished scream that made the hair on the back of his neck stand. Several men in the crowd cowered and retreated. Colista rushed out of the house, pushing between Michael and Joe. She ran into the crowd, struggling against the human wall of resistance, until finally the men stepped aside and let her pass. Michael watched, momentarily stunned, thinking of how the Red Sea had been parted for Moses.

"Sweet Jesus!"

Joe's breathless comment drew Michael's attention, and he turned to find the sheriff staring at the open doorway where Adele Hebert stood, her wild eyes roving over the crowd of men and settling on her sister.

"Get her!" someone in the crowd shouted. The mob lurched forward, and Michael ran down the steps, raising the gun as he went. Before he could fire, the crowd was on him. Someone slugged him hard on the side of the head, and he felt himself falling but was caught by the hands of the mob, his body an effective block against the tide of angry humans. The gun was pulled from his grasp.

Raymond saw the priest pulled into the angry mob. Adele stood in the doorway, an expression of confusion on her face. She reached out a hand toward her sister. Her mouth moved, her words indistinguishable in the roar of the mob.

The sheriff made a grab for the priest's cassock and missed. Unable to assist the priest, Joe pushed back, trying to force Adele inside the house. "Get inside!" Joe screamed at Adele as hands reached from the mob and grabbed him.

Adele didn't move. Her gaze was locked with Bernadette's.

"Kill her!" Bernadette's voice rang over the roar. "Kill her now!" Bernadette raised a pistol from her side. She held it with both hands, pointing at Adele.

Raymond pushed against the crowd without success. The press of bodies held him at the edge of the mob. Bernadette meant to kill Adele. Had always meant that she would die. It was the only way to guarantee Adele would take the blame.

"No!" He screamed the word. "No!"

Amid the uproar of the crowd, Raymond heard the cry of a hawk. He glanced into the cloudless sky, searching for the red tail feathers and open wings. The blue vista was unbroken. He thought of Antoine, the brother he hadn't protected.

He brought the pistol up and squeezed the trigger in one smooth action. The loud report of the gunshot confused the mob. They churned forward, then fell back, their mouths moving but no sound coming out. Bernadette clutched her chest and staggered. She turned to face him, disbelief touching her features before she fell, disappearing in the mob.

Raymond stood with the gun raised. The sheriff scooped Adele into his arms and stepped inside the house. The door slammed, and suddenly Raymond was engulfed in a stampede of men pushing to get away from the priest's house.

They scattered in all directions, and Raymond was left alone with Bernadette. She lay on the grass on her side, her back to him. He walked forward, stopping when he was only inches from her. He knelt and rolled her onto her back. Her sightless eyes gazed into the sun, as if she, too, sought to catch a glimpse of a hawk.

31

———

Raymond stood outside the bedroom he'd occupied only two days before. Doc Fletcher was with Adele. Had been with her for most of the afternoon and evening. He wouldn't leave her side—except to consult with other doctors on the phone. He'd ordered everyone except his wife from the room.

A small, screened porch offered Raymond a place to sit in privacy, and he eased his body into an old rocking chair. The pain in his back was constant, a grinding of bone. He tilted his head back and closed his eyes. He'd found Marguerite's car and determined that the tires matched the tread marks he'd found in Madame's yard. He couldn't be certain now whether Bernadette or Marguerite had paid a visit to Adele at Madame's and slipped her more of the fungus-laden bread. Unless Adele came to her senses, he'd never know. Not that it mattered to anyone but him.

He'd been waiting for hours for word on Adele. John had rushed to Baton Rouge with the grass, bread, and jar of meal. He'd twisted arms at the university, calling in favors from colleagues, and had called back to report that the fungus was indeed ergot, common enough in grasses and grains in the Dakotas but also found in Southern states. Severe hallucinations, and a few other unpleasant side effects, occurred when it was ingested. Deadly in cattle if eaten for long periods, the effects in humans hadn't been studied. There might be the possibility of recurring episodes. Blood vessel constriction might cause a form of gangrene. The best anyone could say was that if Adele lived long enough the effects might wear off. Might.

The coroner had collected Bernadette's body. There would be no autopsy for her. The Bastion boys were on the way to the home of their Mandeville relatives in New Orleans. Joe had packed them off posthaste, and Raymond suppressed a smile as he thought of a refined New Orleans family attempting to deal with their lawlessness. The boys needed discipline and love, and he could only hope someone would supply both for them.

The sound of footsteps approaching on the wooden floor halted his thoughts. Clifton Hebert stepped onto the porch.

"She going to live, her?" he asked Raymond.

"I don't know." Raymond stood. "She's on the edge, Clifton." He hesitated. "I didn't have a choice with Bernadette."

Clifton shifted so that his gaze rested on the Teche. He cleared his throat. "Bernadette was jealous. Of Adele. Of Rosa. It was a sickness with her. Maybe now she can rest."

"Why did she do this?"

"When Bernadette took up with Henri, I knew bad times were comin'. I talked to her, but she wouldn't listen." Clifton sighed. "Henri hankered for Adele, but she never had no use for him."

"Were the twins his?"

Clifton rubbed his beard. "Adele never said. If she'd said, I woulda kilt him for her."

Raymond reached into his pocket for his cigarettes. "All along, it was Bernadette who was the wolf. Never Adele." He struck a match and lit a cigarette.

"Praytor was greedy, him," Clifton said. "He argue with Henri 'bout the money from the liquor. Praytor say Henri was cheatin' him. I heard them. Praytor say he gone get even. Henri, he just laugh like a big joke."

"This information might have been useful earlier." Raymond was too tired to chastise Clifton further. "So Praytor had the motive, and Bernadette came up with the scapegoat. Adele. She hated Adele because Henri fancied her."

"Adele never wanted more than to love her babies, but Bernadette could never see that, her." Clifton walked to the edge of the porch. "I never thought Bernadette would harm Adele."

"All Marguerite had to do was convince that fool Praytor that she'd marry him once Henri was dead." Raymond walked to the edge of the porch beside Clifton and dropped his half-smoked cigarette into the dirt. They both stood looking over the Teche.

Clifton hesitated. "You won't take my dogs, you?"

"Your dogs?" Raymond saw the truth in Clifton's eyes. "Doc said the bodies were bitten by an animal. Not a wolf, though. Bernadette borrowed your dogs the night Henri died, didn't she?"

Raymond could see it clearly. Henri walking down the road in his usual pattern after having sex with Bernadette. Except this time Bernadette followed him to the place where Praytor was waiting with the dogs. Praytor accosted Henri, striking him hard enough to bring him down. "Once Henri was mortally wounded, Bernadette got the dogs to attack him."

Shifting his weight slightly, Clifton took a breath. "My dogs do only what they told to do, them."

Raymond lit his cigarette. "Keep those dogs out of town, Clifton. I don't want to see them again."

Silence stretched between the two men. Raymond considered all that had been lost. Bernadette, Marguerite, and Praytor were all dead. He'd put together the pieces of the puzzle and created a picture, but he would never be certain who'd first come up with the scheme. Even if Adele survived, Doc said she probably wouldn't remember.

"Thank you, Deputy Thibodeaux." Clifton stepped down

from the porch and disappeared into the darkness. "Adele will thank you, if she lives."

Raymond remained standing. Sitting was hardest on his back, and though he felt a need to walk, he didn't want to leave Adele. It was an illusion that his presence helped her fight to live, but he clung to the notion.

A shadow stepped into the moonlight on the lawn and Raymond's body grew still. The figure of a woman walked toward him, a figure cast in the silver glow of light.

"Madame," he said when he recognized her. "You gave me a start."

She took the hand he offered as he assisted her up the steps of the porch. "How is Adele?"

"Doc won't say. It's a waiting game now." He hesitated. "Would you look at her?"

"Dr. Fletcher might not like an old woman from the swamps meddling with his patient."

Raymond couldn't see her features, but he heard the amusement in her voice. Madame had never greatly cared what men of the medical profession thought of her. "It can be our secret," he said. "She's right in here." He led her to the casement windows that opened wide and deep enough to be used as doors.

Florence sat on one of the benches in the small city park. During the summer the oak-shaded playground was filled with the laughter of children, and Florence avoided the place. Today, though, the chill November weather had sent the children home to fireplaces and kitchens filled with the smell of cooking gumbo. The park was empty, the swings creaking in the occasional breeze that fluttered more oak leaves to the ground.

Stella and Vincent Matthews were at the church where Michael Finley was attempting to console them about their mother's death.

Their father had been found in Houma and was on his way back to New Iberia.

Florence had chosen to avoid that scene. Death was always the visitor that stole away loved ones, and Florence had no real comfort to offer the children. Telling them that Bernadette was a murdering bitch wouldn't help. No matter what she'd done, the children still loved her.

All parents marked their children. Sitting on the hard park bench, Florence saw how her life had been shaped by the scars of her own mother's guilt and remorse.

Even so, Florence wanted a child. Two actually. A boy and a girl. No matter that she'd convinced herself otherwise in the past, she knew her heart now. She would make her mistakes, and the children would suffer for her past, but there would also be love. And love compensated for all the errors.

She pulled her sweater closer around her neck. The day was long gone, the temperatures dropping steadily. Across the park and beyond the Teche, stars scattered across the black sky. It was time to go home.

Florence stared at her hands, still plump and youthful. They were soft hands, because she'd done little manual labor. She'd chosen a means of making a living that didn't require calluses on her palms. In doing so, she'd lived within the boundaries of her scars. That was over and done.

She shifted on the bench. Either Raymond would come or not. If he had feelings for her, he'd act on them, and together they'd begin to build the future. If his love wasn't strong enough, she would move on. There was a house in a neighborhood of quiet streets and soft shade. That was her destiny, and she would claim it.

Standing beside Adele's bed, Raymond picked up her hand and stroked the torn flesh and slender fingers.

"Call her, Raymond." Madame stood at the window, almost more shadow than real. "Call her back. She can hear you."

"Adele." Raymond leaned close to whisper her name. When he looked at the window, Madame was gone. "Adele, can you hear me?"

Doc had said she might lose her fingers and toes. Only time would tell how Adele would heal. "Adele." He whispered her name.

The light from a lamp warmed her face, and though Raymond knew it was a trick, he was glad for it. He touched her cheek lightly.

"Adele."

Her eyes opened, and her gaze found him. Confusion touched her face. "What have I done, me?" She started to struggle, but Raymond touched her chest, lightly pressing her back into the bed.

"Don't," he whispered. "You're very sick. Stay still."

"My babies." Tears touched her eyes.

"Tomorrow Father Finley and some men are going to find your babies, and Rosa, and bring them to the church cemetery."

Tears slipped down her temples. Her hand, so weak, pressed his fingers.

"You were poisoned, Adele."

She glanced at the window, transfixed for a moment by the darkness.

Raymond stroked her hand. "Bernadette is dead."

Adele closed her eyes, and for a moment, Raymond thought she'd gone to sleep. "Henri was the father of my babies, but I didn't kill him."

Raymond cast about for something he could say, something he could hold out to her for a lifeline. She'd lost everything she ever loved. Her own sister had tried to kill her. And then he remembered. "I saw Dugas. He's well."

Her eyes fluttered once, twice, and opened.

"Armand." Her voice was little stronger than the wind whispering through the dying leaves. Her eyes closed.

He put her hand on the sheet and stood. "Sleep well, Adele."

He closed the door softly and walked through the house and out onto the lawn. The town had settled into winter quiet. As he walked the streets, his footsteps echoing on the sidewalk, he wondered how the violence of the afternoon could fade away so quickly. He walked past the sheriff's office, past the movie theater, past the drugstore. His feet moved toward Florence's house. He had no idea if she would welcome him or not. He'd given her so little of himself in the past, because so much of him had been dead. Adele had taught him something. He chose life. Through all the death and loss and the pain that crept down his spine, he wanted to live.

He turned back toward Main Street. Before he did anything else he wanted to wash up. Florence liked a neat man, and if he was going to try to convince her to give him another chance, he wanted to be clean.

John and Chula walked toward him, arm in arm. He'd never seen Chula happier. "You made a quick trip to Baton Rouge," he said.

"Amazing what a man can do when a woman inspires him."

Raymond pulled the pack of cigarettes from his pocket and shook one out for John.

"Thanks." John took the smoke and the matches and lit up. "It's a vile habit, Thibodeaux. I'm going to quit as soon as Chula and I say our vows. I was wondering if you might stand up for me as my best man."

The invitation caught Raymond unawares. "Are you sure?"

"You're the best man I know, so you're perfect for the job." John patted Raymond's arm. "We hired a lawyer today to start adoption for Sarah Bastion. She's asleep back with Thomasina."

"Looks like you're getting a wife *and* a family." Raymond felt a knot in his throat. "Congratulations."

"We saw Florence in the park."

"In the park?" Raymond was surprised. "I was planning on talking to her after I cleaned up."

"She looked like she was doing some serious thinking." Chula reached out to straighten the collar of Raymond's shirt. "I think you'd better get over there right now and see if you can't turn her thinking toward you. Else you might lose her."

"Thanks." Raymond glanced down the empty street toward the park. "Thank you both." He started walking. Behind him he could hear Chula's clear laugh and John's soft chuckle. The cold November night bit his ears and nose, and he increased his pace. Ahead of him a pale crescent moon tipped the treetops.